THE CAR HORN REVOLUTION

THE CAR HORN REVOLUTION

AJ ABERFORD

This edition produced in Great Britain in 2024

by Hobeck Books Limited, 24 Brookside Business Park, Stone, Staffordshire ST15 0RZ

www.hobeck.net

Copyright © AJ Aberford 2024

This book is entirely a work of fiction. The names, characters and incidents portrayed in this novel are the work of the author's imagination. Any resemblance to actual persons (living or dead), events or localities is entirely coincidental. Malta is a small island and three-quarters of the population share one hundred of the most common surnames. As a result, there's a chance the author has inadvertently given a character the same name as someone known to a reader (living or dead). If that the case, the author apologises.

AJ Aberford has asserted his right under the Copyright, Design and Patents Act 188 to be identified as the author of this work.

All rights reserved. No parts of this book may be used or reproduced by any means, graphic, electronic, or mechanical, including photocopying, recording, taping or by any information storage retrieval system without the written permission of the copyright holder.

A CIP catalogue for this book is available from the British Library.

ISBN 978-1-915-817-61-7 (ebook)

ISBN 978-1-915-817-62-4 (pbk)

Cover design by Josh Collins

Original concept for series design Spiffing Covers

www.spiffingcovers.com

Printed and bound in Great Britain by Clays Ltd, Elcograf S.p.A.

PRAISE FOR THE INSPECTOR GEORGE ZAMMIT CRIME SERIES

"I thought I knew everything about murders in the Med – not so – this series is a fantastic read!" *Robert Daws, bestselling author of The Rock crime series*

"Can stand up against many accomplished best-sellers such as Gerard Seymour and Ken Follett." *Nik Morton*

"A Hollywood blockbuster just waiting to be made … exhilarating." A *Mother's Musings*

"Utterly engrossing. Unputdownable. George Zammit, unstoppable." *Ken Usman-Smith*

"The Maltese equivalent of Frost … such a lovely character … LOVED IT!" *Carole Gourlay*

"George is such a likeable character, it's impossible not to love him, even as you're squirming at the thought of the snacks in his pocket and the mess they must be making." *Moonlit*

"Absolute belter of a series. Can't rate them highly enough!" *sarahehigginson*

"I'll say it over and over again, a fantastic series and highly recommended!!" *BooksandBacon*

"A fast moving drama. These books should be made into a TV series." *Frank Needham*

"I'd compare [AJ Aberford's] abilities to the post-Cold War novels of John Le Carre ... an educational as well as entertaining read." *Hilary Haskins*

"I love George – he's like a cross between Victor Meldrew and John Wick, if you can imagine such a thing!" *Kerry Young*

"Moments of light relief which will make you laugh out loud." *Alison M.*

"A different take on crime in Malta – loved it!" *I. Paterson*

"What started as a cross between *The Godfather* and *Midsomer Murders* soon developed into a twisty thriller, full of humour." *Angela Paull*

"Imagine an action packed film blockbuster of a book because that's what this is!" *Debbie Young*

"If you like Inspector Montalbano, Commissario Guido Bonetti and Aurelio Zen, you're going to love this ... couldn't put it down!" *Danuta M. Zalega*

"All the chapters come to life on the page ..." Lynnech

"An absolute joy ... !" *John*

There are crooks everywhere you look now. The situation is desperate.

The last words written by Maltese journalist and blogger, Daphne Caruana Galizia, before she was murdered by a car bomb in October 2017.

PROLOGUE

ZAGORI IS a remote region of north-western Greece, famous for its inaccessibility and the forty-six fairytale villages that surround the central massif of Epirus. They cling to the hillsides, connected by narrow roads that follow deeply incised valleys, with arched stone bridges over deep ravines. It was to one of these remote villages, Aristi, that Nikos Caragea, an old man who lived in the forest at the mouth of the famous Vikos Gorge, had brought the foreign woman.

Nikos was her nearest neighbour, although he lived over a kilometre away. The woman had first appeared in the area over a year earlier and moved into a two-roomed cottage, near a disused stone chapel surrounded by a ring of oak trees that were believed to have magical powers. Local myth had it that the long-deserted chapel was one of the many back doors into Hades and, in consequence, the woman had been shunned by the community, whose members were suspicious of her solitary existence and proximity to the unholy temple of necromancy. It was said that this was a place to which the dead returned, once their bodies had decayed and their spirits were released.

This suspicion and fear meant nobody realised that she had succumbed to an intense and prolonged psychotic disorder.

As winter had gripped the region, turning the rivers to ice and causing the forests to hang heavy with snow, Nikos Caragea noticed the woman's SUV had not made any fresh tracks along the two-kilometre drive and smoke from the house's stone chimney had ceased. In an environment where people relied upon the goodwill of neighbours to survive, he slowly laboured through the knee-high snow, up to the cottage, to check if all was well.

Living where he did, in this isolated community, he was no stranger to erratic and eccentric behaviour but, on seeing her, it was obvious to him this woman was in no position to care for herself. Understanding her need, he took it upon himself to deliver her a box of food once a fortnight and replace her LPG gas cylinder when needed. In return, she seemed to have an endless supply of fifty-euro notes, which she thrust at him, without care or thanks.

As spring came, the first yellow crocuses pushed their way through the melting snow, birdsong could be heard once again and the forest tracks turned into long rivers of mud. One day, Nikos found the emaciated woman at the end of her drive, filthy and delirious with fever, suffering from deep infected cuts up her arms. She was barely conscious when he lifted her into the front seat of his dilapidated Peugeot van and drove into Aristi. There, he found Police Sergeant Thanassis Galanis lounging in his two-roomed station, smoking and with the KingBet newspaper open on his desk. A wood burning stove raged in the corner of the first room, pumping out enough heat to bake bread. The sergeant's rosy face showed no expression when Nikos staggered inside the super heated station, half carrying the wretched woman, whom he slid onto a wooden bench by the door.

Nikos explained the circumstances that had led him to bring her in. Sergeant Galanis, angry that his morning had been disturbed, said: "She looks like she needs an ambulance – or a priest, if she's been inside the old chapel!" He shrugged. "What do you want me to do?"

Nikos huffed in exasperation, as the woman started to slide sideways off the bench. He lifted her muddy feet so she could lie on her back, then stood looking down at her, sighing. He lit a cigarette and passed one to Galanis, who took it, despite already having one burning in the ashtray. The pair of them sat in silence for a minute, considering the problem, drawing on the tobacco and exhaling elaborate clouds of smoke into the hot, stuffy atmosphere of the station.

"She's half dead and nobody here knows who she is. Can't you phone somebody and find out? Or search her or something?" said Nikos.

The woman lay on the bench, staring up at the ceiling, oblivious to their conversation. The sergeant heaved his bulk out of the chair, put the cigarette in an ashtray, alongside the still smoking one from earlier, and approached the woman.

"Excuse me, miss, but we need to go through your pockets and see if you've got any identification on you. Do you mind?"

The woman showed no signs of registering what had been said to her and remained impassive, staring at the ceiling through half-closed eyes. The policeman looked hopelessly at Nikos, who nodded vigorously, urging him to go ahead with the search. Galanis gingerly went through her coat pockets and immediately pulled out a basic telephone.

"Well, go on! Try it."

It was dead, but the policeman rummaged in a drawer and pulled out an old multi-charger that had the correct fitting. After a minute or so, the phone flickered into life. Galanis scrolled through the call history and found the unit had only ever made one call. He showed the green string of numbers to Nikos, who said: "Well then, what're you waiting for? Do it!"

The call rang out for what seemed like an age, but eventually it was answered by a woman's deep, hesitant voice, with an Italian accent: "Natasha? Is that you? Where've you been?"

"Er, this is Sergeant Galanis of the Hellenic Police in Aristi. I think we might have the owner of the phone with us right now, but she's … um … uncommunicative. Can you tell us who she is?"

There was a pause on the line. Eventually, the voice said: "Well, Sergeant Galanis, you'd better describe the woman you have in front of you and I'll see if I recognise her. Actually, better still, WhatsApp me a photograph to this number. I'll get back to you."

With that, whoever had answered the call cut the conversation.

Greca Rossi was shocked to see the photograph that arrived five minutes later. The woman she had known was barely recognisable. She was wide-eyed, dishevelled, her hair matted and hanging in untidy dreadlocks. Her face was thin and wizened. It looked like some of her teeth were missing. She seemed to have aged more than ten years, although she had only been missing for two. A pair of hands was visible, belonging to a male person out of shot. He was holding her wrists, turning them so that the palms faced the camera. Her sleeves were pushed up to over her elbows, showing crisscross scars, some dark red, ridged and healed, some bright red, angry looking and swollen. The cuts started on both wrists and went nearly to her elbows.

It took a while and half a bottle of Fragolino wine before Greca could think clearly and return the call, but when she finally did, she was brief.

"I know the woman in the photo. I'm a cousin of hers. I'll get in touch with her father and he'll contact you. In the meantime, please get her to a hospital. It will take a few days to arrange to collect her. Don't worry about any expenses. The family are loaded. Thank you for calling me."

"Er ... miss ... she's hung up! She didn't even give us a name or anything!"

Galanis rang the number back, but the telephone had been turned off.

He and Nikos looked at each other. The old man shrugged and stubbed out his cigarette into the overflowing metal ashtray. He said: "Well, then. That was easy. You watch her, I'll go and get the doctor."

CHAPTER 1
ACTING ASSISTANT COMMISSIONER GEORGE ZAMMIT

HOSPITAL OF ST ANTHONY OF PADUA, RABAT, MALTA

ACTING ASSISTANT COMMISSIONER George Zammit drove down the long, tree-lined drive, up to the double-fronted palazzo ahead of him. The wrought iron gates, which swung slowly open after he announced himself into an intercom, bore the eight-pointed cross that was the symbol of the Knights of St John of Malta. The limestone blocks of the palazzo were the colour of Gozitan honey and the pale blue outer shutters were closed against the cruel Maltese sun. Behind the shutters, the windows were open, to allow fresh air to circulate, displacing the fustiness of age and illness.

George entered the cool, shaded hallway of the nursing home through a baroque doorway, framed by columns, scrolls, floral motifs and cherubs' heads. He signed the visitors' book on the large wooden reception counter, noting the Perspex screens from the Covid years still remained firmly in place. The building exuded peacefulness, with the nun on reception speaking only when necessary, maintaining the aura of dignity and calm.

The room he sought was on the first floor. George climbed the ornate marble staircase, walked down the mosaic-tiled corridor and knocked gently on the hardwood double doors. Hearing nothing, he slowly entered.

George's former boss, Assistant Commissioner Gerald Camilleri, was seated in an upright armchair next to a neatly made bed. He wore paisley pyjamas, with a thick woollen dressing gown drawn tightly around him. He had a scarf wrapped around his wizened neck and thick socks on his feet. His thin hair had all but disappeared and his head seemed disproportionately small to the rest of his heavily insulated body. Classical music played gently in the background and a heavy biography of Gamal Abdel Nassar, the former Egyptian president, lay open on his lap. The long, floor-to-ceiling windows were open, filling the room with the heavy, pine scent of the woodlands outside. Strips of light shone between the closed shutters and the bedside reading lamp was switched on, casting a pool of gold around the seated figure.

He lifted his head and, recognising George, raised a hand in welcome.

"You caught me dozing. I cannot tell whether I spend most of my time asleep or awake these days. How are you, George?" He shuffled in his chair to sit himself straighter.

"*Mela*, I'm alright, I suppose. The family's good and the department seems to run smoothly – even with *me* in charge. Mind you, Chelotti's a good man and takes a lot of the paperwork off me."

Camilleri smiled.

"I am glad you finally accepted the job. I know you had your doubts, but I was sure you were the right man for it! And, yes, it was a smart move to bring in Chelotti. I heard you had done that. Horses for courses, eh?" Gerald gathered the dressing gown closer around him. "I can never seem to get warm these days – most strange. I'm glad you've popped in, I was meaning to have a chat with you. Something on my mind … but first, indulge me, fill me in on the gossip. I do not hear much in here about what is going on."

Before his retirement on health grounds, Gerald Camilleri had held the rank of assistant commissioner in charge of the Financial Crime and Anti-Money Laundering section of the Malta *Pulizija*. In fact, he had been so much more than that. Many said, in his time, he had secretly run the island and that his connections had reached right to the heart of government.

Camilleri's secret was that he had long accepted Malta would always have more than its fair share of shady enterprises. Successive governments had encouraged businesses run by the wrong sort of people, and the cash that flowed through the island's banks was all too often of uncertain origin. Its controversial 'passports for sale' scheme had allowed a host of dubious business types access to the red EU passport, enabling them to wander at will around Europe's Schengen Area, as long as they filled the coffers of the Maltese government and those who served in it.

But, if the government wanted to create this type of economy, Camilleri had chosen not to interfere. While politicians robbed the public purse, bent the workings of the state to their own purposes, the electorate knowingly voted them back into power, time and again. Everybody knew what went on and, if the electorate and those responsible for good governance tolerated such behaviour, who was a policeman to crusade against it?

However, Gerald Camilleri had his red lines, which could never be crossed. He had waged war on the drug gangs, the people traffickers, modern slavers and those who used the country's lax banking regime to fund terrorism. Anyone who created trouble for the islanders, or disturbed the tourists on the sun-baked summer streets, soon felt his hand upon their collar.

George was a different creature altogether. While Gerald was tall, pale, stork-like and urbane, George was short, round and, usually, faintly dishevelled. Gerald ate plain fish and vegetables, sparingly, while George filled his stomach, then his pockets, with *pastizzi*, the island's signature pastry snack, pasta, *ftira* sandwiches, and all manner of carbohydrates. If he was still peckish, he was partial to a couple of sticky *cannoli*, pastry tubes of sweet ricotta and mascarpone cheese. Gerald ate because he had to, and it gave him no pleasure. George ate enthusiastically because it was one of the great pleasures in his life. Gerald had lived a solitary, ascetic existence, with his music, in a bungalow high on the Madliena Ridge, overlooking the sea lanes to Sicily. George, on the other hand, returned to the chaos of family life in the congested urban suburb of Birkirkara, with his wife, the domineering Marianna, and their son, Police Sergeant Denzel Zammit. More often than not, their second child Gina was also to be found in the family home, together with her rumbustious child, known as Baby Joseph, despite having her own apartment around the corner with her husband, Giorgio, son of the local butcher, Joe Mifsud.

George smiled and started to recount the goings on within St Calcedonius Square, Malta Police's General Headquarters. He found it strange that the two of them should be sitting here, like old friends, gossiping about fellow officers, happy in each other's confidence. For many years, George had been terrified of his aloof, sarcastic and condescending boss but, over time and as a result of many shared adventures, the two of them had developed a bond of trust and respect, although George always suspected that until Gerald's last day in the office, he had only ever known a fraction of what his boss was up to or what he was thinking.

George gossiped for a bit, but then came to the subject that had really spurred him to visit the all-knowing Gerald Camilleri.

"*Mela*, there's something going on here, which I think's weird and I'd like your take on it. The Russians …"

"Now we get to it." Gerald laughed weakly, breaking into a cough. "I can always tell when something is troubling you. Pass me that glass, would you?"

He took a sip of the tepid water.

"Yeah, I'm sorry, Gerald, I don't think it's fair to come and add my woes to your problems, but this is serious. Maybe you've heard that the Russians are everywhere on the island these days. Everywhere you go, you see them. The Radisson up at Golden Bay's filled with them – they're even accepting payment in roubles! There're three Russian naval ships permanently in the Grand Harbour, on goodwill visits – so they say. But one's in the dry dock! The ratings ... about a thousand of them ... have been raising hell in Paceville and Sliema. And, worse – you know the Strand Park Hotel and the Beaches, in St Julian's? Well, they've just been requisitioned, taken over by the Armed Forces of Malta, for the use of Russian mercenaries – volunteers, as they call them – from all over Africa. You can imagine the problems they're going to bring with them!"

"Ah! I can indeed. Get me some juice, will you? They insist I drink a jug of water a day; it is ridiculous. Go on, this is interesting."

"*Mela*, I was talking to Xuereb, the assistant commissioner in Vice, and he's saying Malta's flooded with a new wave of East European hookers, trafficked over for the sailors and the Russian tourists. He says the Russians see Malta as the new Thailand. This isn't some backstreet set-up in Marsa – these girls blatantly operate out of the big hotels and nobody dares do anything about it. There's something big going on – everybody at HQ agrees, but nobody knows what. I've even asked Commissioner Mallia what we should do about it... well, as you can guess, I didn't get much change from that!

"Even the street gangs are feeling the squeeze. Russian heavies, ex-military types, have cleared the way for these new businesses. Then, of course, there're the drugs. New stuff, Afghani heroin, via Turkey ..."

A knock on the door stopped George's flow. It opened a fraction and the nurse from reception poked her white-coiffed head into the room.

"Excuse me, Gerald, but you seem to be having a busy morning. A gentleman has just phoned to see if he can visit you in fifteen minutes or so. He said he was in the area and thought he'd pop in. You're not too tired, are you?"

"Good gracious, no! Actually, I was expecting him to call, but not just yet. Yes, tell him I'd be delighted to see him. You don't mind, George, do you? An old friend."

George said, "Not at all, Gerald," and sat back, waiting for Camilleri to respond to what he had been told.

"It is all very strange, I will give you that. One thing I did notice was an article in the *Malta Telegraph*. I do not know why I remembered it especially, but I did. A new Russian ambassador to the island was appointed recently, a chap called Grigori Buzilov. Previously he was the Russian Permanent Representative to the United Nations and before that their ambassador to the UK. So ... a big fish. I wondered what sins he had committed to get himself posted to a backwater like Malta. Now, having heard what you have to say, I suspect there is something we are not seeing that brings a man of such experience here.

"Anyway, thank you for the visit, it has got my brain turning, which is never a bad thing. There is something else I need to talk to you about, but I do not think there is time today, it sounds as if my next visitor is just about to arrive. If you could find time to come back for another chat, it would be much appreciated."

George stood up to leave.

"Of course, Gerald. It's always good to see you. I'll come back as soon as I can. I'm glad to see you looking so ... well."

Camilleri managed a thin smile at the clumsy comment. As he reached the door, George turned and raised a hand in farewell, but he noticed Gerald's head had already slumped to his chest and his eyes were closed. He left, quietly closing the door behind him.

George walked outside, leaving the quiet and cool of the

nursing home, into the glare of the late morning sunshine. Like all sensible Maltese, he had parked his car in the shade, under a sandarac gum tree on the far side of the car park. It was further to walk, but it would be cooler once he got into it. As he made his way across the hard-packed gravel, he saw a white Mercedes pull into the car park and come to a halt. Having assessed the options, the driver reversed and parked in a shady spot against a wall.

George was curious about Gerald Camilleri's visitor. There was something familiar about the car and, given where he had parked, he guessed the driver was Maltese. George stood, partially concealed by his own vehicle, and waited for the man to get out. He reached into his pocket and pulled out a brioche bun with an apricot filling, which he had snaffled from the breakfast table. As he munched on it, he noticed that, despite the heat, the driver of the Mercedes was wearing a heavy tweed jacket and corduroy trousers. George smiled as he spotted the visitor's trademark blood-red brogues.

Marco Bonnici was Maltese aristocracy, his family line going back centuries. He and Gerald Camilleri had been friends and associates for as long as George had been a policeman. It cheered him to think their friendship still continued.

George knew, however, that Marco Bonnici was also de facto head of 'the Family', an organisation that had its origins as a Milanese financial guild, dating back almost to the High Renaissance. There were records of it financing trading expeditions to the Far East; a series of wars in central Europe and funding enormous dowries for royal marriage alliances. It also made loans to popes and bishops, to build monuments to themselves, and to the nobility, so they could acquire lands and estates across Europe.

After the First World War, they said it had been Marco's grandfather who had reinvented the Family as a shadowy organisation, operating across borders, and restored the fortune it had lost in the cataclysm of Europe's Great War.

Marco and his daughter, Natasha, had continued its work, with Gerald as its chief protector and adviser on the island – a fact that had often left George, as a committed upholder of law and order, conflicted and exposed.

A disagreement with Natasha had led to Marco's departure from Malta and his stabilising influence there had been replaced by the ruthless behaviour of his daughter, who had thrust the Family, and Malta, into the limelight, with the stratospheric rise of the businesses she headed up. But, as often happens, her earlier misdeeds had caught up with her. Neither the Family, nor the ailing Camilleri, could protect her from the consequences of her own actions and she had fled the country in disgrace. Since that time, George had enjoyed a halcyon period when he no longer needed to worry about the Family or the Bonnicis. Now, it seemed Marco was back and George felt a creeping sense of unease.

CHAPTER 2
MARCO BONNICI
CASTELLO BONNICI, IL-WARDIJA, MALTA

FOLLOWING his visit to see his old friend, Gerald, Marco drove his white Mercedes back to Castello Bonnici, reflecting on how good it was to be back home. He had just returned from a lengthy spell on his Serbian estate, high on the Zlatibor plateau, and was now making a round of visits on the island, to re-establish contact with old friends and business associates.

Castello Bonnici was an eighteenth-century fortified stately home, complete with small bell tower and crenelated battlements, which sat on top of a long ridge that bisected the island at its narrowest part. From there, you could look both east and west and see twin flashes of deep blue, as the Mediterranean Sea lapped against the two coastlines. Like most Maltese buildings, the *castello* was constructed from local limestone which, in the flat winter light, could look drab and uninviting. However, in the summer sunshine, it came alive when the granular stone took on the warm hue of freshly baked biscuits.

The *castello* was where, all those years ago, Marco had taken his new bride, Sophia. It was also where she had died, only six years later, sprawled across the marble staircase, having taken an unexplained tumble, which had not only cost her own life, but also that of their unborn second child.

Marco's first child, Natasha, had grown up there in the care of her father, helped by a variety of governesses and housekeepers. There had been no shortage of women interested in the good looking, well-mannered and wealthy Marco Bonnici, but he had never remarried or found another woman to equal Sophia.

As Natasha grew into an intelligent and capable young woman, she also acquired the best of her mother's beauty. However, there was something in her nature that, from an early age, had unsettled Marco. As she matured, her ruthlessness and lack of empathy became painfully apparent.

In time, she became involved in the Family's activities, using her undoubted business skills. But, when the scale of her ambitions led to untimely deaths within the organisation's most senior ranks, clearing the way for her ascendancy, Marco realised he had lost all control over her.

Feeling a mixture of revulsion and fear, he had disowned her and left his home, his friends and the Family, to live in his Serbian hideaway. Several years later, when the past had caught up with Natasha and she had become a danger to the continued existence of the Family, its senior members begged Marco to return from his self-imposed exile. They pleaded with him to assume control and lead the organisation back into the shadows, away from public scrutiny, where it could operate privately and with impunity. He realised that, to secure her own rise to the top, his daughter had removed the next few likely leaders within the Family and it was the guilt he felt about that, as much as his sense of duty, that had brought him back into the game.

He entered the *castello* through impressive wooden double doors, making his way down the marble-flagged hall, passing enormous wall tapestries and the watchful suits of armour, before stepping out onto the rear terrace. He became aware of Asano, the Japanese housekeeper, approaching him across the terrace, carrying a tray of tea. The man was so prescient it was almost spooky. Marco had learned from him that Asano had been hired by Katia, their former housekeeper, whom Natasha had finally managed to scare so badly that she fled home to Poland. Unlike Katia, who had jangled her chain of keys everywhere she went around the house, bouncing off her hip, Asano was as silent as an assassin. Although Marco had no complaints about his abilities as a housekeeper, he found his soft-footed omnipresence disconcerting.

Marco glanced left, to where he had once enjoyed tending his acclaimed collection of cacti and succulents. He had hoped it would one day become part of his legacy. With proper care, the slow-growing plants could have outlasted him and he had hoped the sight of them might be a source of pleasure to future generations. But after he had left the *castello* to live in Zlatibor, Natasha had spitefully bulldozed the garden and laid a tennis court, on which, she took pleasure in telling him, she had never struck a ball.

Nowadays, the only person to be found on the court was Asano, who used the space to practise the martial art of *qigong*. He had told Marco that he found the exercises helpful for meditation and movement which, he said, forged 'inner connectivity'.

Asano said quietly, "Mr Marco, I serve Earl Grey tea, for refreshment, but fear peace is disturbed. There is a visitor at front gate."

Marco looked longingly at the tea and raised his eyebrows, enquiring who the visitor might be.

"She comes without appointment. Says you know her. Her name is Greca, your cousin Sergio's daughter. Do I admit her?" Marco nodded.

"And bring another cup, please."

To his surprise, he felt slightly nervous about Greca Rossi's unannounced appearance on his doorstep. He had not spoken to her since the hot muggy day of what had been his cousin Sergio Rossi's *second* funeral, among the Gothic mausoleums of

Malta's Addolorata Cemetery. Greca, Sergio's daughter, had appeared just moments before the interment, arriving in a black limousine, and had spoken only to Marco. She had stood beside the casket for a few seconds and mumbled some words, a prayer perhaps, then left.

Several years earlier, the Family had decided Sergio had become a liability and, much to Marco's horror, had ordered his cousin's assassination. But Sergio had foiled the Family's gunmen, faked his own death, and then joined forces with Natasha to take his murderous revenge on the Family's hierarchy. A tear-stained Greca and her hard-faced stepmother had unknowingly interred a weighted coffin at the *Cimitero Monumentale* in Milan during Sergio's first funeral, unaware that he was alive and well. But, while hiding in Malta, Sergio had found that fate could be a cruel mistress when he was murdered outside the gate of Castello Bonnici, by a car bomb meant for Marco.

At the Addolorata Ceremony, Greca had told Marco that any emotion she had felt for her father had been exhausted by his fake funeral in Milan and that one such service was quite enough for anybody. So, she thanked Marco for overseeing the arrangements, promised to send a cheque to cover the day's expenses and promptly left. A cheque for 20,000 euros had duly arrived and was still sitting in Marco's desk drawer, uncashed.

The sound of Greca's heels clacking down the stone corridors of the *castello* announced her arrival. No doubt Asano was silently leading her through the house, his rope-soled sandals making not a squeak. She appeared in a flurry of movement, almost flouncing onto the terrace. Marco could not stop a grin spreading across his face.

"Well, then, my first cousin, once removed! Look at you, *bellissima*! How are you?"

Greca had a statuesque figure, with large calves, a bulging rear and an oversized body, which she liked to dress in long flowing skirts or caftans. She had dark Sicilian skin, with naturally rosy cheeks, and black corkscrew curls down to her shoulders. Her best feature was a pair of the most amazing green almond-shaped eyes. She was a beautiful woman who commanded the attention of any man she met.

Glancing towards the tea tray, she turned to Asano, who was standing attentively to one side, hands clasped in front of him, and said: "I'm not sure I'm in the mood for tea. Bring two wine glasses and an ice bucket, please."

Asano glanced at Marco, who nodded almost imperceptibly.

Greca watched the housekeeper leave the terrace, walking with quick silent steps.

"Well, he's certainly an improvement on that miserable Pole you had before – Katia, wasn't it? How're you two getting on? You need someone good to take care of this crumbling pile." Marco was surprised by her interest.

"Okay. To be honest, I have only just met him. You seem very familiar with this household. I did not know you had visited before."

"Oh, yeah, I lived here for several months after Natasha and I became friendly. But it's a long story ... maybe for another time. Anyway, I haven't come here to discuss your staffing arrangements!"

She reached into her voluminous designer bag and pulled out a bottle of wine in a dark green thermal sleeve, presenting it to him. "I've come to have a drink with you. And, since I've travelled from Sicily, I thought perhaps we could have dinner together, if that suits you?"

Marco smiled graciously at his uninvited guest and said: "I would not have it any other way. You must stay here tonight, of course. And please, do sit down."

He examined the bottle Greca had put on the table.

"Fragolino ... my word! It is illegal to produce that, is it not? Something to do with the vines and phylloxera plague?"

"Rubbish – all of that's ancient history. I'm the biggest grower of Fragolino in Sicily. Rome banned it years ago, but it's perfectly legal now. I sell primarily to the US; they love it and pay me a fortune! 'Illegal' Italian wine – great marketing ploy! This one's a sparkling red, a little sweet, but with hint of strawberries. Natasha would freeze it so you couldn't taste a thing.

This is lightly chilled, it's better that way."

Asano returned with glasses and a corkscrew, expertly opening the bottle with three twists. Marco took his glass, sucked in some air and rolled the wine around his palate.

He looked at Sergio's daughter and she held his gaze. He had had very little contact with her when she was younger, which he had thought a shame. He tried to imagine her as a child but found he could not.

For a young woman, alone in the world, she was supremely confident and had developed a fearsome reputation in Sicily where she was the main supplier of casual agricultural labour, which she sourced from the waves of migrants who made their way there from North Africa. She was what was known as a *capobanda di caporalto*, or a gangmaster of illegal labour, with strong links to the Nigerian Mafia – the Black Axe Gang or Aye Axemen. This alliance enabled her to coexist with the Sicilian Mafia and the 'Ndrangheta, on more or less equal terms. The Axemen also acted both as her personal security and as enforcers amongst her huge labour pool.

"So, how is business in Sicily? Has the drought affected you?" Marco enquired politely.

"Yes, it's been tough. We harvested early in the South: grapes, olives, tomatoes, fruit, even though yields were low. Low yields mean fewer pickers are needed and I make less money. We're harvesting the almonds now, shaking the trees to get them to drop!"

"And what about Natasha? I assume that is why you are here. You have news of her? If you were here before she left, you two must be in touch."

Greca knew father and daughter were estranged, but had always believed Marco was, at heart, a sympathetic and kind soul. Since their meeting at the cemetery in Malta, she had kept in touch, sending him cards at Easter and Christmas.

Greca and Natasha had had their own reasons for ending their brief friendship. Greca's second-in-command and lover, Ituah, had tried to sleep with Natasha, encouraged by Greca, who had thought she was doing their hostess a favour. When Ituah refused to take no for an answer, Natasha fought back. She had found a long knife strapped to Ituah's calf and had not hesitated to bury it deep into his chest.

That was the end of the attempted rape and the end of Ituah. Natasha had fled to Sicily, and Greca was faced with disposing of the body of her lover when she had woken up the next morning. It had been the beginning of Natasha's self-imposed exile and her slow slide downhill in terms of her mental health. Greca sighed and exhaled.

"Well, I don't know how much you're aware of, but Natasha and I aren't exactly friends anymore. We fell out – big time. As much my fault as it was hers, but it ended with me having to dispose of the corpse of my dead boyfriend. So, you could say it was serious."

Marco sighed. Another name to add to the long list of men who had angered Natasha and not lived to regret it.

Greca flashed a glance at him and took a slow sip of wine. Eventually she said: "I've had a call about her. From a Greek number – a police station. It's time to go and get her, bring her back to civilisation. It's been nearly two years without a word from her. I think she's in trouble. You can't just leave her, not any longer."

Marco stared back at her, as her green cat's eyes drilled into him. They assessed each other for several seconds. Finally, Marco was forced to break the silence.

"You do not know what she has done to me. I owe her nothing. She destroyed everything in my life I held dear, my wife, your father, my colleagues in the Family. She even concreted over my bloody garden! She is a serial murderer. My own daughter – who I still love, by the way – is a murderer! And not once or twice. There is a pile of dead bodies that she is responsible for. How am I supposed to deal with that? Do I want to restore her to what she was? No, I do not! I would rather leave her in Greece, foraging for nuts and searching for firewood, or whatever it was she was doing there." Greca edged forward in her seat.

"I've got a suggestion for you. I'm not getting involved any further. This is for you to sort out, as her father. They contacted me, asking for help, because mine was the only number on her phone. I've found a secure Swiss clinic. Once she's in there and her next-of-kin – that's you – has signed the papers, they won't release her until they think she's no longer a risk to herself or anybody else."

Marco looked up, interested.

"It is not one of those places celebrities go to dry out, is it?"

"No, it doesn't deal with addiction problems. Just severe cases of psychosis and schizophrenia. It's the real deal and very expensive. But that's not a problem for you, is it?" Marco ignored the dig.

"When she spoke to you, what did she say?"

Greca made no reply but took out her phone and flicked the screen for a moment or two. Then she passed the phone to Marco.

"That was how she looked last week."

Marco examined the photograph Greca had received from Sergeant Galanis. He put his head in his hands and shuddered, as a bout of tears overtook him.

"Where is she?"

"I told the police to take her to a local hospital. They'll hold her there until you collect her. Go get her, Marco, she's your damn daughter, after all. Take her to the private clinic and write a cheque. Is that asking too much?"

Later, they settled down for dinner, which Asano served in the library. Marco was well aware what was to be the principal topic of conversation. Greca had previously approached the Family claiming her entitlement to her father's share of the joint assets. But, given Sergio had been the one who had murdered the organisation's council of three, known as the Wise Men, the Family was adamant that any claim he might have had to any of the wealth was forfeit. Marco knew Greca was unwilling to accept this and guessed it was, in part, the reason she had made the trip to Malta.

He had asked Asano to prepare something Italian and informal for their supper, though he was just as capable of producing Eastern-inspired dishes a Michelin chef would be proud of. On this occasion, Asano produced a classic platter of antipasto, followed by roasted quail breast, wrapped in thin slices of prosciutto.

Greca clapped her hands when the quail arrived.

"Ah, my favourite! Asano, we can wash it down with some more of my Fragolino rosso. Can you open one? The driver left a box in the hall. People say the best Fragolino rosso comes from the Veneto, but wait until you taste mine!"

Asano clasped his hands in front of him and said: "Please, the favourite wine is already decanted for the breathing and is recommended with the quail. I bring at once, so sorry for the delay."

Marco dabbed his lips and watched the enigmatic housekeeper fade out of sight.

Greca smiled.

"Isn't he a sweetheart? And this is all very civilised. But the island seems to have changed for the worse. What on earth's going on with all those Russians? They're everywhere." Marco sighed.

"I know. Yesterday, I was out and about and saw them at the entrance to the Parliament building, the Law Courts …

they even have a presence at the airport. It is quite intimidating.

"If you go to the Grand Harbour, there are gunboats, minesweepers, a frigate, a fancy reconnaissance ship, even three submarines. Though what submarines have to do with an alleged search and rescue brief is beyond me."

Greca arched her eyebrows, her green cat's eyes flashing in the low light, watching him intently. Marco was lost in his reverie, trying to make sense of the Russian presence.

"In the evenings, groups of sailors hit the bars and clubs. They do exactly as they please. Fighting, abusing women, smashing places up. The *Pulizija* cannot handle them. As you can imagine, it is ruining the tourist trade."

"Hmmm. The papers in Italy are making a massive thing of it. And you don't know why they're really here?"

"I can guess what is in it for the Russians – but for us Maltese, I have no idea how it has been allowed to happen."

Asano silently ghosted into the room, his light frame and sandals not making a sound on the polished stone floor, a starched white cloth over one arm and the decanter of wine in his other hand.

"I serve the wine. If temperature not correct, I apologise." They sat in silence while he poured.

Greca nodded to him and then broached the subject that had been on her mind for too long.

"You know I've approached the Family about my claim for compensation for the loss of my father's share?"

"Yes, and I heard Von Wernberger was blunt in his response. Even though Sergio was a friend and my blood, as are you, I can see the argument that a man who murdered three heads of the Family and an heir apparent, loses any moral claim to a share in our communal wealth. I must say, Greca, it confuses me why you cannot see that." She twisted her mouth to one side and set her jaw.

"I can see the argument, but I think it's shortsighted. You've seen what I can do. I've tamed the 'Ndrangheta and the Sicilian Mafia. I've built a business using muscle and guile. Natasha was mentoring me. I was her prodigy or whatever the French word is. She saw my potential. You did it for my father, knocked the rough edges off him, polished him up a bit, showed him how your boys' club worked. Took him out of Sicily and put him in Milan. Natasha was doing the same for me. But then … well, it all went wrong."

Marco sat back and sipped some wine.

"I was not aware of that. It was good of her. But what do you want from me, Greca? You will never get Sergio's shares in the Family, that is not going to happen. I am sorry. Even if you and I are blood, there is nothing I can do about it."

"Well, there is, you see. Aside from the money, I want you to pick up where Natasha left off. Bring me inside. I can help you."

Marco looked at her. Her vivid green eyes were so bright and alive.

"Well, well, Greca. You surprise me. I do not know quite what to say. But you must realise, the Family operates very much in the shadows these days. Our enterprises are not nearly as profitable as they were. We make a point of doing nothing contentious. So I am not sure the opportunity you are looking for is even there.

"One thing Natasha taught us was how much peril there is in flying too close to the sun. Someone destroyed the Croce Bianca, our palazzo in Milan. It was not just a body blow to our organisation; it touched our soul – it will forever be a stain on this generation of Family members who allowed it to happen. We will be remembered as the generation that lost the most beautiful Renaissance palazzo in Milan and some of the most priceless treasures in the Western world. So now we are ashamed almost to the point where we have rendered ourselves invisible. Again, I am sorry, but I am not going to be able to help you with this request, either."

Greca kept her face absolutely still. She wondered if he knew, or even suspected, that it was she who had struck that magnificent fatal blow in an act of pure vengeful spite, destroying centuries of accumulated history and the arrogance of the precious building's custodians.

She sliced into the quail, scraping her knife across her plate in a subconscious gesture of frustration. Asano was pouring more wine and flashed her a sideways look with his impenetrable black eyes. She understood nobody in the Family was going to help her just because she felt it was the right thing for them to do.

CHAPTER 3
ARTICLE IN THE MALTA TELEGRAPH

Reporter: Justine Galea

Date: 22 May 2025

Russian Sailor Dies in Paceville Attack

A Russian sailor was beaten to death last night on the Santa Rita Steps in Paceville. Seaman Sergei Gusev was nineteen and served in the crew of the Admiral Butakov, *a guided missile frigate from the Russian Black Sea fleet, currently on a goodwill visit to Malta.*

A spokesperson from Armed Forces Malta confirmed that Seaman Gusev and three other sailors were on shore leave in Paceville, when they were the subject of an unprovoked attack by four Albanian doormen from the Club Marbella. Bystanders saw the young seaman beaten and kicked to death.

Later, several of the sailor's shipmates arrived at the club, to try and lend assistance to the stricken man, but he had been pronounced dead at the scene. Police were later criticised by the manager of the Club

Marbella, Henri Vassallo, for the length of time the Santa Rita Steps were closed.

"Not only did we lose a lot of business over the evening, but the Pulizija took so long to tidy up the scene, large crowds gathered at the top and bottom of the stairs. In the hot evenings, this can be unpleasant and dangerous. It's not a great advert for the island."

The visit of the Admiral Butakov is the latest in a series by naval vessels from Russia's Black Sea Fleet. There is now some evidence that Russia is making overtures to Malta with a view to securing the use of its ports for refuelling and access to its repair facilities.

Frequent 'goodwill visits' by Russian naval vessels, and reports of several high-level meetings with the prime minister, suggest that relations between the two countries are growing closer. This is also evidenced by the high-profile appointment of the new ambassador, Grigori Buzilov, previously Russia's Permanent Representative to the United Nations and a former ambassador to the UK.

CHAPTER 4
PRIME MINISTER EDWARD REFALO

OFFICE OF THE PRIME MINISTER,
VALLETTA, MALTA

THE FLAMBOYANT, baroque Auberge de Castille is perhaps the finest building in Valletta and, as such, a fitting place to house the office of Malta's prime minister. Unfortunately, its current occupant did not have a history as illustrious as the building's. Edward Refalo was a weasel of a man, with a long, pointed nose, close-set, shifty eyes, and a slender, diminutive figure. His thinning grey hair was brushed back from a peak on his forehead and lay plastered across his skull.

Refalo had been a minister in an earlier Maltese government, but proved repeatedly incapable of recognising a conflict of interest if it bit him on the nose; a lack of judgement that had eventually forced him out of office. In Malta, redemption within a political career is never impossible, as memories are short and today's political scandal is soon forgotten. So, Edward Refalo was duly rehabilitated and, to the surprise of everybody but himself, rose to become prime minister of the European Union's smallest country – top of the pile, in the land of opportunity.

That afternoon was stiflingly hot and even the air conditioning struggled to cool the high-ceilinged Cabinet Hall where Refalo and his chief of staff, Raymond Farrugia, were meeting a visitor. The recently appointed, high-powered Russian ambassador, Grigori Buzilov, was a well-dressed gentleman who modelled himself on certain British Civil Service mandarins, for whom he had the utmost respect. He spoke English without any trace of an accent and had already overstayed his thirty-minute appointment by more than an hour. His three-piece suit remained buttoned and there was no trace of perspiration on his forehead.

The ambassador had presented the politicians with two smartly bound folders, stacked with financial accounts, records of bank transactions, company registrations, even some photographs of meetings between the two of them and a variety of third parties. Each folder also contained a small hard drive that the ambassador assured Refalo and Farrugia contained video and audio recordings of some of the meetings.

Satisfied that he had checkmated the pair, Buzilov sat back in his chair, crossed his legs and folded his arms across his chest. He had an olive complexion and swarthy jaw, a testament to his family's connection with the Caucasus, and could hold a man in his gaze for several minutes straight with unblinking dark brown eyes, a technique Prime Minister Refalo found deeply unnerving. The files had set out a full and complete legal case against the two men. The ambassador let them stew for a few seconds more, then reached into his pocket and took out two buff-coloured envelopes that he waved at them.

"You are aware of the Extradition Treaty between the United States of America and the Government of Malta? Well, this is a copy of a letter we intend to send to the American Embassy in Attard, purporting to be from an anonymous whistle blower.

"It is my guess that, when the Americans find out what you two have been up to: facilitating sanction busting, leaking official US military secrets – I think that counts as espionage, by the way – accepting bribes to commit breaches of international anti-terrorism laws, it will only be a matter of time before the outrage in the US will make your extradition a mere formality. Certainly, your colleagues in the Ministry of Justice here will be extremely happy to wash their hands of the unpleasant task of prosecuting the two most senior officers of state, don't you think?"

Raymond Farrugia could not contain himself.

"But that's ridiculous! All we did was offer you help when everybody else shunned you. We did you some favours – that's all!"

"Yes, and we paid you substantial amounts of money for that help. Refuelling our naval ships is always helpful, buying the artillery munitions stock from the Nigerians certainly aided our military in the Donbas offensive, and we thank you for the 'problems' with the VertWay pipeline. Libyan gas would have proved most useful to Europe that winter. It was a particularly cold one, if I recall correctly."

Grigori Buzilov smoothed back his glossy black hair so not a strand was out of place. He adjusted his perfectly positioned tie and looked up at the plasterwork on the ceiling, as if musing about happier times.

"And, thinking back, the information about the planned US and EU exercises allowed us to plant some nice surprises, but the veto on the petroleum related sanctions ..." he smiled, shaking his head "... that was your best work!" He leaned over and tapped the pack of documents nearest Refalo. "But extremely expensive, as these folders show. It would have been most unfortunate had the European Council extended the sanctions regime in that particular area. We particularly thank you for vetoing that in Brussels. A nice irony, no? The smallest country in the EU, bringing the Germans, the French and the Poles to heel. It played very well in the Kremlin, I can tell you!"

Farrugia leaped to his feet, as quickly as a rotund man in his sixties could, his chair sliding noisily on the polished wooden floor. Refalo raised a hand to steady the man, but he ignored it. He was livid, panicking, and on the verge of losing control.

"That ruined our political careers! We're pariahs in Europe and even our own colleagues won't speak to us. My own son calls me a traitor, the press vilifies us. Politically, we're dead men walking – and now you rub our faces in it?"

The Russian smiled and rubbed his first finger and thumb together, mockingly.

"We all have choices in life, Raymond. You have made yours." Buzilov stared at him for a moment, the smile gone, coldly examining the hapless man before him. "When it is time, you can disappear somewhere nice and spend all your money. But not now. No, now is not that time."

Farrugia sat down, the anger draining out of him, like so much dirty bathwater.

Refalo usually had a pallid complexion, but his skin had turned the colour and texture of a cold, gutted candle. The surface moisture on his face made it look oily. He was a short, thin man who rarely perspired, but he felt an unusual cool sticky sensation spreading under his shirt. Refalo spoke to Farrugia, struggling to keep his voice steady.

"We're a non-aligned country, remember that. We remain neutral – our constitution says so. Half our population has no idea where Ukraine is, and doesn't care. Vetoing the sanctions resolution in Brussels was perfectly natural, given our unique constitutional position." Refalo shifted in his seat to face his guest. "Anyway, you haven't just turned up here to threaten us. What do you want?"

Grigori Buzilov smiled.

"Ah! That is better. Just your continued help, that is all. We had noticed a certain, shall we say, cooling in our friendship. I thought I would try to get the energy and enthusiasm back into it. Our relationship is not an 'on–off' affair. You cannot simply fill your pockets, then walk away. That is not what friends do, is it?"

Ray Farrugia snorted. Grigori Buzilov glared at him. He said menacingly: "Listen to Edward, Ray. You get it, don't you, Edward? Why don't you explain it to your colleague, he seems to be struggling."

Refalo looked at the man through the hooded eyes of a cobra. He said softly: "Oh, yes, Grigori, I get it. I get it perfectly."

The men sat in silence for moment or two. Finally, the visitor said: "Good! Well then, there is nothing more to say, is there? I will leave you to discuss the material I have left and prepare yourselves for our next, more substantive, conversation. I will arrange something for next week. There are exciting times to come, believe me!"

With that, the Russian ambassador left the pair of politicians rooted to their chairs. He slid out through the double doors, which clicked shut behind him. Ray Farrugia pulled himself to his feet, tucked his shirt back into his trousers and went to check the door was properly closed. He returned and slumped back down, his whole body witness to the despair within him.

"Oh, God! Edward, what the hell do we do now?"

Refalo said grimly: "We shut the stable door, that's what we do. We sweep every room, every car, our homes and phones, our wives' phones, the kids' phones ... we clean up our computers, delete everything we can. We get some of the most stupid policemen on the island to start shredding as many papers as we can find. Get them to sign the Official Secrets Act and threaten them, and their families, with what we'll do if any of this leaks. We clean house. Then, if we're asked, we deny everything – as usual." Refalo held his chin, deep in thought. "Speak to the police commissioner and see if you can get that man Zammit onto it. I'm not sure he's that bright, but he's loyal and senior enough these days. They can start in my office. Keep the Public Service people out of it. We'll say it's a criminal matter."

"But what about ... him?"

Refalo glanced towards the door, as if to reassure himself that the ambassador had really left the room.

"We do exactly as he asks. Whatever it is." Refalo paused for a second, fixing Farrugia with a steely stare, to make sure he understood.

CHAPTER 5
ACTING ASSISTANT COMMISSIONER GEORGE ZAMMIT

ZAMMIT FAMILY HOME, BIRKIRKARA, MALTA

The Zammits lived in Birkirkara, one of the most densely populated neighbourhoods in Malta. The majority of the three-storey blocks were split into apartments, and the family considered itself lucky to have a ground-floor property with sole access to a small central courtyard, where George's wife Marianna could dry washing and tend her pots of herbs, and he could grab the occasional after-lunch nap. In Malta, families tended to stick together and, more often than not, remained living in the same tight-knit neighbourhoods. So, although there was mutual support within the area and lifelong friendships were forged, everybody also knew everybody else's business, their secrets and their comings and goings. And nobody paid more attention to these, or was better informed about local goings on, than Marianna Zammit.

Unbeknownst to her, the drama that was to unfold over the coming weeks and months, and that would be talked about in the neighbourhood for years to come, was taking shape in her very own kitchen.

Denzel Zammit was steaming with anger. He threw the *Malta Telegraph* across the kitchen, shouting: "It's lies! Damn' lies!"

Rummaging on the floor, he picked up a sheet of newsprint and scoured the article for the quote.

"It says, '*The sailor's shipmates arrived on the scene later, to try and lend assistance ...*' They were almost on the point of raping two bar girls when I got there! And that manager guy, Vassallo ... I'm going round there again tonight, and I'll find some underage drinkers, you'll see! And then I'll have his licence!"

Marianna was alarmed by the outburst.

"Sit down, *bravu*! I'm sure you did your best, but that Paceville ... well, it's a Godless place. You should get danger money for even going there. Anyway, I don't want talk about such nasty things in my house!"

But Denzel was not to be placated. He smoothed the paper over the table, covering the bottom of the page with tomato and caper sauce from his pasta, as he angrily read aloud.

"'*The* Pulizija *took so long to tidy up the scene that large crowds gathered at the top and bottom of the stairs ...*' It was a crime scene, for God's sake! Someone had been murdered, but Lord forbid it should be allowed to get in the way of a night out.'

George stirred from his seat and went to stand behind his son. He put his arms gently on the young man's shoulders. Denzel was tall for a Maltese man, at just under two metres, and exceptionally tall for a Zammit, none of whom had ever before broken through the 1.75-metre barrier. Where his father was short and squat, Denzel carried his height well and his figure was athletic, in contrast to his father's increasing portliness.

"Listen, Denzel, where did that witness statement come from?"

He glanced back to the top of the page.

"A spokesperson from Armed Forces of Malta?"

"Exactly. I think AFM have become far too cosy with our Russian friends, ever since they gave us those three patrol vessels. They were worth tens of millions and there's talk of more to come. Tomorrow, we'll have a chat with our own PR people and tell them about the forty-eight sailors who've been banned from future visits to Malta and who were handed over to the Russian Navy to be disciplined. Plus, the two who were charged with sexual assault and ended up in Corradino. That should put a different spin on the story. Leave it to me."

George winked at him. Denzel was still not appeased.

"It's still not right, is it? How can AFM just do that? Christ, they're such liars! It's getting more like Moscow every day here!"

"Listen, calm down. We need a little chat after dinner. You won't mind if we don't do the dishes tonight, will you, Marianna? Denzel and I need to talk shop for half an hour."

He caught his wife's eye and winked at her. She huffed and said:

"Doesn't bother me, as long as it stops all this shouting and blaspheming. Father Peter wouldn't be pleased to hear you using the Lord's name like that. You bear that in mind at your next Confession, young man!"

"Oh, Ma, really! Confession? I haven't been since I told Father Peter about me and Bella Brincat, and that was over fifteen years ago, so I'm hardly going to start now."

His mother turned her back on Denzel and started clearing dishes.

"*Uwejja*! C'mon! Did you hear that, George? You'd better have a word with him about being a good Catholic. I don't want any more shame brought on this family." There was a pause while Marianna clattered some pots and pans. The men looked at each other and Denzel mouthed to his father: 'What shame?'

George shrugged.

The pair went outside to sit in their easy chairs in the back yard, George taking an espresso and Denzel a can of Cisk, the local lager. The rest of the apartment block overlooked the yard in the central well, but only George's apartment had access into it. Being summer, the evening was still very hot and muggy.

The air felt thick and damp and, during the hotter parts of the day, a thin sheen of moisture covered every brow and neck. With George, it also covered his back, his chest and his scalp. He hated the summer months, but noticed Marianna's pots of herbs, the three small lemon trees in their large ceramic tubs and the rows of tomatoes in long wooden planters, were all doing well.

In the summer, once at home, the Maltese had no qualms about getting rid of as much clothing as possible. George was wearing some well-washed baggy shorts of an indeterminate colour, an undervest stained with Marianna's tomato *zalza* and some of his son's old sliders. Denzel wore his football shorts and an old basketball vest. He leaned back in his wicker rocking chair and enjoyed a moment, just gazing into the square inky black of the sky above the courtyard. All the windows of the other apartments were thrown open to try and catch some of the cool evening air. The voices and chattering televisions of a dozen families rang out around the yard and the smell of a dozen dinners gently mingled and slowly dissipated into the night.

George and Denzel had tuned out the background noise, which served to conceal their conversation.

George said: "*Mela*, for your ears only – and I mean it. It's serious stuff. Promise you'll keep this between the two of us?"

Denzel was, of course, intrigued and immediately agreed, without further thought, if only to hear what was to come.

"Yeah, sure, Dad. Promise."

"There's more to this Russian thing than meets the eye. I think there's some kind of arrangement that the Russians have offered. I can't say much more, but I've been up to Castille, and they've asked me to do a clear out of records …" his voice fell to a whisper "… from the PM's personal office! The stuff I've seen! You wouldn't believe it! Anyway, that's not the point.

This Russian thing's bigger than that poor lad getting killed in Paceville."

Denzel was alarmed.

"But, Dad, you can't just go in there and start shredding the PM's papers! That's illegal. Look what happened to Trump when he flushed his papers down the toilet. All political records have got to go to the National Archive. Everyone knows Refalo's a crook – of course he wants to clean up the nest from time to time – but he can't ask you to help him. He has the Public Service for that – why you?" George shrugged.

"I don't know. Perhaps they won't do it?"

"Exactly, or else he's too scared to ask them. What does Mallia say?"

Deputy Commissioner Mallia was George's boss and someone he had surprisingly little to do with. They exchanged pleasantries in the corridor when they met and George had learned to punctually deliver all paperwork to his desk, so some subordinate could tick a box saying everything was in order. But, on the important issues, the deputy commissioner seemed to have no view, so long as the names involved were not in his circle of friends. Deputy Commissioner Mallia enjoyed his regular long lunches, trips on private jets to watch Manchester United play in the capitals of Europe, and summer breaks on property developers' yachts, sailing around Sicily and Croatia. His associates were the property magnates and other local business types who used the deputy commissioner's friendship to maintain their stranglehold on the commercial life of the island.

"Well, I haven't raised it with him," George admitted.

"Maybe you should? I don't want to see you going to jail, Dad."

"Perhaps I'll have a quiet word with Gerald. I'm due to visit tomorrow anyway. He likes to hear what's going on."

"How's he doing?"

"Last week, not so good."

Whereas Deputy Commissioner Mallia indulged his taste for the good things in life at the expense of others, his supposed subordinate, the former Assistant Commissioner, Gerald Camilleri, had effectively run the island. Camilleri always seemed to know exactly what was going on in Malta at any point in time, as well as having an uncanny sense for people and events. George found himself missing those insights more and more.

"All I'm saying, Den, is that it's a difficult time. I feel a bit lost. Gerald always knew what to do when things became tricky. I'm just not the same sort of man as he is. I don't have his people skills or experience. Or presence, for that matter. I know what people think – I'm still the inspector who got lucky, promoted above his ability when there was a quota to be filled."

Denzel looked straight at him.

"Well then, you'd better do the best you can to change that, hadn't you? Because from what I can see, there's nobody else who is going to step up."

"*Mela*, God help us!"

"Oh, Dad! Better remember to confess that blasphemy to Father Peter!"

"Yes, your mother wants me to have a word with you about that …"

"Oh, shut up, I'm getting another beer. Do you want one?"

George called after his son: "Anyway, what did happen between you and Bella Brincat? As I remember, she had big thick glasses and braces on her teeth …"

CHAPTER 6
PRIME MINISTER EDWARD REFALO
LAZARETTO, MANOEL ISLAND, MALTA

THE PENINSULA upon which Valletta sits separates two extensive, similarly sized, natural harbours. The larger, deeper and more famous is the Grand Harbour, which lies to the south of Valletta, while to the north is Marsamxett Harbour. The Grand Harbour is surrounded by the ancient forts of St Elmo, Ricasoli, St Angelo, St Michael and the mighty sixteenth-century limestone bastions that tower over the water's edge.

Marsamxett Harbour is not without traces of early fortifications for those who care to look, but sketchy twentieth-century development and the recent commercialisation of the Gzira and Sliema waterfronts have given the second harbour a very different feel. In its centre, just off the coast of Gzira, lies the leaf-shaped mass of Manoel Island.

This small, flat land mass, less than half a square kilometre in extent, is linked to the Gzira promenade by a short bridge. The island has a rich history with an imposing eighteenth century star fort on its south-western tip that was in the hands of the British Navy from 1802 until their final withdrawal 1979.

Next to the restored fort is the now derelict Lazaretto area, originally a medieval quarantine hospital to protect Malta against the arrival of plague, carried by seafarers and imported cattle. Later, it became a British submarine depot, with a network of concealed tunnels that wove their way through the limestone beneath the island. This maze of tunnels and underground rooms had housed a field hospital and fuel bunkers, protected beneath layers of rock from the German bombardment that had almost flattened the island during the Second World War.

The British Navy had soon realised that this was the deepest part of the harbour, with thirty metres of water beneath the surface. It was here that their submarines refuelled, were serviced and lay concealed, safely submerged, while the German bombers flew above, dropping their lethal loads.

Over the years, most of the buildings on the island, except for the restored fort, had become derelict and dilapidated. Their courtyards and flat roofs were overgrown with waist-high vegetation. The service roads had crumbled, as years of heat softened the tarmac and cracked the concrete. Wooden fence posts rotted, and wire fencing corroded to dust. It had taken decades, but the wind and the sea had fought back and reclaimed large tracts of the island.

A large black minibus and small accompanying convoy of police vehicles came to a halt outside the entrance to the derelict Lazaretto complex of buildings. It was nearly midday, and the concrete slabs reflected the heat back into the already hot air. Less dense as a result, it curved the light upwards, causing the ground beneath to shimmer and form black pools of illusory water.

Prime Minister Refalo and Chief of Staff Farrugia got out of the minibus, followed by Ambassador Buzilov and a new arrival on the island, the man-mountain, Admiral Aleksandr Berezovsky. Within seconds, Farrugia was wiping condensation off his glasses and dabbing his forehead with a handkerchief. He pushed his shirt tails into ill-fitting suit pants.

The Russian admiral was enormous both in height and girth, towering over Edward Refalo. The admiral knew how to use his height, moving in close to whomsoever he was addressing, forcing the listener to raise his or her head and look up to him. The heavy, double-breasted uniform jacket he wore, with its eight brass buttons, was cut to allow room for the admiral's expansive gut, while the bands on his cuffs and rows of colourful medals on his left breast indicated he had been in the navy long enough to gather an impressive array of honours.

Ambassador Buzilov was untroubled by the heat and maintained his usual immaculate appearance. His jet-black hair, held back in place with a hairdresser's product, glistened in the harsh sunlight. The lower half of his olive-skinned face was shaded with black stubble, which grew at the speed of bamboo.

As a diplomat, he had glided between the world's embassies, delivering the most outrageous untruths and boastful propaganda in just the right effortless way so that his audience were well aware he was merely saying what officially had to be said. This was diplomatic stock-in-trade and should not interfere with good relations between educated and refined people.

The admiral was a less cultivated creature. He swayed back on his heels and pushed out his jaw pugnaciously. He swivelled right, then left, as he would when standing on the bridge of his favourite carrier, the grandly named *Admiral of the Fleet of the Soviet Union, Putin*, surveying his battle group. Pulling up his sleeve, he adjusted a bezel on his watch, to check the bearings of the approach to the harbour from the open sea.

"Yes, Grigori, I like it. I like it very much. I've looked at all the charts and maps, and studied the depths in the approach, and it all seems good. We'll do our own survey, of course, but the local geological studies say we can safely construct our submarine pens at twenty metres below sea level?" The ambassador nodded. "Well, in that case, yes, we'll take it."

The ambassador smiled broadly. "Excellent, I thought you would."

"When can we take possession? I mean, who else would want it? Look at it! It's a complete mess! Like this whole country."

The ambassador puckered his lips in thought.

"Well, to be fair, there are still one or two small details to be ironed out. There are some Maltese who have an interest in developing it – for apartments, that sort of thing. And the Maltese Parliament needs to come onside. But I would say you can start construction within the next month or so, at the outside. If you want, you can probably begin site clearance even sooner."

Refalo and Farrugia looked at each other in bewilderment. Refalo said: "Mr Ambassador, what's going on here? What on earth are you talking about? This land isn't for sale – not even to you. I couldn't sell it, even if I wanted to. The government granted a nine-hundred-and-ninety-nine-year development concession on the island. It isn't some town house in St Julian's, it's Manoel Island. The fort's a World Heritage site!" Ambassador Buzilov smiled at him.

"Well, you should have taken better care of it, is all I can say! Anyway, your first job is to clear the way for a lease to us for … say … umm, you mentioned nine hundred and ninety-nine years?" He turned to the admiral. "What was the Guantánamo lease? That was the same, was it not? I do not see why we should get a worse deal than the Americans. That would never do!" The ambassador smiled at Refalo and continued: "Buy it back, cancel the concession, do something – you are the government!

"Also, we have arranged for our own security to protect the site, so there is no need for you to worry about that. The detail should arrive from Libya next weekend. Meanwhile, we will need you to requisition a local hotel to house them. I noticed one or two likely properties on the promenade there. Can you look into it for me?"

Farrugia's face was a picture. He wiped some beads of sweat from under his eyes, with a slightly soiled handkerchief.

"Are you mad – a seafront hotel? It's the start of the school holidays. Everywhere's full! We can't just whistle up an empty hotel. Surely you understand that much?"

The ambassador looked at him, face expressionless.

"This is a new world we are living in, gentlemen. Just get it done, please. Make arrangements to accommodate, say, two hundred men from the *Russkaya Volonterskaya Gruppa*. They are a combat-ready volunteer force who help us in certain situations. Very useful people. Basing them here in Malta will be much more pleasant for them than hanging around in Libya, Mali, Niger or Sudan. Those places are so bad for the nerves – there are civil wars there, you know? Poor fellows!

"Better be warned, they will have weapons with them – so tell your customs and the airport police. And, just so you know, they do not react well to being told what to do. They will also need vehicles, so a transporter plane is landing tomorrow at Malta International, coming from Tripoli with some of our trucks and jeeps in its hold." The ambassador smiled, oozing charm. "We would not want to presume too much and take yours now, would we?" His expression shifted.

"We will also keep a small force at the airport – say two dozen men or so. Oh, and at the docks and ferry terminals too. They will need their own office and facilities. Nothing to worry about, just there to keep an eye on security. Can you tell the appropriate people?"

Refalo glanced at Farrugia, who shook his head in disbelief, but took his phone from his pocket to make a note of Buzilov's requirements. The admiral, meanwhile, had wandered off, peering over the walls and looking down into the lapping, cobalt blue waters. He liked what he saw. He liked it very much.

Farrugia could not believe what was happening around him. He sidled up to the admiral, who saw him approach and quickly took a step towards him. The chief of staff reacted by taking a step backwards. The admiral took two short steps ahead and peered down at the sweaty crown of the politician's scalp. Farrugia blinked frantically behind his spectacles and scuttled another step back. The admiral closed in on him again.

"Stay still, man! We're not doing *kalinka*!"

"Er, yes." Farrugia tilted his head upwards so the admiral could look straight down his long broad nose at him, as he had intended.

Farrugia stuttered: "How much of the island do you think you might need? Maybe just the Lazaretto buildings?"

"Certainly not!" the admiral boomed, with an implacable smile. "We want all of it! Every last square centimetre, including the boatyard and that stupid duck sanctuary. Come to think of it, I know some very good recipes for duck..."

After a while, they headed towards the minibus, Refalo's mind working at double speed, envisaging the trouble that lay ahead: from his cabinet, the government, the press, the president, the EU, and not least, the electorate. Feeling nervous and agitated, he fell into step and matched the pace of the ambassador.

"Grigori, if we're to do this, or try to do this, it has to be for a reason. I can't just say I was blackmailed into it. If there's no good reason, there'll be confidence issues in the government that I can't control and the president can invoke the constitution, if he so chooses. You know how these things work. What do I say when objections are raised?"

"Edward, first, blackmail is such an ugly word which should not be spoken between friends. Second, we say Russia is delighted to be able to help a small, beleaguered state that hitherto has been ignored by its supposed European brothers in the fight against the impact of African migration. Italy has failed to support you in controlling mass population movement and the new right wing has shown no interest in stepping up.

"We Russians are a humanitarian nation, with years of experience in Africa, and we are appalled by what we see happening here. That is why we have supplied the patrol vessels, to aid your search and rescue work. To be doubly effective, we are basing part of our fleet in Malta, to fill the gap that the European navies have ignored. To do that, we need facilities. Also, you need to protect your homeland, since the camps in the south of the island cannot hold the numbers of desperate people you have allowed in and Europe will not accept any onward transfers. What choice do you have but to improve your own security? Yes?"

Refalo just stared at the ambassador, who continued his lecture.

"You are a small country with limited resources – how many men are there in your navy? A few hundred, if that. Tell them, Edward, that drought, Islamic State, famine in the Sahel, the wars and unrest endemic in the Middle East, will only make this situation worse. The whole of Africa is heading this way, and you are the most southerly country in Europe – well, apart from those silly Italian islands! You must act. And so you have done. You will be viewed as heroes."

Buzilov smiled, smoothed his hand over his hair, then across his stubble, as if surprised by its growth rate. Refalo looked sceptical.

"You think people will believe that?"

"It is up to you to make it work. We have people who can facilitate things. We will send some over, to help your office get properly organised. I am glad we agree that there is a PR exercise to be managed here."

Refalo turned his head to one side and saw two young boys on bikes, weaving down the service road, laughing and chatting. They had fishing rods strapped to their down tubes, waving in the air like giant antennae. Multi-coloured rucksacks no doubt held their reels, lines, stale bread, crisps and Kinnie, the island's favourite fizzy drink. Refalo remembered, in more innocent times when he was a boy, how he too loved to while away his summer holidays here, playing in the maze of derelict buildings, throwing stones at any remaining panes of glass, exploring the tunnels and leaping from rocks into the blue waters of the harbour. He smiled to himself.

Grigori Buzilov followed Refalo's gaze.

"How on earth did they get in? I can see our men will be arriving just in time!"

The admiral was incensed. He screamed something in Russian at one of the Russian naval security guards. The man unholstered his pistol and fired a shot into the air. The boys froze. One of them put his hands in the air. Admiral Berezovsky screamed at Ray Farrugia: "Tell them to go home or the next shot will be through their kneecaps!"

With no need for further threats, the boys turned their bikes around and fled back the way they had come.

CHAPTER 7
ACTING ASSISTANT COMMISSIONER GEORGE ZAMMIT

POLICE HQ, FLORIANA, MALTA

GEORGE WAS AT POLICE HQ, making his way down the corridor leading from the large first-floor conference room. There, the Commissioner of Police had just read to the most senior officers the bombshell of a memo that he had received that morning.

To: The Commissioner of Malta Police and his Senior Command
From: Michael Cini, Minister for Home Affairs and Security

Please note that tomorrow, at noon, we expect to welcome Colonel Igor Fedorov of the Russian Military Police at Malta International Airport. On the orders of the prime minister, he will sit alongside the Commissioner of Malta Police ...

"That's me, of course," the commissioner had said with a wry smile directed at the assembled officers.

"'... and share the equivalent rank and superiority within Malta Pulizija *as our current commissioner.*'"

Nobody paid much attention to the rest of the memo, given how stunned they were by the news that the *Pulizija* was henceforth to be commanded jointly by the Russians.

George turned and saw Mallia making a beeline down the corridor towards him. The deputy commissioner pushed his face close to George's, so he could smell his coffee breath.

"Well, my God! What the hell was all that about? Don't you worry, I'll find out. I'm in shock."

Mallia was shaking his head in confusion and George could not help but watch his drooping jowls flap around his jaw.

"Did you know anything about this? It's outrageous!" George shook his head.

"Listen, I'm glad I've found you – you've not been at Castille lately, working in the PM's office? Questions have been asked."

George stood firm and stuck out his jaw. The previous day, he had told one of the prime minister's junior advisers that he was returning to his normal duties at police headquarters, as he felt he could no longer be of assistance in helping with the "reorganisation" of the PM's office. He had only been there for two days but had quickly realised he was becoming part of something that made him deeply uncomfortable.

He looked around to be sure they would not be overheard and spoke softly, yet urgently, into Mallia's ear.

"*Mela*, I don't want to be there because I'm being asked to destroy papers that should, as a matter of law, be preserved and sent to the National Archive. I don't understand half of the stuff, but there're contracts about energy supplies, provision of health care arrangements, certain land deals – including compulsory acquisitions and sell offs – that just don't look right to me. This isn't the PM's personal stuff, they're government records and not his to destroy! It occurred to me that I could be shredding valuable documents that a magistrate might want to see. You know what he's done in the past. Who's to say it's not going on now?"

"For God's sake!" Mallia clapped his hands on his head in shock. "You're not supposed to read the stuff, just get rid of it. Do as you're told!"

"But that's the point, Carmel. If it's just a case of 'getting rid of it', why has that become a police matter? I'm not doing it. The PM could easily ask the Public Service to do it. It's their job. But he won't because he's scared of them. He thinks we're more ... biddable. And I've heard it's all linked to the Russians. How, I've no idea. If there're repercussions, so be it. I'm referring my concerns to you. You can take them up the chain – *if you dare*!"

George was shaking. He hated conflict, but here he was convinced he was in the right.

The deputy commissioner spluttered, "How dare you? You ... you haven't heard the last of this! I haven't got time to stand here arguing with you, Zammit, but watch your step. You're one pronouncement away from receiving an official warning!"

George took a deep breath and hissed: "Deputy Commissioner, I'm perfectly entitled to raise a formal grievance that I've been ordered to undertake duties that put me in contravention of this country's legal code. Would you prefer me to do that?"

The deputy commissioner looked at him, aghast. He whispered urgently: "What's got into you? Have you gone mad?"

Without another word, George moved off and returned to his office, slightly shaken, but secretly proud of how he had handled a tricky situation. A nervous sweat had sprung out across his brow.

On his desk was a message from the Hospital of St Anthony of Padua asking if he could visit Gerald Camilleri, saying that the patient was becoming very weak. He immediately took his jacket and made for the car park, his head still spinning.

The drive to Gerald's hospice, outside Rabat, was about twenty minutes to the north. On leaving the congestion of the harbour area and the intensively developed Central Belt, the countryside opened up. In the central plain, fields appeared to either side of the road and he could see farm labourers working on the red clay soil, covered with rows of vines, bushy potato tops, cabbages, and even a large field scattered with pumpkins, lying around like so many forgotten basketballs.

Many of the labourers were black and George thought that it was not so long ago that it would have been rare to see migrants from Africa working in those family-farmed fields.

He entered the nursing home and waited in the reception area while a nun silently ascended the stairs to the first floor. A few minutes later, she appeared on the landing and beckoned him up.

"Please don't tire him, he's getting very weak." George nodded.

Camilleri was in bed, lying very still, propped up with a pile of pillows. As George entered the room, Gerald shielded his eyes against the light from the corridor that silhouetted his friend in the doorway.

"Ah, George, I would recognise that profile anywhere – you need to lose a little weight. Come, sit with me. Tell me what has been happening."

George briefly updated him on everything he knew, including the instruction to clear documents from Refalo's office, and the remarkable memo from the minister himself. He finished by explaining that he had stormed out of headquarters, having threatened to file a grievance against Mallia for ordering him to destroy government property.

Gerald had slid back on his pillows and George feared he had fallen asleep again. But the minute George had finished speaking, he opened his eyes and raised his head. "My word! That is quite a tale. How exciting!" Gerald's voice was a rasp.

"I thought it might come to this. It seems the Russians are coming to save us from being overrun by migrants. I do not believe that is the truth for a moment, but others will, no doubt. So, what is it they really want, do you think? A jumping off point for their Libyan campaign? A foothold in the Central Mediterranean? A poke in the eye, aimed at NATO and the EU? Hmmm. Probably all of those things."

He lay quietly for a while, his eyes closed, breathing deeply. George waited patiently for him to continue.

"They will need Refalo and his cronies in their pocket, but that is only a question of money. Playing the migrant card is interesting. If it came down to it, maybe the stupid electorate would go along with it. It is too depressing.

"Your file-cleaning exercise also suggests to me the Russians might have something on Refalo, which is why he is so belatedly trying to weed out his paperwork. If that is the case, it would be too late now for him to start covering his tracks. You are right to want nothing to do with his clearing of the Augean Stables. Stay well away from that little game. You have your talents, George, but you are no Hercules!"

George leaned forward, amazed Camilleri's forensic brain could so quickly gather together the pieces and create the bigger picture. But what Hercules and those stables had to do with anything, he had no idea.

"So, what do I do? *Mela*, I can't just sit around doing nothing, can I?"

"Well, there is something I have not told you. Now, listen carefully, I think I know what it is the Russians have on Refalo and Farrugia. And Cini come to that. Some time ago, papers were stolen from my office. Incriminating papers. I do not think now is the time to use this information, but that time will come soon – let us keep this our secret for now. You will have to be ready to act on your own initiative – my days are coming to an end.

"But there are people ... well, a person ... whom I trust will help you, when the time is right. I knew something big was coming, but such a storm ... I never expected ... this."

Gerald sighed and closed his eyes. George was certain he had fallen asleep. Then he rallied. His milky eyes opened, and he tried to raise himself while he spoke.

"I cannot share names with you, as it would put the person I trust in danger, and I promised I would not do that. But keep your eyes and ears open. You will work out who I mean, and when he, or she, is ready to act, then they will need your help."

George stood up and put his arm under Gerald, to lift him higher. He seemed to have said all he was inclined to say about the theft of his papers. George had a thousand questions still, but the subject was closed. There was another thing Gerald needed to talk about.

"Listen, while you are here, indulge me a little, will you? There is that matter I intended to talk to you about before Marco Bonnici's arrival intervened. Now is a good time." Camilleri pulled the bedclothes tighter around him and lowered his voice, until it was no more than a breathy whisper. "You know I am a Catholic, I have been all my life. I even have a modicum of faith, which is convenient knowing what is shortly to come. But I need to make a temporal confession, to an officer of the law." He saw the look of consternation on George's face. "It is true, a priest will not do for what I have to say. The old crows would flap around, wringing their beads and grabbing at their crucifixes. So, will you hear my confession?"

George was confused.

"If it's what you want, then I'm happy to be your confessor. But I'm pretty inexperienced and I've got no power of Absolution, if that is what you need."

A tired smile spread across Camilleri's face.

"No, George, I doubt even you can grant me release from my burden of sin. To start with, I am not a contrite sinner, as you are about to hear. You remember, a little while ago, I told you about my younger years? How my father was a brute, in his work as a policeman and as a husband and father? My mother, my sister and I hated him. He hurt us and belittled our mother in front of us. I dread to think how he earned his reputation as a policeman, because when I joined the force, years after his death, I was treated with outright suspicion, because I was his son.

"He died, I think I told you, in 1974, around the time the republic was declared. I suggested to you then that he was involved, somehow, in the politics of the time. That was a lie. My confession, George, is that it was I who killed him." Camilleri had a thin smile on his lips. "He was a drunk and he went to the roughest bars near the shipyards, where he would bully and brutalise anyone he took against. If there were objections, or anyone took advantage of his inebriated state and fought back, he would take his revenge, sober and backed up by others in uniform, the next day. He was a monster and was widely hated in Paola.

"I was young, around twelve years old, when I decided I had had enough. One evening, he had left Mother on the floor of the kitchen, weeping and bloody. I, too, had a bloody nose, the price of my intervention. I waited for him with a length of timber in a back street in Paola, outside a bar, between the shipyards and our house. As he staggered out of the bar drunk, I clubbed him. I could hardly reach his head. He took the blows, laughing at first, not realising my intent. When he fell to his knees, I set about him again and beat him until he was unconscious. Then, fearful of what would happen when he regained consciousness, I took his pistol from his holster, fumbling with it, and eventually shot him, twice, in cold blood. My own father!" Camilleri sighed. "It was terrible, unforgivable even. At first, I struggled to get the gun from the holster, then I tried to fire it but could not. I had not released the safety catch. So there were plenty of chances for me to relent. But I did not, I struggled on until I succeeded.

"After I had taken the shots and Father lay on the pavement, with blood coming from his head, three men came out of the bar to see what all the noise was. They soon realised what I had done. One of them knew who I was and they also all knew who, and what, my father was. They took pity on me. One took me home and spoke to my mother. Never a word was mentioned about it in our house. The other two took my father's body and threw it into the dock. Such was his reputation, nobody thought it strange that he should meet his end that way. His death was what it was. Who those three men were, I never knew. It is unlikely I will ever meet them, at least not in this world, but should it ever happen, I would throw myself at their feet in thanks."

He sighed and smiled weakly.

"There, I have told a representative of the law what happened when I was twelve. Do you think you can understand why I did what I did? Or will you arrest me, as I deserve? I know I cannot be absolved; I would have to tell a priest I am an insincere penitent." A rueful smile spread across his gaunt face. "I say to myself, I have no idea why it troubles me so much but, then again, I do know. As death comes nearer, I think what this confession could do for me when I am finally called to judgement."

George took his thin, cold hand.

He was mortified. There were so many sides to this man. George had seen the best of them, but he had also seen the worst. He had been right, as a young policeman, to be scared of the enigmatic, aloof assistant commissioner whom he now knew had carried this terrible burden for all those years. George wondered if guilt had eaten away at him, to make him the austere, solitary man he had become.

He swallowed hard and said: "I hope you telling me this gives you some comfort, Gerald. It takes courage to speak out after so many years of silence. I respect that. I'm just sorry it's taken you so long to share your burden."

"Thank you, George. I know I will shortly be judged, and, in His court, no sin is secret, no matter how long concealed. There will be no smart lawyers to help me and all I can do is throw myself on His mercy. I find myself thinking of that moment more and more."

George sat in silence for a moment, until Gerald's thin hand squeezed his. He looked up with a start and saw the other man's lips moving. George listened hard and realised he was murmuring the Act of Contrition.

"O my God, I am truly sorry for having offended You, and I detest all my sins because of Your just punishment, but most of all because they offend You, my God, who art all good, and deserving of all my love."

George joined him, speaking softly, and together they completed the prayer.

"...I firmly resolve, with the help of Your grace, to sin no more and to avoid the near occasion of sin. In the name of the Father, and of the Son, and of the Holy Spirit. Amen."

George sat there until the shallow breathing became rhythmic and he was certain Gerald was asleep. Then, he slowly released Gerald's hand from his, raised himself from the bedside and left the room. In his heart, he knew he would never see his mentor and friend again.

CHAPTER 8
SERGEANT DENZEL ZAMMIT

MALTA INTERNATIONAL AIRPORT, MALTA

THE FIRST FLIGHTS of Russian volunteers were due to land in Malta the weekend following the meeting of the senior command.

With a wicked smile, the commissioner had put Deputy Commissioner Mallia in charge of managing the day-to-day relationship between the Maltese *Pulizija* and the Russian military and, in particular, the Russian Military Police, when it came to law enforcement. Given that the deputy commissioner himself never actually did any real work, he immediately summoned George to his office. He, of course, had left headquarters to visit Camilleri, so the only lackey to be found lingering around headquarters was Inspector Karl Chelotti.

Chelotti had been told to put a team together and make all necessary arrangements to go and meet the Russian volunteers. By one of those quirks of fate, Denzel happened to be passing the outer door to Mallia's office just as the deputy comissioner was explaining to the inspector what was needed. He spotted Denzel out of the corner of his eye and, as he desperately grasped at straws to rid himself of the responsibility that had been laid at his door, said to Chelotti: "Take young Zammit and some constables. He'll help you. He's bright enough."

Chelotti shouted out into the corridor: "Zammit! In here!"

Denzel stuck his head into the room and Mallia pointed to a chair.

Chelotti thought through the logistics of the arrangements.

"They'll land and get out of the planes at the Air Wing's hangars, I assume?"

Armed Forces Malta's Air Wing had less than a dozen fixed-wing planes and half a dozen helicopters. They operated out of six hangars on the periphery of Malta's International Airport.

Mallia squirmed in his chair.

"Well, no, actually. The ambassador was quite insistent that he wanted to welcome the volunteers himself, at the main terminal building, along with the prime minister." Chelotti could not believe his ears.

"The prime minister! And he's agreed to that? Those guys are mercenaries ... hooligans."

Denzel nodded his head enthusiastically.

"You bet, sir. I've seen what they get up to."

Mallia snapped back: "Yes, Jesus save us! That's what I was told. We might as well tell the airport to hoover the red carpet and let's have a civic reception at Castille, while we're at it!

And don't call them mercenaries – they're volunteers." Denzel pulled out his notebook to record the instructions.

"No, you fool! I was being ironic, for God's sake." Mallia paused and ran his hand across the film of sweat that had formed on his brow. This all sounded very tricky indeed and he still had four more years to serve before he could retire on a full pension.

Suddenly, Mallia's phone rang. It was loud and insistent, causing him to jolt backwards in his seat. He looked at it for several seconds, almost not believing it was for him, until he forced himself to lift the receiver.

"Deputy Commissioner Mallia here. Who's speaking ...?

Oh ... oh, good morning, sir. Yes, sir ... I understand, sir ...

completely ... Really? Me? Well, of course, I'd be proud to serve ... Tomorrow? No, I mean, yes! Ha, ha!... Of course. Thank you for your confidence in me, sir ... yes, tomorrow. I'll see you then, sir."

The deputy commissioner's jowls sagged and settled over his collar when he had finished speaking. His head slumped, as though someone had physically deflated him. Denzel thought he might cry.

"Four more years," he muttered. "I only had four more years." It seemed he had forgotten Denzel and Chelotti were in the room. Denzel swallowed noisily.

"Sir, on the phone you mentioned tomorrow. Does it concern our arrangements?"

Mallia twitched, realising he still had subordinates in front of him.

"Er, yes, I'm afraid it does. That was the minister. The commissioner of police has just resigned – doesn't like the way things are going apparently – and it looks like I'm going to be his replacement. How about that?" he said with a thin smile. "And, Chelotti ... you'd better get that carpet hoovered after all. "

The next morning Denzel was waiting behind the dignitaries in the VIP area of Malta International Airport. As agreed, over 300 new Russian volunteers were arriving from Benghazi, on two of Malta Air's Boeing 737 aircraft, and the formal greetings were to be made in the main arrivals hall. A dozen scheduled flights had been diverted to the Air Force hangars where customs and border control officers, who were all part of the police establishment, had been ordered by Mallia to make the best job they could of processing the arriving tourists in the sweltering, airless buildings.

Once the planes had landed, Denzel went through to the baggage reclaim area, where the volunteers would collect their kit and weapons. He waited nervously, with six of his officers, for the Russians to arrive. The plan was to have them gather in the arrivals hall where the Russian ambassador and Refalo would give a short welcome address. They would then return airside where vehicles were waiting, out of sight, to form the convoy that the police would escort to Buggiba. What happened after that, he had no idea.

Twenty minutes after the planes had touched down, the first volunteers came down the escalators into the baggage reclaim area. He heard them before he saw them. Their loud gravelly voices and laughter echoed along the corridors. He was not quite sure what to expect, but certainly not 300 combat-ready, filthy troops, dressed in a variety of camouflage uniforms, with tactical belts and some wearing military helmets. Their faces were lined with ingrained dirt, as if they had walked straight off the battlefield.

It struck Denzel that he was the first Maltese official these Russians would meet, so he had to set an example. He walked out and stopped in front of the first volunteer, who looked like a fifteen-year-old, with a shaven head and a good dose of acne across most of his face and forehead. The young man looked at Denzel and walked straight past, without a second glance, leaving his outstretched hand hanging. After that, the volunteers descended the escalators thick and fast, adding the clatter of heavy boots to their shouts and cries.

Denzel was approached by an older man, dressed in a neat uniform and with a clean-shaven face. He wore the bands of a senior non-commissioned officer on his combat jacket. He smiled at Denzel and said: "Good morning!"

Denzel had spent a little time on the internet and answered in Russian.

"*Dobroye utro!*" returning the greeting. Denzel then noticed his new friend was smoking, as were a lot of the volunteers. Denzel pointed to the cigarette and wagged a finger.

"*Zapreshchena*! Forbidden." Something was evidently lost in translation as the new arrival fished around in his pockets and, with a wide smile, forced a packet of cigarettes on to him. "*Sigarety russkiye* ... good, good! For you!"

Realising that was the limit of what they could say to each other, Denzel clapped the soldier on the shoulder and said: "*Spasibo! Spasibo!*" Thanks, thanks.

Pleased with the start he had made on establishing good relations with their new guests, he turned his attention to what was happening in the baggage reclaim area. There were huge military rucksacks and duffel bags falling off the luggage belts and piling up everywhere. The crowd of volunteers pushed and jostled each other to try and hear the names that were being called out.

Somewhere in the chaos, Denzel heard a high-pitched female scream. It was not immediately clear where it was coming from, but it was definitely the sound of someone in distress. He pushed in amongst the mêlée and looked around, until he spotted a group of volunteers in the small duty-free store in one corner of the baggage reclaim area. They seemed to be helping themselves to cartons of cigarettes and bottles of spirits. One already had an open bottle and was greedily pouring whisky down his throat.

Denzel looked around for his team and, seeing no familiar faces in the jostling crowd, radioed for back up. It was then he noticed the young assistant who had been serving in the shop. She was sitting on the floor, with blood coming from her nose. Denzel immediately rushed across to help her. As he neared the shop, he crossed paths with a volunteer cradling an armful of bottles of spirits. He was laughing with a friend, who was also carrying a handful of bottles. Denzel saw red and swiped the drink out of the volunteer's arms. The bottles hit the floor and smashed at his feet. There was a moment of silence, then a loud cheer from the surrounding men.

The smashing sound seemed to alert the other volunteers to what was available in the duty-free shop and more of them started to make their way towards it. To his disappointment,

Denzel saw his newfound friend, the NCO, laughing with the others, while stuffing Marlboro cigarettes down the front of his jacket. Denzel managed to get the shop assistant onto her feet. With one arm around her shoulders, he tried to usher her through the crowd, towards the exit. To his horror, he saw a small group of volunteers had effectively barred this by threading their belts through the handles, making it impossible for the police backup he had requested to get in from the arrivals hall. He saw the doors flexing against the restraints, as those on the other side tried to push through.

A second group of Russians had raced up the stairs, to the top of the escalators, and effectively blocked the route into the hall from the upper level. They were hanging over the balustrade, shouting encouragement to their comrades below, who were busy glugging spirits and showering each other with shaken bottles of Prosecco. The rest of Denzel's team had fled up the escalators to the safety of the upper levels of the terminal, leaving him alone with the mob.

By this time, the duty-free shop was being systematically stripped. The baggage hall resounded to cheers and shouts, as the volunteers filled their rucksacks and duffle bags. Some had even had the cheek to load bottles and cigarettes into the large duty-free branded plastic carriers held at the checkout. Denzel approached the exit door to the arrivals hall with the assistant still hanging on his arm. He started undoing the belts in a bid to escape the mayhem, only to feel a stiff blow to his left ear. He reeled to one side, rendered deaf for a moment, not hearing a word the scrawny, bony-faced Russian was shouting at him. His assailant came at him again, fists flailing, catching Denzel a blow to the side of his face.

Denzel dropped the girl and unclipped his holster, raising his weapon in front of him. He screamed at the Russian to step back but, to his horror, the volunteer smiled and drew a long-serrated knife from his belt, waving it at Denzel. Then, the man suddenly leaned forward and grabbed the shop assistant by the hair, roughly pulling her towards him. She screamed, Denzel screamed at the volunteer and the volunteer screamed back. The Russian was backing into the crowd, keeping a good handful of the shop assistant's hair twisted round his fist. He pulled the woman with him and a crowd of men began to close in around, protecting him. Denzel moved forward, keeping his weapon trained on the man, their eyes locked onto one another's. Then, slowly and deliberately, the volunteer gently ran the blade of his knife down the side of the cowering woman's face, his eyes still fixed on Denzel, daring him to retaliate.

Denzel's world went silent. He was oblivious to the crowd around him, the faces swimming in front of him as one moving mass, and the voices forming one low-frequency roar. All he could see was the thin ribbon of blood that ran down the terrified woman's face and the twisted, silently screaming face of the beast who had done that to her. The Russian was waving the knife madly in his direction, jabbing it and slashing the air just centimetres from Denzel's nose. Then, the Russian turned to the woman and grasping ever more firmly onto that fistful of hair, pulled her head to one side and put the knife point into her ear. Laughing into Denzel's face, he started to gently twist the point. The woman screamed again. Something inside Denzel snapped and he squeezed the trigger.

CHAPTER 9
GERALD CAMILLERI
HOSPITAL OF ST ANTHONY OF PADUA, RABAT, MALTA

GERALD JOSEPH CAMILLIERI died in the early hours of a Wednesday morning, in his darkened room, in the small nursing home in the woods. When the young Nepalese nurse entered to open the wooden shutters and let in the light of a new day, she immediately knew that all life had already left the room.

She approached the bed to check for a breath or a heartbeat, noticing the strange phenomena that death worked on a body. It had stolen all colour from the corpse, drawing the blood quietly to the depths of its internal organs, but also seemed to draw the colour from the bedclothes, the deceased's nightwear, the wallpaper, curtains and any other surface nearby. Everything had become grey and neutral, as if all life had soaked away, through the cracks in the floorboards, under the ill-fitting windows and doors, and between the cavities in the walls.

Gerald Camilleri had largely lived and worked alone. It was not a state of affairs that he had planned, but the manner of his father's death and the secret he had carried with him, until the very last, had set him apart. In his heart, he had never considered himself worthy of respect, or even love. Besides

George, only his sister Carmella knew the truth about him and that unique bond had sustained him throughout the years.

It was not until he shared his secret with George that he found any peace. George never understood why Gerald had felt it necessary to unburden himself in that way. But had he known the profound sense of release the confession had brought the dying man in his last hours, he would have recognised the value of the service he had given to his friend.

The funeral of Gerald Camilleri was held in St John's Cathedral, Valletta. Although the cathedral was originally built by the Order of St John in the late sixteenth century, its real moment of glory arrived one hundred years later, when the Knights applied some of their considerable wealth to richly adorning the interior, turning it into a baroque masterpiece to rival anything to be found in Rome or elsewhere in Europe. Given Camilleri was not only a respected member of the Order of Malta, a senior officer in the *Pulizija*, but also a man who had, over the years, done favours and provided service to nearly every politician, businessman and financier on the island, it was a large and eclectic crowd that gathered to pay their respects.

His heavy mahogany casket was laid on the catafalque before the altar, draped in the State Flag of the Sovereign Order of Malta, a rectangular red field with a white Latin cross. This flag had flown since 1291, when the Order left the Holy Land for Cyprus, hoisting it over all its ships.

After the service, it had been arranged for the body to be cremated in Sicily, Malta having no cremation facilities. Gerald Camilleri's funerary urn would then be returned, to be placed in the family's columbarium in Malta's sprawling, gothic Addolorata Cemetery, on the outskirts of Valletta. A bronze tablet would later be engraved in remembrance of him.

As he had grown older, Gerald had come to appreciate the action of his late mother in arranging for his father to be buried in a small, cheap plot in a distant corner of the cemetery. She had said she did not want any family member to have to spend another minute in that man's company, let alone eternity, a sentiment that Gerald had wholeheartedly endorsed.

Marco had visited the chapel of rest and spent some quiet moments with his friend before the funeral service. Afterwards, he had travelled with Gerald's sister, Carmella, her daughter Silvia and Silvia's partner Lucy, to the funeral home, where the casket was made ready to be sent for cremation in Sicily. It was here, in the heavily ornamented, stuffy little chapel, that the small party said their final emotional farewells to one of life's gentlemen.

Forty-five minutes later, Carmella, Marco, Silvia and Lucy returned to the funeral reception hosted by the Lieutenant of the Grand Master, Fra' Ernesto de Belvoir, at the Order's sovereign territory in Fort Saint Angelo, in Birgu. The gathering of the great and good was the perfect opportunity for Marco to canvas opinion, talk to some of the politicians and find out what the body politic was thinking. There was a large turnout, all milling around the magnificent reception rooms. Marco became aware that the crowd was conversing quietly, creating a low collective hum, quite unlike the resounding chatter and laughter that was usually the case when a hundred people were left to chat between themselves and enjoy a glass of wine or two.

He supposed the subdued atmosphere was because the elite group felt frightened. They were the ones who had the most to lose from the Russian occupation, as he now thought of it. They were the members of the House of Representatives, the ministers, the judiciary, the *Pulizija* – those whose autonomy was now under threat. Someone had welcomed the Russians into the parlour and now they were proving to be poor house guests.

At the back of the hall, standing with an uncomfortable looking Ray Farrugia, was the newly arrived Colonel Igor Fedorov, head of the Russian Military Police, who was responsible for managing all security issues on the island. He looked resplendent, standing erect in his formal dark blue uniform, a gold braid aiguillette draped across his right shoulder. He and Farrugia were not speaking, but Fedorov was scanning the room, his cap held stiffly under one arm, revealing his cropped straw blond hair. Marco watched him closely. He immediately took a dislike to the arrogant half smirk on the soldier's chiselled face as he surveyed the room.

The colonel seemed to sense he was being watched and his pale blue eyes immediately alighted on Marco who had no alternative but to hold that gaze, resolving not to be the first to turn away. For no more than a couple of seconds, they studied each other across the room. Eventually, the colonel nodded his head, almost in greeting, and turned away. Marco had not realised it, but he had been holding his breath.

He had entered the room with Silvia and Lucy. Heads turned at the sound of a shriek of joy from Silvia, who bounded through the room to throw herself at George, standing at the buffet with his mouth full of hors d'oeuvres and pockets stuffed with vol au vents. Silvia was a tall woman, a head higher than him, with broad shoulders and wide hips. She had caramel-coloured skin, dark smoky eyes and strong features. Her manner was confident and assured, without any sense of arrogance. Despite being a scientist – a marine biologist – she was led by her heart, a trait that her more reserved partner thought made her impulsive, exciting and, sometimes, exasperating to be with.

It was that impulsiveness that had led Silvia to leave their flat in Catania and meet up with a section of the Maltese resistance movement, *Democratica*, who were being trained by the Americans at the US base at Signorella, in readiness to strike back at the virtual occupation of their country by the Russians.

"George, George, I was hoping I'd find you here! I'm sorry …"

George had been the one who had pulled Silvia out of the tunnels under Mount Etna, when she had been kidnapped by the 'Ndrangheta. Her uncle, Gerald, had sent him to Sicily to help find her and landed him in all manner of trouble, culminating in his reluctant involvement in the rescue mission while the volcano was erupting. Fortunately for George and his reputation as a man of many heroic deeds, the rescue had succeeded, and he had emerged with the lion's share of the credit.

George hurriedly wiped crumbs from his mouth and gave Silvia a hug, then embraced Lucy. He turned back to Silvia and took her hand.

"No, we're all sorry today. Your uncle was a great man. We all know it, don't we?"

He looked behind him at his colleagues from the *Pulizija*, who were watching the exchange.

"This is Silvia Camilleri, Gerald's much-loved niece," he announced. There were murmurs of commiseration from the group.

Lucy put an arm round George's shoulders and the three of them stood locked together for a few moments. Then Silvia pulled them away from the group of *Pulizija*.

"My uncle always spoke very highly of you, George. That's why he sent you to rescue me from the volcano!" George blushed.

"Well, that's one assignment I don't want to repeat. He caused me some trouble, that man!" They laughed.

Silvia's expression shifted to a serious one. She and Lucy moved him further away, to one side of the hall. In hushed tones, Silvia said: "Look, I've heard about Denzel, and I just want to say, I'm sorry he's in trouble but he did the right thing, shooting that Russian rapist. He did us all a favour!"

"Well, it wasn't quite like that ...'

"George, it doesn't matter. It teaches them they can't come here with their filthy manners and medieval attitudes and do as they please. But listen – all I'm going to say is, if he's hiding somewhere and needs anything, or if there's any problem, we can ... well, we've got friends who'd be honoured to help. Not everybody's just sitting around and letting them walk all over us. You understand me?"

George noted her careful choice of words and glanced around.

"Don't worry about Denzel. He's safe. But I hear you. I know he's itching to come back, but I really don't think ..."

"George, we need good people." They were looking out of the window into the courtyard below, their backs to the room. Silvia was whispering.

"People with the balls to stand up to these bastards. What are they really doing here? Why do we put up with it? Tell Denzel to follow Democratica online. If you need to contact me, for now, I'm at my mother's." George shook his head.

"*Mela*, you ladies had better be incredibly careful who you speak to like that. These are tough times. Nobody knows who's thinking what. With me, you're safe. But there're others who would hand you over, just to get into their good books..."

George's heart suddenly turned to ice, as a hand lightly touched his shoulder. Lucy stepped back in alarm. Silvia turned to look at the newcomer, her deep brown eyes widening in surprise, while the muscles in her face tightened.

A man's voice said: "Get into whose good books?"

Colonel Igor Fedorov stood behind them with a crooked smile playing around his mouth. His blue eyes were narrowed in suspicion. The three of them were speechless. Stepping forward unexpectedly, Marco Bonnici joined them, saving the situation by saying with easy charm: "Well, your good books, of course, Colonel! We all need to be in your good books, do we not? But, let me introduce myself. I am Marco Bonnici." The colonel tried to dredge the name up. It rang a bell.

"Ah, yes, I've heard of you ... or perhaps I should say, I've heard a lot more about your daughter." Marco shrugged.

"Unfortunately, that would not surprise me. But let's not talk about her. It upsets me too much. I am her father, after all. Tell me, how are you finding Malta ..."

Marco and the colonel made small talk for several minutes, until the Russian got bored but, before he left them, Marco had managed to invite him to the *castello* for dinner.

George, Lucy and Silvia had drifted off to one side, leaving Marco to continue making conversation. After Fedorov left, Marco came across to join them. He looked directly at Silvia and asked quietly: "Tell me, is there any organised resistance developing against these hoodlums? Or are the young content to allow the Russians to corrupt our government and steal our country? If there was such a group, I would be extremely interested in knowing more about it."

Silvia shrugged. "Why would you ask me?" Marco smiled.

"Just a feeling – and the contents of a letter your uncle left me, which was given to me by his notary. I am honoured that Gerald had sufficient trust in me to make me an executor of his estate. He mentioned you were always one to favour direct action in times such as these and asked that I contact you after you returned from Sicily, to make sure you stayed safe." With a twinkle in his eyes, Marco added: "Though what you might have been up to there, I cannot possibly imagine!"

CHAPTER 10
MARCO BONNICI
THE WEBER CLINIC, BERN, SWITZERLAND

THE WEBER CLINIC WAS A PRIVATE, twenty bed, specialist inpatient unit located in Bern, Switzerland. It had been opened thirty years earlier by leading psychiatrist Dr Hans Weber. The clinic had not only become world famous for the size of its fees and its strict ethos of confidentiality, but also for the specialised treatment of patients who were acutely ill with schizophrenic or psychotic conditions and in need of twenty-four-hour supervised care. Dr Weber's daughter, Laura, had followed in her father's footsteps and now ran the clinic. She had had several calls and consultations over Zoom with Marco and seen the distressing photograph of Natasha's current condition.

Marco spoke at length with Laura Weber and, under a vow of strict confidentiality, told her about Natasha's disturbing pattern of behaviour. He was reluctant to spell out the worst of her history but spoke in such terms as to suggest she had no compunction about harming others, appeared to have no conscience and lacked any ability to express remorse for any of her actions.

Marco explained that he believed a period of intense stress, when she had been subjected to extraordinary pressures, including the risk of criminal prosecution, had finally pushed her over the edge and led to her hiding away and living a solitary life in the forests of north-west Greece, where she had experienced some kind of emotional collapse.

The doctor was fascinated by what she had heard and agreed to treat Natasha. Over the next few days, they had several further video calls, where Marco explained as much as he could about Natasha's background and history. The process exhausted him, and he began to feel the sessions were as much about him as they were about Natasha. After one conversation, they had sat in silence, looking at each other on their respective screens. Then, Dr Weber had asked: "Are you, or were you, married, Mr Bonnici?"

"Well, yes, I was, many years ago. Unfortunately, my wife died. She fell down some stairs. She was pregnant and died of haemorrhaging after a miscarriage. Natasha was the only witness – she was five years old."

Expressionless, the doctor scribbled another note.

"I am sorry. That is dreadful. And yet you raised your daughter and the two of you lived together until she was in her mid-thirties?"

"She is my only child. I am afraid I learned how to love her and hate her at the same time."

"Did you ever seek professional help to reconcile a huge conflict like that?"

"No."

"Was her presence in your life the reason why you never remarried?"

"I never dared disturb our relationship. I felt anyone coming between us might ... well, I do not know what would have happened. But also, for many years, I could not remove myself from Natasha's life. As she grew older, she became more bold, reckless even. It seemed she felt that normal rules, and laws, did not apply to her. I was worried what might happen if I left her to follow her own path. But, of course, there came a point when I could not bear it anymore, so I left. And then all this happened."

The doctor smiled sympathetically.

"You blame yourself?"

"I do."

"Once we have Natasha safe in the clinic, would you consider speaking to a colleague of mine, to explore your feelings about all this? I think it would help."

Marco sighed and steepled his hands under his chin.

"I will consider it. But in the past, it has been more convenient to push all this out of my mind and try to concentrate on other things. We will see."

"You are right, Natasha should be the focus of our attention at the moment. Okay, this is what we are going to do.

"Under Swiss law, I quote, 'A person may be detained in a suitable institution in the case of mental disorder or serious self-neglect, provided there is no other way to ensure her personal welfare.' This is the best way forward and I am happy there is sufficient evidence that Natasha's personal welfare is a serious cause for concern. I should be able to obtain the court order for her detention within the next twenty-four hours. The photograph taken in the Greek police station and the circumstances in which she was found should be enough to convince a court to make the order. The fact that her next-of-kin wants her treated here in Bern is sufficient for the court to have jurisdiction."

Two days later, Marco boarded a small, chartered jet at Malta International Airport, noting, with a sigh, the heavy presence of Russian troops around the terminal and even in the VIP suite. The jet then flew to Bern, where it collected Dr Weber and two nurses, one male and one female. From there, it was a short flight to Ioannina airport, in north-west Greece, where Natasha was in hospital. A people carrier waited at the private terminal to take them onwards, to the hospital.

In the people carrier, Dr Weber sat next to Marco. When

they arrived at the hospital, she turned towards him and placed her hand briefly on his shoulder. She said, in a soft reassuring tone: "I believe it is best if you go in first and make contact with Natasha. Try not to startle her. Remember, she has had no contact with friends or family for two years. She may even find the act of speech physically difficult at first. Just sit for a while and say nothing. See how she reacts. It will take time for her to work out how to behave with you."

Marco nodded along. He had never considered how they were going to persuade Natasha to come with them. He had half-expected that the two nurses would wrestle her to the ground, sedate her and bundle her onto the private plane. As the doctor continued to speak to him, he became aware of the faint smell of her floral scent, as her straight, ash blonde hair brushed against his shoulder.

"Try to win some trust. Speak softly to her and without emotion. Above all else, do not try to make physical contact. If no progress is made today, tell her you will return tomorrow. We have time."

He first saw his daughter through the narrow slit of a window in the door of her single room. She was sitting beside the bed, in a pale blue armchair. She was very thin and wearing an oversized jumper and some jeans that were obviously not hers. Her matted hair was tied on top of her head, in an untidy mess. She was not wearing any makeup, and her head sagged slightly forward. The weight loss had made her cheekbones more pronounced, and the narrowness of her face accentuated her large dark brown eyes. She looked gaunt and neglected.

Almost as if she sensed his presence behind the door, she slowly turned her head, and her eyes met his.

CHAPTER 11
ACTING ASSISTANT COMMISSIONER GEORGE ZAMMIT

POLICE HQ, FLORIANA, MALTA

A WEEK after the fiasco at the airport, George was hauled before Acting Commissioner Mallia and the newly arrived Fedorov. The acting commissioner was a nervous, sweaty mess. He had a handkerchief in his hand and was constantly wiping his brow as well as the rolls of flesh around his neck. He and Colonel Fedorov sat in the large conference room, to either side of the top end of the table.

Mallia nodded at George, who saw the shifty look in his eyes and the dripping perspiration. He knew he could not trust this man to fight his corner or, more importantly, Denzel's corner. George stood to one side of the table, unsure whether he should sit or not. Fedorov looked at him through his close-set, slanted eyes, which were the palest shade of blue. His blond hair was shaven at the sides and cut short and neat on top of his head. A sharp, well-defined parting separated his scalp into two distinct sections. His face was thin and his nose long and straight. The shape of his skull gave prominence to his jaw and cheekbones. He was slightly built but, even seated, had a strong physical presence. Every inch a fighting man, today Fedorov wore his less formal, olive-green field uniform, with a zip-up jacket.

George guessed he could only have been in his early forties, which was young to be sporting three stars on his shoulder boards, showing his elevated rank. George pretended not to be intimidated and sat next to Carmel Mallia, facing the Russian.

After the shot had been fired in the baggage hall of the airport, all hell had erupted, and Denzel had nearly been torn limb from limb by infuriated volunteers. He had been dazed and horrified by what had happened and had stood there taking the blows, until his legs gave way beneath him, and he had fallen to the floor, where the rioting men continued to beat and kick him unconscious. It was only the arrival of Chelotti and some Russian Military Police, who had forced open the doors from the arrivals hall, which managed to restore calm to the ugly atmosphere. Chelotti summoned two other officers, and, between them, they carried Denzel away from the scene, after which Chelotti personally drove him to Mater Dei, the main hospital on the island.

Fedorov took charge of today's meeting.

"So, this was a serious assault – no, let's call it what it was, a *murder* – of one of my men, ruining the welcome ceremony that our heroes so richly deserved and giving encouragement to subversive forces, with possible links to the Maltese *Pulizija* and Armed Forces."

George stammered and stuttered: "I ... I d-don't think that is ... t-t-t-totally correct, if I may say so."

"You don't? How interesting. When one person shoots another in the head from point blank range, I think we can call it murder. Unless of course the person pulling the trigger is a policeman's son – then, I can see, there will be a different explanation.

"We have fifty statements, each saying the same thing, Assistant Commissioner Zammit. Andrei Khatuntsev, the deceased volunteer ... he has a name ... took a souvenir from the duty-free store, but found he had no euros to pay for it."

Fedorov took a statement from a pile in front of him and started to read aloud.

"'Frightened by the aggressive attitude of the Maltese policeman, Khatuntsev was asking the shop assistant if she would accept Libyan dinar in payment, when the policeman grabbed the girl, pulled her away from him and then deliberately shot him in the head, execution-style. I didn't see any knife and Khatuntsev did not harm the shop assistant, as far as I could see.'" Fedorov dropped the statement on the table in a show of disgust.

"Fifty witnesses attested to this!! What am I supposed to think? They're all wrong?"

George did not answer him. Mallia fidgeted with his pen. It was Fedorov who broke the silence.

"When did you last see your son?"

George said nothing but looked at Mallia.

"Carmel, what's the status of these questions? Should I be taking legal advice? Should you be cautioning me?" Mallia shook his head.

"George, you're here voluntarily to help us ..." Fedorov cut in.

"Your son murdered one of my men. I want some answers. It's your duty to answer me. I repeat, when did you last see your son?"

George looked him straight in the eye, his hatred of the Russian blazing across the table. Finding courage, he never knew he had, he said: *"Mela*, I don't answer to you. I refuse to answer."

Fedorov turned to Mallia.

"You see? Is this how it is going to be?"

Mallia made a gesture with one hand, lowering the palm to the table, to urge the colonel to calm down.

"George, please. Answer some simple questions?"

"I last saw my son three days ago, in ward fifteen of Mater Dei Hospital where he'd been taken on leaving the airport, having suffered serious injuries. He was nearly beaten to death while trying to rescue a young girl who was being held hostage by one of your men. He'd already cut her with a knife and was threatening to do more harm to her. I'm sorry one of your men died in the incident but, before we use words like 'murder', I think we need to see, and hear, a lot more about what really happened that morning, not a pile of fabricated rubbish like this! "

He flicked his hand dismissively at the pile of statements that sat on the desk in front of Fedorov.

"And for the record, my family and I have not seen him since, nor do we have any knowledge of his current whereabouts. And that's all I have to say to you, Colonel."

Chelotti had spoken to George, and they had both agreed it was only a matter of time before the Russians took matters into their own hands and made an example of Denzel. Chelotti had a cousin who worked at Mater Dei as a porter and had him arrange a secret meeting with one of the doctors who was from Tbilisi, Georgia, and no friend of the Russians.

Denzel had been brought out of the induced coma the hospital had placed him in, with no lasting ill effects. He was taken to an outpatients' entrance in a wheelchair, where he had been bundled into a waiting car and driven to Chelotti's uncle's house in Hamrun, a densely populated, working-class district outside Valletta. The doctor had agreed to visit and treat Denzel at the safe house and fix the hospital records, so it looked like he had discharged himself and walked out of the hospital unaided.

George felt slightly nauseous and a little shaky after giving his statement. He was not good at telling lies and knew it showed. He clasped his hands together under the table to control the tremors in them. He could feel the colonel's eyes boring into him.

"Are the palms of your hands damp, Acting Assistant Commissioner?" Fedorov challenged him. "I was with the FSB for several years and I know when someone's lying to me. Be careful, Zammit, I've got my eye on you. Don't think you can hide behind that uniform. If I want to get the truth out of you, I will. I want to talk to Sergeant Denzel Zammit in connection with my murder enquiry and neither you, nor the acting commissioner here, will stop me."

The colonel sat back, narrowed his eyes into slits and folded his arms. With a contemptuous look at Mallia, he flicked his wrist and dismissed the witness.

George walked out of the conference room with as much dignity as he could muster. He felt ill and realised he had to get out of headquarters before his legs buckled underneath him. He hurried through the hushed atmosphere of HQ, noticing nervous colleagues avoid making eye contact with him. The Russians had moved about twenty officers into the building and allocated an officer to each of the squads. They had only been there for a week, but it already felt like they ran the place.

Every time George arrived home, he faced a barrage of questioning from Marianna and Gina. This time was no different.

"Have you heard anything more?" started Marianna. "I need to go and see him."

Gina appeared at her mother's shoulder.

"I do too. So does Baby Joseph, he misses him so much."

Baby Joseph, nearly two years old, was busy tearing a newspaper into the smallest pieces he could, before stuffing them in his mouth.

George looked at the child, his lips blackened by the wet newsprint.

"Have you seen what he's done? Who's supposed to be watching him?"

Gina hurriedly picked up the little brute and prised the paper out of his mouth.

Marianna said: "Oh, you can't watch him all the time." She shook her head and patted the boy's head indulgently. "He's such a good eater!"

George had had his own weight problems as a child but thought Baby Joseph needed his jaws wiring or his hands tying behind his back. The child never stopped eating, and it showed.

George slumped into a kitchen chair. He was exhausted, so the last thing he needed was another row with Marianna and Gina.

"*Mela*, I don't know any more now than I did last night. The best thing we can do, the safest thing for Den, is to pretend we know absolutely nothing. Okay? We don't talk to anybody, no matter who they are. Got it?""

Both the women nodded, but George wanted to make sure they really understood.

"So, if somebody asks where Den is, what do you say?" Gina piped up.

"Well, he's staying at Karl Chelotti's uncle's house in Hamrun, isn't he?"

George banged his fist onto the table.

"*Madonna mia*! How stupid are you? You'll get him killed, girl!"

Gina's face crumpled, tears pooling in her eyes. She wiped her face and went to give the child a biscuit.

Marianna's face was like stone.

"They're not going to do that, are they? Kill him?"

"No, no. They're not." George felt another wave of nausea sweep over him. He recovered himself. "He just has to stay there until he gets better. Then we'll work something out."

"No, no! He needs his mother. I'm not going to just sit here. I'm going to see him tomorrow and that's that." George exploded.

"For God's sake! Have you not listened to a word I've been saying? You're not going anywhere near him. The chief

Russian dragged me in this morning. He doesn't believe I don't know where Den's hiding. And he's right, of course! He said he was watching me, which also means he's watching you two. He's not stupid. And what? You're going to lead them right to Den, are you? Is that your plan?"

Marianna cast her eyes down and her bottom lip started to tremble.

"'Course not."

"No, good."

Gina had gone noticeably quiet. Marianna frowned at George and nodded over at their daughter, who was giving Baby Joseph another biscuit.

George said: "Sorry, love, I didn't mean to snap. I'm just so worried, you know? We have to be very careful."

Gina looked up; her eyes still full of frightened tears. "There was this man..." George felt himself go cold.

"What man, Gina?"

"The man who came here this morning, asking about Den. Said he was a friend. Was he?"

"I don't know. Did you recognise him? *Mela*! What did you say?"

"I didn't recognise him, no. He spoke funny, sort of like the Polish boy who works in Giorgio's shop. I said nothing. I was busy feeding Baby Joseph. I said not to worry, Den was okay, and he was safe. That's alright, isn't it? I didn't say where he was."

George and Marianna looked at each other. George shook his head.

Marianna said: "Gina hurry and get packed. We're going to stay with Aunt Stephania on Gozo. It'll only be for a few days.

George will tell Giorgio."

CHAPTER 12
ARTICLE IN THE MALTA TELEGRAPH

Reporter: Justine Galea

Date: 21 June 2025

Constitutional Crisis as Malta gives Manoel Island to Russians

Two months after the Russian soldiers and naval vessels first arrived, the Maltese government has signed a 999-year lease with the Russian Federation for the whole of Manoel Island, set in Marsamxett Harbour. The Russian Navy has secured the island and begun a two-billion-euro construction project to turn it into a base and facility for the newly formed Russian Central Mediterranean Fleet. This base is of crucial importance to the Russians, allowing it to compete with NATO and the US in the Mediterranean theatre and also wield influence in North Africa.

The granting of a lease of sovereign Maltese territory is controversial and, on the face of it, illegal, as it is in contravention of the Maltese constitution that entrenches the country's neutrality and non-alignment. The constitution expressly forbids the presence of foreign mili-

tary personnel or facilities and further prohibits the use of its shipyards by foreign naval powers.

The government argues that the current migration crisis is only the beginning of a larger threat arising from climate change within Africa. This anticipated intensification of the crisis is so grave as to constitute a threat that legally justifies the request for a limited number of Russian armed forces to come to Malta's aid at this time of peril.

It also argues the humanitarian assistance being provided by the Russian navy, in helping Armed Forces Malta patrol the extensive Maltese Search and Rescue Area, is non-military in nature and is permitted within the constitution, given it is assisting in the performance of civil works or activities.

The mood in Brussels is one of shock and surprise. The President of the European Commission, Noémie Minaud, said: "Make no mistake, the behaviour of our partners and EU members, the Maltese government, in inviting the Russian fleet to take up permanent residence in our backyard, is an international crisis of the gravest proportions. Malta's actions could well be in breach of the EU's Common Security and Defence Policy and have given rise to widespread alarm on the scale of the Cuban Missile Crisis of the 1960s. Urgent talks have already been arranged during which we hope common sense will prevail."

CHAPTER 13
MARCO BONNICI
IONANINA UNIVERSITY HOSPITAL, GREECE

Marco opened the door and slowly walked into the hospital room. It smelled of the stale food that Natasha had refused to eat, which lay on a plastic tray on the bedside locker.

Marco spoke to his daughter in a soft voice.

"Natasha, you have had us all very worried. I am so glad to see you. How are you?"

She said nothing, turning her head away to look out of the dirty window, peppered with dead bugs and flies, onto a view of the parking lot. Slowly, she lifted herself off the chair and started to move towards the door. There was no weight or flesh to her. Her baggy denims could not hide the outline of the bones of her pelvis, as she walked ahead of him. The formerly lustrous deep brown hair was now a dry and brittle pile of tan and greying dreadlocks. When he looked into her nut-brown face, the first thing he noticed were the cracks and ulcers around the corners of her mouth and the missing teeth on the left hand side of her jaw. Her eyes, usually so bright and full of mischief, were milky and her eyelids appeared red and inflamed.

Marco was grateful that the long sleeves of the simple grey jumper she wore hid her wrists and forearms. He did not feel strong enough to see them just yet. She seemed neither pleased nor surprised to see him, her face expressionless, except for a dull, faraway look in her eyes.

He said to her: "I have come to take you away, if that is what you want?"

She stood still, looking at him, as if considering the offer.

"Away? Where to?"

"First to a clinic, a nice place. Then, when you are a little better, we can decide what to do and where to go next. Somewhere safe."

"So not the *castello*?"

"I do not think it is safe for you just yet."

"Will Katia be there?"

"No, Katia is not with us anymore."

"I'm glad. She used to say nasty things about me."

With that, she turned and waited for Marco to open the door and let her leave. Marco gestured to the nurse who had waited outside. She opened the door and ushered them out. Slowly, they walked Natasha to the car park, where Dr Weber and the two nurses were waiting by the black people carrier.

Natasha saw the vehicle from about fifty metres away. Dr Weber opened the sliding door, then stood to one side of it, with her hands clasped in front of her. Natasha stood stock still, like a creature of the woods, not moving, watchful.

Marco appeared behind her and put his head close to her shoulder. He spoke softly into her ear.

"Do not worry. That lady is Dr Weber. She will be looking after you. She is nice. I like her."

On hearing that, his daughter jerked her head around to face him. The minute he said it, Marco regretted it. He had not wanted to reveal anything of himself to Natasha until he knew more about her mental state. The moment passed. Natasha stayed put, not moving, warily watching the doctor and two nurses. Nobody moved.

"Do we have to go with them?"

"Yes. We are going to get into the minibus and go to a house nearby, but only for one night. There you can have a long bath – remember how you used to like those? Then, tomorrow, we will take a small plane and fly straight to Dr Weber's clinic."

"In Malta?"

"No, in Switzerland."

"Yes. Malta's no good for me now."

Marco handed Natasha over to the medical team, who settled her, while he headed inside to see the administrator. She presented him with a bill for a few thousand euros, for which Marco offered a credit card, and then pushed a small rucksack towards him.

She sat back and said: "Your daughter's a mystery, but please take care of what's in that bag. There's a small fortune in cash, gold and jewels in there. The police were interested in the three forged passports and identity documents. They have them, by the way. Perhaps you can call in on your way past? They'd like a chat with you. "

Marco said: "Thank you for your help. Please give my apologies to the police. I fear I would be of little help to them."

The trip back to Bern passed without incident. Laura Weber and the female nurse gently took Natasha in hand and, once in the clinic, she offered no resistance to being bathed and dressed in new clothing. She ate two bowls of soup with a little bread and peacefully submitted to everything that was asked of her. Dr Weber had suggested Marco spend less and less time with Natasha, to allow her to get comfortable interacting with the other members of staff, as well as to prepare her for his departure.

On Marco's last night in Bern, he visited his daughter and told her he was going back to Malta for two weeks but would return after that to see how she was doing. She asked if she could go with him but, when he told her she had to stay with the doctor, she seemed content. Her appearance was already beginning to improve, after several baths to soak off the ingrained filth and a visit from a hairdresser to cut out the worst of the knots and colour her short hair a deep chestnut brown. Her skin was already looking better, as the infected insect bites had started to heal, and a course of vitamins was starting to bring some life back to her complexion.

Dr Weber had asked a dermatologist and a plastic surgeon to examine Natasha's arms and, while both said the scarring could never be completely removed, they could, over time, significantly improve the appearance of her arms. A dentist was also on hand to start preparing some implants for the teeth that she had lost.

Natasha had been prescribed a course of antipsychotics and, in the following days, Laura, as Marco now addressed Dr Weber, would introduce a program of psychotherapy to begin to help Natasha explore her emotions, thoughts and behaviours, and how these factors had shaped her life. Only when that was complete could she start to think about reintegrating herself back into mainstream life.

Marco had taken every opportunity to spend time with Laura, ostensibly to discuss Natasha's treatment, but he realised it was also because he liked to be with her. He sensed that, despite her cool professionalism, she might feel the same way. On his last night in Bern, he had invited her out for dinner, and, to his surprise, she had accepted. She said: "Is this a business dinner or dinner with a friend? I need to know how to dress, you see."

"Well, it is certainly not a business occasion. Other than that, we will have to wait and see what fate has in store for us."

"Oh, no! You are not a determinist? I believe firmly in making my own luck. If there is something I want, then it is up to me to go and get it!" Marco laughed.

"Well, in that case, I hope you get whatever it is!"

Laura met him in a restaurant in central Bern. She looked stunning in a calf length cream suit, the exact colour of her fine shoulder length hair. She wore a simple white blouse and a string of pearls, which glistened pink and blue in the low restaurant lighting. She was elegance personified. Marco, on the other hand, had only brought a limited wardrobe for his travels and wore the same old Harris tweed jacket with leather elbow patches. He had changed into a heavy Tattersall check shirt and a rather racy pair of salmon pink moleskin trousers. He would have fitted in perfectly against a country setting in Yorkshire or the Cotswolds but looked rather out of place in central Bern.

The conversation inevitably started with Natasha and Laura mentioned that she already seemed to be repressing or forgetting memories of her life in Greece.

"She asked a nurse where she had been for the last few weeks. This afternoon, I asked her about her life at the cottage and she told me she could not remember very much. However, she did tell me all about your life together in the *castello*. It sounds a wonderful place." Marco smiled.

"So, what do you make of it all?" he asked.

"At this point, I honestly do not know. The process of making memories and forgetting is still not wholly understood," Laura said. "It used to be argued that threatening material is repressed in the long-term memory, so it cannot gain access to consciousness. You can understand that where, say, a patient has suffered historic child abuse, but it seems strange in Natasha's case, when the memories are so recent. We could be looking at amnesia, I am not sure.

"Most people with amnesia have problems with short-term memory – they cannot retain new information. Recent memories are most likely to be lost, while more remote or deeply ingrained memories may be spared. I would have thought the period in the forest would have been indelibly ingrained! So, we will have to keep an eye on that.

"She also asked me if I liked you. The way she said it was rather strange. It did not seem like a casual enquiry."

Marco felt that familiar hollow start to open up in the pit of his stomach.

"Honestly, Laura, you do not know her. Be incredibly careful! She is highly manipulative, dangerous and jealous. I hate to say it but, if she thinks someone is stealing somebody away from her, she is capable of anything. Especially in the condition she is currently in."

"Ah! So that is what I am doing, is it? Stealing you away. If so, I had better get on with it! Tell me about the *castello*. I would love to hear more."

"I would be delighted to. And maybe one day you could come and visit it – and me, of course?"

"Who knows? One thing I must bear in mind, Marco, and I take this seriously, is how to manage my professional obligations to Natasha. A friendship with you could put me in a tricky position. Let's just take it one step at a time."

CHAPTER 14
ACTING ASSISTANT COMMISSIONER GEORGE ZAMMIT

ZAMMIT FAMILY HOME, BIRKIRKARA, MALTA

GEORGE KNEW he could not keep Marianna and Gina in Gozo indefinitely. His sister was not a woman of infinite patience, and he suspected that, eventually, sparks would fly and the two women would fall out. He had accepted that Denzel was always going to be at risk if he stayed on the island, especially if Marianna and, more particularly, Gina, knew of his whereabouts. They loved Denzel as much as he did; it was just that they were naturally gullible and apt to say the wrong thing at the wrong time. He simply could not trust them with Denzel's life.

He had spoken to Chelotti and thanked him for what he had done. They had shaken hands and George had embraced his colleague, even suggesting they have an early evening beer. The pair had walked up to the Bocci Club, around the corner from Police HQ, where they had sat with two yellow cans of Cisk lager, watching some of the locals from the neighbouring tenements play the Maltese version of *boules*. They laughed about the petty feud the two of them had shared over the years.

"'The 'use it or lose it inspector'!" George said. "That nickname stuck with me for years! Thanks *very much* for that!"

"Well, you've had the last laugh, Acting Assistant Commissioner, sir! Who would've thought it? An office on the third floor, no less!"

"Hey, enough of the cheek!" George paused and looked around him. It was not unknown for the occasional group of Russians to turn up at the club. "*Mela*, listen, I need to get Den off the island. This new guy, Fedorov, he's a piece of work."

"Yeah, I've heard. A really *nasty* piece of work!"

"How's my son doing?"

Chelotti brought his head closer to George and whispered.

"My uncle says he's getting stronger. He can walk about, but he's not sleeping so much. He's getting pretty frustrated at being cooped up all day and night. But that's how it has to be."

"Well, it's the least of his problems. If I can get him off the island, I know someone who'll take good care of him."

"I suppose it's a good plan, but tricky. The Russians are all over the airport and the ferry terminal. How're you proposing …" Chelotti's face dropped, as he realised what was being asked of him. "Oh, no! George, you can't ask me that!"

"Karl, listen, you're the only person I know who has a boat and can sail. Also, the only person I'd trust not to shop me and Den to the Russians. These are strange times. You don't know who to trust anymore."

Karl Chelotti took another swig of his beer and asked:

"Where're you thinking of?"

"Libya."

Chelotti laughed out loud.

"Forget it! I'm not sailing to Libya, it's miles away." George shushed him.

"Quiet, you don't know who's listening," Chelotti huddled closer.

"Be serious, George! There're Russian and Maltese search vessels everywhere; Libyan coastguards, who're worse; migrant boats filled with desperate people – who you can't just ignore if they're in trouble. No, George, it's an absolute nonstarter."

He pondered.

"How about Lampedusa then? That's in Italian waters and the trouble only starts to the south of there. And it's half the distance."

It was Chelotti's turn to think.

"Maybe. It's more of a possibility than Libya, for sure. It's a long trek for me though. About ninety nautical miles, something like one hundred and seventy kilometres. At five, six knots or so, I don't know how the currents work, but it's a good eighteen hours' sailing. Possible though. You're going to have to let me think about it. And even if he gets to Lampedusa, it's nearly a hundred and forty nautical miles from there to Libya."

"Karl, I know I'm asking a lot. But it's the only chance of getting him away from here. They'll catch him, sooner or later, if he doesn't leave the island. If you can get him to Lampedusa, I can take it from there. It'd be such a relief."

That evening, George sat by himself in his kitchen. It was silent in the flat and he was lonely. The kitchen usually resounded to the chatter of the women, the banging and clattering of pans and, recently, the wails of Baby Joseph. Now, everything was still, and he hated it. He even opened the door to the back yard, so he could hear the faint chatter from the other apartments and listen to the background buzz of their televisions.

With a sigh, he steeled himself. He knew he could not delay having this conversation any further. He settled down at the kitchen table and opened his contacts. The list was alphabetically sorted so, almost every day, the name stared him in the face, but it had been several years since he had called the number. He felt ashamed at having left it so long, particularly as he was now ringing because he needed something. He had no idea how his call would be received. He pressed the number hoping, after all these years, it had not changed, and sat back.

It beeped and beeped. Then, there was the sound of someone coming on the line – There was a deep, rough voice barking something in Arabic.

George ventured to speak. Maltese was a Semitic language, as was Arabic, and he had spent several years working in Libya, so the language was not a problem. "Abdullah? Abdullah Belkacem?" There was a moment of silence.

"Yes, who are you?"

It was him alright. His voice was heavy with suspicion.

"Don't you recognise my voice, you old villain?"

There was a second, longer silence, then a throaty chuckle.

"Allah be praised! He has brought you back to me. I cannot believe it! Every night, I lie awake and cannot sleep. I think: where is my friend, George? What have I done to offend him so much? Why must we always be apart? What are you doing, George? Is the lady wife well? Has time made her speak any more kindly of me? Tell me, are you speaking the Russian now and drinking the vodka? I see the television and I am much confused."

"*Mela*, no, of course not, I wouldn't speak Russian, even if I could, and I hate vodka. But, Abdullah, it's good to hear your voice. I wish I was ringing in better times. I hate to say it, but I've got trouble. Trouble with the Russians. I need to ask for your help."

"Ha! Troubles you say? George, if I lived a hundred years, I could never repay the debts I owe you. So, you will tell me your troubles and, I swear, I will make them my own. Then I will make them disappear. Like a puff from a donkey's arse, they will go. But first, you must speak to this person I have with me ..." his voice went faint as he spoke to someone at his end of the line "... yes, yes, it is him... just a minute, woman." He spoke over the line again. "George, if you do not speak to her now, she will eat her own fingers with excitement."

A woman's voice came on the phone.

"George, George! Is it really you?"

"Rania, yes, it's George. It's been too long, I'm sorry." He felt himself getting emotional. Rania, Abdullah's wife, had always had a special place in George's heart. She was a good and generous woman, and one of the few people who had the strength to stand up to Abdullah and, when necessary, keep him in check. She had looked after George during his time in Libya, welcoming him into their family, treating him as one of her own.

"What is happening? I heard the word 'troubles'. Do not let that fool of a husband of mine lead you astray! You talk to me, okay? You know he might have the strength, but I have the sense! What are these troubles?"

"Rania, you sound just like my wife! But listen, I must ask for your husband's help first. He will tell you all my news." Abdullah must have snatched the phone back.

"George, speak with me of these troubles. Then we can tell each other our news."

George had first met Abdullah nearly ten years earlier, when he was a powerful militia leader in Libya. He had saved Abdullah's life in a gunfight at the Vai Vai Café, on the Libyan border and, despite Abdullah being a people trafficker and militia leader, the two men had become good friends. The pair had escaped Libya, being pursued by IS fighters, in one of Abdullah's inflatable boats, together with a crowd of migrants, all of them surviving a perilous Mediterranean crossing.

In the years that followed, George had helped Abdullah to return to his family in Libya and re-establish his militia as a powerful proxy force for the Americans, guarding Libya's vast energy reserves in the west of the country. This had made him a very wealthy man. Even more so than when George had first met him. George had also reluctantly travelled across Libya with him to hunt down Abu Muhammad, the leader of IS in Libya, who had gunned down Abdullah's brother.

Their adventures had not stopped there. The pair had stormed Abu Salim, Tripoli's infamous high-security prison, in a daring raid to free Abdullah's son, Jamal, who had made an attempt on the life of Hakan Toprak, a Turkish fixer and intelligence officer, known as the Hawk.

It was the storming of Abu Salim that George knew Abdullah would remember most, as he told him Denzel's story. Abdullah listened carefully, muttering his approval at certain points. When George had finished and told him what he needed to know, there was a silence on the phone. For a terrible minute, George thought Abdullah was going to refuse to help him. Then he said: "George, this story makes me very happy. Not because your boy was beaten and now must hide, but because I can see he is a good man, like his father. Your son protected the woman and shot the Russian dog in the face, which is no more than the shit on my shoe deserved. It is only a shame the Russian did not live for a few moments longer, so he could know the ugliness of his own face.

"I will go to Lampedusa myself and carry your boy on my back, swimming, if Allah wills it. You get him there and we will speak again, my friend. Now, tell me ... what of my friends in Malta? How is the old policeman, the man named after the camel? Or the Lady Mantis, Natasha ... has she bitten the head off another mate? And that Turkish turd who calls himself the Hawk – Hakan Toprak – *you gazma*, he is the bottom of a shitty shoe ... One day I will meet him again, and then ..."

George told Abdullah about Camilleri's death, and then about Gina and Baby Joseph, whereupon Abdullah shouted out: "Rania, George is a grandfather! We must call him *jadd*!"

George then had to pass on all the details to Rania: gender, name, weight, whether the birth had been easy or hard, how old he was now, if he was a good eater ... all the details that were thought important following the birth of any child.

Finally, Abdullah said: "George, this grandson of yours is

nearly two years old and I never knew of him. You are a *jadd* and I never knew. This must never happen again, my old friend. As you saved Jamal from the killing in the prison yard, I will take Denzel and keep him safe from the Russian scum.

"Now Rania will make me tea, to celebrate our friendship. You, too, must make some tea and think on our friendship and the bringing of our sons together. May they be as true to each other as their fathers have been."

Smiling, George put down the phone and went into the kitchen to put the kettle on, wondering why on earth he had left it until now before making the call.

CHAPTER 15
PRIME MINISTER EDWARD REFALO

OFFICE OF THE PRIME MINSTER, VALLETTA, MALTA

IT HAD BEEN three months since the first volunteers had landed at Malta International Airport. It had taken only three months for the number of Russian 'advisers', volunteers and their associated security detail to swell to over 2,000. In addition to this, there were another 1,000 Russian naval officers and ratings, also taking daily coffee and enjoying life on the promenades of Sliema and St Julian's.

The naval types were either involved in the Search and Rescue patrols, in Malta's designated area from Tunisia to Crete, ferrying the volunteers back and forth to Libya, or accompanying an increasing number of tankers from Russian ports to Hurds Bank, the shallow stretch of water fifteen kilometres from the Maltese coast.

Refalo had long been aware that Russia had historically aided many sanctioned countries, including Venezuela, Iran, Syria, Libya and even North Korea, by managing a network of ship-to-ship transfers of their embargoed petroleum products from the coral and sand shallows of Hurds Bank. Since these waters were thirty to forty metres deep, shipping could safely drop anchor there and avoid paying port charges. More importantly, Hurds Bank was in international waters, so the Maltese authorities could conveniently ignore whatever sanction-busting business was being conducted.

The 999-year lease of Manoel Island to the Russians had now also been completed. There had been ructions in the Maltese Parliament, with legal and constitutional challenges still pending in the courts. Manoel Island had been completely closed, with the newly restored historic fort only remaining open to the public on a limited basis. Even then, access was confined to authorised, pre-vetted visitors, who arrived on a Russian Navy 'courtesy launch' and received a one-hour guided tour. The increasingly disgruntled population and frustrated tourists could do little but stand on the Sliema promenade, only a few metres away across the harbour, and watch the erection of ugly security fencing and a five-metre wall of corrugated steel sheeting that marred their picture-postcard view across the cobalt blue waters to the bastions of northern Valletta.

In the office of the prime minister, in Castille, Refalo was desperately explaining his problems to an unsympathetic Ambassador Buzilov. "This is it," he said, slapping a sheaf of papers onto the table, "here's your bill that has to go before the House. They won't pass it. I've taken soundings."

The ambassador took the papers and, with downturned mouth, read the headings.

"Yes, *'the removal of the principle of neutrality and non-alignment'* ... *'removal of prohibitions on foreign military forces entering the island'* ... this all seems to be in order. What is the problem?"

Refalo was exasperated.

"This bill amends the constitution. It's not some minor piece of legislation; there's hell on about it. It needs a two-thirds majority and it will fail to win one. I've already told you that. Anyway, I've done what you asked – I'll probably be kicked out because of it – there's talk of a vote of no confidence. Then you'll be in trouble. They're saying we've been *invaded by stealth*, and this is the latest turn of the screw."

Grigori Buzilov, immaculately dressed in a shiny, two-tone light blue suit, was looking at Refalo with a steady gaze.

"Is that what people are saying? '*Invaded by stealth*'? Hmm. Interesting. Is that what you believe?"

Refalo said nothing but glowered at Buzilov from across the highly polished cabinet table.

The Russian made a clicking noise with his tongue and said: "Well, I have been waiting for this moment. I knew it was coming. We need to show the dissenters, and those who would destroy our good work, that we will not be blown off course. Our project must succeed. Denying the seriousness of the crisis facing Malta, does not mean it does not exist. If we give in to these sorts of people, the country will cease to exist as a functioning European Catholic state within ten years. It will be overrun by African migration. Agreed?"

"Well, yes, I see your point, but how do you propose to do that? It's a democratic country. You can't force people to vote for a new constitution, just to suit your own ends."

"Really? You do surprise me, Edward." The ambassador ran one hand over his oiled, black hair. "In my country, the representatives in the Duma and the Federation Council would not dream of standing in the way of proposals to improve the security of the nation. Give me the names of those who you think are *most unlikely* to vote for the changes. We can start there and try to change their minds. We need to do this for the good of the country."

Buzilov put his hands behind his head and leaned back in the antique, mahogany elbow chair.

"How about the members of the House who went to the rally in the square outside here? The protest organised by that group ... Democratica. Yes, I think they will do, to begin with. And while we are on the subject, I think we should have a word with the leaders of that civil society crowd of nay sayers.

They are a danger to public order. Perhaps you can ask Michael Cini to join us? I think this conversation might have some implications for his ministry."

Refalo had no idea where Buzilov was going with this line of thinking, but he had given up trying to second guess the mercurial ambassador. He picked up the phone and summoned the minister for Home Affairs and Security to his office. The PM and Buzilov sat in silence, looking at their phones, while the minister left the meeting he was chairing and walked the 300 yards from his office, behind the courts on Strait Street, up Valletta's main thoroughfare of Republic Street and to Castille. Cini arrived, looking hot and flustered, plonking himself down with a loud exhalation of breath.

"My God, it's hot out there!"

Buzilov looked at Cini, and then at Refalo. Cini read the mood in the room and immediately felt nervous. The sweat that bristled across his forehead and trickled down his cheeks was not just due to the speedy uphill walk.

The ambassador smiled at them both, which did not help.

"Right, gentlemen. Forget about the weather, it is time to up the stakes. Michael, how much room do you have in Corradino?"

The Corradino Correctional Facility was Malta's only prison, built by the British colonial authorities in 1842, based on the model of Pentonville in London.

"Well, the prison's full to bursting. I can't say for certain ... about a dozen places, I'd guess. I'll have to talk to the governor."

"We will need ... at least fifty. No, we can begin slowly, say with thirty, by tomorrow evening. We are going to have an anti-corruption round up. It will only last a week at most, to give us a chance to talk to everybody concerned. You can release remand prisoners ..."

Michael Cini interrupted: "But that's the judges' job ... who're we rounding up, exactly?"

Fedorov fixed him with a steely glare.

"I am sorry, you must not have heard me correctly, Michael. I said, 'release the remand prisoners'. And, to answer your question, we are rounding up corrupt Members of Parliament. I mean, from what I can see, that is most of you!" He beamed at Refalo and Cini. "We will arrest them and walk them from the police cars straight into Corradino. Oh, and make sure the press knows the time of the first arrivals. It is such a powerful signal!" His hand rasped against his black stubbled chin.

"Then we have facilities on *RTS Yeltsin*, the destroyer anchored on Hurds Bank. We can take a dozen or so of the more high-profile interviewees there. That is a strong move. We will *disappear* them for twenty-four hours. In the interests of national security and all that. Get the press down on Pinto Quay. Ray Farrugia is top of the list. I have sensed a deterioration in his attitude in the last few weeks."

Refalo looked askance at Cini. He said to the ambassador: "You're doing a round up of Members of Parliament? Ministers even?"

Buzilov raised his eyebrows and said in a tone of affected innocence: "Only those who will not vote for the constitutional changes. What else do they expect us to do?" Refalo was horrified.

"But you can't do that!" Buzilov was enjoying himself.

"I know, I am not going to. You are!" Refalo almost laughed in amazement.

"You want me to order the arrest of Ray Farrugia, my friend and chief of staff? On what grounds?"

"Have you forgotten the folders, Prime Minister?" Buzilov sighed. "This is why I will never attain high office; I am too reasonable. I suppose we can make an exception for Ray. But still, bring him in with the rest. Remind him what is in the folder and tell him we expect his ongoing co-operation. We will let him sweat for a bit first – then you can release him. Make sure he knows where his loyalty should lie. Fear is everything."

Michel Cini looked on, his furrowed brow showing confusion.

"What folders are we talking about? Who's going to do the interviews? On what grounds are we going to make arrests?"

Buzilov laughed.

"Michael, Michael! Relax. Edward will show you your folder when he has a minute. It will explain everything, will it not, Edward? To more important business. The Russian Military Police will work with the *Pulizija*. We have a list of misdemeanours we have collected. They all seem to be common knowledge – in the public domain even. It only took us a couple of weeks to gather the dirt. It was not hard. Most of it is in your newspapers. Incredible! And yet still you get away with it. Malta – it is definitely my sort of place!" Michael Cini was visibly nervous. "What sort of things are we talking about?" Buzilov pulled a face.

"Oh, nothing serious. Just low-level corruption. Favours granted to associated parties in the planning process; direct orders for goods placed outside of the tendering rules, where certain people who should not have, have benefited; appointments of friends and family to posts that do not exist or are at overly inflated salaries; backhanders in exchange for contracts; abuse of government funds for entertaining and hospitality; mistresses travelling on ministerial trips abroad – you know, the usual. Well, for Malta that is. But all in breach of the law, if you are inclined to look at it that way.

"And if you, that is, this office, is to continue to allow these 'perks', then ..." Buzilov leaned across the table and shouted aggressively into Refalo's face "...we damn' well expect people to do what they are told to do and vote for the constitutional changes!"

Buzilov sat back and laughed at the horrified expressions of the pair of politicians.

"Oh, come on. Did you lot all think this could carry on forever? Actions have consequences. Anyway, that is how the interrogations should go. Just tell them they have to vote for the changes, or ... they will be attending *your* special magistrates' anti-corruption court, to expeditiously press through these cases in a matter of days. Actually, it will be so fast, there will be no need to release them ahead of the proceedings."

Refalo could only say: "*My* special courts?"

Michael Cini said: "You're joking, surely?"

"No, Michael, sadly not. And, come to think of it – I recall your son, Anthony, qualified as a surveyor six months ago. Give him my congratulations, will you? I hear he is doing very well. He works in the Ministry for Public Works and Planning, if I am not mistaken? Sixty thousand euros is a large salary for one so young and just starting his career, would you not say? Maybe we should bring him in and ask him how he got the job? Or maybe we should ask the person who appointed him?"

CHAPTER 16
SERGEANT DENZEL ZAMMIT

ABDULLAH BELKACEM'S HOUSE, MARSABAR, LIBYA

IT WAS A PITCH BLACK, moonless night when the *Dragut* set sail from Marsamxett Marina, with Karl Chelotti at the helm and his brother-in-law, Joe, keeping look out on the prow. Denzel was below deck, in the saloon, where there was an empty space beneath the semi-circular seating, ready for him to hide in, in the unlikely event anyone should come aboard to inspect the vessel. The boat edged out into the harbour, having had to sail straight past Manoel Island itself, to pass the headlands of Valletta and Tigne Point and get out into the open sea.

Construction work on Manoel Island continued twenty-four hours a day, the floodlights shining over the dozens of construction sites, blinding all those on the island to the passage of an unlit yacht, quietly navigating the dense, impenetrable blackness of the harbour waters. Nobody noticed the fifteen-metre vessel slip out, past the green and red lights of the breakwaters, into the choppy Mediterranean. The wind was behind the *Dragut*, from the north-east, blowing steadily. Karl Chelotti was happy he would make timely progress on the outbound leg. Once he had unloaded his human cargo, he could relax and enjoy the return trip. The fridge was well stocked with cans of Cisk lager.

As they headed south, Karl kept the lights of Malta close to his starboard side. To go too far offshore would mean sailing amongst the ships moored on Hurds Bank. That night, it looked like the coastline of a small city, with hundreds of lights emanating from the dozens of vessels, flickering on the near horizon. Fishermen had reported their boats being boarded, and even seized, by overly aggressive Russian gunboats that patrolled the area, protecting the naval assets riding at anchor. The *Dragut* sailed on, past Delimara Point and the bright lights of the Freeport, turning south-west, on a beam reach, heading straight for Lampedusa.

Once they were clear of Malta, Denzel came out from below deck and settled down in the cockpit with Karl and Joe for the long haul towards the small Italian island. They took turns to keep watch over the screens of the automated vessel tracking system and in scouring the horizon for telltale navigation lights on other shipping, while the others dozed on the bunks below. The time passed peacefully and by the early evening of the next day, the *Dragut*, sails furled, motored into the small harbour at Lampedusa. As soon as the boat had been tied up in the marina, a swarthy looking, middle-aged local, in cut-off denims and a soiled white vest, with a cigarette hanging out of his mouth, ambled down the pontoon and nodded to Karl.

"Zammit?" he asked.

There was no respite. In only a few minutes, Denzel was crouched in the back of the wheelhouse of a twenty-metre, noisy *mator* fishing vessel. At first, he gagged and fought the urge to vomit – the smell of dried fish mixed with diesel fumes was almost overpowering. He never learned the name of the skipper, or of the two crew who busied themselves dropping the trammel nets and hauling in meagre catches of sea bream and other assorted species. Everything was thrown into the ice boxes below deck. Nothing went back over the side, no matter how small.

After almost two full days at sea, Denzel wearily climbed

over the side of the fishing boat, feeling empty and dehydrated. The beat of the boat's engine had never stopped, and the minute he had two feet on the slimy Marsabar quayside, the boat slid away into the gathering dusk. The skipper watched him from the wheelhouse. Denzel raised a hand in farewell, but the man turned his head away and took the odorous, battered boat, together with his stinking catch, back towards the open sea.

George had packed Denzel a sports bag containing the bare minimum of his possessions. When he had looked inside, in a quieter moment on his journey, he was surprised to find his football boots. He had played football to a high level in Malta, being the centre back for Birkirkara St Joseph's, but what he was supposed to do with them in Libya he had no idea. He gazed forlornly along the dockside, wondering whether Abdullah had forgotten about his arrival. A feeling of hopelessness and panic started to build inside him.

After about ten minutes, by which time Denzel's nerves were in pieces, a pickup truck drove along the quayside and stopped about twenty metres away. In the half light of the early evening, he saw the rangy figure of Abdullah, dressed in the traditional long *djellaba* robe, get out of the passenger side, followed by the driver, a young man in jeans and a polo shirt. Once Abdullah had convinced himself that the lonely soul with the sports bag was indeed Denzel, he strode towards him, beaming from ear to ear.

Abdullah had changed in the years since Denzel had last seen him. His beard and hair were now streaked with grey, and he had lost a tooth or two, but he was still thin, with strong wiry arms and lithe movements.

"*Wa Alaykum as-salam,*" he said.

"And unto you, peace," Denzel replied with the traditional response.

Abdullah held him by the shoulders and looked him up and down.

"You have grown to be a fine man now, not short and fat like your father!" He laughed and dragged Denzel towards the young man in jeans who stood a little behind him.

"This is my son, Jamal." The young man smiled.

"Welcome, Denzel." The two appraised each other. Jamal was a little younger but held himself with assurance. He approached and held out his hand. "Your father saved my life in Abu Salim Prison, so anything I can do for you, I consider my sacred duty."

Abdullah gravely nodded his approval.

"Thank you," Denzel said, "you must tell me that story. There's a lot about my father I don't know. He never ceases to surprise me."

Abdullah guffawed.

"Come, come, I will tell you everything I know about George. There are so many stories, it will be a long night. But first, we must eat. Rania has made her lamb dish; it was your father's favourite – do you like lamb?"

Denzel had not eaten anything decent for days and his legs went weak at the thought of it.

Back in Malta, things were not going quite so well. George had driven up to the ferry terminal at Čirkewwa, on the northern tip of the island. Marianna's relationship with Stephania, his sister, had deteriorated to the point that she had announced she was returning to Malta. Stephania had been horrified by the rate at which Baby Joseph was gaining weight, and tried to suggest a visit to the children's clinic might be a good idea. The women had argued, and Marianna had told Gina to pack her bag, while she rang George.

"I will not be told what to do by *your* sister!" George sighed.

"I'm sure she was just trying to be helpful."

"She made our Gina cry, saying Baby Joseph was a *ħanżir tat-trabi*! She should look in the mirror; she's got nothing to talk about! A little pig? I ask you? Mind you, it doesn't surprise me – you Zammits are all the same. Your mother had a nasty tongue on her, God rest her soul ..."

And on it went, until they met in the terminal building on the Malta side of the crossing.

The first question, inevitably, concerned Denzel's wellbeing. George braced himself.

"Well, we ... that is, Den and I ... decided it'd be best if he took some time out, until things died down."

Marianna said: "*Time out?*"

"Yeah, time out."

"Well, hasn't that already happened? It's been weeks! Things *have* died down."

"No, Marianna, nothing's died down. *Mela*! He shot a Russian dead. They're still after him and they won't stop.

Anyway, he's safe now, we can all relax." Gina smiled broadly.

"Oh, that's good! Thank God. Baby Joseph and I have been so worried."

Marianna smelled a rat.

"So, where is he? Where's this *time out*, safe place?" George took a breath.

"He's left the country."

There was silence for a moment, until Gina said: "Without saying goodbye?"

Marianna hissed at George.

"You sent us to your sister's so you could whisk my son away without me knowing!"

"*Mela*! I wanted to keep him safe. If nobody knows where he is but me, that's best."

He inadvertently glanced at Gina.

Marianna glared at her husband.

"You tell me where my son is, right now!"

"Honestly, it's best if I don't."

An inhuman screech came from Marianna.

"You will tell me, now!!"

Heads turned towards them throughout the terminal building. George shook his head. There was no denying her.

"If you must know, he's safe. He arrived last night. He's with Abdullah, in Libya."

Marianna staggered slightly and grabbed Gina's arm. His daughter's other hand covered her mouth in horror. Marianna said, in a small quiet voice, "You sent him to *that* terrible man? And you didn't tell me – and you didn't let me say goodbye. You've broken our family, George. You'll regret this for as long as you live – I'll make sure of that!"

CHAPTER 17
ARTICLE IN THE MALTA TELEGRAPH

Reporter: Justine Galea

Date: 14 July 2025

Ministers and MPs Held in Corradino and on Russian Ships as Part of Anti-corruption Crackdown

In a shock move, Prime Minister Edward Refalo and the Minister for Home Affairs and Security, Michael Cini, have asked the Pulizija to question over twenty ministers and MPs, as part of a so-called anti-corruption enquiry. The MPs, who are members of both main political parties, were brought into Corradino Correctional Facility this morning and held for questioning. Some were taken by police launch from Pinto Wharf to the Russian destroyer, Kosygin.

None have been formally arrested, but their detention has caused outrage. Retired Judge Mario Zahra said taking MPs outside of Maltese jurisdiction, to a foreign ship on Hurds Bank, was illegal rendition. Lawyers working for those taken to the Russian ship are currently petitioning the courts for their immediate return.

It has been noted that all the MPs involved are vocal critics of the proposed bill to alter the Maltese constitution. Leader of the Opposition, Alfred Fiteni, said, earlier this morning, the move was 'political intimidation at its most blatant'. Mr Fiteni's family later informed us that, shortly after making his statement, he was asked to accompany the police and also taken to the destroyer, the Kosygin.

The President of the European Commission, Noémie Minaud, said: "We are deeply concerned about what is happening in Malta. The recent action of the Maltese government in the treatment of its elected representatives appears to be an act of intimidation contrary to the laws of the European Union, which we condemn in the strongest possible terms."

We approached the offices of the prime minister and the commissioner of police, both of which declined to comment.

CHAPTER 18
ADMIRAL OF THE FLEET OF THE SOVIET UNION, PUTIN

THE GRAND HARBOUR, VALLETTA

THE AIRCRAFT-CARRYING CRUISER, *Admiral of the Fleet of the Soviet Union, Putin*, was the flagship of the Russian navy. It arrived just off the mouth of the Grand Harbour during the night following Gerald Camilleri's funeral. At 300 metres long and with a draft of 10 metres, it was simply too large to be accommodated within the harbour itself, but it made for a magnificent sight for those who had gathered at Tigne Point and Fort Ricasoli.

Although it had the shape and appearance of an aircraft carrier, the *Putin* was designated a battle cruiser, which meant it could legally access the narrow Bosphorous and Dardanelle Straits from the Mediterranean to the Black Sea naval base at Sevastopol, in Crimea. Aircraft carriers were banned from the channels under the 1936 Montreux Convention, while a battle cruiser fell within the permitted categories.

The importance of the Montreux Convention was highlighted following the Russian invasion of Ukraine in 2022. The Convention, 'in time of war', allowed Turkey to limit the transit of Russian warships from the Mediterranean into the Black Sea, denying Russia the opportunity to strengthen its forces close to the conflict zone with southern Ukraine. The

Russians had also had to deploy their Kilo-class submarine fleet into the Mediterranean, to avoid the strategically important vessels becoming locked into the Black Sea.

To announce the arrival of the flagship, the flight aircrew of the carrier spent the afternoon setting up the catapults that threw the Mikoyan Mig-29 fighters off the flight deck and up into the air. All afternoon, the east of the island reverberated to the sound of the jets blasting their engines and building thrust, to scream around Malta in a low-level exhibition of aerial prowess. The skies rumbled like thunder as the jets passed out of sight, only to return silently flashing across the island, travelling from coast to coast in a matter of seconds, skimming rooftops. As they soared upwards into the cloudless azure sky, they would be followed a moment later by the roar of the sound waves from the jets' powerful engines. Crowds gathered, as the schools emptied and thousands lined the seafront at Qui-si-Sana, where the best views of the take offs and landings were to be had. At one point, the *Pulizija* decided to close the road, as the crowds watching the performance had spilled over onto the carriageway. It seemed half the island had crushed themselves onto the Sliema seafront.

In the evening, orange service vessels towed a series of barges out of the Grand Harbour and anchored them around the carrier. Once darkness fell, a massive firework display illuminated the vessel, which responded by firing flares and tracer shells high into the sky to contribute to the celebrations. The carrier had a crew of 1,650. This brought the total number of Russian service personnel on the island to over 6,000.

Malta was not unique in the EU in still considering television to be the main and most trusted source of news on national political matters. However, it was unique in that its three main channels, operating in the Maltese language, were a state-controlled public broadcaster, and the other two being owned by one or other of the two main political parties.

In the Zammit household, Marianna was an unquestioning

supporter of Refalo's *Partit Laburista*, the Maltese Labour Party, so the channel of choice for the news was ONE TV.

"My father voted Labour and, if it was good enough for him, it's good enough for me. It's only the stuck-up Zammits – who think they're better than anybody else – who vote for the *Partit Nazzjonalista*," she taunted them.

George would try to challenge Marianna on the government's record, its integrity and delivery, but the response was always the same.

"Well, one lot are as bad as the next, aren't they? It's hardly worth bothering with the vote."

On the evening the aircraft carrier *Putin* was putting on its firework display, George was sitting in the stifling summer heat of the kitchen in his vest, reading the paper, while ONE TV droned on in the background. He noticed Gina was transfixed by what she was seeing.

"What are you watching, *pupa*?"

"Look, it's the Russians, they're putting on free fireworks and an air show. Isn't that nice of them? They've just been showing a football match between Russian sailors and some of the migrants. Did you know, the migrants in the Safi camp are teaching the Russian sailors to speak English? It's good, isn't it?"

"Gina, please don't believe that stuff. It's what they want."

Marianna was at the sink, tidying away the last of the dishes.

"Well, Joe Mifsud's doing alright out of them. He's having to buy frozen chickens from North Africa to keep up with the Russian orders. He got the Manoel Island contract, you know.

He's becoming an important man, George." Gina was not totally impressed.

"It's not so good for poor Giorgio. He's up all hours, my poor husband, jointing, slicing and chopping. He's got butcher's wrist."

George looked at her.

"Butcher's wrist?"

"Yeah, from too much chopping."

"I've never heard of that before!" Marianna rounded on him.

"They work hard, the Mifsuds. Morning till night. Our Gina knows, don't you, my *ħanini*? Not everybody has it as easy as you, George."

He could not believe what he was hearing.

"And what about our Den? Having to hide out, away from his family, for doing his duty and then being accused of murder by those manipulative b—" Marianna frowned at him, and he stopped himself in time. "And you're won over by a few fireworks and some phoney TV? What's happening in this house?"

There was a brief silence. Then Marianna said, "Gina, turn the channel over. Your father's having one of his turns. And better get your stuff ready, Giorgio will be here soon to pick you up. Unless his wrist is playing him up. George, why don't you take your daughter home? Do something useful for once!"

CHAPTER 19
MARCO BONNICI
THE WEBER CLINIC, BERN, SWITZERLAND

ONE AFTERNOON, while Marco was taking a coffee, sitting quietly with Natasha in the clinic's grounds, he thought to mention Camilleri's death.

"Do you remember Gerald?"

"Of course I do." Natasha paused, then added, "He never liked me."

"Well, I'm afraid he died a few weeks ago. I will miss him. He was a good friend of mine."

"He became no friend of mine. I think, in the end, he was frightened of me."

Marco thought it a strange conversation and mentioned it to Laura, as they lay in bed that evening. They had secretly become lovers. Over the last few months, he had made several visits to Bern, partly to enjoy more of her company. Laura had made it clear that they should avoid their relationship becoming known within the clinic and, most certainly, make sure Natasha remained unaware of it.

It had been many years since he had been with a woman, and it had taken some time before he regained the confidence to fully enjoy the experience. Once he had found how he could make Laura happy, he embarked upon a new era of lovemaking. Not as energetically as in his youth, and on the understanding that, every other night or so, there had to be a break in proceedings. In any event, the relationship brought him joy and put a spring in his step that did not go unnoticed by Natasha.

She seemed unfazed by his arrivals and departures. Over the months, her appearance had improved, thanks to a healthy diet, some cosmetic dentistry and the ongoing attention of a hairdresser. Regardless of her outward appearance, she still maintained she had only the sketchiest recollection of her time in the cottage in Greece.

Laura had said to Marco: "It is difficult. What is happening is that she is either deliberately, or subconsciously, refusing to talk about her experience. Denial of itself is not a mental disorder, but there is an illness called anosognosia psychosis. This is often used to describe people who are not denying mental health problems but are unaware of their condition. It is why it is so difficult to get many schizophrenics to take medication. They are not aware that they need to. They have no insight into their own illness."

Marco considered the possibilities.

"Could it also be true that she is just playing us along? Pretending she does not remember?" Laura was not sure.

"Why would she do that? What has she to gain? Remember the state she was in when we found her. She had been there for close on two years! I dismiss nothing, but deceit at that level would be an impressive performance!"

The next day, after her surgery had finished, Laura told Marco she had a treat in store for him. The sun was shining brightly, and the temperature was in the mid-twenties. Laura was dressed in a light thermal top and stretch exercise pants, with her hair pulled back into a tight bun. She gave Marco a carrier bag from a sports shop and sent him into an examination room to change. Marco looked in the bag, at the shorts, T-shirt and tracksuit top. He took fright, fearing some fiendish

After much persuasion, Marco stripped down to his new swim shorts, the label still attached, and negotiated the landing stage. With a shiver, he climbed down the iron ladder into the clear, cool flowing water. With a shriek, Laura dived over his head and disappeared beneath the emerald surface. In no time, the pair of them were lying on their backs, hand in hand, as the current carried them downstream, the clouds drifting past above.

Laura's perfect pale complexion had taken on a healthy pink hue, though Marco would swear his toes had turned blue. He saw the city's Botanical Gardens pass by on his right, while on his left the fifteenth-century Witches Tower cast its menacing shadow across the river. Together, they drifted through the heart of the old city. They were not alone. It seemed half of Bern was in the river that afternoon. Groups of people floated by in multi-coloured swimming caps, chatting and joking. A few energetically swam past them, moving quickly downstream, the speed of their strokes aided by the current. When they got to the high Lorraine Bridge, which loomed above them, carrying the main railway line heading south to the Alps, Marco found himself waving up at those in the passing carriages, like a twelve-year-old schoolboy. At the Lorraine pool, they left the water and Laura pulled two small micro towels from her bag.

"There, you see? Wasn't that wonderful?"

With his hair still plastered to his head and the river water running down his body, Marco took her hands and drew her to him, delicately kissing her cool, bloodless lips.

"It was one of the best experiences of my life! Thank you."

As Marco and Laura had left the clinic and walked down the wooded drive, they had been watched from a small upstairs window. The window only opened so far, to admit air, but not so wide as to allow a body to squeeze through. Natasha had wondered what on earth her father was doing dressed in shorts, shoes and socks.

plan to get him into a gym, a place he had never had
visit. He reappeared, with his white spindly legs pol
from under a pair of black swimming shorts. After a
giggling, Laura reassured him they were going to enjoy
the privileges of living in Bern and he would not look
place.

"Now you look like a real Bernese!"

Marco had tanned arms and a wiry, strong physiqu
his years of manual work in his Alpine gardens in Serb
by no means could he be described as athletic.

"What is this? I cannot go out like this – I look ridicu
She put a hand on his arm.

"But you are with me! How is that even possible?"

She pushed him out of the room and the pair of
walked out and down the clinic's main drive. One thing
had forgotten was footwear, so Marco clattered down the
stone steps of the clinic in his shorts, worn with dark b
socks and blood-red brogues.

They strolled through the old town, Marco wonderi
people were quietly laughing behind his back. Eventually,
reached the River Aare that ran through the centre of the
There, they followed the riverside paths until they were u
the old Altenbergsteg latticework suspension bridge.

On the concrete landing stage, Laura confidently strip
off her thermal top and stretch pants, down to a black
piece swimming costume.

"The current is not as strong here. It is perfectly safe. Co
on, undress! I do this all the time."

As a Maltese, Marco was a competent swimmer, but only
the summer months, when the sea reached the temperature
bathwater.

"You must be joking! There is no way …" She thrust
waterproof bag at him.

"Put your clothes in there, it will act as a float. We tal
them with us."

She had noticed he was walking close to the doctor, their shoulders even rubbing together, as one of them whispered something into the other's ear. They were laughing, sharing a joke. At one point, Dr Weber actually laid her hand on Marco's – briefly, but it certainly happened. They were lovers, Natasha knew it. At first, she smiled with the satisfaction of having her suspicions confirmed. Then, her mood changed.

Her breathing became more rapid and deep, as anger started to build inside her. She had watched them closely until they disappeared behind some dense linden trees. The emptiness that had hollowed her out over the past months had gone. She had never felt more alive and awake, burning up inside, as anger and jealousy roused her from the state of drugged, docile submission she had lapsed into in recent months.

Were they laughing at her? She felt her captivity bite into her, imprisoned and helpless as she was, while they set off on whatever ridiculous frolic they had planned. Those two people, the only two in the world she had thought she could count on to put her first, were together. Without her. Behind her back. The old feelings of abandonment, self-pity, betrayal, hatred for those closest to her, which had been absent for so long, awoke and started to fester within her.

CHAPTER 20
SERGEANT DENZEL ZAMMIT

AL AHIL MARSABAR FC, MARSABAR, LIBYA

DENZEL HAD BEEN with Abdullah for some weeks and was getting into the Belkacem household's way of life. His strength had returned, and he had started going for early morning runs with Jamal, to restore his fitness.

Abdullah ran security for the American and Maltese owned oil and gas companies operating in western Libya and took pleasure in explaining his work to Denzel.

"So, you see, your father helped me make this business, which has been so good for my family. Me and Jamal and my cousins, and their cousins, and the cousins of the cousins – we are many people – all of us look to Allah, to help us keep the refinery at Marsabar safe and all those pipes that run across the empty desert from the oil fields."

Abdullah spat on the ground. They were standing next to his Land Cruiser, as he showed Denzel and Jamal a pumping station, in a desolate area some kilometres south of Marsabar, which had recently been the subject of an attack by a militia linked to Islamic State. The wind was blowing red dust from the Sahara, causing grit to stick in their hair, collect in their ears and sting their eyes. Abdullah pulled his *keffiyeh* across his cheeks.

"You see," he said, looking at the twisted and scorched metal and broken pipework, "if we sleep, or get fat and lazy, the IS *chelb* from Chad, Mali and Niger will raid the wells, take the hostages, demand ransoms, capture well heads, blow up the oil and gas pipes and make the doing of business difficult. Then, the Americans will be much unhappy with me, and I will be unhappy with Jamal, and the cousins will be unhappy with their cousins, and all that. Nobody will be happy! The militia people are no good, just good for the blowing up the things, not making the jobs, not making for people's better lives. They are not thinking people."

He tapped the side of his head with one finger.

Denzel had heard about MalTech, the successful Maltese business that Natasha had run, and wondered where it all fitted in.

"So, this is the gas that is piped to Malta and MalTech sells around Europe – the stuff Dad was involved with?"

"Ah, yes. George has done much to make all this happen. He has many medals for fighting the scum from Islamic State. Then, when you were young and not interested in such things, he worked with the Lady Mantis to set up all the legal arrangements, the counting of the money and such. I do not understand this work. Me, I do the simple things. I stop the stealing and the blowing up of things." Abdullah scowled, as he looked at the damaged pumps and twisted wreckage. "But not today. Today is not a good day."

"Who's the Lady Mantis?" Denzel asked.

Abdullah livened up.

"Ah, yes, the Lady Mantis ... the Maltese *contessa* who eats her mates alive!" He laughed loudly. "It is my name for her. It suits her well."

Denzel was none the wiser.

"Now," said Abdullaah, "let us talk of other things – like the football!"

On a Sunday, if all was quiet, the young men played soccer

together. Jamal was an accomplished midfielder for Al Ahil Marsabar FC and Denzel had played for Birkirkara St Joseph's as a centre back. It was only when he went to watch the first training session that he realised why his father had packed his football boots for him. After the session finished, Abdullah came up to the boys. Denzel had proved himself to be a strong and skilful player, adept at responding to the erratic bounce of the ball on the rough Marsabar pitches.

"Jamal tells me you are much better than that useless Jubayr. He is no good, eh?"

"He has the injury, Father, but yes, Denzel is much stronger, so we play together on Sunday," Jamal said.

"Excellent, excellent. You cannot lose if you both play. I am sure of it."

Abdullah accompanied the boys, as he still called them, to the match on Sunday, where he shouted nonsensical instructions at them from the touchline, and random abuse and oaths at the referee and their opponents.

At halftime, the referee had had enough of this local in a turban and *djellaba*, shouting the odds. He stormed towards the team's huddle to have a word with Abdullah, who had pushed the coach to one side and had taken over the halftime team talk. He had his back to the touchline and was unaware of the approaching referee. Jamal saw the man striding purposefully across the pitch, with Abdullah in his sights, and nudged Denzel, alerting him to the fun to come. Unfortunately, one of the linesmen saw what was about to happen and ran to take the referee's arm and quietly explain who it was he was about to berate. The man turned away.

Within ten minutes of the second half, Al Ahil Marsabar was winning comfortably, so Abdullah was happy to leave them to their game, as he had business to attend to. As the boys were coming off the pitch, full of excitement at their win, Denzel saw Abdullah deep in conversation, at the back of the small concrete stand, with a short middle-aged Western woman dressed in a black trouser suit and a brightly coloured headscarf.

Jamal also spotted the pair and walked alongside Denzel, saying: "Have you seen that? Those two are up to something. I know the signs. She's in the American military – Father takes his instructions from her."

At that moment, Abdullah and the woman turned to look at the boys and Abdullah flicked his wrist to beckon them over. He introduced the woman.

"This is my friend, Mary-Ann Baker. She works for American government. You work for American government, Denzel, and …" He looked at Jamal, pointing his long nicotine-stained finger at him. "…you work for American government. She is boss, yes? We do what she says. Is that not right, eh?" The woman smiled.

"Well, sorta right. It's more we all try 'n' do the right thing in a difficult world, you know?" Jamal sneered.

"So, you're CIA?"

The woman said, "I can't answer questions like that." Jamal scowled.

"So, if you're not CIA, why're you watching the football? You going to sign us for a Major League soccer team?"

Abdullah barked at him: "Be quiet! Show respect! Mrs Baker will speak to Denzel. Go, and let us talk quietly."

Jamal glared at the American and skulked off to join his other teammates.

Mary-Ann Baker explained how the American government saw the situation in Malta.

"Abdullah has told me a little bit about you, Denzel. You know better than most what's going down on your island. We've got a phrase for it – *country capture*. So, we're mightily pissed off by the whole picture. You've got the Russians using Malta as a base for their North African ambitions. That naval base, in your beautiful Grand Harbour, changes the whole military dynamic of the southern Mediterranean. Politically, it blows a hole in the EU's coordinated defence strategy, whatever that is, and gets up close and personal right at NATO's back door. So, yeah, we don't like it."

Denzel thought she had missed an important part of the argument.

"Well, yeah, but what about us? The Maltese? They've taken over our country, run riot in our streets, use us as some sort of ... I don't know, playground with no rules – they've destroyed our democracy. What about that?" Mary-Ann Baker continued patiently.

"Sure, Denzel, all of that too. You've seen what's going on, there's no point you telling me what's at stake for Malta – I know only too well. It's my job to know. Abdullah's told me you've already had a few brushes with the Russians. You're police, or probably *ex*-police these days, weapons-trained, some experience with the Green Berets in Syria, am I right? So, I guess you know how to handle yourself. My question is, what do *you* want to do about it?"

There was a pause as Denzel tried to read the subtext here.

"What can I do?"

"Help us get rid of them?" She smiled and shrugged. "Amongst the other shit shows I run, I organise support for the Maltese resistance movement, Democratica. We're training and helping recruits with American-sourced weapons and munitions – well, maybe not *all* American, can't be too obvious."

"What? You want me to become a terrorist?"

"No, that's not it. If you want to be a part of getting rid of the Russians, you have to start making life difficult for them. And that means breaking some eggs! We've already started to build an operation, over in Sicily, and there're some good people involved, but not many – I'll be honest, not many at all. But, from little acorns and all that ...

"You're in the shit in Malta anyway – there's no going home for you, unless it's undercover. We know what you did, and who your father is. The Maltese Machine Gun, yeah?" It was a nickname that George had picked up when he had helped defend a band of American contractors and soldiers from being overrun by ISIS fighters in southern Libya. "That's why, when Abdullah mentioned you were here, I thought I'd look you up.

You come from good stock. You've already been through the Green Beret induction course in Syria and you've got some combat experience, plus a medal for valour – not everybody can say that! Anyway, that's what I'm offering, if you're buying."

Denzel found he had been nodding along throughout her pitch.

Abdullah looked down his long Roman nose and spat into the dirt.

"Denzel, this woman speaks the truth, but you will do nothing without your father's blessing. I do not care how old you are. You are in my house; I will not let you leave my side without his consent, *Inshallah*." He glared at Mary-Ann Baker, who merely raised an eyebrow.

Denzel did not have to think for long. He still bore the scars of the beating he had taken at the airport and had seen enough of the Russian occupation to know where his loyalties lay. He put his hand on Abdullah's shoulder and said:

"Uncle, thanks for your hospitality and protection. You've been a true friend to our family. But I can make my own decision on this. Of course, I'll speak to my father and tell him what I've decided. Subject to that, Mrs Baker, I'm in!"

CHAPTER 21
PRIME MINISTER EDWARD REFALO

OFFICE OF THE PRIME MINISTER, VALLETTA, MALTA

EVERY FRIDAY AFTERNOON, Edward Refalo, Raymond Farrugia and Michael Cini met the Russian officials in the large baroque Cabinet Room in Castille. From the other side, the attendees were Ambassador Grigori Buzilov, Admiral Aleksandr Berezovsky and Colonel Igor Fedorov. As usual, the meeting would begin with a list of requirements from the Russians.

However, not everything was running smoothly. One afternoon, the admiral was in a particularly bellicose mood. There had been several instances of low-level vandalism against Russian property and vehicles, which he seemed to feel was the direct responsibility of those Maltese in the room.

"It's unacceptable!" he roared. "It starts with slashing tyres and daubing paint, next there'll be roadside bombs, suicide attacks – you know how it goes! You've got to act."

Grigori Buzilov sought to calm the bull of a man.

"Aleksandr, it is only to be expected. An element of protest is entirely predictable. However, I agree with you, the *Pulizija* must be ready to deal with all attacks on our property or our people, and we must have contingency plans for if such protests escalate. In fact, I have an idea."

Buzilov got up and went over to the side table where coffee and water were laid out. He poured himself a coffee.

"Can I help anybody?" he asked, with the look of a shark, trying to tempt a swimmer off a beach.

Refalo glanced at Colonel Fedorov and could tell by the phoney, beatific expression on his face that he knew exactly what was coming next and was enjoying the way Buzilov was toying with them. Refalo lost patience.

"Well, what's going on now?"

The ambassador returned to his seat and glanced around the table to ensure he had everyone's full attention.

"I think we can see from the tenor of this conversation that we need more facilities to accommodate those who may be opposed to our plans; to avoid further disruption. Given the desperate state of your prison – the one and only prison on the island – we propose to fund and build a new facility to hold those lower risk offenders whose crimes are of a more, let us say, political nature."

Here Michael Cini interjected.

"I'm the Minister for Home Affairs, National Security and Law Enforcement, and I know nothing about this."

Buzilov smoothed his hair, then ran one hand over his afternoon stubble. He smiled.

"No, you would not. We have only just decided to do it." Cini was incensed.

"And where do you propose to build this ... illegal prison camp?"

"Well, on the site of the collapsed Azure Window, on Gozo. There is nothing there anymore. We will close the road. There is a natural plateau, it is out of the way and quite secure. People will soon forget there is even a camp there."

Buzilov opened his arms and beamed at them. Fait accompli. The Maltese contingent was speechless. The Azure Window had, until 2017, been one of the iconic sights of Malta – a thirty-metre-tall arch that jutted out into the sea on the north-west of Gozo. It had even featured in *Game of Thrones*. One March morning, it had collapsed into the sea during a powerful storm. The early hour had saved the lives of countless tourists, who would otherwise have insisted on clambering along it, despite warnings of its perilous condition.

Ray Farrugia mumbled: "People won't stand for it."

The admiral's chair legs screeched against the tiled floor, as he jumped to his feet.

"People will do what they're damn' well told! D'you not understand?"

Buzilov sighed.

"There may be those who do not understand the good we are doing here. But, in future, they will be the ones behind the wire at Camp Azure. Be careful, Farrugia, you have already had your final warning – you would not want to be among the first to arrive there."

Ray Farrugia seemed to shrink back in his chair. The admiral scratched the side of his belly and stifled a belch.

"Now, Ray, can you organise the acquisition of the site, please? Also, we'll need to acquire the Ta Qali car park."

Ray was chastened, his face a pale grey. He said nothing. Refalo looked at the Russians.

The car park was actually the old World War II runway from which Hurricanes and Spitfires had defended the island in its darkest hours, when Malta had the dubious honour of being the most bombed place in Europe. Today the huge concrete runway and apron served as parking for those wandering amongst the woods of the national park, fans watching football at the national stadium, and visitors to the huge concert and exhibition centre.

Refalo saw the smirks on the Russians' faces.

"And why, might I ask, is that required?"

The admiral shifted in his chair, hands resting on his huge belly.

"You've no air defences. You're wide open to attack. We

need space to build some missile platforms. Also, we can adapt the runway to allow us to bring in some of the larger unmanned aerial vehicles – drones, and some of the smaller military aircraft.

"Malta International Airport's fine for the time being, but we need our own space. We've got MiGs that can operate on less than a kilometre of runway, so a few minor adaptations and Ta Qali will be perfectly suitable. We'll have to close a few of the access roads, and that useless little craft park – nothing for the Maltese to be concerned about – but the Libyans in Tripoli might be in for a few surprises!"

Buzilov was not laughing. He glanced at Refalo and said: "So, this is what we want. We need to be able to defend our installation at Manoel Island. We would not want another Pearl Harbor, would we? Can Ray sort out the legal work? We need to move onto the sites immediately."

"This is going too far, Grigori. You're deliberately provoking the Americans and the EU. What do you think they're going to say about it? You're militarising the entire island."

The ambassador fixed a smile to his face, as he said reassuringly:

"Edward, Edward. Do not worry about these things. It has all been very well thought through. Your little republic is not in NATO, so we can forget about them springing to your defence. The belligerent British have left the EU, and you are not treaty partners. The right-wing Italian government is very friendly with our president and shares our view that the African migrant problem needs to be firmly addressed." Grigori examined the moulding on the ceiling before continuing. "So, that only leaves the French and the Germans. When have they ever agreed on anything, let alone done anything about it?

"Anyway, who is going to interfere in the affairs of an independent sovereign country? I take it there has been no change of thought about the welcome you have extended to us, has there?"

Michael Cini sat at the end of the table, as if trying to distance himself from the others. He said in a soft voice, "There's still the question of the vote on the constitutional amendments. Until then, the EU view is that, invited or not, your presence here is unconstitutional and therefore illegal." There was an animal noise of disgust from the admiral.

"The EU can..."

Colonel Fedorov held up his hand to prevent a further outburst.

"Is opposition to the changes well organised? Is there a person around whom opposition has – what's the word – coalesced?"

There was silence around the table, until Cini said: "President Michael Mizzi is known to oppose the changes. That gives encouragement to others."

The admiral and the ambassador turned their gazes to meet Colonel Fedorov's, as he said: "Interesting."

CHAPTER 22
SERGEANT DENZEL ZAMMIT

SIGNORELLA US AIRFORCE BASE, SICILY, ITALY

THREE WEEKS after the conversation with Mary-Ann Baker, following tearful farewells with Abdullah and Rania, Jamal took Denzel west along the coast road and secretly crossed the closed border to Tunisia's Carthage airport, where Denzel boarded a plane for Catania, in Sicily, via Rome. He was met at Catania by a young American man with a buzz cut, heavily tattooed arms and a body as solid as a redwood tree. He introduced himself as Huck, speaking in a Tennessee twang through his bushy red beard. His outfit of brightly patterned, short sleeved shirt, cargo shorts, flipflops and sunglasses, made him look like any other poorly dressed tourist transiting through Catania's airport. After introducing himself, he never spoke another word while driving Denzel to the American military base at Signorella, the hub of US naval air operations in the Mediterranean, some forty kilometres south of Mount Etna.

In a discreet low-rise block, on the western edge of the large, fortified US airbase, Huck introduced him to Billy, another American from the southern states. Billy was tall, thin and rangy, with a scraggly beard, and he too was heavily tattooed. He wore wrap around Oakley sunglasses but, in his case, never removed them, even when indoors. He had an unstable energy about him that found release in permanently tapping his right foot when seated and drumming his fingers on any available surface. Denzel was not surprised when he later found out that, back home, Billy had played a mean snare drum in a well-known rockabilly band.

Just as the three of them were taking their seats around the table, a figure appeared at the open door and Huck said, "Okay, Denzel, it's show time. Here comes the boss."

Through the door came a tall, broad-shouldered woman, with dark, curly shoulder-length hair. Her thumbs were tucked into the waistband of her jeans, and she stood for a minute looking at Denzel. She took off her sunglasses, revealing a face with a firm jaw and piercing dark eyes, before making her way across.

"Denzel Zammit?"

He nodded, looking at her suspiciously.

"I'm Silvia Camilleri, Gerald Camilleri's niece. Your father saved my life in Sicily."

Denzel held out his hand and smiled at her.

"Ah, my God! I thought I knew you! You're the woman he rescued from the volcano. We met – at my sister's wedding."

"We did, I remember. That was quite a night!"

"I'm afraid I can't recall much about it! So, anyway, now we're going to stick it to the Russians?" Silvia nodded.

"I hear you already have."

"Well, yeah, sort of. But I ended up in a bit of a mess. So, I need them gone. How come you're here?"

"I'm a sucker for a cause and when someone invades your country … well …" she shrugged "… you don't get a bigger cause than that!"

Huck said: "Hell, Billy, don't ya just love it when something beautiful happens? I'm all wellin' up here, but shall we get down to business?"

"Sure thing, Huck. My heart's fit to bust. Now, take a seat,

Silvia. Denzel, Silvia's already a bit ahead of you in basic insurgency training. In Fort Bragg, where I got my Green Beret, the Special Forces Qualification Course takes sixty-one weeks. Huck here, he's a US Navy Seal. His training was just learning to hold his breath and swim, real fast. But even that took eighteen months." Billy winked at Huck, who sat impassively. Billy let his smile drop. "We've got about twenty days before we send you home. So, no pressure."

Billy started drumming his fingers. Huck took over the briefing.

"We're guessing you can find your way around the little ol' island of Malta – it's only the size of Central Park – so we'll skip all the navigation and communications bit and focus on the survival, evasion, resistance and escape exercises. And especially on advanced special operations techniques. That's the bullets, bombs and guns bit. Y'all up for that?"

Denzel and Silvia looked at each other. Denzel swallowed and nodded. Silvia looked Huck square in the eyes.

"Sure we are. Let's get on with it."

The next twenty days were a blur. There was a group of twelve enthusiastic young Maltese, from all walks of life, who had signed up for the training program. The group started that afternoon with basic firearms training. Denzel had been on the police range many times but, by the end of the first week, his shoulder was black and blue from the recoil of the myriad weapons they had to master. They learned how to enter buildings and not end up shooting each other; how to assess the best way to approach a target; how to behave so as not to attract attention. In an isolated quarry, they practised setting off small charges of plastic explosives, pulled the pins on grenades, experienced the shocking sensory impact of a stun grenade. They learned to recognise different interrogation techniques and how to respond to them. Billy tested them endlessly with pictures and profiles of Russian ships, planes, weapons, armoured vehicles and helicopters.

Twenty days later, both Denzel and Silvia admitted they were exhausted. Billy was worried the group was approaching information-overload point but told Denzel and Silvia they were close to returning to Malta and he was worried there was still some way to go in their preparation for live operations. Given their rookie status, he and Huck had been ordered to accompany them back to the island, to act as in-field advisers.

"This most definitely does *not* mean we can pull the trigger on any Russkis or stick any bombs up their tail pipes. But Huck and I'll be on hand to show you guys how to do exactly that, without killing yourselves or, hopefully, getting caught. But, if shit goes down, Huck and I are outta there, double quick, and Uncle Sam ain't never heard of you. Got it?"

Denzel nodded his agreement and could have kissed the pair of them.

It was not long before they were given a departure date. The plan was for Silvia to take a commercial flight, directly back to Malta. As Denzel was a wanted man, he would travel by sea with Huck and Billy, along with a small armoury of weapons and materials. Denzel sent a coded email, giving the date and time of their arrival to George, who had promised to make sure there were no problems once they docked at Valletta. On the morning of departure, Huck demanded Denzel go to the bathroom and get himself all good and empty, then led him to a battered, light green fourteen-metre container that was on the back of an articulated lorry. Denzel clambered aboard and squeezed his way through pallets of goods tightly wrapped with layers of shrink wrap.

The back section of the container had been modified to house a narrow compartment, with its own filtered air supply and climate control capability. There were four narrow bunks at the far end of the space. Strapped to the frame of the container wall, Denzel was impressed to find a full range of communications equipment, bullpup assault rifles, concealable urban sniper rifles that fired rounds capable of piercing cinder block walls more than a foot thick, and a rack of body armour.

In the main section of the container, buried behind pallets of tinned tomatoes, pasta, wine and beers, and other household goods, ostensibly bound for Malta's wholesalers, there were Smart tube-launched grenades that, once fired, would seek a laser-guided target. Secreted among the crates of tomatoes were a number of explosive charges and incendiary mines with which to conduct modern guerrilla warfare.

They drove south, to the Sicilian port of Pozzallo. It was from there that the high-speed catamaran, *Jean de la Valette*, departed from Sicily for the ninety-minute journey to Malta. The huge catamaran carried over a hundred cars and twelve articulated wagons, as well as 800 passengers.

Like all soldiers, Huck and Billy were used to passing long hours of inactivity, waiting for something to happen. They relaxed on the bunks in their boxer shorts, displaying their impressive range of tattoos. Billy was on top and Huck below. At first, they slept. Then, after an hour or so, the truck came to a halt. Huck watched the screen of his laptop that showed images from the concealed cameras positioned on all four corners of the container. He could see the lorry sitting in line, along with the other commercial vehicles, waiting to board the catamaran. Huck broke the silence by announcing he was hungry.

Then he said: "Billy, can I ask if you've ever been to Isaacs's Steak and Chop House in Nashville, Tennessee?" There was a pause before Billy answered.

"Huck, I can't say that I have. Tell me. What is it about that, no doubt, very fine establishment that brings it to your attention, right at this moment?"

"Well, I was thinking about their T-bone steaks, which are perfectly well cut, no less than an inch thick and seared on a red-hot skillet, leaving the meat in the middle still pink and, for me, a little bloody. I do believe a well-cooked T-bone's America's best steak."

Billy was shocked by the casual extravagance of the statement.

"America's best steak? That's a truly outrageous claim, my friend." Huck waited for Billy to develop his thinking. "You can't say a thing like that when we've not even discussed the soft-textured, subtle-flavoured filet mignon, or the beauty of a well-marbled ribeye, where the fat melts into the fibres of the muscle. And what about New York strip? Cut from the sirloin of the beast, with that rich layer of fat to add umami flavours – which you've also ignored. No, no, there's much more to be said before we can agree on *America's best steak*."

In the privacy of his bunk, Huck smiled and settled down for the discussion. He had struck the first blow and Billy had responded, just as expected. Such arguments were their favourite way of passing dead time.

Within half an hour, Denzel was asleep, lulled by the roar of the giant catamaran, as it sped across the smooth water towards Malta, and the lazy drone of Huck and Billy's voices, arguing about the merits of charcoal grills and red-hot skillets.

He was woken by Billy shaking his shoulder.

"Quiet now. We've arrived."

As the *Jean de la Valette* docked in Valletta, a call came through to the *Pulizija* sergeant on duty, who tipped off the customs officers that the battered green container on the Volvo truck was under covert police surveillance and should not be subjected to any random checks.

The truck used its HIAB crane to unload the container in a securely fenced compound of an abandoned coastal quarry, away from the congested southeast of the island. The quarry would be used as a base where the newly formed resistance could learn how to handle the resources at their disposal. Given that Denzel was still being sought by the Russians for the killing of the volunteer at the airport, he would remain with Huck and Billy, based in a rented flat in the nondescript town of Siġġiewi.

Within a day of landing, donning a baseball cap and sunglasses, Denzel took the bus to Valletta and went to the Herbert Ganado Gardens, a little-frequented park formed within the bastions of Floriana, overlooking the Grand Harbour. As had been arranged with George, his family were sitting on a bench at the far end of the main pathway.

He walked towards them, watching Gina, as she rocked a baby buggy backwards and forwards. His mother perched on the edge of the bench, dressed in her church coat, despite the summer heat. She was animated about something or other and, as usual, seemed to be haranguing his father. He smiled. Nothing had changed.

It took a little while before Gina spotted Denzel's familiar gait walking towards them. She jumped to her feet and rushed along the path towards him, quickly followed by Marianna, and the women tearfully embraced him.

His mother was ecstatic.

"So, does this mean you've come home? George, what're we doing hanging around in this park? It's for drug addicts and prostitutes. Why aren't we all at home?" Denzel put an arm around her.

"Listen, Ma. I can't come home until the Russians leave. You know that – it's too dangerous for all of us. Anyway, it's lovely to see you. How have you all been?"

"*Uwejja* ... if you only knew! I've been a nervous wreck. First your father banished Gina and me to that horrible aunt of yours, in Gozo. She was cruel to our Gina and said awful things about Baby Joseph. Then she threw us out! My own sister-in-law! So, your father ... pah! It was hell, I tell you."

George interjected, "*Mela*, that's not quite true ..."

"You be quiet. I'm talking to my son. You're the one who banished him to Liberia, so I'm entitled to have a word with him, now he's back."

"Libya, Marianna. Liberia's a different place, remember?" murmured George.

Denzel looked at the strapping child who was busy chewing a *ftira* – a large flat breadcake, filled with tuna, tomatoes, capers and sweet white onion, from the picnic basket. He observed: "Well, whatever happened, it doesn't seem to have done him any harm. He eats capers at that age? I hated capers as a kid!"

Marianna had not finished with her list of gripes.

"I bet it's been terrible living with that awful man in Liberia. It's a horrible place, all dirt and flies. A bit like Gozo, really. Do they have electricity?"

"Look, Ma – Abdullah and Rania have been great to me while I was in *Libya*. Rania's a wonderful cook, I think you'd really like her. They kept me safe and treated me as one of their family. They couldn't have done more for me. Dad said we should all go to see them, once this is …"

"What's this, George? Me, Gina and Baby Joseph, go to Africa? To that house, where *they* live? No, no, no – we're all going to Spain, to Nerja. How dare you even think about treating your family like that. It's Spain for us, that's final!"

George looked at Denzel and shook his head. Denzel grinned back at him.

"Look, Ma, I'm only here for today. I've just come to see you and make sure you're alright. So let's enjoy our lunch, shall we?"

"*Uwejja!*? You're going back to live with that horrible man – he's not even a Christian, and … I'm sure his wife is perfectly respectable, but … well, she's married to him!"

"Look, you know it's not safe for me here," Denzel said, crossing his fingers behind his back. Better that his mother should believe he was well off the scene with Abdullah. "The Russians would shoot me as soon as look at me."

"Not while I'm here, they wouldn't! Anyway, George said

he'd bring lunch. That probably means a dozen *pastizzi*!" George was shocked.

"What's wrong with *pastizzi*?"

He grabbed what was left of the *ftira* from Baby Joseph and Gina put him into his pushchair, where he promptly fell asleep. Marianna was correct. George produced a large brown paper bag, filled with oily ricotta and pea *pastizzi*. He had brought cans of Cisk lager for the men and Coke for the women. They settled down on some benches and chatted for the next hour or so.

Marianna brought Denzel up to speed on what was happening in the family, the street and, finally, her take on the state of the country. Gina added her own unique spin to the political goings on, until everybody was thoroughly confused. George then distributed some *cannoli*, the Sicilian delicacy of puff pastry cones, filled with a delicious mix of heavy cream, mascarpone and ricotta cheese, dusted with powdered sugar. Coffee was poured from a large thermos and the chat continued, until the feast was interrupted by Baby Joseph waking up from his nap and immediately grabbing at the food.

Denzel chased the excited, sturdy toddler around the narrow tracks between the flower beds, growling and barking like a rabid dog. The child squealed in delight, until Denzel grabbed him and swung him round and round in circles, whereupon he was promptly sick.

Overall, it had been a fine afternoon but, like all good things, it had to end. Denzel told them it was time for him to leave. Amidst more tears, he made his way out of the park and took the bus back to Siġġiewi. He had things to do and his mind had begun to focus on the week ahead. The Zammits put Baby Joseph into his pushchair and packed the picnic basket. Marianna and Gina forlornly walked off to the car park, arm in arm. George trudged behind, pushing the heavy child, the pungent smell of vomit floating in the air behind him.

CHAPTER 23
SILVIA CAMILLERI
CASSAR'S QUARRY, SIĠĠIEWI, MALTA

THE SUN WAS SINKING. The dusty quarry floor was already shrouded in evening gloom, while the high, sheer limestone walls were still lit in shades of butter yellow and flax. The place itself was deep in the country, north of Siġġiewi, and rarely visited, except by hunters trying to shoot rabbits or birds. Malta's built heritage was based on the easily worked limestone that had been cut from the ground since Neolithic times. The countryside was covered with small disused quarries such as that.

Denzel was excited and nervous. He had seen action before – when he had stormed an ISIS *madrassa* in Syria with American special forces – but he knew, no matter how many times it happened, he would never lose the sick feeling in his stomach, as the pre-mission nerves began to bite.

He suddenly stopped cleaning his rifle and listened intently. In the distance, he heard the faint sound of a car's engine. It grew louder and eventually he saw it nose its way over the lip of the quarry and slowly start to descend the rough track, terraced into the vertical walls. Denzel leaped to his feet and began to quickly reassemble the rifle.

Billy stuck his head out of the container and shouted: "Relax, Den. The boss is here."

The car came to a halt and Silvia got out, followed by an older man who slowly unfolded himself from the back seat. The new arrival stretched, cleared his throat and gobbed a ball of phlegm onto the rock floor of the quarry. Silvia wore dark clothing, while the older man had baggy jeans secured around his skinny hips with a thick belt, and a hooded sweatshirt, bearing the logo of some English university. Around his neck and over his head, he had a red-and-white-checked *keffiyeh*. Silvia took off her sunglasses and made her way across to Denzel.

"Hiya, how's it going? You look a little pale."

"No, no. I'm fine. It's good to have a few nerves, you know."

"You're right. Only the stupid or liars say they don't suffer from them. It'll be fine."

Denzel merely nodded suspiciously.

"Anyway, I brought someone you know." She turned to look at the older man who was surveying the quarry and the two Americans who stood cradling their weapons.

"Ha! This is a no good place. One way in, one way out." He turned to look at Denzel. "So, you let Americans choose the camp, eh? I see I am here only just in time."

Denzel looked at the man he now recognised as Abdullah. "What on earth …?"

"I speak to Mary-Ann Baker and I say that there is no way George and his son can do this resisting thing alone. It was the voice of Allah Himself that told me to come. Jamal is home in Libya, he is now the big boss, and me … I am just humble soldier in resistance. I too am here to resist! George will be much pleased."

He beamed, very pleased with himself.

Billy and Huck looked unimpressed.

"Well, isn't this just dandy?" Billy said. "I heard, Huck, we were getting a seasoned veteran; a fighter trained in guerilla warfare. A real wild tiger. Isn't that what you heard?"

"Sure was, Billy. And this here, Huck," he pointed at Abdullah, "he ain't no soldier like I've ever seen."

Abdullah slowly walked over to Billy, who stood his ground and, in one lightning-fast move, grabbed his automatic rifle, put Billy flat on his back and trained it on Huck.

Huck had his hands in the air. He smiled down at Billy, who lay prone in the dirt.

"Well, I'll be damned!" Huck was staring at Abdullah. "How in the name of the Lord did you manage to do that? Guess the Green Berets ain't all they're cracked up to be. Can he get up now?"

Abdullah spat on the ground, forcing Billy to roll over to avoid being hit. He held out his hand, to help the American up.

"Take my hand. It is offered in friendship. And learn the lesson – old dogs still bite."

Billy was furious. He had bet Huck a month's pay that the whole resistance thing would go to shit in less than a month.. Huck shared Billy's concerns and thought he was probably right but, for the sake of being a good sport, had taken the bet. However, the arrival of this Abdullah dude cast their wager in an entirely new light.

Billy took Adullah's hand and shook it, after getting to his feet.

"Well, I can't say I'm mighty pleased being put down like that, but it was some move. Maybe you could teach it to me sometime? Anyways, let's get started. It's gonna be a busy night."

Denzel took Abdullah to one side.

"Uncle, I'm always pleased to see you, but this isn't your fight. You didn't have to come. Does Dad know you're here?"

"Any fight of yours is a fight of mine. I have come to pay off but a small part of the debt I owe your father. If I stayed and fought for a thousand years, still I would owe him a fortune. I am here because Rania made me promise I would make sure you are returned to your mother, alive and unharmed, as George made sure Jamal was returned to us. So do not waste the breath on the talking and arguing. And it is best if George does not know that it is you and me who are giving these Russian dogs a kicking – because then, there will just be more of the arguments. Now, there is work to be done."

Huck pulled out three long canvas bags and started filling them with the weapons and equipment that Denzel and Silvia had become familiar with when on the airbase in Sicily. The two Americans then unrolled a detailed map, together with additional hand-drawn site plans, and outlined the mission and their respective roles.

An hour later, having taken questions, they all made themselves as comfortable as possible and Huck suggested they take some personal downtime before zero hour. Denzel lay on the wood-panelled floor of the container, his head resting against a pallet of plum tomatoes, counting the minutes, as they ticked away. Abdullah rolled his coat into a pillow and settled down on the rough floor of the quarry, looking at the stars, trying to work out the direction of the Qibla, the fixed direction towards the Ka'bah in the Grand Mosque in Mecca, Saudi Arabia, which all Muslims face when performing their prayers, wherever they are in the world.

At midnight exactly, Silvia drove the Fiat back up the zigzag track out of the quarry, with Denzel in the passenger seat and Abdullah squashed in the back. In the rear of the car were eight twelve-kilogram anti-tank mines and a rucksack of incendiary hand grenades, with sufficient power to cause considerable damage to unarmoured vehicles. Huck and Billy remained in the container to control the Delta quad drone with thermal imaging and night vision capabilities that would give the team added security when they reached the site of the attack.

The plan was to destroy the Russian vehicles parked in the

depot in the Marsa Park and Ride, in Qormi, part of the urban conglomeration on the east of the island, five kilometres inland from Valletta. They would approach on the road that ran parallel to the back straight of the racecourse, park the cars next to the children's play area, then enter the car park through a gap in the largely ornamental fencing. The cast iron railings had been severed earlier and wedged back into position by a road crew working an angle grinder, pretending to be making pavement repairs.

It was a low-security target, chosen to bolster confidence in the team and provide a highly visible demonstration that the resistance was in business. The three or four Russian guards were in a small cabin at the gate to the car park and those who had been observing them said they rarely ventured out at night, except to smoke or urinate against a nearby wall. Huck and Billy would manage the drone that would hover overhead, to alert the party of any movement from the cabin.

They arrived a little after 00:30 and turned the car around, facing back the way they had come for an easier getaway. The large anti-tank mines were weighty, so each of the men carried two, in a rucksack, and had to make two trips to get them to the car park. Silvia took the lighter incendiary hand grenades. The severed railings came apart just as they were supposed to. Within minutes, the three of them were in the car park.

They had chosen a moonless night and that, with the weak street lights, conspired to conceal their presence. Once they were inside the car park, it was easy to move between vehicles and keep out of sight of the cabin at the entrance.

Backed up against the fence, in a row, were four tracked armoured vehicles, each capable of carrying eleven men. Next to them were four T-90 tanks, still on transporters, which had never been moved the entire time the Russians had been on the island. The vehicles were intended to be available to deal with civil disturbances or used as a show of strength, if the occasion demanded it. The Americans thought the tanks were just for show and had laid bets with Denzel as to whether they could even move.

Abdullah unloaded the anti-tank mines and placed them beneath the targets. His teeth gleamed in the dark, as he gleefully went about his mischief. At worst, the mines would blow the tracks clean off. At best, the blast would penetrate the armour and completely destroy them. The T-90 was a small, lightly armoured tank and Huck was confident the mines had enough explosive power to smash them to pieces.

It took ten minutes to place the mines and attach the remotely operated detonators, which took the place of the more conventional pressure triggers. Denzel ran a wire across the car park to the trigger mechanism, which he placed near to the gap in the railings. Once all was set, he launched the drone that Huck and Billy would control remotely. Silvia distributed the incendiary grenades and they began to roll them under the military trucks, ambulances, and, most importantly, the six riot-control vehicles. The grenades had a six-second fuse and there was no doubt that, as soon as the first one exploded, the Russians would be alerted and rush out of the guard house, leaving seconds for the saboteurs to make their escape. Their plan was to destroy the vehicles but avoid taking human life.

The team worked together, moving backwards between the vehicles. Denzel prepped each grenade, getting it from the bag and identifying the next target, while Silvia and Abdullah took the bomb, pulled the pin, released the lever and rolled it under each vehicle. The fuses only allowed a maximum of six seconds before the thermite ignited at 4,000° Centigrade. The casing of the grenade was composed of magnesium, a metal that itself burned at an extremely high temperature. Once the anti-tank mine charges had been set and the grenades distributed, they put on ear protectors and, despite poor visibility, dark goggles.

The first grenade exploded under a large riot-control vehicle, with a deafening roar and a blinding white light, stronger than any of them had imagined possible. They all stood stunned for a moment. Once they had recovered themselves, they kept retreating towards the fence, keeping the grenades rolling and exploding. Denzel rolled another beneath a bus that was already alight from an earlier blast.

"Jesus, all of Malta must be wondering what's going on! Give me another one ... come on, come on!"

The scale of the damage was incredible. Flames leapt up everywhere, illuminating the whole car park. Denzel's ears were ringing from the blasts. His bag was empty.

"Silvia, now! Let's blow the tanks."

She found the small ignition switch that would trigger the detonators. It was a simple rocker model. She checked Denzel and Abdullah were safe and flicked the switch. The anti-tank mines exploded with less theatricality than the incendiary grenades. More of a dull 'crump', not the high-pitched shriek of the flaming grenades. The armoured hardware just seemed to collapse in on itself. The tracks burst outwards and the body of the tanks sank to the ground. Turrets were blasted off some of the tanks, and one of the armoured personnel carriers was lifted into the air and toppled onto its side.

Denzel became conscious of a light just above their heads as Huck flew the drone low across the car park to record the damage. Silvia caught Denzel by the arm, her chestnut brown eyes alive with excitement.

"We did it! Come on, Denzel, Abdullah ... hurry! Let's go before it's too late."

They squeezed through the railings and ran across the road to the waiting vehicle.

Silvia's car sped away, with Denzel twisted round in the rear seat, checking for signs of a chase behind them. They all laughed and screamed with relief.

Abdullah said: "Allah be praised! That was a very fine explosion. It is a shame George was not there to see it. He would have been much pleased. I knew I was right to return and help with the resisting!"

CHAPTER 24
NATASHA BONNICI
THE WEBER CLINIC, BERN, SWITZERLAND

THE SIGHT of her father and Dr Laura Weber walking down the clinic's drive together, obviously on close terms, had a profound effect on Natasha. She realised that, despite her absence, the world was moving on and there were things happening around her that she had no ability to control or influence, certainly not while she was locked up in the Swiss prison masquerading as a clinic.

The antipsychotic drugs had made her feel woozy, thick-headed and lethargic. She had argued with Dr Weber that they made it more difficult for her to engage with the cognitive behavioural therapy and the supportive psychotherapy Dr Weber was such a believer in. It was true that most of the manifestations of her illness – the hallucinations, short-term memory loss, delusions and disturbing thoughts – had disappeared and she had become more cooperative and willing to engage with those treating her. Natasha made a concerted effort to maintain a calm exterior and was especially polite and courteous to her allocated nurse, Wilhelm, an English-speaking German from the Rhineland.

In their patient review meetings, Wilhelm impressed upon Dr Weber how well Natasha seemed to be responding to treatment, how cooperative she was and how, in his view, she could become one of the clinic's most successfully rehabilitated patients. Dr Weber also noted how much improved the patient's physical appearance had become.

It was part of Natasha's therapy to improve her cognitive responses, so she and Wilhelm played chess in the afternoons. Natasha never mentioned that, until her early twenties, she and Marco had regularly played chess and that he had taught her the game from an early age. Defeating Wilhelm was an easy matter, but she toyed with him, enjoying how much his victories pleased him.

Marco had always maintained that chess developed the skills to find creative solutions and put a plan into action. At that moment, she needed a solution to get her out of the Weber Clinic and put a stop to Laura Weber taking advantage of her father. Something at the back of Natasha's mind realised that Wilhelm might be the key to that. She had noticed him watching her between moves, in a way that was more than just one chess player observing another. Before their sessions, she would check her appearance and apply a little make up. She was aware that, now her hair had grown into a short pixie style, her figure had filled out and her complexion had been restored, she was nearly back to the woman she had been, before the Greek years – as she began to think of them.

One afternoon, as Wilhelm's hand reached to move his bishop, Natasha decided it was time to make an approach. She reached out and put her hand on his, resting it there for a second or two.

"Are you sure that's the best move?" she asked.

Wilhelm froze.

"Please," he said, "you know there's no physical contact allowed within a patient's room." Natasha sighed.

"I'm sorry, you're right." She adjusted the collar of her blouse, revealing a little more of her lower neck and running her fingers across her sternum.

"Sometimes a bit of human contact, just to feel somebody, is exactly what I need." She glanced at him to gauge his reaction, a playful expression on her face. His pale blue eyes were fixed on her, his facial muscles pinched. He was a little older than Natasha, showing signs of weight gain, with a healthy, tanned complexion and receding blond hair. In his younger days, Natasha thought, he would have been a good-looking man.

"Relax, Wilhelm. I'm not making a pass at you – not yet, anyway. Just don't move that bishop. I know you're trying to tempt me with the Greek Gift, but I'm not going to go for it." Wilhelm swallowed and shifted position in his chair.

"I think we should call it a day, Natasha. You're making me uncomfortable."

She sat back from the board, looking amused.

"Well, I can fix that and make you a lot more comfortable, if you'll let me."

Her look of amusement broke into a seductive smile.

"You know what I mean?"

Wilhelm did not move. He sat transfixed, staring at her.

"I find it difficult to sleep at night. Playing chess seems to soothe me. Maybe we could finish this game later this evening? It would be an immense help to me."

She raised her eyebrows, inviting a response.

Wilhelm did not say a word, but he never took his eyes off her.

She knew she had him.

CHAPTER 25
ASSISTANT COMMISSIONER GEORGE ZAMMIT

ZAMMIT FAMILY HOME, BIRKIRKARA, MALTA

IT WAS George and Marianna's thirtieth wedding anniversary and preparations for a family meal had been underway all week. Marianna had invited the Mifsuds, Gina's in-laws, to dinner on the Friday evening. On the preceding Wednesday, the Mifsud butcher's van had pulled up outside George's apartment and the driver had presented Marianna with sufficient meat to feed a banquet at the Presidential Palace. In terror, she had returned half of it, as she had neither the skills nor the oven space to roast a full rib of beef, two legs of lamb and a long loin of pork wrapped and tied in a boned-out pork belly. That was before thinking about what to do with the bloody heap of unplucked chickens and unskinned rabbits that lay on her table in a large plastic tray.

In exchange for a rabbit and a chicken, a neighbour had agreed to let Marianna use her oven, and George had rigged the barbecue to slow cook the *porchetta*. With those arrangements in place, Marianna thought she and Gina would just about be able to manage to serve enough meat to sate the carnivorous appetites of the Mifsuds. George had thrown a further spanner in the works when he had bumped into his elder brother, Albert, in Hamrun and gone to the Band Club for some beers. In a rare and uncharacteristic act of drunken bonhomie, he had invited Albert to the feast.

Marianna considered her brother-in-law the black sheep of the family, since he had a penchant for wine, coarse humour and bothering the ladies. Albert had readily accepted the invitation – after all, he had been the best man at their wedding.

The evening of the celebration arrived. The meat took centre-stage on the table and a red-faced Marianna and Gina sat down, triumphant, presenting a banquet the like of which had never before been seen in their apartment. George rose and kissed Marianna on the cheek, to his wife's shrieks of delight. Toasts were made and Albert discovered, not for the first time, that his glass was empty. Joe Mifsud was perspiring heavily, as he addressed the piles of meat in front of him. Everything was going splendidly.

Then, Giorgio raised his glass and said: "We need one more toast. Don't think we've forgotten about Denzel. He should be here with us tonight. Gina and I think about him all the time. Don't we, love?"

Giorgio raised his glass while Marianna's bottom lip protruded, as she fought a sudden welling of emotion. George cast his eyes down, but also raised his glass. Joe Mifsud did not release his cutlery but merely stopped chewing and waited for the moment to pass, so he could resume his ferocious assault on the plate before him.

Then his wife, Josette, who was as round as she was tall, flashed her dark eyes around the table and said: "Well, he could've been here, if he hadn't shot a Russian. I can't raise my glass to him – the boy was stupid."

There was a moment of complete silence, broken by the clatter of cutlery on china, as Marianna struggled to take in what she had just heard. It was too much for her. She pushed her plate away and stormed out of the dining room.

At the door, she turned and shouted: "How dare you come into this house and say a thing like that? Shame on you!"

Then the sound of sobbing started from the corridor.

An argument began raging around the table, with Josette shouting at Albert and Albert shouting back. George tried to calm the guests, but to no avail. Joe Mifsud continued eating, his fork spearing lumps of lamb and beef, his other arm around his plate, as if to protect it. The argument moved from the cause of Denzel's absence and on to the reason for the Russians' presence. Gina clung to Giorgio in tears. Josette Mifsud proved herself to be a fierce adversary and a strong backer of the pro-Russian party.

"Do you want to be overrun by African migrants?" she demanded to know. "Because I don't. They'll change the churches into mosques, they'll open the border and there'll be thousands of them. It'll be the end of us, the Maltese, I promise you. And what a welcome! To start shooting the Russians just because they got a bit excited at the airport." George tried to intervene.

"*Mela*! *Mela*, wait a minute. Denzel was acting in defence of …"

The drink was getting the better of Albert, who shouted over his brother's words.

"I don't know about what happened with Denzel and I'm sure he did his duty and made us proud, but she's right about the migrants. These Africans from Chad, Sudan, Iraq, all those places, they've not got a cent, no trade and they can't look after themselves. Once they know the gate is open, there'll be thousands coming. Look, how many migrants there are in Malta already? Five thousand? But most of them are young men. Wait until their wives and the kids arrive – eh? We'll see some numbers then. No, the Russians see it as it is – but listen, I agree, they shouldn't be here. They're an army of occupation, it's true. It's wrong …" he banged the table with his fist "… and it's illegal!" Glasses tumbled and two smashed on the tiled floor.

Gina sniffled into the crook of her arm and slid out of the

dining room to comfort her mother. It had all gone horribly wrong. She could not stay and listen to it a moment longer.

Albert paused to consider his own rambling argument, then, deciding it all made perfect sense, poured and drank a glass of wine, becoming more animated, as he proceeded. "Look at Germany, they let in millions, and Sweden the same. They regret it now. Oh, yes! No room in the schools or at the doctor's, decent areas turned into slums. No money for anything. They wished they'd never let in a single one of them!"

George held his hand up to quieten them. Josette Mifsud was now sitting, subdued, while Albert ranted. The heat had gone out of the discussion, and he saw his opportunity to quell the unpleasantness around the table.

"Josette, please, listen to me. Den fired his weapon at a young man holding a knife to a woman's head. He'd already cut her face and she'll be scarred for life. She was bleeding. My son warned the soldier to drop the knife, but he refused and started to push it into her ear, with a mob egging him on. Her ear started to bleed. So ... *Mela*, we know the rest. Den would have done the same if it had been a Maltese, an Englishman or a Swede. Unfortunately, it was a Russian and there were political consequences.

"But Denzel's a victim here as well, forced to flee to avoid retaliation. All because he had to do his duty. He had to make a near impossible decision. I just hope I'm never in that position. We've got to support him. It has nothing to do with the rights and wrongs of the Russian occupation, migration or any of that. Don't you see?"

Josette was a proud woman and not minded to back down.

"Well, I still think he was wrong. But, I'm sorry I upset Marianna. I'm a mother too, so I'll apologise. What sort of people would we be if we didn't stand by our children? But listen, Mifsud Family Butchers supply the Russians. They buy a lot of meat from us, they pay on time ... so we say, the longer they stay, the better. Isn't that right, Joe? He's very friendly with the local officers and helps them find their way around. Helps them out with information about the town too and who's who, that sort of thing. Don't you, Joe? They all seem like nice people."

Joe Mifsud glared at his wife and mopped his brow with a crumpled handkerchief. Albert finished a glass of Gozitan red in one long slurp. He was highly animated and had begun slurring his words. The glass tumbled over, when he dropped it onto the table. He was back on his feet.

"What does that mean, 'helps them find their way around', gives them 'information about the town and who's who'? Are you a snitch or something, Mifsud? My God, an informer for the Russians, is that what you're saying? Tell them nothing, or if you have to, better it's lies. For God's sake, don't do their dirty work for them!"

Joe Mifsud laughed nervously.

"No, no. Nothing like that. I just … just … help them out, you know."

Albert was angry, waving his arms about, as he began shouting.

You *are* a snitch! You come here, to our family occasion, while behind our backs, you're helping turn us into slaves of the Russians. Well, to hell with you!"

Albert lunged forward to grab at Joe Mifsud's shirt but collapsed across the table, covering himself in the bloody juices from the platter holding the beef rib. Josette was quick to defend her husband, jumping up and striking Albert across the head with the metal serving tray that had held the *porchetta*. It made a loud clanging noise, as it resounded off his head, remnants of the meat flying everywhere. Gina peeked in from the corridor and gasped. She ran to Giorgio and the two of them scurried out to the kitchen, to cower there out of range.

Josette moved quickly around the table, beating Albert's head and his back with the dish, hot gravy and meat juices showering everyone. With one final thump, the tray flew out of her hands and knocked several more glasses onto the tiled floor, where they shattered.

Marianna had been hovering in the corridor, her ear to the dining room door, not wanting to miss a word of who said what, to whom, during the argument. Just as she had placed her hand on the doorknob to enter the room, George noticed Josette pick up the long carving knife he had sharpened only that morning. Whether she had any intention of causing harm would never be known because, at that very moment, his wife walked through the door and George – alarmed by the prospect of Josette choosing to use the knife – threw the entire contents of a jug of iced water into the face of Gina's mother-in-law.

Time seemed to stand still. In the shocked silence, all eyes turned accusingly towards him, standing there open mouthed, the empty jug in his hand.

It had turned out to be a wedding anniversary to remember.

CHAPTER 26
COLONEL FEDOROV
OFFICE OF THE PRIME MINISTER, VALLETTA, MALTA

It was a scorching hot morning and Colonel Fedorov, seemingly oblivious to the heat in his heavy grey military jacket, had convened a meeting with Edward Refalo and Ray Farrugia. In addition to the prime minister and his chief of staff, the meeting was also being attended by the new Maltese State Advocate, Christa Baldacchino, who was responsible for bringing the government's case before the Constitutional Court, asking it to declare the presence of the Russians on the island legal, despite the country's constitutional commitment to neutrality and non-alignment.

Christa Baldacchino was young, attractive in a prissy sort of way, and had been one of Gerald Camilleri's protégées. As State Advocate, she enjoyed constitutional independence and was not subject to the direction or control of any other person or authority.

Fedorov, on the other hand, seemed to think differently and assumed she could be a useful tool in putting pressure on her uncle, the president of the Republic, when it came to constitutional reform. He had immediately included her among his 'Maltese Cabinet', where it appeared she had no hesitation in becoming an ally of the Russians.

Fedorov was furious at the recent raid on the Qormi Park and Ride and was determined to make a point to Refalo, whom he sought to blame for the débâcle. Refalo was expecting trouble and kept nervously brushing back his thinning hair.

"Prime Minister, I feel there're forces at work within the Maltese government that're not only encouraging public dissent but are also supportive of these crazy acts of violence, which serve no purpose other than to inflame local passions. We'll not tolerate it."

Refalo furrowed his brow, as though deep in thought.

"Well, it's inevitable that not everybody will see your presence here as ..."

Fedorov was having none of it.

"It's up to you to make sure the right message gets out and we're fully supported in our efforts to assist you. That's what our presence here is about, after all."

Refalo did not like the direction this conversation was going in.

"But you're being rather heavy handed, if I may say so. People're arriving at Camp Azure daily, without charges being made, and it's creating ... problems. The camp isn't even ready yet. The EU's Commissioner for Human Rights, along with Amnesty International and a dozen other NGOs, have been on to me. Really ... you've got to give me a chance here!"

Fedorov threw his hands into the air.

"I don't think we can successfully accuse those in Camp Azure of treason or sedition, which goes too far, but I do feel it's time we considered enacting some emergency regulations to try and ensure public order. What do you say, Miss Baldacchino?"

Fedorov looked at her. She smiled sweetly back at him. "It depends. What exactly do you have in mind?"

"Well, for the sake of argument, when the Russian Federation's been in similar situations, say Chechnya, for example, we've found that invoking an Emergency Powers Act can be quite helpful. A good starting point is crimes against public safety." He rubbed his hands together and looked at her with his blue gimlet eyes. "Maybe you could put something together about offences of, say, subverting friendly forces; destruction and damage of property belonging to said friendly forces; suppression of not just riot, but assemblies likely to cause nuisance; disseminating false and misleading information damaging to the state; local and national curfews ... and even giving certain officers of the Russian Federation the power of arrest, perhaps? You get my drift?

"I think we're heading in the right direction, aren't we, Miss Baldacchino. It is Miss, isn't it?"

Christa Baldacchino dropped her head so he could not see her roll her eyes.

"Yes, Colonel. I am unmarried."

Ray Farrugia glanced at Prime Minister Refalo, who was glaring at the by now pouting State Advocate. Fedorov leaned closer to her.

"How soon can these new laws be enacted?"

"Well, I'll have to do some research but, if you can persuade the president to proclaim a state of public emergency, we can bring in a raft of orders of the sort you've been discussing." She smiled sweetly. "But I don't know how he'd feel about legislating for sweeping powers like that – I really don't. After that, unfortunately, the House of Representatives has to vote on the continuation of the orders and would agree only on the grounds that democratic institutions in Malta are threatened by subversion. But, given what's happened to Michael Cini, his detention ... well, I'm not sure that's going to be easy to achieve."

Refalo and Ray Farrugia were confused, although they had noted Cini's absence from the meeting.

Ray said: "I don't understand? The president's one of the main opponents to amending the constitution. How can he be bounced into proclaiming a state of emergency and saying that democratic institutions in Malta are threatened by subversion? Christa's right, I don't think President Mizzi is actually our greatest fan at the moment."

Refalo added: "And, please, tell us ... what's happened to Michael? As prime minister, I naturally have an interest in the whereabouts of my ministers."

At that moment, the door swung open, and they were joined by Admiral Aleksandr Berezovsky, who apologised to Fedorov for his lateness.

"So sorry, Igor, a small discipline problem needed attending to. I had to come down hard on some civilian contractors. I think they took my point!"

"Well, Aleksandr, I was just explaining to our Maltese friends that Ambassador Buzilov and I paid a short visit to the president." He turned to Refalo and Ray Farrugia. "I must say how much I enjoyed strolling through the St Anton Gardens. It's not exactly Moscow's Aleksandrovskiy Sad, but still a pleasant enough little haven. Anyway, after our ... what's the word ... chat, I think, Edward and Ray, you might find the president now has different views to those he held previously."

The admiral smiled, his lips curling back to reveal yellowing teeth. Fedorov continued speaking.

"As for Minister Cini ... Well, I feel that you, Ray, should assume that office of state. Michael Cini is taking some time out, enjoying our hospitality. We didn't feel he was committed to the *team*. Isn't that how you put it?" Refalo gasped.

"You can't meddle in our political process like that! You've got no right. What're you doing to him?"

"Outrageous! You've overreached this time, Fedorov!"

Farrugia agreed.

The admiral stirred in his seat, shifting his bulk forward, and suddenly slapped one meaty fist down onto the mahogany table, causing even Colonel Fedorov to jump, along with the collection of porcelain coffee cups, monogrammed with President Putin's initials, a gift to the prime minister of the Maltese Republic from the people of Russia.

"Almost the exact same words Cini used when we locked him in a cabin on the frigate *Admiral Makarov*. I've told the captain to clear the next three cabins, in case we've got to entertain any other high-profile guests. So, mind your manners, gentlemen."

Colonel Fedorov smiled.

"Please, Aleksandr! I'm sure our friends understand the situation now. We're all *friends* here, aren't we? There's no need for threats, is there, Edward?" Fedorov leaned back in his chair. "Yes, a state of public emergency. That's exactly what we're dealing with here." He looked coldly at Refalo. "I think you will find your president agrees and is fully prepared to be supportive.

"Now, let's come to the appointment of local liaison officers. Ray, what progress?"

The chief of staff sighed deeply. He had argued against the formation of a network of informers, seeing the likelihood of small-minded behaviour and other abuses of position. Of course, he had lost the argument and Fedorov had told him the benefits of having such officers far outweighed the disadvantages.

"We've appointed thirty local liaison officers, people who're central to their communities and are known to be in favour of your support of the Maltese government." Ray Farrugia was pleased he had managed to say this without a hint of irony. "It was also helpful to identify people who've vested commercial interests in your presence. I couldn't find many who would do it otherwise. Some are local politicians or council staff. Some are businesspeople, community leaders, local suppliers to the military, or people who hold government contracts. We've even got a couple of priests – from the Orthodox Church, naturally. But, in every case, they're closely connected to your forces and to their communities and are willing to keep an eye on things for us.

"As I said before, we've got to be aware of people using their position to settle personal scores and cause trouble for business rivals, but the network should prove useful. They've all been vetted by the *Pulizija* and are of good character. Well, as good as we can expect." Fedorov nodded his approval.

"And have these people been giving us the names of protesters and Democratica terrorists?" Ray Farrugia hesitated.

"Well, not the Democratica activists. The people we're after are too clever to let their whereabouts be known. We've questioned and detained a few university lecturers, journalists, local hot-heads, even some retired expats, but none of them are men or women of action, if I can put it like that."

Fedorov was not convinced.

"Well, for the time being, keep them at Camp Azure, to dissuade others from becoming involved. Once Christa's got our new laws in place, we can charge them with something. You know how it is? I expect to see results from this initiative this week, particularly arrests for the Park and Ride outrage. Otherwise, I'll have to let my own security people do their work and, I warn you, they're not the gentle type."

CHAPTER 27
MARCO BONNICI
THE WEBER CLINIC, BERN, SWITZERLAND

MARCO WAS FURIOUS.

"Natasha was nearly raped, Laura! In a secure hospital, of all places. She has the scars to prove it, defensive wounds. He attacked her, in her bed, and the man was found naked in her room! What more do you want? I cannot believe you are questioning it?"

"Marco, I am mortified about what has happened and my first duty is always to our patients. But the thing that concerns me greatly is that the facts also fit Wilhelm's version of events – well, some of them. He is in the wrong, there is no doubt about that, for even thinking of taking advantage of one of the patients. By definition, they are not legally capable of giving consent."

Laura was agitated and upset, struggling to make sense of the facts, even after twenty-four hours. She had phoned Marco, as soon as the night team had alerted her to what had happened. He had insisted no police be called and that both Natasha and Wilhelm wait in the clinic until he arrived. Natasha had no choice but to comply, and Wilhelm was so desperate to prove his innocence, he would do anything he was asked. Laura was confused and desperate to call the police, before too much time passed.

"It is a black mark against him that he came into the clinic late at night and let himself into her room. That alone is enough to get him fired and give the police the basis of a case. But he says, not only did Natasha consent, she enticed him … entrapped him. I told him, she is a patient so why on earth would he ever try to excuse himself? He says he is convinced that she knew exactly what she was doing. She suggested he visit her late at night and then she undressed him, aroused him and took him to bed, not the other way round. Then, she attacked him."

"Come on, Laura, listen to yourself. It is the rapist's oldest defence. The woman wanted it, led him on and said, 'yes, please'."

Laura held up her hands in capitulation.

"I know, I know. But there is also the mystery of the room's CCTV camera. It is in perfect working order; we have tested it. Yet somehow it doesn't show anything, until the pair of them are naked, on the bed, with Natasha beating up Wilhelm. He is just lying there, passively, hands covering his head. Our IT manager says the camera must have been covered, only for whatever it was to suddenly fall off at the very point where Natasha is seen resisting, which seems oddly convenient, from her point of view."

"Well, who knew it was there? Who could have covered it? It cuts both ways, Laura. Clinic employees know the score about the use of CCTV. Anyway, this is about Natasha and her future wellbeing. Sorry to be dismissive, but I do not care what happens to your orderly."

"He is a nurse, Marco, a highly trained, psychiatric nurse, with twenty years of unblemished experience. I just do not get it. If Wilhelm wanted to do this, without consent, which I struggle to believe, he would have known there was a camera in the room and a big red button by the bed, which Natasha could have used to summon assistance at any time. And she knew that call button was monitored, that it would be answered immediately – especially late at night – but she never used it, until she had finished defending herself. Why wait, when she knew it was there, easily within reach? Wouldn't it be the first thing you would do? Summon help?

"What's more, Wilhelm left his car in the car park, in plain sight of the exterior cameras. Why would he have done that, if he was sneaking in to commit a crime? It does not make any sense. There are things I just do not get, but I will leave it there. Whatever happened, we have let you and Natasha down. I am profoundly sorry for that." Laura wiped tears from the corners of her eyes. "Actually, I am devastated. Professionally, of course, but also personally, that this should come between us."

"I know, me too. I am sorry, Laura, but right now, I must do what is right for Natasha. I am going to take her home. We need to put our own feelings to one side for now."

"I understand."

"You said you thought she was nearly ready to leave anyway?"

"Yes, yes … on the face of it. But I was giving it another week or two to make sure …"

Marco heard the doubt in her voice.

"Make sure?"

"Yes. I do not know whether it is just me … others have not seen it … but I have a lurking suspicion her turnaround has become almost too good to be true. She has scored full marks for everything she did. Has she worked out how to play the system? Could she be faking a full recovery? I might be doing her an injustice, but your warnings about her have always been at the forefront of my mind. Maybe they have clouded my judgement?"

Marco sighed and leaned back in his chair.

"It is always good to be wary around Natasha. But I have to

take a chance and get her away from here. You do understand?"

"Of course. She cannot stay, after what has happened. I am afraid poor Wilhelm will have to take his chances with the law."

"There will be no need to involve the police. Speak to Wilhelm and tell him, if he signs a letter of confidentiality, which I will send to you, no official complaint will be made. How you deal with him then is up to you. You have my word, nothing about this incident will ever be mentioned by Natasha or myself."

"Well, thank you. I had not expected that. May I ask why?" Marco smiled and gently took her hand.

"You know Natasha's history. If she needs further support, then perhaps we can talk again."

"I would be more than happy to. Please keep in touch, Marco. I do not want this to be the end for us."

The next afternoon, he found Natasha dressed, made up and waiting outside Laura's office, with her small suitcase. There was no sign of the previous night's trauma. Marco asked his daughter if she was ready and she smiled, saying: "As I'll ever be."

Outside, as they were taking their leave of Laura, she shook Natasha's hand, saying: "I am so sorry about how this has ended. You have my best wishes for the future and, if you need me, you know where I am. Call me at any time." Marco stepped away to speak to the driver.

It was not the fact that Natasha did not respond to her words that Laura remembered afterwards, but her expression on receiving the apology: knowing, triumphant, smug, calculating. Laura thought about that look for a long time but could neither understand it nor get it out of her mind.

CHAPTER 28
THE RESISTANCE
ST ANDREW'S BASTION, VALLETTA, MALTA

LIFE in the small cramped flat in Siġġiewi had started to become boring and oppressive. On the surface, the Americans seemed calm and relaxed, spending most of their spare time discussing food and its preparation, while Abdullah impatiently paced the floor, like a caged animal. There were arguments every day.

The previous day, Abdullah had demanded: "Why is it all the time waiting? There are Russians everywhere, no? They are in the hotels, in the bars …" he thought for a moment "…why not take a rope and wait for a drunk one to go piss, then …" He made a chopping action with his hand. "Or I can be waiter and do 'yes sir, no sir', in their restaurant and, while they eat their swill, like pigs, then I roll grenades that rip their bellies apart! Ha! Will much scare the others and kill many Russians. It is good, no?"

Huck sighed.

"'Cos, you bloodthirsty dude, it ain't just about killing Russians. It's about humiliating them. And, more importantly, we don't wanna go blowing up Maltese bar staff, stray English tourists or, worse, anybody American!"

"Huh. Then I must seek refuge from anger in Allah's perfect words – but this waiting and nothing doing is making me crazy!"

Abdullah had sloped off to sulk in a corner, while Huck and Billy reverted to their favourite way of passing the time, arguing about food.

That morning, the wrangling revolved around the best cut of bacon. Billy had commented, quite casually, that he understood the European preference for lean back bacon, from the loin of the pig. The seemingly casual comment had hung in the air like an unexploded grenade.

Huck, of course, had to respond. Billy drummed his foot, eager to get the debate going.

"Well, Billy, I respect your opinion, of course I do, but I've gotta disagree. The problem with back bacon, as I know you're aware, is the lower fat content. That has all kinda consequences. For one thing, when cooked, your back bacon goes hard, not crispy, so there's the problem of texture, which can be a really big deal, say, in a burger. Now, your American bacon, streaky bacon, preferably from for the pig's belly, has an exceptionally high fat content, which gives both texture and flavour. In my opinion ... and it's just an opinion, mind ... that makes streaky the superior cut."

Billy nodded along sagely, but Denzel knew from experience he would never agree. The game was that he would simply bide his time until he had an opportunity to respond.

"Well, I find that mighty interesting, Huck, but not necessarily convincing. So, would you be prepared to compromise and say, maybe, the middle cut ..."

At which point Abdullah had jumped to his feet and said: "You should not eat the pork at all! No part of it – it is unclean, this is known. Everybody knows pigs eat the carrion, rubbish, many foul things and are unclean. So, stop the pig talk! It is *haram*!"

The two Americans looked at each other with raised eyebrows.

Billy said: "Yeah, interesting point of view. Okay, Huck, maybe we talk about *toe-foo* next? Whadda ya say?" The pair of them grinned at each other.

The atmosphere was thick with testosterone and ill will. Abdullah glowered. Denzel had to leave the room. When he returned, sometime later, he noticed the Americans were looking at drone footage of Marsamxett Harbour and whispering between themselves, so he knew something was afoot. After Billy suggested he meet up with Silvia at St Andrew's Bastion, he guessed it was to be the beginning of their next operation.

That afternoon, Denzel and Abdullah were leaning against the walls of St Andrew's, the imposing block of high fortification that was the main defence of the entrance into Marsamxett Harbour. Part of Valletta's huge defensive walls, it was on the north side of the peninsula on which the city stood and looked out over Manoel Island onto the shores of Sliema. Abdullah breathed in the warm salty air, savouring the deep musty smell of the seaweed collecting on the rocks below and the sharp metallic tang that blew in on the breeze.

"Oh, it is good to be out in the world again. I cannot be an animal in a cage. The talking about the food – it makes me want to ... aaargh! Shout and scream!" Denzel laughed.

"I know what you mean. It drives me crazy too."

Silvia was standing a little apart, taking photographs with her phone, watching the tower cranes swing their loads through the skies, while the contractors busied themselves building the Russian naval port on the island. In the middle was a steel-lattice communications tower, probably fifty metres tall, that had only recently appeared on the skyline.

They peered out across the rippled jade waters of the harbour. The low cloud base obscured the sun, and the dull light leached away the usual vibrant colours of the bay. But Silvia's dark brown eyes were sparkling with excitement.

"You see that mast over there?"

"You can hardly miss it, can you?" Denzel replied.

"It's the Russians' new encrypted 5G tower and it's central to their military communications. Both the fleet on Hurds Bank and all the military here on the island rely on it. The tower can handle huge amounts of data and links to all the existing cell towers, allowing full coverage of the island. Take that out and ... well, they won't like it."

Abdullah cackled.

"We cut down the Russian's manhood, yes! Is good."

Denzel looked at the old fortifications and the new Russian built sea wall defences around Manoel Island. There were guard posts, searchlights and high fencing along all points of access to the water.

"It's also a very visible, symbolic target. The whole island would know, if we could get at it. But look at the defences. How would we get anywhere near it? The island's sealed off."

Abdullah looked suspiciously at Silvia.

"You know I cannot do the swimming? The water is for fish, not men.

She laughed.

"I have a plan. You're not claustrophobic, are you?" Abdullah looked puzzled.

"Fear of small spaces. Like getting stuck in a lift."

Both men were silent while they tried to work out what Silvia had in store for them.

"Come on, answer me! You don't panic when a lift jams or anything like that?"

Abdullah said: "Why, we take lift to cross water?"

Silvia pointed at the building immediately to their left, adjoining the bastion.

"No! You see that building?" Denzel knew it all too well.

"Of course. I did my police entrance exams in it. It's now a museum, though I've never been in it. Too many bad memories."

"It's now the Fortifications Interpretations Centre. Models of Maltese military architecture – you should take a look, it's interesting. It was built in the sixteenth century, just after the Great Siege, and underneath it's got a large water cistern and an underground grain store. Most people don't know the store exists."

"Okay, but how's that going to help us?"

"Well, Uncle Gerald was fascinated by the history of Valletta. He was a Knight of St John. Did you know?"

"Yeah, Dad told me."

"As a knight, he had access to a lot of the old papers in the National Library. They preserve all the documents produced and received by the Order since its origins in the twelfth century, up until the end of its rule in Malta in 1798. Uncle Gerald was always digging about in them, and he told me about an old tunnel that ran from the cistern, under the museum, to the old quarantine hospital in the Lazaretto, on the south side of Manoel Island. The Knights used Turkish slaves to dig it in the late fifteen hundreds so, if Manoel Island was ever taken by sea, they had a secret route they could use to mount a surprise counter-attack." Denzel was surprised.

"Really? And it's still there?"

"Yep! Years ago, Uncle Gerald took me exploring. We didn't get all the way along. I was only twelve. I got frightened and started crying, so we came back." She smiled to herself at the memory. "But I went there again two nights ago. I forced the door open and it's still as it was. People were smaller back then, so it's low and tight. The roof has crumbled in places, but it's dry ... well, the first bit is. Later on, it's a bit wet and very spooky! But it gets us onto the island. We just have to break down the metal door at the other end. We'll need something special to do that – I don't know what. The door won't have been opened for years and I've no idea what's on the other side."

Abdullah said: "You go down this tunnel, just you? In dark?"

"Yeah, I mean ... I had a torch ... but you know the strange thing? I bet nobody's been down there since Uncle Gerald and I went exploring, nearly twenty years ago. Amazing, isn't it?" Abdullah was not convinced.

"How do you know that?"

"Uncle Gerald slid a piece of paper between the top of the door and the jamb. It fell to the ground when I opened it. It was a sweet wrapper I'd given to him from my pocket." She fished around in her coat and pulled out a folded Rowntree's Fruit Pastels wrapper. "There! Twenty-year-old proof!"

Denzel took the paper and unfolded it. He immediately recognised the dark green paper, with the Rowntree's branding and pictures of miniature oranges and lemons. He handed it back to Silvia, shaking his head.

"I believe you. So, how's this going to work? We go down this secret tunnel, carrying what – all our gear? How long did it take you to walk down it?"

"Forty minutes. It'll be quicker next time."

"Okay. So, then we break down this ancient door, leading to who knows where, and then ...?"

"Then, we improvise. It's about two hundred metres to the mast from the Lazaretto buildings. There's rough ground up the hillside with some bushes and trees, so we're not totally in the open. The mast's got three-metre, metal-palisade security fencing around it. But we can bring a car jack or something, force open a space to get through. Billy and Huck will know what works. The three of us should be able to do it." Denzel's heart jumped. She continued: "The drone shots don't show any guards inside or around the perimeter. Your American flatmates can supply some of their mines or explosives, show you how to use them – then bang, and we run home."

She shrugged, the wind tossing her hair. Denzel saw the strength in her. The resolve.

"Sounds really easy," he said, forcing a smile. "What can possibly go wrong?

Abdullah looked down his hooked nose, grimacing at them. "Remember, no swimming time!"

CHAPTER 29
PRIME MINISTER EDWARD REFALO
OFFICE OF THE PRIME MINISTER, VALLETTA, MALTA

EDWARD REFALO WAS FIDGETING in his seat at the end of the long mahogany conference table in the Cabinet Room. The President of the European Commission, Noémie Minaud, rightly considered herself a woman of some importance and, when she spoke, she expected to be listened to. For the last twenty minutes, she had been making her views about the situation in Malta very clear.

To Refalo's left sat Ray Farrugia, who had just stared at the highly polished tabletop throughout the meeting and had yet to speak. To Refalo's right sat State Advocate Christa Baldacchino, who was there at Colonel Fedorov's request, to advise on any points of law. Two of the Commission's many anonymous supernumeraries sat at the bottom of the table, silently tapping on their laptops, creating a contemporaneous record of the conversation, which so far had more the feel of a lecture to a trio of miscreant teenagers.

"... and you ... well, not exactly you, your learned and respectable predecessors ... signed up to the Treaty on European Union. Your little country – undeveloped and inward looking, rejected by the British, your shipyards closed, your farmers grubbing around in your few centimetres of topsoil – we took it in. Made it part of the European family, helped it develop. We gave Malta jobs, access to our member countries, skills, money... oh, the money! You were happy to take that. Take it and pocket it! It makes my blood boil. Filling your coffers with your sale of EU passports, letting all kinds of undesirables flout our borders, looking away as dirty money floods our financial system. You are a gaping back door through which anything unpleasant can creep in.

"Do you know what Article Two says?" She glared around the table, looking at them over the top of her wire-framed spectacles. Christa Baldacchino's face was red with embarrassment. She had never heard anyone talk to senior ministers like that before. Edward Refalo soaked it up. He had had more dressing downs than he could remember, and it helped that he had no sense of shame and the skin of a rhinoceros. Ray Farrugia, on the other hand, was a broken man, not knowing what to say or do from one day to the next. Mentally, he had already joined Michael Cini, in a rocking cabin aboard the Russian prison frigate.

Christa knew exactly what Article Two said. She had studied European Law at Malta's university, and so, oblivious to the rhetorical nature of Minaud's question, she confidently replied: "Article Two of the Treaty is founded on the values of respect for human dignity, freedom, democracy, equality, the rule of law and respect for human rights ..."

"Oh, be quiet, for God's sake! If you all know what it means, what the hell is going on in this country?"

Minaud sat back and looked at the three of them. It was obvious they had no response to any of her accusations. They were in government, but certainly not in power. Before arriving, she had heard from her aides, and read in the briefings, that the situation in Malta was serious, but had not expected it to be anything like as bad as it was.

The cavalcade from the airport had been deliberately directed along the Great Siege Road, around the periphery of

Valletta, giving Noémie Minaud views of the works on Manoel Island. She saw the Russian fleet, at anchor in Marsamxett Harbour, and the cruisers and frigates berthed in the Grand Harbour. The *Admiral of the Fleet, Putin* had been especially brought inshore, trailing its sooty blue exhaust behind it, to conduct exercises, its MiGs shooting up off the ramped deck, to roar around the island's skies.

At road junctions, the local police lounged against their motorcycles, while Russian soldiers stood to attention in lines, saluting as the president's motorcade passed by. She was horrified. This was a country under occupation.

She sighed. It was no use blowing off steam against these three. She was talking to the wrong people. It was obvious that the island had been quietly captured and a situation had developed that was beyond the Maltese politicians to rectify. She cleaned her glasses and thought about her next move.

"So, how deep have the Russians got their claws into you? This camp on Gozo ... How many people is it holding? I've summoned the Maltese Permanent Representative a dozen times – he says he knows nothing!".

There was silence. The President of the Commission sighed. She leaned forward across the table, relaxing her tone, trying to connect with the two men. She paused, until she had eye contact with Refalo and Farrugia.

"So, what do you have to say?"

The silence hung in the air like an unpleasant smell. She sighed.

"Okay, say nothing. This is where we are. You remember the bad old days in the seventies, following independence, when Prime Minister Mintoff played the Cold War card, cosying up to China and Russia? Of course you do. Is that what is happening here? Well, if it is, let me tell you, we are not going to tolerate it.

"We believe Malta is acting contrary to Article Two of the Treaty. As a result, the Council of Ministers and the Commission are taking steps to suspend the Republic of Malta from the European Union. Do you understand? *Suspension!*" She paused to let the gravity of her pronouncement sink in. "It is an international humiliation. As you know, there is no mechanism to expel a member state, otherwise I would have pushed to expel you, so this is the next best thing. My colleagues," she glanced at the men in suits at the bottom of the table, "have all the paperwork with all the necessary resolutions and so on. As you might guess, it is not a quick process, so you will have plenty of opportunity to respond and make your objections. I am sorry, but you have left us with no other choice."

Refalo and Ray Farrugia sat in silence. The president of the European Union could not believe it.

"Have you not heard what I just said? We are suspending you from the Union because you have disregarded our founding values. No country has ever been suspended before. Are you not ashamed that this has happened on your watch?"

Ray Farrugia wearily lifted his head and said: "What can we say? You've made your mind up."

"Listen, I have no idea how you got yourselves into this position, or at what point you realised there was no going back and that the Russians were here to stay, but this situation is now escalating dangerously. You know the Lisbon Treaty contains a clause – the 'mutual defence clause' – which states that, if a member state is the victim of an armed attack on its territory, it can rely on the aid and assistance of the other member states, which are obliged to help?

"And, as an EU country, you have access to all the top-secret information shared amongst member states! So, I am sorry, but from now on that privilege is withdrawn and we want all the papers and data in your little secret room returned – immediately."

The EU president saw Refalo imperceptibly shake his head. He raised his hand and seemed to scratch his ear. Then she realised the reason for the prime minister's lack of responsiveness and the presence of the showboating little toady, Christa Baldacchino – this conversation was being monitored! She thought for a moment.

"Listen, it is a lovely day, let's go for a walk, shall we? Get some fresh air. Walking always helps me think. Miss Baldacchino, I think we can manage without your contribution."

Ray Farrugia jumped to his feet with a show of energy that had been lacking all morning.

"Yes, why not? I'll organise some security."

The president was a step ahead of him. The last thing she wanted was some Russian minder on her shoulder, listening to every word.

"No, I don't think so. *Allons-nous faire une petite promenade.* I am sure we will be perfectly safe, and it will be good for our spirits."

Twenty minutes later, they were in Hastings Gardens, on top of St Michael's Bastion, on the west side of the City Gate, a short walk from the Parliament building. Unlike the nearby Upper Barrakka Gardens, which offered spectacular views of the Grand Harbour, Hastings Gardens were altogether less glamorous, but had the advantage of being quiet and free from tourists. The three politicians spoke freely now they were away from the ears of the Russians.

"Edward, please be straight with me. What on earth is going on? Do you have no control over your country? Have all democratic processes collapsed?" Refalo sighed.

"Noémie, we've been weak. The truth's just as you said – the country's been captured. We let them in when we shouldn't have. We gave them a foothold. But now, to all intents and purposes, they're firmly in control. They're ruthless, militarily strong – you've seen that – and seemingly not scared of anybody. They've imposed a rule of terror: arbitrary detentions, suspension of court sittings, dismantling all the protections conferred by the state. We don't know what to do."

Ray Farrugia pulled up the waistband of his sagging pants and wiped perspiration from his brow. He was bursting to speak.

"You've got to help us! Michael Cini, our Minister for Home Affairs, spoke out and he's been taken, disappeared, being held on one of their frigates. Union leaders, journalists, lecturers, anyone who speaks against them, they all get taken to Camp Azure. It's a concentration camp they've built on Gozo. They've even nobbled the president. He was leading those in the House of Representatives who were going to vote against the amendment, you know, to ditch neutrality and non-alignment. Then, overnight, he changed his mind. We've got no idea what happened, but now all opposition to the vote has crumbled.

"The court case will fail; the constitutional amendment will pass and the Russian presence will become perfectly legal. And, just so you know, suspending us from the EU plays right into their hands. That's what they want. They'll step forward on the international stage, as Malta's new best friend, offer us all sorts of aid and deals... and, before you know it, we'll be part of the Russian Federation, another Crimea or Donbas. A satellite territory, under their yoke."

The president shook her head. Her mind went back to the time of the Second World War when the British had interred the island's top politicians who were thought to be too close to the Italian government of Mussolini. It seemed that across its history, foreign powers had no compunction about invading Malta and imprisoning its people. And now it was happening again, on her watch. She clenched her fists and said angrily:

"I cannot believe it. This is an outrage! My God! Does anyone here have a cigarette?"

Refalo put a hand inside his jacket pocket and took out a box. He offered the president a Marlboro and lit one for himself. She inhaled deeply and took in the view over Manoel

Island, the tower cranes and the barges going about their land-grabbing business.

"Edward, I propose Ray comes with me, now, and tells your story to the people who matter, in Brussels and Washington. We need a governmental voice, otherwise it will seem as if it is we who are meddling in the affairs of a sovereign country – not the Russians. We need evidence that what is happening here is without the consent of the Maltese Parliament or people."

Ray Farrugia's mouth fell open.

"Er, I don't know about that. What if they won't let me leave?"

"Who are *they*? The Russians? Look, get in my car, accompany me to the airport, then we will simply walk up the stairs together onto my waiting plane. We will be in Brussels in less than two hours. It is time to stand up to them, Ray. Or are you just going to keep letting them piss all over you and your country? It is up to you. What can they do about it?"

CHAPTER 30
ASSISTANT COMMISSIONER GEORGE ZAMMIT

RESISTANCE FLAT, SIĠĠIEWI, MALTA

George trudged up the stairs to the third-floor flat in the rundown block where Denzel, Abdullah and the Americans were based. He had agreed to do their shopping, so the men could limit the amount of time they were seen out and about.

Luckily, two of the flats in the block were empty and two were occupied by elderly residents, who were happy to mind their own business. The only problem was a nosy car mechanic who lived on the ground floor and always seemed to be out in the street, fixing a vehicle, when George arrived.

Sick of his questions and curiosity, George had told him the people in the flat were Serbian gangsters, who were witnesses at a forthcoming trial and were best left well alone. After that, the mechanic moved his repair operations to the rear of the block, out of sight.

That evening, as soon as the sun had gone down, George arrived at the top-floor flat with his four shopping bags. He tapped the pre-arranged knock onto the door and waited. The door opened as far as the security chain would allow. All he could see were some bared teeth and a long grey beard. It was only when he saw the twinkling eye through the fissure that he could picture the familiar face in his head.

"*Madonna mia*! You madman – let me in!"

The shopping fell to the floor and the two men embraced, tears in their eyes. George was trying to be cross. but failing miserably.

"What're you doing here, meddling in things that don't concern you?"

"What? Meddling, you say! How can there be dangers for you and your son that do not concern me? We are brothers ... not of one blood, but of one mind, one heart, and it is said in the *Hadith*, one brother is better than a thousand friends! So, do not go saying about the meddling – I am here to fight by your side. As I said to the Baker woman, 'I will not be stopped!'" Billy was leaning over the back of a sofa, smiling.

"Well, ain't that about the size of it? Hell, he's a fighter alright, and the Lord knows, we need some of those."

Abdullah smiled and held up his arms at the rightness of it all.

George looked at Denzel who stood sheepishly against the kitchen door.

"And you knew? All this time?"

"No, he just turned up with Silvia. No one was more surprised than me. But here we are! You'd better not tell Mum – or anybody else, for that matter." Abdullah's face fell. His jaw dropped.

"The lady wife is still not much liking me?" He shook his head morosely. "What can I do?"

"Let's not worry about that. We'll have tea and we can talk."

And talk they did. First, about the Russians, the raid on the Park and Ride, Denzel's exile, Abdullah's promise to rid every Russian from Malta. Then about their families, what they would do, once the Russians had left, how George and Denzel – and maybe even the 'lady wife' – should visit Libya where Rania could cook the lamb dish George liked so much. George talked about the death of Camilleri, the man with 'the name like a camel', and then, much to Abdullah's delight, how he had chased the 'Lady Mantis', Natasha Bonnici, out of the Sliema Tower Hotel, with two knitting needles sticking out of her neck, courtesy of her sidekick, Savi Azzopardi's girlfriend, who had turned out to have bigger balls than he did.

Finally, the sun set, and George had to take his leave. He promised to return, and bring green tea, mint tea, all sorts of tea. He promised to save Abdullah from this crazy flat, where all the talk was of food they could never eat.

CHAPTER 31
ASSISTANT COMMISSIONER GEORGE ZAMMIT

POLICE HQ, FLORIANA, MALTA

HELPING Denzel with provisioning the flat was the least of George's troubles. As a senior policeman, he had been required, on Commissioner Mallia's instructions, to arrange the arrest and transportation of several high-profile individuals to Camp Azure. He had numerous conversations about it with Mallia and expressed his reluctance to get involved in the persecution of Maltese citizens by the Russians. Mallia was terrified of Fedorov and told George, if he did not do their bidding, the pair of them would also end up in Camp Azure.

The transportations were grim, depressing affairs, usually involving tears, cursing and handcuffs. Many of those taken had no idea why they had been selected, other than on the say so of the local liaison officers, who were proving to be enthusiastic supporters of the Russian occupation. On more than one occasion, George suspected business or political rivalry may have had a hand in their selections. Distraught wives and, on occasion, husbands, railed and protested against the seizures, but all George could do was brandish the paperwork and try to assure them it was all a terrible mistake that would be sorted out in due course.

Ever since Inspector Karl Chelotti had taken Denzel to Lampedusa on his yacht, George and he had become friends and confidants. They shared a similar view of the Russian occupation of the island and were in despair at the round ups and illegal detentions. Eventually, they had agreed to develop a strategy to frustrate the process. Together, they had devised a system that whenever George received instructions to pick up an individual bound for Camp Azure, he would notify Chelotti, who would then have a quiet word with the person involved and give them a chance to slip off the island or go into hiding. If Chelotti got word of a forthcoming arrest, he would speak to George, who would do the same. The system was not entirely foolproof, as Commissioner Mallia explained to George and Karl Chelotti one day, in his office.

"Listen, I'm getting reports from Colonel Fedorov that there's a problem with the detentions. We've got a leak. Somebody's tipping off the subjects, who're disappearing before we can get to them. Fedorov's furious and he's threatening me! *Me*, of all people! What's going on?"

George felt himself turn white, as the colour drained from his cheeks and a pit opened up in his stomach. Inspector Chelotti seemed to find it funny. He asked Mallia with a smile: "So, what're the instructions, sir, if your name is on the next list?"

"That's not funny, Chelotti. You don't joke about things like that. Not in this country, anyway." Mallia wiped a film of sweat from his brow. "I wish Assistant Commissioner Camilleri was with us. He was just the man for times like these."

George wished Camilleri was with them too, but ignored the comment, saying: "There're a lot of people involved in compiling the lists. Admin officers, junior and senior police officers – it could be anybody. Where do we start?"

"Quite! That's what I said to the colonel."

Chelotti was more open about saying what he thought, often recklessly so, in George's opinion.

"These detentions aren't popular, and the mood has certainly turned against our friends from the east. With a bit of luck, they'll be off soon. Whoever's doing this, good luck to them, I say."

Mallia's eyes darted around his office.

"Inspector, one more comment like that and you'll be guarding the Freeport, in sergeant's stripes!"

"Well, it's true, sir."

"Walls have ears, Inspector; you'd do well to remember that."

As an assistant commissioner, it was George's responsibility to give the top man a solution. He remembered the words Camilleri had always used in such circumstances.

"*Mela*, Commissioner Mallia, leave this with me. I'll give the matter my most urgent attention and report back to you as soon as possible. But I'll have to make the most thorough and searching enquiries."

Mallia looked at him, with a trace of a smile.

"That's exactly what Gerald used to say when he had no intention of doing anything."

That afternoon, George decided to return home early. He felt out of sorts and could not summon the energy to do any meaningful work. It was ironic that since the arrival of the Russians, crime on the island had all but disappeared. Organised criminal gangs from Sicily and the Italian mainland had quietly left. The Russians had taken control of the island's regulators and, after a short but brutal purge, installed a cabal of Cypriot, Azerbaijani and Arab bankers. The island was now awash with all manner of money, as the Russians used Malta's local banks to trade and finance transactions with Syria, Iran, Democratic Republic of Congo, Venezuela, Libya and Russian Ukraine, as well as North Korea, in flagrant breach of the EU autonomous and UN transposed sanctions regimes.

Beneath his apartment, he was lucky enough to have a basement garage for his sole use – not a common facility in

Birkirkara – where he kept a small fridge for the perishable food he delivered to Denzel and the Americans. The garage was a dusty place, with dark corners where spiders and the occasional cockroach lurked. Marianna and Gina refused to enter it. So George felt his secret stash was safe from prying eyes. Neither Gina nor Marianna had any idea Denzel was secreted only a few kilometres away from them, and George intended to keep it that way.

He planned to go over to the flat that evening to take a delivery of food and a suitcase of clean clothes. As he turned off the street and drove down the ramp into the underground garage, he was surprised to find the light on and even more surprised to find his daughter sitting on a beach chair that was thick with cobwebs, her eyes red from crying. He parked the car and went across to her.

"Now, now! What's all this about? What's up?"

Her jaw set and a frown settled over her brow, as she glared at the suitcase sitting by the fridge.

"What's this case of clothes? What're you up to? I came down looking for light bulbs. Does Mum know? I don't think so or she would've told me. You've been creeping off recently in the evenings and you won't tell us where you go. Don't lie to me – you have! There's something going on. Have you got another woman somewhere? Are you leaving us? You are, I know you are! What's going to happen to Baby Joseph, his granddad living with a ... one of those women!" She started sobbing.

George could not understand how she had arrived at such a conclusion.

"*Mela.* None of this is what you think, Gina. Go and get your mother and send her down here. You stay upstairs while we have a chat. Relax, everything's fine. Just go and get Mum. Please."

Gina scooted off upstairs. Soon, a worried-looking Marianna poked her head around the top of the stairs.

"George, I'm not coming down. You know how I hate spiders."

"Marianna, please, I've got something to tell you. It's about Den."

Without hesitation, she appeared at his side.

"He's alright, isn't he?"

"Yes, yes, he's fine."

She took a step back, folded her arms across her bosom and squared up to George.

"What's all this about then? You've got that look on your face."

"What look?"

"That stupid, guilty look." George sighed.

"As I said, it's about Den!"

She surged forward, so her face was almost touching his.

"You've already said that. Now, you tell me everything! And don't you lie, 'cos I'll know and then … then …"

George hastily began to explain how Denzel was helping the resistance; just running errands and using his local knowledge. Not involved in anything directly, so she did not have to worry. He said, in times like these, everybody had to do their bit and hers was to keep quiet and not tell Gina anything.

She bit her bottom lip and pondered. George could tell she was thinking things through. Finally, she said, "Yes, I think you're right. You don't know this, but Joe Mifsud's become one of those local liaison people. He asked our Gina how Den was doing, whether he was safe and alright."

"What, he's spying for the Russians?"

Grim-faced, Marianna nodded.

"I used to like that man. I used to think how lucky Gina was to marry into such a nice family, being butchers and everything. But now … What've things come to? What sort of man does that? I don't suppose it matters much – you ruined things between our families anyway, throwing that jug of water over

Josette, then trying to fish the ice cubes out of her top. I've never been so embarrassed!"

George bit his bottom lip.

"Let's not talk about that *again*. We can't tell Gina anything, you know what she's like? I love her to bits – she's my daughter – but, God bless her, she can't keep a secret."

Marianna nodded in agreement just as a voice from the staircase suddenly said, "Yes, I can!"

They looked at each other in surprise.

Marianna went and grabbed Gina, dragging her down the remaining stairs, into the garage.

"It's rude to listen into other people's conversations, you snoop! How much did you hear?"

Gina looked sulkily at the floor.

"Most of it. I thought Dad was leaving us ... for another woman."

Marianna scoffed.

"Another woman? Don't be ridiculous! In the name of the saints, who'd have him?" George looked at his wife, slightly taken aback. Marianna continued talking to Gina. "But listen, young lady, from now on, any conversations about Denzel take place here, in the garage. We never mention his name upstairs. And you never mention his name to Giorgio – you don't want to come between your husband and his father, do you? That wouldn't be fair on Giorgio, would it? If Joe Mifsud says anything about our Den, you just smile and be nice. Then you come home, and you tell me or your father. Yes? It's very important. Do you understand?"

George was quietly impressed with Marianna and grabbed her hand in support.

"You just do what your mother says, Gina. Den's doing the right thing – that's what you need to remember – and *we've* got to do everything we can to protect him."

Marianna said: "Right, Gina. Baby Joseph'll be awake from

his nap soon. You'd better go up. George, you get this stuff into the car. I'm getting my shoes, then you're taking me to see my son. Don't even think about arguing."

"*Mela*, there's one more thing you should know – umm, it's about Abdullah ..."

CHAPTER 32
THE RESISTANCE
FORTIFICATIONS, INTERPRETATION CENTRE, VALLETTA, MALTA

ABDULLAH AND SILVIA met Denzel outside the museum, next to St Andrew's Bastion, in the early hours, leaving their vehicles parked nearby. Denzel had brought two rucksacks. One was for Silvia, containing a quiet electro-hydraulic pump and flexible oil reservoir, mounted inside a purpose-built backpack. In total, it weighed less than 10kg. This piece of equipment had a range of door-breaching tools that they would use to force entry into the museum and open the iron door at the other end of the tunnel, to gain access to the Lazaretto buildings.

His own rucksack was heavier and contained the demolition set to bring down the communications tower. Denzel had been taught by Huck, who seemed to know everything there was to know about explosives.

Abdullah carried an M4 American assault rifle in a padded nylon bag, slung across his back like a rucksack. Silvia had cryptically mentioned that they could get wet and any weapon below shoulder-height could be compromised.

Abdullah looked sceptical and said: "But there is no swimming?"

Silvia said: "Not swimming ... but definitely some wading." Abdullah looked at her suspiciously.

"*Wading*? What is this 'wading'?"

Silvia laughed.

"It's like swimming, but your feet are on the bottom. Come on, you're not afraid of a bit of water, are you?"

Abdullah was very much afraid of a bit of water, but he clenched his teeth and said nothing.

Denzel watched as Silvia took a moment to check over the equipment in the rucksack. He was not sure what he feared more – the trip down the four-hundred-year-old narrow tunnel under the waters of the harbour or being captured at the other end by the Russians. There was a terrible rumbling sound from his guts.

They went round to a side service entrance and Denzel fitted a hydraulic door-breaker to a hose that ran from Silvia's pack. Abdullah went a little way up the street to keep an eye out for any late-night wanderers. The electric motor hummed quietly and, after the tool had been wedged between the door and the jamb, easily snapped the lock. Once in the museum, they made their way into the cellars and then down a further narrow staircase, with enormous treads, deep into the foundations of the bastion. From there, they found the old door to the stone cistern that Silvia had forced open when she had gone exploring previously.

They fitted head torches and lightweight yellow plastic helmets, which they had covered in black masking tape, and set off into the darkness. The air in the tunnel smelled musty and vegetal. Denzel felt the humidity starting to settle on his skin and soak into his clothing. The roof was low, and they had to stoop, making the going more strenuous than he had imagined. Abdullah was a tall man and the crack of his helmet on the jagged stone roof and his curses in response became a common refrain, as they progressed down the tunnel. Nervously, he ran his hands along the striations on the tunnel walls, where Turkish slaves had hacked out the limestone to form the passage. He was alarmed to find they were dripping wet.

The tunnel narrowed as they progressed, sometimes barely wide enough for them to squeeze through. Denzel had to fight hard to keep his nerves under control. He did not dare dwell on what he knew was above them, wondering whether those who had dug the tunnels knew how close they were to the waters of Marsamxett Harbour, only a few metres above. All around was the sound of running water, dripping from the roof and pooling on the floor, before forming rivulets that disappeared down sinkholes.

There were loose stones beneath their feet. At one point the ceiling had collapsed, leaving a pile of rubble as high as Denzel's chest blocking their way.

Silvia said: "We'll have to take off the rucksacks. You can slither across the top of this to reach the other side. It's only four or five metres."

Denzel was horrified.

"You actually did that when you were here by yourself? You're crazy!"

Abdullah was bringing up the rear, eyes wide with fear revealed by the beam of Denzel's headtorch.

"So now the water is ... up there?" He looked at the roof of the tunnel.

Silvia said helpfully: "Yeah, there can only be a few metres of rock between us and the seabed. Weird to think that, isn't it?"

"So, this water here, wetting my feet, this is from ..."

"Yeah, there must be a leak."

She heard Abdullah muttering under his breath.

"In the name of Allah who with His Name nothing can cause harm in the earth nor in the heavens, the all-Hearing, the all-Knowing, keep us safe from the waters, as I cannot do the swimming ..."

"Okay, we're about halfway, it's a bit trickier from now on.

But I didn't turn back, having come this far, so neither will you, right?"

After another fifteen minutes, squeezing through narrow sections of tunnel and negotiating further rockfalls, Denzel became conscious he was splashing through deeper water. Behind him, he heard Abdullah muttering his own version of the *dua* for safety.

"*O Allah, guard me from what is in front of me and behind me, from my left, and from my right, and from above me. Oh, yes, especially from above me ... I seek refuge in Your Greatness from being struck down – or drowned, because I do not have the swimming. But, if it is Your will, I promise I can learn ...*"

"There is much water, it is getting higher," he called out. "Is it safe to be moving forwards?"

Silvia did not falter, pushing on through.

"Hold your bags high, we're coming to the deepest part." Denzel felt the grip of panic seize his stomach and twist it.

"Oh, shit! Are we nearly there?"

"Yep, this is as bad as it gets. We start climbing soon."

Silvia was right. It only took a few more moments and they were on a staircase that widened to a point where they could move alongside each other and stand upright. After a few minutes of hauling themselves, and their kit, up the stairs, they approached a steel-riveted door. Denzel ran his hands over his clothing, trying to squeeze out some of the moisture that had soaked and chilled him. Abdullah leaned against the wall, panting, as the adrenaline drained out of him and the panic receded.

"They say *Jahanna*, the world for sinners, is a place of fire – but I have seen it, and it is a dark tunnel of water. Now, I do not care if we must fight a thousand demons, it is better than that hell."

Silvia put her index finger to her lips.

"Quiet, we don't know what's on the other side of this."

They edged towards the sliding door and placed their ears

against it but heard nothing except the sound of dripping water.

Denzel said: "Do you think it's safe?"

"Nothing about this is safe, Denzel. How're we going to get this open?"

"The spreaders will force it open. Huck says they exert six tonnes of force."

With much screeching of tortured metal, the long-time rusted steel plates were forced to slide back on the narrow iron rail. The metal door gave access to a small pitch-black room with an uneven floor. Denzel tried to imagine where they might be. Over time, as the Lazaretto's use changed and it finally became derelict, the existence of the tunnel had passed from memory into myth. He wondered if, apart from themselves, there were any others still alive who had made the journey through the subterranean passage.

They used the spreaders again to exit the room through a flimsy wooden door into heavy undergrowth, overwhelming what had once been a courtyard. They were now within the old plague hospital and Abdullah had never been happier. All around him there was clean air, scented with the salty iodine aroma of the sea. A stiff breeze blew, dispelling the moisture from their wet clothing. Abdullah looked up and saw the darkness of the night sky, his sense of relief dissipating at the thought of what lay ahead of them.

CHAPTER 33
NATASHA BONNICI
CASTELLO BONNICI, IL-WARDIJA, MALTA

THINGS HAD CHANGED at the *castello* during Natasha's absence.

The most obvious difference was the absence of Katia, the housekeeper. Natasha could not blame her for taking the considerable savings she had amassed over the years and returning to her home city of Krakow. But she knew, from the first moment she saw Asano, Katia's replacement, that he was going to be a problem.

When Natasha had first arrived and gone to her room, she found her bath had already been run, hot and foaming, with lavender-scented candles placed in sconces on the walls. There was a note on her bed, written on thin rice paper, in an elegant Japanese-style font, saying:

'I do not wish to presume or intrude and please forgive the running of bath – is gesture of welcome. I am here to serve. Asano.'

She had laughed. He did not fool her, but nevertheless, she slipped off her clothes and slid into the welcoming, scented water.

During the rest of the first week, Natasha learned of the Russian presence on the island and was genuinely flabbergasted. She was amazed so much had happened of which she had been totally unaware. In ordinary times, it might have been shocking enough just to hear that Edward Refalo had attained the office of prime minister. He had been the deputy chair of her energy company, MalTech, until her departure and subsequent self-imposed exile in Greece. Her low opinion of his abilities and character made it all the more difficult for her to believe he had achieved so much, in so little time.

Marco said with a smile: "You must remember, Natasha, there is a particularly shallow pool of talent on the island. Also, I remember a past prime minister saying that only a thief, a fool or a madman would dream of standing for election. If memory serves me, he was kicked out of power shortly afterwards! I have still not decided which one he was – possibly all three!"

Over the next few days, she insisted he drove her around the island and showed her the extent of the Russian occupation. They took the ferry from the landing stage at Sliema, to Valletta, to get the best view of Manoel Island, where he pointed out the works on the new naval base. They passed two of the Black Sea Fleet's Kilo-class attack submarines, moored on pontoons alongside the Lazaretto, and saw minesweepers tied to large orange buoys to the side of the main channel.

Marco said: "Wait until you see the Grand Harbour."

"I'm shocked. I've got so many questions. Like, how has this even been allowed to happen?"

"I know. Every day they become more entrenched. The longer it goes on, the harder it will be to get them out. The EU is outraged, but the Russians have played a clever game. They gained a foothold initially, I believe, by blackmailing Refalo and Farrugia. Once they were ensconced, they started to crush dissent, political and civil, and attack the constitution. They quickly built their military presence and assumed control of the island. We are not members of NATO – what could we do to stop them? Once the constitutional changes go through, and with the round ups of the politicians who oppose them, there is talk of taking us out of the European Union, if we are not thrown out first!"

Natasha could hardly believe what she was hearing. Marco had been quiet on the journey back to Malta, unsure whether she would welcome general conversation. He had thought it best not to disturb her with details of the changes back home. So, he had given her time to adjust and let her sit quietly, speaking only to reply to her questions or to give brief instructions about the journey. Natasha, for her part, was happy to sit in silence and enjoy being free from the confines of the clinic.

Marco thought a little family news might interest her.

"Oh, and your cousin Greca called here a few weeks ago."

Natasha immediately went on the alert. She knew Greca rarely did anything without a prior motive.

"Really? How was she?"

"Very well." Marco laughed. "She still has a bee in her bonnet about Sergio's entitlement to a pay out from the Family's coffers and believes she deserves a seat at the table. I told her to forget it. You know, she is a highly intelligent woman. It confuses me why she cannot see that what she wants can never happen."

"Yes, she always thought something was due to her."

"... she asked me to mentor her, you know, along the lines of what you were doing for her ..."

"I hope you said no!"

"Of course. I knew it was just a poor ruse to try and get into the Family through the back door. How come you two fell out anyway? Apparently, you were as thick as thieves. I did not know she had moved into the *castello* for a while?"

"It's a long story – it was a mistake – but not now, Dad. Anyway, these Russians, what're you doing about it? It's not like you to sit by idly. Or maybe the years in Serbia have softened you?"

Marco looked at his daughter and smiled.

"I have to be careful, but shall we say, I monitor the situation closely. In fact, I am on good terms with the head of the Russian military on the island, Colonel Fedorov, who dines with me occasionally at the *castello*. He has a penchant for Maltese red and Italian grappa. They rather loosen his tongue. He enjoys what he calls a 'robust exchange of views'. I find those views are mainly his." She laughed.

"I'd be interested to join you next time the colonel accepts an invitation."

He cast a quick glance in her direction.

"We will see. Your recovery seems to be coming along nicely. Maybe returning home was the best thing for you."

The ferry had nearly reached Valletta. They planned to climb up, through the old narrow streets, into the city centre, then descend the other side of the peninsula, to the ferry stop on the Grand Harbour. The steepness of the incline left Natasha short of breath and she made a mental note to start an exercise regime. It was a short trip across the Grand Harbour to the Three Cities on the opposite side, the original home of the Knights Hospitaller, who had ruled Malta for 250 years through their Order of St John of Jerusalem.

Marco intended to ignore the fast catamaran to Bormla and instead take one of the small *dgħajsa*, the gondola-like water taxis that, for a few extra euros, would wander, usually unchallenged, through the Russian fleet berthed in the Grand Harbour itself. Several of the larger naval vessels, which formed the Admiral of the Fleet, Putin battlegroup, were anchored out on Hurds Bank, but there was still an array of frigates and destroyers, alongside a dozen smaller tankers, patrol boats and supply vessels.

The star of the show was the Pyotr Velikiy, the Peter the Great battle cruiser, the flagship of the Northern Fleet that had recently arrived in Valletta from the North Atlantic. It had tied up at Pinto Wharf, just below the Upper Barrakka lift, and groups of schoolchildren were being shown around by jolly ratings, chosen for their friendly demeanour and command of English.

Their weather-beaten ferryman, a cigarette hanging out of his mouth, asked them: "Do you want to see warship? It's very big, we can go close?"

Marco nodded and flashed a twenty-euro note, so the small, brightly painted dgħajsa, with its 6 h.p. outboard, spluttered its way towards the waterline of the massive ship looming above them. They sailed so close to the hull, Natasha could almost run her fingers across the markings of the Plimsoll line. She craned her neck to look up, but it was impossible to see the anti-ship guided missiles or the radar-aimed cannons. The vessel had a lethal capability and was specifically designed to destroy American ships in an all-out naval war. She was surprised they were allowed to approach so close.

Marco turned to her and said: "Impressive, isn't it? This is what we are up against."

She looked thoughtful.

"Not really. What we're up against is the apathy of half a million people who're letting this state of affairs continue. Is there no resistance, no public backlash? It makes me livid, seeing what's going on!"

Marco looked at her and saw the anger on her face.

"That is probably not a conversation for today."

Suddenly, a large but highly manoeuvrable Russian patrol boat emerged from behind the vessel and spun in front of them, creating a wash that sent them grasping for the side rails of their taxi. Two sailors were on the prow, shouting and gesticulating at the taxi driver who remonstrated with them, shrugging his shoulders and pointing to his passengers. But knowing the game was up, the water taxi turned and headed away from the battle cruiser.

The ferryman took them back to the landing point in Valletta, where they disembarked and travelled by taxi to Sliema, to retrieve Marco's parked car. Once inside, Natasha said to her father: "Is it safe for me to be back in Malta? If I remember correctly, I left under a bit of a cloud. What's the situation with that anti-Mafia prosecutor in Rome – Tozzi, wasn't it? Am I still in trouble with him?"

"Hmm, yes, I think you might have got lucky there. Signor Tozzi is no more. I am afraid he stood on too many toes and was gunned down in Ponticelli, Naples, by some young Camorra foot soldiers, out to make names for themselves."

"Well, that's good news. And on a local level, is Superintendent Zammit likely to cause any trouble?"

"As I think I mentioned to you in the clinic, Gerald died earlier this year, so there has been a shake up in the *Pulizija*. Superintendent Zammit is now Assistant Commissioner Zammit, unbelievably."

Natasha raised her eyebrows and smiled for the first time since her return to Malta.

CHAPTER 34
ARTICLE IN THE MALTA TELEGRAPH

Reporter: Justine Galea

Date: 25 August 2025

Russia Suspected in Murder of Maltese Politician in Brussels

Belgium has officially declared it believes there to be Russian involvement in the brazen assassination in Brussels at the weekend of Raymond Farrugia, chief of staff to the Maltese prime minister. Farrugia, aged 62, was believed to be in Brussels to give evidence to high-ranking European and US officials about the Russian presence in Malta, which some believe amounts to an illegal occupation. Mr Farrugia was shot in the back, as he was sightseeing in Train World, a railway museum in the north of the city, and died shortly afterwards.

A Russian national and former security services officer, Vadim Strakhov, was arrested, having been caught on CCTV disposing of a Glock pistol in the nearby Brussels Canal. The weapon was later recovered by police divers.

The President of the European Commission, Noémie Minaud, said the murder of a foreign minister of state was an attack of the most serious nature, verging on an act of war.

A Kremlin spokesperson denied any involvement in the attack, but claimed to have evidence Mr Farrugia was in Brussels to pass on intelligence about Russian naval matters to NATO, which is also headquartered in the city.

He added that the Russian security services had been assisting the Maltese Pulizija in investigating serious allegations of corruption at the highest level within the Maltese government, in which Mr Farrugia had been a prime suspect.

CHAPTER 35
THE RESISTANCE
MANOEL ISLAND, MALTA

As soon as Abdullah, Denzel and Silvia left the courtyard, they found themselves on the concrete service road that ran around the south side of the island, towards Fort Manoel. Opposite them were some derelict, flat-roofed buildings, dating from the Second World War. Abdullah took the M4 assault rifle from the bag and loaded a thirty-round magazine. He felt much better now that he could feel the wind in his face and was cradling a rifle in his arms.

Silvia knew exactly where they were going and led them across the road in the lee of the buildings. They worked their way around the back and set off over the rough scrub of the hillside. It was a dark night, and thorny bushes caught their hands and faces. The mast was visible from all over Sliema and beyond, its red aviation warning lights flickering amongst the dishes and antennae. Close up, it looked even more enormous.

The three-metre-high palisade offered no resistance to the spreaders and, within seconds, they had passed their packs through the gap they had made and squeezed themselves through. Huck had told Denzel that the best approach to bring down the tower, which was a substantial steel structure, was to use shaped charges to sever it at its joints and angles, so the cumulative effect of the blasts would weaken the base and its own weight would bring the mast crashing down.

Denzel and Silvia carefully positioned the TNT, taping blocks to the girders at the base, while Abdullah patrolled the perimeter, using a night-vision rifle scope on the M4 to look out for trouble. Denzel screwed the detonators into each of the packs of TNT, which would be ignited by an electric match, triggered by a radio signal from a handheld transmitter.

When he had finished, he was sweating heavily. He gathered his equipment and wondered why he still had one pack of TNT left over. Deciding he had covered the entire base of the mast with explosives, he dismissed it as unimportant. He took his rucksack and squeezed out through the gap in the fence. The whole operation had taken them twenty-five minutes.

They prepared their packs, Denzel's considerably lighter now that most of the TNT was strapped to the mast, and headed back towards the Lazaretto. Abdullah was ahead of them, moving quickly and stealthily across the rough terrain.

As they approached the derelict buildings, they heard a dull, mechanical thump-thumping noise. Abdullah held his fist in the air, and they all dropped to the ground. Creeping forwards, they looked down the slope to the service road that lay between them and the entrance to the overgrown courtyard. There was a work party of some sort feeding a reel of cable through a trench. They did not look like military, but Denzel could not be sure. Next to them, a mobile generator banged away, providing the power to a series of brutally bright arc lights.

"Great! What now? They're just contractors, aren't they?" Denzel hissed.

Abdullah was kneeling, lining up the men in the night-vision scope.

Silvia tapped his shoulder and shook her head furiously, indicating they must think this through.

"I don't know who they are. Even if they're just workers,

they could summon soldiers. We can't assume they'll be friendly, and we can't take any chances." She chewed on a knuckle. "Well, we need to blow the mast, that's the first thing. That'll attract their attention and then, while they're wondering what the hell's going on, we'll try and get behind them and into the courtyard. We can't hang around here, it'll be sun up in an hour or so."

They crept down to the service road and worked their way a little further along it, so they could cross with less chance of being seen. Denzel took the radio controller out of the side pocket of his rucksack and turned it on. He entered the password, then the PIN and the screen came to life. The menu came up and he started the detonation sequence. Silvia looked over his shoulder, as he entered the final details. A large red square appeared. He reached round and offered her the handset, saying: "Go on, push it, and let's see what happens!" Abdullah nodded.

"Yes, cut off the Russian manhood!"

She bit her bottom lip and looked at them both, a devilish grin on her face.

"Here goes!"

For a second, there was one almighty shaft of blue-white light from behind the hill, then a deep resonating boom, which seemed to echo across the harbour and bounce back at them from the bastions of Valletta. They saw the red lights on the tower shake, then start to flicker, as the mast slowly listed to one side, before accelerating on its downward trajectory. It landed out of their sight, but they heard the screech of twisting metal and the crash of the impact.

Despite the need for them to start moving, they kept still for a few seconds, before Abdullah urged them forwards.

"Come on, let's get out of here. Cross the road, slowly, don't run," Silvia ordered. They were nearly on it when she held up her hand. "Hang on, they're going."

The workers had dropped their tools when they heard the

blast and were gathering around their van, looking up the hill towards the fallen mast, deciding what to do. At that moment, one of them turned and looked directly at the three figures standing immobile by the roadside. Abdullah slowly put the M4 to his shoulder, causing the man to shout and alert the others, who dived behind the van.

Abdullah kept his weapon trained on the van, while they walked across the road. They had not got halfway across when a military SUV came speeding around the bend, blue lights flashing. For a second, the headlights caught them, as they scrambled to reach the rough terrain in front of the courtyard. They squatted low and held their breath but, after a few seconds, they heard the high-pitched whine of the vehicle reversing. Abdullah dropped onto one knee and let loose a short volley of shots, which stopped the SUV in its tracks.

The three of them ran, jumping and leaping amongst the scrub and mounds of fallen masonry. They managed to find and open the storeroom door, just as torch beams appeared behind them at the entrance to the courtyard. Again, Abdullah slowed the pursuers down with more shots that slammed into the limestone walls and showered splinters across the courtyard. Part of him would rather have stayed and fought it out in the open than retreat down the tunnel.

Denzel gently pulled him into the storeroom and shut the door behind them. Their helmets were on the floor where they had left them. They quickly fastened the chin straps and turned on the head torches. As Denzel pulled the tunnel's sliding door towards him, the jarring grating of metal on metal rang out loud and clear.

They made their way down the stairs and entered the tunnel itself. As before, they waded through water and scuttled along the narrow passage, scrambling over the rockfalls where necessary. Denzel was breathing out great clouds of vapour in the dank atmosphere and his heart was hammering in his chest. Silvia stopped and put her finger to her lips.

"Shhh." In the distance, they heard loud shouts and the rattle of falling rocks. "Shit, they're onto us! Let's hurry. Remember, we've got the advantage, we know how far it is and what's ahead of us, and they haven't got head torches or helmets."

Just at that moment, she lost her footing when stepping into a small depression in the tunnel floor.

"Ah, God, that hurts!"

Abdullah tried to support her, as she tested her ankle. She grimaced.

"It's no good. I can't put any weight on it."

Denzel threw an arm around her, and they started to stagger down the passage.

"C'mon. We can't hang around."

Due to the narrowness of the tunnel, it was almost impossible for the two of them to move side by side. Improvising, Silvia went behind him, with her hands on his shoulders, and hopped her way down the tunnel. They could hear the sounds behind getting nearer and, when the tunnel was unobstructed, the distant glow of their pursuers' torchlights became visible. Abdullah turned to face the oncoming group, the M4 at his shoulder.

"You go." He smiled. "They are rats in a sewer!"

Denzel and Silvia hurried away down the tunnel. Abdullah turned off his head torch and waited, letting the pursuers advance. As the light of their torches brightened the passage, he fired six shots towards them, the loud cracks resounding off the tunnel walls. There was silence. He waited until he heard rocks shifting underfoot and then he fired again. This time there was a shout and a scream.

Ahead of him, Denzel and Silvia were reaching the end of the tunnel.

"Come on, Silvia, we're nearly there. We're almost at the cistern."

"It doesn't matter. There're all those stairs to climb and the car is miles away. They're going to get us."

"I don't think so. Let's get to the cistern, then we'll see. Give me a minute!"

Silvia was panicking.

"We haven't got a minute!"

He opened his rucksack and fiddled around for thirty seconds or so.

Silvia was becoming hysterical.

"Come on, Denzel! Stop messing! We haven't got time for this."

He called for Abdullah to hurry along and, when he appeared out of the mouth of the tunnel, pushed him to one side, against a wall. Then he threw something along the tunnel and heaved the metal door partially shut. Between them, he and Abdullah carried Silvia across the base of the cistern as far as the bottom of the stairs.

She sat down, her head in her hands. The voices of their pursuers were getting nearer. A shot echoed down the tunnel, hitting the metal door with a bell-like clang. Abdullah clipped a new magazine into the M4 and grimly trained the rifle on the entrance to the tunnel.

"You know, we nearly did it." Silvia was on the point of tears.

Denzel took the radio controller out of the side pocket of his rucksack, opened the app and jabbed the big red square, detonating the last block of TNT. There was a huge roar from the mouth of the tunnel, as the door was blown back onto the opposite wall and a hail of rock clattered around the cistern. A cloud of dust filled the room, temporarily blinding and choking them.

Silvia grabbed Abdullah's arm. He turned to her, coughing.

"In the name of the Prophet, may peace be upon Him – what is this new hell?"

Denzel poked his ears to try and stop the ringing of a hundred bells.

"I had a packet of TNT left over." He grinned. "Just as well!"

"Truly Allah is with us today. *Inshallah*."

Silvia's face, in the light of his headlamp, was white with dust, but her eyes shone brightly again.

"Hang on, where's all this water coming from?"

The three of them looked towards the mouth of the tunnel where the light of their headtorches caught dark foaming water streaming into the cistern at an alarming rate. It was already lapping over the ankles of their boots.

"My God, Denzel, you've blown a hole in the bottom of Marsamxett Harbour!"

Abdullah, a look of pure horror on his face, was already scuttling up the stairs, as more water came pouring in.

CHAPTER 36
ASSISTANT COMMISSIONER GEORGE ZAMMIT
OFFICE OF THE PRIME MINISTER, VALLETTA, MALTA

MARIANNA WAS THRILLED to hear George had been summoned to a meeting with the prime minister and immediately made him try on the trousers from his best blue suit, to ensure they still fastened comfortably around the waist.

"We don't want you to be giving the prime minister what for and suddenly find yourself all constricted."

"Er ... no, quite." He smiled. "Can't go there ... all constricted."

She ran a finger around his waistband, checking for tight spots.

"*Uweijja*, don't go holding your breath. You'll only suffer for it later; it'll give you wind. And you don't want that! What does he want with you anyway?" She approached him and put her mouth to his ear, whispering. "It's not about our Den, is it?"

"*Mela*! Of course not. And we don't talk about that here – do we?"

"No, we don't. But it was so nice to see him. Don't you think he's lost some weight? He's not getting fed properly, is what it is. I've done some baked pasta in a tray for tonight's dinner. All he's got to do is heat it up. He can share it with those other boys. Can you pop it across?" George was exasperated.

"No! The less I go there, the better. The less I see of him, the safer he is. Look, you need to understand that I can't wander around the island with trays of food – people will wonder what's going on. A bag of shopping's different."

"Well, take more food. He's looking hungry, if you ask me. Maybe those other boys are taking it all? Then, of course, there's that Abdullah. What you were doing bringing him along, filling our Den's head with nonsense, I don't know."

"I didn't bring him along! He just turned up. I had no …"

"Oh, yes? You expect me to believe that? I know you, George Zammit. He'll turn our Den against me, I know he will. Whispering in his ear all day and nothing I can do about it. He's a terrible man!"

A few hours later, George was sitting at the bottom of the Cabinet Room conference table, as far away from Edward Refalo and Colonel Fedorov as he dared. Hanging on the wall opposite him was a portrait of a disgraced former prime minister who had resigned after buckling under pressure following various corruption scandals. The shamelessly self-important figure hung next to the portrait of another former Labour PM, Dom Mintoff, father of the Maltese Republic. George sighed, wondering what Mintoff would have thought of the Russian occupation. It was he who had embedded the principles of neutrality and non-alignment into the Maltese constitution, adamant that the proud new Republic would never be beholden to any world super power, whether western or eastern. "George, are you with us?"

Commissioner Mallia glared at him.

"Er … *Mela*, of course."

Fedorov addressed him then, blue eyes bright behind his narrowed eyelids.

"Assistant Commissioner, I have reviewed your file, and it seems you're a man of action?"

George stuttered, "Well, I wouldn't ..."

"Oh, yes, most certainly! Rooting out insurgents in Libya, breaking international oil-smuggling rings, arresting IS leaders in Syria, thousand-metre sniper shots, sinking Greek naval vessels, rescuing young ladies from blazing volcanoes? Medals and awards from the Americans! Is there anything you can't do?"

There was a smattering of polite laughter. George was still wary – he had the feeling that something bad was coming.

"You're aware, of course, that Ray Farrugia was leading the programme of local liaison officers, gathering intelligence about the activities of the so-called Resistance? Although what they think they're resisting, God only knows.

"Well, as you know, Mr Farrugia is no longer with us, which is just as well, as he could have done a great deal of harm. So, farewell, Mr Farrugia. And, Edward, just so we're clear – no state funeral for him and nobody from the government attends any private service. Please make that plain. Ray Farrugia was corrupt and a disgrace to his office. Can we release a statement to that effect before he becomes some sort of martyr? I understand his death may be related to his nefarious business activities. You can also say that. As for his wife and family, I think some time in Camp Azure would be appropriate – to discourage any others who may be similarly inclined to take a vacation in Brussels."

The room went quiet. Edward Refalo glanced around the table, but all eyes were cast down, examining papers, fingernails or the whirls in the highly polished mahogany tabletop.

"Yes, of course," Refalo murmured. "He was corrupt and a disgrace, but the family ... really?"

"Camp Azure – really!"

Fedorov then took a slurp of his barely warm tea from a fine bone china cup.

"So, Assistant Commissioner Zammit, we come to you. Commissioner Mallia has every faith in you, and, because of his increased workload, he's suggested you head up the newly formed Home Security Command. You'll report jointly to the commissioner and to me."

George opened his mouth and tried to make the words shape themselves. Commissioner Mallia had dropped his head and joined those studying the tabletop.

"The Home Security Command?" ventured George. "I've never heard of it."

Fedorov sighed.

"Assistant Commissioner, for all your great deeds, you do sometimes come across as being a little slow. You've not heard of it because, until now, it didn't exist! Newly formed. Did I not make myself clear?"

"Yes, yes, certainly. Very pleased, sir, thank you ... er ... what does it do, this home security thing? Is it domestic insurance type of security ... or commercial as well?"

Fedorov scowled at him, just for a moment – then burst out laughing.

"Very funny, George. You nearly had me for a moment there!" He banged the table. "This is what we need around here – someone with a sense of humour!"

George managed a confused smile in response.

"Just to help you order your priorities, I'm making you personally responsible for finding out who's leaking those arrest notices. We failed to collect two more potential subversives yesterday. One had gone to Spain on holiday, apparently, while the other had left for medical treatment in Switzerland. I want this stopped."

"Of course, sir. It must be stopped."

"Excellent! That's the spirit. Take note, all of you. It's more people like Zammit we need."

Later that night, the telephone by George's bedside rang at 04:00. He fumbled the large black acetate receiver to his ear, knocking over the bedside lamp, as he did so. It was an irate Fedorov, screaming at him to get himself to Manoel

Island as quickly as possible. There had been a terrorist attack, and the main communications mast had been destroyed.

Halfway through the conversation with Fedorov, Marianna had leaned across the bed, urgently tugging on George's pyjamas, asking:

"It's not about our Den, is it?"

Once George had put the phone down, he took a long look at his wife and asked:

"Do you know who that was?"

"Somebody with no manners, ringing here at this time of night!"

"He was the head of the Russian security services in Malta. The man ultimately responsible for catching Denzel. And what did you say?"

There was a moment's silence.

"Nothing important. I never said where he was, did I?"

"*Mela*! You probably said enough to put all our lives at risk. It's just lucky he was shouting at me and not listening to you. Anyway, I've got to go. I'm the man responsible for catching everybody in the resistance."

"At this hour? What about our Den?"

"*Madonna mia*! I don't think he'll last long – unless his mother learns to keep quiet!"

Forty minutes later, George arrived there with Inspector Chelotti in tow. They showed their ID to a surly rating, with a shaved head and tired eyes, who directed them to the scene. Lights had been positioned to shine onto the wreckage and the hilltop was swarming with Russian Military Police and engineers, trying to salvage the communications gear from the tangle of metal. The fallen mast looked like some mighty mechanical beast that had been torn apart in mortal combat with a dinosaur.

Karl Chelotti stood, hands on hips, watching the dozens of personnel tramping all over the hilltop.

"Well, that's the crime scene gone. What're we supposed to do here?"

"Let's find out how they got in and maybe where they came from."

It took George and Karl a few minutes to identify the gap in the palisade that had been forced. The panels of railings were scattered all over the hillside, but the clear symmetrical buckling of the two uprights and fresh scratch marks were sufficient for George to conclude commercial spreaders had been used to force the fencing apart. They photographed the fence and moved on.

A Russian policeman had recovered the remnants of a detonator and George made a note to find out whether such detonators were used in any of the island's many quarries. The Russian also pointed them in the direction of two communications engineers, who, whilst hiding under their van, had seen three civilians running across the road, into the Lazaretto, immediately following the blast, chased by three soldiers.

George spoke to the two who gave a brief description of two men and a woman. The man was tall, nearly two metres, dark-haired and around thirty years old. The other, a marksman, was equally tall, thinner and older, with a grey beard, possibly Arab-looking. The woman had long wavy dark hair and was also tall. She had a big build and was wearing a thigh-length military jacket. All of them carried backpacks. As the descriptions of the trio emerged, George felt a constriction start to squeeze his throat.

The Russian Military Police had spent half an hour trying to find the soldiers who had been chasing the fugitives – their SUV still sat on the roadside by the Lazaretto, its engine running and blue light turning. They had discovered the names of the men who had signed out the SUV, but they seemed to have vanished.

The Maltese policemen walked the perimeter of the site, giving George time to gather his thoughts. As they followed a wall down the hillside, he said to Chelotti: "Life's getting very complicated." He sighed and shook his head.

"What? You *know* who they are?"

George did not say anything but stared at Chelotti, who mouthed back at him: "Your Denzel?"

He nodded. "And Gerald Camilleri's niece and another friend of ours."

"You're joking? Wow! Good work, I say."

George and Chelotti went down the hill to where the trio were last seen crossing the service road. By the thin first light, they poked about in the undergrowth for a bit, making a show of doing something, until Chelotti said: "We're wasting our time here. Why don't you just go and ask Denzel how he did it? Get us something to give to Fedorov, to keep him off our backs."

George laughed.

"You know, that's not a bad idea. I'll see him later today. I suspect he'll be getting some sleep just now. Speaking of getting Fedorov off our backs, I need some help nailing the informer who's tipping off all the arrest subjects." Chelotti was confused.

"But that's us?"

"*Mela*, I know that! But we need to give Fedorov a sacrificial offering. He's made me responsible for catching whoever it is. I know just the person who should take the fall – or shall I arrest you and save myself the bother?"

"Don't joke about things like that, it makes me nervous."

"Look out for the next arrest list and I'll highlight a name and address. You go round and pick this chap up. Just take him straight to Camp Azure, no need to interrogate him or anything. We can tell Fedorov we've got our snitch. Then, we'll have to be more careful in future. We won't be able to help everybody we want to."

CHAPTER 37
NATASHA AND MARCO BONNICI
CASTELLO BONNICI, IL-WARDIJA, MALTA

ASANO HAD EXCELLED HIMSELF. Good Japanese cooking was hard to find in Malta and Colonel Fedorov admitted he had little experience of it. Asano had started with sake-steamed local clams, followed by yakitori chicken skewers, with a delicious salty sauce. This was followed by a fresh clear miso broth, some creamy tuna rice balls and thin slices of marinated wagyu beef fillet, cooked at the table on a teppanyaki grill.

The colonel had refused the sake and started on the special section of Marco's cellar, which held the island's best vintages. Asano moved like a ghost, drifting around the table with small, precise, movements, appearing first at Natasha's shoulder, then manifesting himself by the colonel, serving him small portions of perfect food in blue and white ceramic bowls. He never spoke, other than to mutter deferential apologies for sins uncommitted: *Sorry for your wait. Please excuse bad service. I forget to serve lady first, so sorry.*

Natasha hated him.

Fedorov was in expansive mood. More so, as the red wine disappeared down his throat.

"You know we want influence in the Mediterranean, of course we do. You've got to consider geography, historical legacy, and the threat the West has always posed to us. Like all things Russian, understanding us is never simple. What did Churchill say: 'A riddle, wrapped in a mystery, inside an enigma'!

"Take Syria, for example. Do we love Assad? No, we don't care what he does. It's his country, his people, to treat how he chooses. What's important is that we're now friends with Syria and Iran. We've got a good naval base in Syria, at Tartus, and we're more able to defend ourselves against the threat to the Russian heartland from NATO, by land, air and sea.

"People say, 'Oh, no, the West would never attack Russia!' But James Baker, when he was American Secretary of State, promised Mikhail Gorbachev, in 1990, that, if Russia accepted Germany's unification, NATO would not expand to the east. What followed? Twenty years of NATO expansion, with five NATO members now sharing our borders. Battlegroups in Poland and the Baltic states hold annual exercises, right under our noses. We can hear the rattle of their Leopard tank tracks. It's provocation, you must agree?"

Marco said: "But, Colonel, the world changes around us. What was right twenty-five years ago, maybe is not so good today."

"Exactly my point! That's why we're here in Malta. Our long-term plan to prevent the Mediterranean theatre falling totally under NATO control. To provide balance, we must protect our southern flank. Also, it's true, it supports operations in Libya and Egypt, opens the doors to the rest of Africa. It shows new friends we've got serious strategic intent in the Southern Mediterranean."

Natasha had been subtly baiting the Russian throughout dinner, receiving warning looks from her father as she did so.

"I understand your argument about needing to protect the entrance to the Black Sea and against incursions from the Atlantic – it's true, Malta's invaluable for that. But what would you want from Africa? Libyan oil's an excellent strategic resource and crying out for investment, but the rest?" Natasha wrinkled her nose in distaste. "Just desert, scrub, famine, IS, failed states – do you really want the Sahel?"

"We want stability and long-term friendships. And, yes, development and economic benefits, too. The West has lost the trust of Africa. Because what does the West do there? It supports regime change, wherever it chooses. Look at what the French have done. That makes for nervous governments. I don't just mean Iraq. You ask the Serbs, or see what happened with the Arab Spring, the Rose Revolution in Georgia, the Orange Revolution in Ukraine in 2004 ... and don't talk to me about Palestine! The West brings nothing but trouble, always trouble."

Fedorov was getting into his stride. He finished his brandy and, without missing a beat, Asano produced a newly warmed balloon and dribbled a splash of Torres 20 into it.

"Or maybe the Chinese are better?" the colonel continued. "The Africans say, 'The Chinese build us a deep-water port, the Americans give us a lecture.' But the Chinese build railways, roads and deep-water ports then, five years later, their loans bankrupt the countries." Fedorov shrugged and raised his hands in the air. "They're worse than the World Bank. Is that better? No, it's financial imperialism. The African governments regret the day they picked up the phone to the Chinese. We Russians, we cause no such trouble. We're long-term friends. It's the better way."

"And Ukraine in 2022?"

Fedorov wagged his finger at Natasha and swirled the brandy around his glass.

"Oh, maybe we speak too much of politics already." Marco shuffled in his chair.

"I agree, but it's always a pleasure to hear your thoughts, Colonel."

Natasha had sparkled throughout the evening. She had pulled out a black cocktail dress and a sequined cashmere shawl and was almost back to her old self. Her hair was still cropped short, and her face and body remained thinner but, despite the shadows and hollows in her cheeks, her eyes were newly alive. Her old wit and confidence had returned. Marco was aware the Russian colonel was paying her a lot of attention. He seemed to enjoy their sparring and political debate.

Marco decided that, as the coffee and brandy had been finished, it was time to bring the evening to a close. The colonel had already drunk a great deal. He dabbed his lips and placed the linen napkin on the table. Asano materialised from the shadows. He made a show of collecting the napkins and removing the coffee cups.

"Signor Bonnici, I know it is late but, if I can, I'd like to raise one other matter with yourself and Miss Natasha," said Fedorov.

Marco made a gesture of acquiescence.

"You are my guest."

"Natasha, forgive the observation, but I'm pleased to note you seem to be in very good health, given your recent problems. I hope you've managed to put the worst of your troubles behind you."

Natasha glanced at her father who was sitting very still, watching the Russian.

She replied sweetly: "I'm not sure it's appropriate to raise such a personal matter, especially as a guest at my father's table."

The colonel kept a poker face, all symptoms of his wine and brandy consumption immediately disappearing.

"Yes, it's rude of me, my apologies, but hear me out. I'm no fool and I make enquiries about all the major players on the island, which of course includes both of you. I was fascinated to read our intelligence report on the Bonnicis, both father and daughter." He smiled knowingly and glanced between them. "Even before the question of offering our support to Malta was mentioned, I was aware of the existence of the Family. So, I was delighted when I discovered that the present head of that illustrious organisation was one of my acquaintances." Marco nodded graciously.

"Fascinating, Colonel. I have no idea what you are talking about, but please go on."

"I was also fascinated to read your curriculum vitae, Natasha. Quite a rise and quite a fall. And the ruthlessness of it all! I'd never have guessed you were a woman of such remarkable talents. It brought me round to thinking that maybe we could all be of use to each other."

Natasha and Marco sat and waited for the Russian to get to the point.

"Marco, you've enough on your plate running the Family's affairs from Switzerland and have never been one to seek a public profile, so my focus must necessarily turn to you, Natasha. Until recently, you ran MalTech, one of Europe's largest public companies, and were a well-known face in the business world across Europe. Your number two was Edward Refalo, our current, sadly inept prime minister. I find myself frustrated and angry at the lack of talent and ambition in your government today. They're small-minded and self-serving people, your prime minister being no exception.

"We have plans for this island. Exciting plans. We see it as the new Dubai or Singapore. An energy-based economy, sitting as a financial hub for Europe, independent of the EU, but a true global player. This country can become a vital intermediary between the North African states and the European markets. We'll use our connections and influence, offering Malta as a route to market for African oil and gas. We can also funnel our own hydrocarbons through your system, avoiding all those troublesome sanctions. In return, Malta can become an investment conduit for money going into Africa. Not to mention the new mineral rush – the quest for lithium, graphite, cobalt, nickel, rare earth elements and the rest of the riches beneath

African soil. It's a grand vision that offers key players access to vast untapped markets."

Natasha was interested. She mused: "They do say Africa's the future. Apparently, one in ten of the world's births will occur in Nigeria in the next twenty years. By 2030, it'll be the fourth most populous country. Congo, Egypt, Ethiopia and Tanzania are all on a similar trajectory. Currently, every one of those countries is desperate for investment partners. You're right, it's a great opportunity."

Fedorov clapped his hands.

"Exactly, I knew you'd understand. This, in part, is why we're in Malta. To consolidate our African Gateway project." Natasha leaned forward.

"Snappy name. But what does it have to do with me?"

"You're Maltese, you can stand for election here. With our help, you'd soon be at the top of the table. Until then, sit in the cabinet, or as it will shortly become, the Emergency Management Committee, as a special adviser. You've run a large public company, not to mention a large international … shall we say, organisation? You can handle Refalo and his friends – certainly, *we* can handle them for you." Natasha smiled grimly.

"Well, it's a very interesting idea, but frankly, I'm not one hundred per cent myself yet and I'm not comfortable with the recent arrests, Camp Azure, disappearing minsters and all that. And you went too far with Ray Farrugia – that'll blow back on you. It's all too heavy handed. You've already alienated the political class, now you're doing the same with ordinary citizens. You're losing the battle, Colonel. All that would have to change for me to be interested in your proposition."

"Over time, it will. Your forthright views are appreciated. They're what we need."

Marco could tell from the twist of the colonel's mouth that he did not really want to hear Natasha's views. He looked in amazement at his daughter, who seemed oblivious to the harshness of the criticism she had just dared to voice to the

Russian. Fedorov rolled his tongue around his mouth, a little tell of his that showed he was thinking hard. He looked at her with a deadpan expression on his face.

"The other thing we can do is rid you, once and for all, of any suspicion of involvement in those notorious murders in Milan ... the killing of your partners in the Family."

"Really? How on earth can you do that?"

"We've a Mafia contract killer under arrest already. It was an ill-advised attempt by the 'Ndrangheta to take over some Russian Mafia drug businesses. Gangland murder, gone wrong. They brought their feud to Moscow. Stupid of them. The man concerned is now in a camp in Norilsk, where his sort don't live long. In fact, in Norilsk nobody does.

"So, if you want those concerned to hear his confession to the murders of the three Wise Men, plus Salvatore Randazzo, you'd better tell me soon. We can provide your lawyers and the Anti-Mafia people in Rome with the officially obtained confession, but, of course, there's no question of extradition. And is there anybody else who's died and whose name we should add to the list of his victims? With any stain lifted from your reputation, you'd find yourself respected and welcomed once more by your peers in the international business community – something that would serve us, as well as you.

"I'll leave you to think about what I've said. Marco, thank you for your wonderful hospitality, it's been a most enjoyable evening."

After Colonel Fedorov had left the *castello*, Marco and Natasha slumped into a pair of the oiled teak armchairs in the new conservatory that Natasha had added to the rear terrace. Behind them, there was the slightest chinking of glasses, as Asano quietly finished clearing the table. Marco swirled another small brandy around his glass, while Natasha poured herself another glass of sparkling water.

Her head was spinning. She had been told by Dr Weber to avoid high-pressure and stressful environments but, increasingly, as her confidence returned, she was doubting the wisdom of the doctor's advice. And what was now on offer to her was remarkable. Notwithstanding the death of Tozzi and her father's vague assurance that it was unlikely she would be pursued by the prosecutors in Rome, the opportunity finally to rid herself of the shadow of prosecution for the Milan murders, which had hung over her for years, was extremely tempting. Although she would never admit it, in the early hours of the morning, when she should have been asleep, her thoughts occasionally led her to contemplate the horror of a lifetime of incarceration.

There was also another thought at the back of her mind. She could see the possibility of personal renewal, a chance of rejuvenation, the ability to rise back to where she belonged. The more the idea took shape, the more convinced she became that she was not someone who was ever going to be happy just sitting quietly, doing nothing. She had made a horrendous mistake in allowing herself to fall so low. All that wasted time, the self-loathing, the self-hatred, the weakness – that was simply not her.

Fedorov had offered her the chance of becoming the number one person in Malta. It did not really matter if, for now, the Russians were pulling the strings – nothing lasts forever. She smiled, pleased with the clarity of her thinking.

That fool of a doctor had had her weeping and sniffling, forcing her to see things not as they were, but as Laura Weber wanted her to see them. Natasha had been manipulated and fooled, made to feel diminished, guilty, exhausted and incapacitated. She had been tricked into seeing herself as a construct of someone else's agenda.

Throughout the treatment, she had been systematically stripped of her freedom and independence of thought. She saw that now. The medication had numbed her, making her thickheaded and stupid. The doctor had seen her pain and then imprisoned her and used the cloak of her profession to twist the knife deeper. For some reason, Laura Weber had set out to destroy her. That much was clear. Maybe it was to leave the way open for the doctor to start her dalliance with Natasha's father. He should have known better. In fact, he should have known better than to take his own child there in the first place.

Natasha felt the blood course through her veins. She felt alive, energised again. How many times in one life do you get the chance to wipe the slate clean and take a seat alongside the most powerful and influential people in the land? To redeem yourself. And that was just the beginning. There was also the Family, which had so unceremoniously kicked her out and abandoned her. This would prove to them she was back, as effective as ever, freed from the weight of her past actions. With all the legal threats removed, they could no longer use the argument that there had to be distance between them. There was no reason why she should not make a play to retake her seat.

Another thought had struck her earlier in the evening. Her father had spoken to her of a troublesome young clique of Family members who had christened themselves the Hussars and were making waves and challenging the hierarchy. He was particularly piqued that his chief of staff, Bernd Kruder's son, Leopold, was their leader. Perhaps they would benefit from some guidance, or even leadership? Maybe this was her route back to the top table in Château San Salvatore? She smiled inwardly. She was feeling so much better.

This whole train of thought lasted less than two minutes in real time. As Marco cradled the balloon of brandy, letting the vapours rise deep into his sinuses, Natasha said: "You know, I think I'll take the colonel up on his suggestion."

Off the back kitchen, there was a pantry. It was not a glorified cupboard, as most people would understand the word, but a small suite of rooms that Asano called his own. The main room had a buttoned futon bed on a tatami mat, with a neatly folded white futon, which was rolled up during the day and kept in a scrupulously clean alcove. A small wardrobe held Asano's summer collection of wide bleached cotton pants and white short-sleeved *haori* tops. In a lacquered trunk was an identical range of clothing, in black, for winter, plus a collection of dark quilted waistcoats and jackets to ward off the chill.

A low door led to Asano's own *kamidana*, best described as a small chapel, where he practised the Shinto religion. The *kamidana* shelf itself was set above eye level and held a range of holy scripts written on stiff card, circular mirrors, and receptacles to hold water and small token offerings of food.

It was in the privacy of his *kamidana*, behind a locked door, that Asano made a phone call later that evening, to recount what he had heard of the conversation between Colonel Fedorov, Marco and Natasha. He concluded by saying: "Yes, if hearing is correct, Miss Natasha said to Mr Marco she would work with the Russians to be *kaichou*, most senior person in government. Yes. I hope this is correct hearing.

"And, sorry to take time but, *shujin* – Mr Marco – was talking of a new faction in Family. Some young man, son of Bernd Kruder is leader, I think. Mr Marco say they cause him troubles. Thought you need to know. If not correct, I am sorry.

"Miss Natasha also receive offer of Russian prisoner to confess to all Italian murders, to clear her name and take away many problems. Think best to tell you."

The voice on the other end said: "Yes, Asano, all very interesting. Keep up the good work. Who was it who made her the offer of a place in government?"

"The Russian, Colonel Fedorov. He say all Maltese politicians no good. Miss Natasha is better."

"He's probably right. And was it the colonel who offered to arrange the confession?"

"Yes."

"Stay close to them, Asano. It looks like things are underway."

CHAPTER 38
THE RESISTANCE
FORTIFICATIONS, INTERPRETATION CENTRE, VALLETTA, MALTA

THE SALT WATERS were rising around Denzel's legs, as he dragged Silvia to her feet. He watched her grimacing in pain when she put weight on her damaged ankle.

"Listen, relax, the water's going to rise to the level of the harbour. Remember, we're at the level of the tunnel, which is obviously lower. Worst case, we'll just float up the stairs."

"If you say so. It hurts like hell. You'll have to help me."

He shouted up the stairs: "Adullah, come back and help! We've got to carry her."

Abdullah peered down from an intermediate landing. All he saw in the cone of light from his head torch was swirling black water rising up the stairs towards him.

"You promised me there would be none of the swimming! All I can see is the water, everywhere!"

By now, it was waist high, and Denzel and Silvia could not even see the foot of the stairs. They thrashed about in a flood that was thick with debris from the tunnel, until Abdullah's strong grip pulled them up onto the staircase. He had Silvia's arms around his neck and together they made the climb, half floating in the cloudy seawater. Once they were at the same height as the top of the cistern, the water level seemed to stabilise.

Abdullah was panting; fear forcing great gulps of air into his lungs, as he wrestled to control his instinct to flee. Then, the hard work started. Twenty minutes later, they were in the side storeroom, dripping wet and puffing. Silvia collapsed onto the floor.

"I can't get to the car. I just can't."

"Let me see what's going on outside," Denzel suggested.

He looked out of the door, up and down the street, confirming what he had hoped for.

"There's no one around. If they'd been told about the tunnel, all this area would be crawling by now. Do you think the guys that followed us are … you know, dead?"

Abdullah was jubilant, enthusiastically proclaiming: "Verily we belong to Allah, and truly to Him shall we return."

The streets were totally quiet but, across the waters, Manoel Island was lit with the glow of dozens of vehicles and the emergency lighting that had been erected to begin the recovery work on the mast.

It was getting light, and Denzel was worried that dragging a dripping wet and protesting Silvia through the streets to their transport would attract attention. He sighed, looked up and down the street and started running. He did not stop until he had reached his car. One or two vehicles passed him, but none slowed or seemed to pay him much attention. In twenty minutes, they were helping Silvia into the front passenger seat of the nondescript Fiat he had bought with fake ID and a bundle of euros, courtesy of the American government.

It was early in the afternoon by the time George arrived at the apartment in Siġġiewi. He parked around the rear of the block and nodded at the mechanic from the ground-floor flat, who lifted his head from under the bonnet of an old Toyota. Without a word being spoken, George went upstairs. Huck opened the door, bleary-eyed, holding a Glock 19 handgun, and told George that Denzel and Abdullah were in bed, asleep.

Huck looked up and down the staircase, holding the handgun behind him, and said: "Don't stand there, come in. Billy and I've got a bit going on just now and Den and Abby were pretty wiped when they got back. But it's all cool. A complete success."

"Does he let you call him *Abby*?"

Huck looked puzzled.

"Sure, why not?"

George put on some coffee and went to wake Denzel, who emerged a few minutes later in a T-shirt and joggers. He spoke to Billy.

"No problems?"

"Nope. One hundred percent success. Good job! The whole island's on The Strand to watch the fun."

He slid a laptop in front of Denzel, who pushed his hair away from his face and sat down in front of it. Online footage from a thousand mobiles showed images of the collapsed mast lying on the hillside of Manoel Island. On the promenade itself, and the Strand, the main road that ran to the north of Manoel Island, a mass of people had gathered, cheering and chanting 'Russians go home!' while waving home-made placards. Billy smiled.

"Yep, you created quite a stir!"

George gathered them together and told them the news of his appointment. Denzel looked concerned, but George smiled at Huck and Billy. As security professionals, they immediately saw the upside of the situation. Huck clapped him on the back. "We've got ourselves a double agent. Great news, George."

"It's not gonna be as easy as it sounds," Billy warned.

"They'll be watching you and what you do. You're gonna have to pull in some people. There's no way round it. The main thing is, you can protect this cell. That's the biggie." He looked over at Denzel.

"So, Den, you're gonna give George something on last night's job? Something that sets him up as an investigator; something that no one else has?"

George said: "That's exactly what I'm here to ask for. How did you do it?"

There was silence for a few moments. Then Denzel said: "Okay. There's a tunnel leading from the basement of the Fortifications Centre ... you know, the museum ... leading down to the ferry and then under the harbour and across to the Lazaretto on Manoel Island. I can give you that. You should go and do another search, now it's light, and 'find' the tunnel. I'll tell you exactly where it is. Oh, and divers might come across some body parts from the missing Russian soldiers, towards the museum end. Or they could be trapped under rocks or washed to the other end, I really don't know."

Everybody nodded except for George, who said in a shocked voice: "Body parts?"

While there was still a little daylight left, George and Karl Chelotti returned to Manoel Island. They made a big show of crawling all over the Lazaretto buildings, demanding ladders, torches and yellow marker tape to isolate areas of interest. Finally, they went into the courtyard and then the storeroom, where they photographed the scratch marks on the doors. Then, after another half hour, they emerged with wet feet, saying they had found a previously undiscovered, flooded tunnel, the door to which had recently been forced open.

Saying they were following up on an old case, the next morning they visited the cistern in the Fortifications Interpretation Centre, with the museum's director, only to find it flooded. This was a shock to all concerned, particularly the director, who swore the cistern had always been dry in all the years he had been involved with the building. Chelotti found part of a severed arm, washed up on the bottom steps, and held it aloft. It was encased in a sleeve that could have been part of a Russian uniform and a Russian watch still encircled the wrist.

It only took another day for divers to fully explore the passageway and bag a variety of human body parts, found floating around at the museum end. They also discovered a recent disturbance to the seabed in the harbour, allowing them to conclude that an upward force had created a fissure, causing seawater to flood the ancient tunnel.

All this enabled the newly formed Home Security Command to report to Colonel Fedorov that the terrorists had entered via the museum and left the same way, while being chased by three members of the Russian Military Police. Once out of the tunnel, the terrorists had let off a charge, possibly the same TNT explosive they had used on the mast, which blew a hole in the tunnel roof, causing it to flood. The blast had immediately killed the three pursuing Russians.

When questioned about what had led George to the discovery of the tunnel, he said that a thorough police search had revealed the entrance on the island and he then remembered hearing rumours of a tunnel, dug by the Knights, under St Andrew's Bastion and extending under the harbour as far as Manoel Island. He had been curious as to where the newly discovered tunnel on the island emerged and it seemed possible there might be some truth in the old story. He and the director of the museum had gone down to the cistern, to see if there might be a link from the museum to the foundations of the bastion and discovered a doorway leading down to the tunnel.

Fedorov said: "Very professional, George. Well done. Now

we know the how, we can guess the why. We just need to know who did this."

"I'm afraid, at the moment, we've got no idea."

"That doesn't surprise me. But we're playing a long game, Assistant Commissioner. The case will remain open until the offenders are caught. As I'm sure they will be."

CHAPTER 39
MARCO BONNICI
CHÂTEAU SAN SALVATORE, LAKE LUGANO, SWITZERLAND

MARCO HAD STAYED with Natasha for well over six weeks after their return from Bern. He had seen it as his duty to remain with her and ensure she had the best chance of returning to health. To his surprise, they had had a pleasant time together. They had walked along the cliff tops on the western side of the island, dined out in Valletta's better restaurants, and Natasha had hired a personal trainer, who came to the *castello* three times a week.

He had been amazed by how fast she seemed to have recovered. Natasha remained on a low dose of anti-psychotic medication, but all her counselling and other support had come to an end when she had left the clinic. The point came when Marco realised that he had to return to Switzerland for a brief time, to deal with some business issues within the Family. He felt confident enough to tell Natasha he was leaving to spend a few days at the new headquarters on Lake Lugano, and she seemed completely unfazed by the news.

Since the destruction of the *Croce Bianca* in Milan, the Family had lost its spiritual home. The management committee was struggling to come to terms with the new, more utilitarian setting of the former seminary and hotel, despite its idyllic location on the Swiss side of Lake Lugano. As part of the deal with the Direzione Nazionale Anti-Mafia in Rome, the Family had restricted its activities and divested itself of all public investments. That meant there was little for the committee to do, and its members were becoming restless and troublesome, squabbling among themselves.

Marco had gathered them together to remind them that, despite the loss of their treasured palazzo in Milan, they remained at liberty, their substantial assets untouched and their reputations unsullied. All of those things had been at risk, primarily because of the attention Natasha and Hakan Toprak had attracted with their dealings in the energy markets. Toprak had positions within the Turkish intelligence organisation, the *Milli İstihbarat Teşkilatı*, as well as the secular, pro-European Turkish government, and was its chief fixer, operating on a long leash. Such was his autonomy, he had been able to combine his official duties with being Natasha's lover and partner, sitting at the head of the Family, where he had skilfully ensured all parties benefited from his activities. Seeing the net closing around Natasha, he had not only ended their relationship, but also secretively acquired a substantial portion of the Family's public investments, allowing Marco to take the organisation out of the limelight and back into the shadows.

As part of the change of direction towards respectable undertakings, Marco had suggested the Family should embark on a new project – the acquisition of works by Italian Old Masters, such as Botticelli, Titian, Tintoretto, Leonardo even. He envisaged one day going beyond paintings and sculptures, suggesting the creation of another library, focusing on rare books and manuscripts, to rival the American University libraries or the Bodleian in Oxford. Such collections were not just marvellous investments but would put the Family back where it belonged as a cultural force within the European aristocracy. There was a short debate, and an initial fund was agreed to start what they all knew would take several generations to accomplish. The Family had been around for a very long time and Marco did not see that changing. He had given this generation the chance to create their own legacy.

More to the point, Marco had noticed that the faction of younger, more restless members, who had formed a splinter group, were calling themselves the Hussars. Historically, the Hussars had been an ostentatiously dressed and prestigious branch of the nineteenth-century Polish calvary, drawing on Central Europe's young nobility to fill their ranks. The fact that the junior members of the Family had chosen that name spoke to a state of mind that had caught Marco's attention.

It was obvious to him that the young men would not be fobbed off with such distractions as curating an art collection. Enquiries revealed their minds were filled with thoughts of avenging the destruction of the Croce Bianca, leveraging the wealth of the Family through a series of higher-risk business investments, and developing links with 'other groups' who could protect the Family from any future humiliations, such as the one they had recently suffered.

Marco had spoken to Bernd Kruder's son, Leopold, and had been surprised by the tone of their encounter. Leopold had his father's arrogance – unsurprisingly, given his privileged upbringing – that stemmed from an unshakable belief in the natural superiority of the old Austrian nobility. One morning, sitting on the terrace of the Château San Salvatore, Marco had asked him to talk about the Hussars and what they were trying to achieve.

"Well, Marco … I can call you that, can I? Or would you prefer 'sir'?" Leopold's supercilious expression was enough for Marco to take a thorough dislike to him. "You ask what we are about? I can tell you what we are *not* about – and that is sitting on our hands, doing nothing, until we are past our prime and a bunch of old men. *That* is most definitely not us." Marco raised his eyebrows.

"Interesting. Well, what are you then?"

"The Hussars stand for all the old values: courage, honour, camaraderie, individuality yet loyalty to the common cause. We want the Family to be what it once was. Not like it is today, hiding in the shadows, ashamed of itself."

Marco nodded along, trying to get a sense of how concerned he should be by this development.

"Well," he said, "we welcome energy, lively minds and new opinions – that is how organisations develop. But remember, Leo – and tell this to your friends, too – loyalty means loyalty to the whole Family, not just to the Hussars. Make your contribution, leave your mark, as is expected, but do not overstep. Remember – the Family is bigger than all of us."

"Are you threatening us, Marco?"

"No, Leo, far from it. Why would you think that? I am just trying to make sure we operate collectively and openly. These are our core values. I do not like factionalism within the Family, it is destructive. So, please, tell your friends not to give me any cause for concern."

The boy had haughtily pushed his chair back and strutted off, without giving any other response. Marco left the conversation feeling unsettled. It had not gone the way he had wanted it to. He sensed the suppressed hostility within the younger members and resolved to speak to Leo's father, Bernd, as soon as he had the chance.

After his business meetings, Marco had taken Laura to the botanical gardens at Parco Sherrer, on the southern tip of the peninsula, where they could look across the shimmering waters of Lake Lugano, onto the heavily wooded hillsides of the Italian side of the lake. They sat amongst the lemon trees and bamboo groves of the hillside villa, surrounded by classical statuary. It was the end of summer and the autumn winds that blew down from the Alps had yet to arrive. It was still warm enough to sit and enjoy the fragrant perfume of the lemons, which hung heavily around them. With Laura at his side, Marco thought this was as near to perfection as he could hope for.

He was in the mood to share confidences and had given her an edited version of the Family's history and how the Bonnicis fitted within it, including his own role as the head of the organisation.

"So, you see, we, or rather I, have to balance the established aims and traditions of the Family against the short-term ambitions of those who only have one lifetime in which to make a legacy. It is not easy to exert patience and think across the generations, when our world lives increasingly in the present. Hence my idea of replacing at least some of the antique treasures that were destroyed in Milan. It is a chance to create a heritage, to be assured of remembrance in the future."

Laura immediately understood the wisdom of the decision and said: "If you have all the money you need, and creating more is not a challenge, then most people *do* start to think about their legacy. Giving the members the opportunity to create their own is a smart move. It prevents their lives from becoming devoid of meaning and indulges their need for external regard. The super rich are impossibly vain. But not everybody will be happy with your scheme. I suppose there will be those who crave the stimulus of a competitive environment, for its own sake. To assert ego, achieve power, test themselves against others. These are not passive types you are dealing with, and you should beware of them."

"Sometimes, I think they are more like a bunch of children: self-centred, demanding, precious, and often downright annoying."

"That is why they asked you back to lead them. Even if they are intelligent, well educated, well bred – emotionally, the rich can be selfish, isolated, at odds with empathy and compassion, narcissistic and totally lost. All the things that you are not, Marco. In many ways, their emotional problems can be more severe than those of the poor."

"Hmm, all too true. But those people, I understand. There is also a group that I do not. They are a new problem. A group of young blades who appropriately call themselves the Hussars! Can you believe it? Their collective personality revealed by their choice of name! They are young, all fired up, wanting action, and have started pushing for change, at the very time I am trying to calm things down. They make me feel old!" Laura laughed.

"Is it really so difficult to understand such a clash of perspectives? It happens in all organisations. Let me guess – they advocate organisational agility, quick decision making, disruption, new thinking and experimentation. Your committee, including you, favour stability, tradition, conservatism, ways of doing things that have always served you well. Come on! Don't tell me you have not seen this before? Remember, you were young once. I don't know what you are worried about. You have to cut them some slack – let them spread their wings – otherwise, there will be trouble." He put his arm around her.

"That is why I like being with you. You think so clearly." Laura smiled.

"I hope there are other reasons." She watched a tourist boat plough its way across the lake beneath them, its wake forming a latticed fan. "It is good to be with you again, but you know, I nearly did not come."

"Why on earth not?" He was shocked.

"Natasha, of course. I do not see how I can be part of your life, having been her doctor. The conflict of interest runs too deep."

"Well, she is much better now. You would be amazed."

"I am, but not for the reasons you think. I should not really talk about this with you, it is unethical and unfair, but I worry about the speed of her recovery. She was an extremely sick woman and one who only partly embraced the treatment options she was offered. I said before – I think she did the bare minimum to persuade us she had recovered and, when things were not moving at the speed she wanted them to, she manipulated Wilhelm into a position that guaranteed her removal from the clinic.

"And before you say anything – yes, he was totally in the wrong to fall for it and has been dismissed without references. But the incident illustrated for me what a ruthless manipulator your daughter is, which no doubt is why she was so successful in the business world."

They sat in silence for a moment. Marco could tell Laura was wrestling with whether to say more. She clasped her hands together and he felt her body stiffen.

"Listen, I hate myself for saying this, but I would hate myself even more if I did not and then something happened."

"Something happened? I am not sure I know what you mean."

"To you. I worry about something happening to you. And I would worry for myself, if I were ever to become a serious part of your life. I believe Natasha suffers from delusional jealousy and that you are part of that pathological condition. She fears losing you and reacts against anyone who threatens her possession of you."

Marco shifted uncomfortably in his chair, remembering the marble steps stained by rivulets of crimson blood, the torment on Sophia's face, as she and the baby lost their grip on life. Laura continued speaking.

"It fits with Natasha's narcissistic traits. Narcissists talk a good game, but actually have very low self-worth and self-esteem. This imperfect sense of self naturally makes it extremely easy for them to become jealous – very jealous.

"I should not say this, but I believe Natasha's real or perceived rejection by everyone close to her: her mother dying in front of her, you leaving her, the Family not taking her seriously, her lovers further diminishing her self-worth, particularly the Turkish guy, and no doubt other events which you either have not told me about, or of which you are unaware, all conspired to provoke the catastrophic psychotic episode that led to where we are today.

"I am sorry, I did not mean to reveal that, but it is my professional judgement that is urging me to speak to you about it. Natasha has *not* recovered, I can guarantee that, because all those issues remain unaddressed. Until they are, I believe you would be safer away from her.

"I think you should return to Serbia, to a life where you were happy. And do it as soon as you can. Natasha is a destructive force. She has killed on several occasions and appears to feel little or no remorse. I know she is your daughter, but she frightens me.

"Call me a coward, but I would hesitate to meet you in Malta, much as I would like to and, the truth is, I would be reluctant to meet Natasha again, unless it is in a purely professional capacity. I am so sorry, but I thought you should know where I stand, both as a doctor and as someone who would love to be close to you."

Marco was stunned, but not surprised. There was little Laura had said that he could argue with. He turned away from her, frowning, wondering when everything had gone so horribly wrong with his child and whether it had all been his fault.

CHAPTER 40
ARTICLE IN THE MALTA TELEGRAPH

Reporter: Justin Galea

Date: 2 September 2025

President Makes Proclamation of State of Public Emergency

The president has today proclaimed that a State of Public Emergency will commence with immediate effect. Speaking from the presidential palace, he said the government would be seeking a resolution of the House of Representatives, declaring that democratic institutions in Malta are threatened by subversion.

This proclamation follows a statement from the office of the prime minister earlier today, claiming a significant attack on the island's communication system on Manoel Island two nights ago was aimed at causing chaos and subverting the disciplined forces of Malta.

The communications mast in question was a tool of the Russian military, allowing its land and naval forces to integrate their systems and communications with those of the Maltese military and police.

There have been no arrests, and no group has claimed responsibility for the attack.

This declaration means that all the fundamental rights and freedoms of each one of us have been suspended and replaced by the rules and regulations of the police and/or the military.

This newspaper has already received notice that, as of today, all newspaper copy, of whatever publication, must be vetted by the Ministry of Home Affairs, before it can be printed and circulated to the public. This is what we can now expect from this regime! This is censorship! This is undemocratic! This is state capture!

CHAPTER 41
ABDULLAH BELKACEM
BIRKIRKARA, MALTA

It was Billy who had to break the news to Abdullah, who was outside on the narrow balcony smoking a rolled-up cigarette. Huck and Billy had begged him to keep the windows shut and the curtains drawn, but Abdullah was feeling the strain of their long days of inactivity. When Huck went to fetch him, Abdullah thought he was about to receive another reprimand.

"Do not start with the telling off again! All I do is stand and look at the sky, the scrubland and the white houses. It remembers my home. If you want to sit in this cave all day and play computers, that is good. Me? I need to breathe!"

"But, dude, someone might see and wonder, who is this guy?"

"People do not think like this. They look at me and think: there is an Arab having a cigarette. So what?"

"Forget about it. Come in, we need to talk. Listen, dude, you're not gonna like it, but you've got some trouble back home."

Denzel was sitting on the kitchen unit, while Huck was at the dining table, on his laptop. Abdullah threw himself onto the sofa.

"What trouble is this?"

"There's been a flood, dude. A disaster. Thousands dead. People washed away into the sea, like Derna last year. A dam burst and flattened half the town. General Boutros is blaming Tripoli and Tripoli's blaming the rebels. The dam's been busted for years, and nobody got round to fixing it, so ... anyway, it's a shit show. It's chaos, and chaos means trouble.

"A hundred Russian volunteers have arrived in Marsabar and are holed up in the university. Our guess is they're planning to take advantage of the disaster and make a move on the refinery. Your guys've had a couple of small firefights, but they've pulled back."

"Yes, my son has told me of this. He says they have given the Russian dogs much kicking!"

"I'm not sure you're getting the whole story. We need you back there, Abby – with *you* kicking ass! Control says having you back there's more important than you sitting around here, smoking an' gettin' a sore butt."

Abdullah closed his eyes and tilted his head upwards. He held his arms apart, opening his palms. He muttered a short prayer under his breath, then walked back towards the window, lighting and smoking another cigarette. Finally, he turned to face them and said: "Allah protects my family and my people from all calamities. But sometimes Allah expects a little help. If Allah wills it, I must return to my home. Denzel, you will forgive me in this?"

Denzel nodded and banged a clenched fist against his heart. Abdullah continued:

"Tell George it breaks my heart to leave work unfinished. But we have started it, Denzel. Have faith, Allah willing, you will kick the Russians back to the stinking pit that is their home. *Inshallah!*"

The next day, Abdullah was due at the airport for the evening flight to Tunis, where Jamal would meet him and smuggle him back into Libya, across the closed border. With some time to kill, he took the bus to Birkirkara with half a mind to try and catch George at lunchtime. Walking up the high street, he saw the ironmonger's shop he had bought when he had first arrived in Malta some ten years earlier. He had managed it and lived in the flat upstairs, until the Americans had come knocking, asking him to lead a militia to protect the oil and gas installations of western Libya from the threat of ISin-Libya and the Russian- and Egyptian-backed army of General Boutros.

He could not resist a look inside and was gratified to see it was still the same jumble of plastic guttering, lengths of timber and racks of fixings and tools it always had been. The top shelf behind the counter still had the half dozen, hugely expensive security locks that he had bought from a crooked salesman, who had promised him they were his bestselling line. When the young Maltese owner saw him looking at them, he hopefully asked if he should get one down. Abdullah laughed.

"By my beard, you will need the favour of Almighty Allah to sell those locks. If not, they will still be here on Judgement Day!"

He left the shop and made his way to George's non-descript front door. He gently rapped on the wooden panel and, before long, heard the flapping of sandals down the corridor. A key turned and a bolt shifted, then Marianna's head popped around the door.

She did not say a word but glanced up and down the street, in case his presence at her door had been noticed by the neighbours. Finally, she stood back and held the door open so he could enter. For a moment, they stood in the hall looking at each other. Marianna did not budge.

"*Salam*, Marianna." He smiled at her stern expression. "You know, our Prophet, may peace be upon Him, says there is no good in the one who is not hospitable. So, can I come into your kitchen and see the new grandson? I was much pleased to hear George was a *jadd*."

Marianna broke her silence.

"A *jadd*? What's that? I'm sure I've heard him called worse. You'd better come in." Reluctantly, she stepped aside.

Gina was sitting on the sofa, eyes wide open, fearful that the terrible Abdullah had shown up and here they were, totally unprotected by any able-bodied man. Baby Joseph was alongside her, asleep, a sticky red substance around his mouth.

Abdullah came into the room and grinned, showing the best of his uneven, yellowing teeth and receding gums.

"Ah, the beautiful Gina and Joseph. I was many times happy to hear your news. I said to my wife, Rania: *George's daughter will make a wonderful mother.* You are kind and generous, and full of love. Indeed, the infant has been blessed with the best of mothers!" He tapped the side of his nose. "I can tell these things!"

Gina smiled coyly and primped her hair.

Marianna made a strange noise and folded her arms under her bosom.

"I was pleased that you named him after the father of your prophet – it can only bring him good fortune."

"The father of the prophet? No, Joseph is Giorgio's father's name. He's called Joe Mifsud, the butcher." Abdullah frowned.

"No matter. I bring small gifts." He pulled a multi-coloured ball out of his bag and laid it next to the sleeping baby Then a box of *imqaret*, the luscious date-filled pastries George was so fond of.

Marianna scolded: "Well, the boy's not playing with that inside the house!"

Then she capitulated, leaning across and taking a pastry.

"Thank you, Abdullah, that is very kind of you." She looked at the battered cabin case he kept close to his feet. "I suppose you've come to see George? Are you leaving?"

"Yes, I have done my helping, and all is well, but now I must return. I have my own work back home. I would much like to see my friend, George, before I leave – do you have telephone for him?"

Marianna rang George's mobile. He did not answer, and the leave-a-message tone beeped.

"George, George? Can you hear me? Don't you pretend you can't!" She turned to Abdullah. "He always does this – thinks I don't know! I've got Abdullah in the kitchen and he's going to Liberia. He wants to say goodbye. George?" He picked up the call.

"Hello, Marianna, yes, yes, it's me. Just ... why's he going to
Liberia?"

"I don't know, I'll pass you over."

Marianna watched a huge smile spread across Abdullah's face.

"Ah, my friend, it is good to hear your voice ... No, I do not go to Liberia ... I go home ... yes, there is some little trouble ... I will fight the Russians in Marsabar and you and Den fight them here. They can never win if we do that ... yes, yes ..."

Marianna glared at Abdullah and shouted from the kitchen chair: "George! You listen to me! You and Den are *not* fighting anybody. No good comes from it!"

Abduallah glanced at her and spoke to George.

"... yes, yes, the lady wife is not liking the talk of fighting. For now, I say farewell, but we will meet again soon, my friend. Remember our promise to each other... in Libya, yes ... I told Rania. She is much excited and much looking forward to meeting the lady ... no, no, I know, between you and me ... she is already waiting, and she will cook her lamb. Yes ... it is mighty fine! Farewell!"

Abdullah handed the phone back to Marianna. There were tears in his eyes.

"I love him like a brother."

She muttered: "Hmmm. George already has a brother, and I think one's quite enough."

Gina asked Abdullah if he would like some tea. He nodded, sniffed and wiped his long, crooked nose on this sleeve. Marianna turned to Gina and rolled her eyes. While the kettle boiled, he chatted about Denzel and reassured the women that the boy was well and a credit to the family. He started telling stories about George's experiences in Libya and how he had inadvertently sunk the Hellenic Navy's patrol boat in Gavdos, which elicited gasps and, finally, smiles. Try as she might, Marianna could not resist her guest's humour and easy charm. Soon, she and Gina were giggling at Abdullah's stories. He recounted the first time he and George met, when George had saved his life during the firefight in the Vai Vai Café. Afterwards, he had noticed, to his surprise, this "brave warrior" was wearing women's cat's eyes sunglasses, which George thought suited him handsomely. He had been duped into buying them at the market, in Tripoli.

Eventually, Baby Joseph caught the scent of the sweet pastries and woke, immediately starting to grab at the box. Abdullah bounced him around, let him tug on his long grey beard and fed him chunks of the sweets. Finally, it was time for the visitor to leave. He kissed the women and pinched Baby Joseph's cheek, leaving a pink imprint.

Marianna said: "It's a shame George was not here to see you. He'll be disappointed, but at least you managed to speak to him. He's very fond of you ... for some reason."

Abdullah looked wistful, saying: "George will not mind; he knows we have a friendship that cannot be told or written of. I am a lucky man that Allah has blessed me so. Tell him those words when he returns."

As the door closed and Abdullah disappeared down the street, pulling his wheelie case, Gina said: "Awww! He's nice."

Her mother replied: "Don't be fooled, he's a terrible man."

CHAPTER 42
THE RESISTANCE
ABOARD THE JEWEL OF THE ISLANDS, GRAND HARBOUR, MALTA

It was rare for Billy, Huck or Denzel to leave the apartment, but recently Denzel had become aware that the Americans had been disappearing for hours on end, in the early hours of the morning. They refused to tell him what they were doing, saying all would become clear at the right time.

Finally, one afternoon, Huck told him to go and 'lay up' for a while, so he would be good and fresh to join them later that evening to help them in planning the next mission. It was after midnight when the three of them got into a Ford Transit van and drove to the rough end of the Grand Harbour, where the disused warehouses and greasy wharfs formed a backdrop to old ships awaiting their last, sad journey to the breaker's yard. There was nothing worth stealing in the area, so it was totally deserted.

As they made their way towards the site of the now demolished power station, the van's headlights disturbed a group of feral dogs that were picking at something lying in the shadows of a high stone wall. Denzel watched a large rat scurry along the quayside, until it ducked over the side of the wharf, to escape the glare of the headlights. Billy drove and Huck peered out of the passenger window, glancing down at his phone occasionally.

"Wait up! Here she is. Wow ... What a beauty."

Huck was pointing to a small coastal freighter that listed against the side of the wharf. The heavy irony raised a ripple of laughter. Even under the thin yellow light that came across the water from the Sicily catamaran terminal, they could see the impact of years of neglect on the little ship. Above, the vessel's waterline had once been black, but streaks of rust ran like tears down its sides. Although secured against the concrete pillars, the empty craft sat high in the water, showing a skirt of peeling, red anti-fouling paint, flecked with dried weed and barnacles. Billy parked the van on the opposite side of the road, tucked into a piece of derelict land between two limestone warehouses.

"Okay," he said. "No lights, no noise, no calling out. We don't want any attention. We've got fifteen minutes before our guest arrives. Let's go on board and get this deck set up."

Huck was an ex-Navy Seal and no stranger to working aboard ships. He immediately found the deck control panel. There was a banging from below, as a diesel generator, which Billy had fuelled and serviced the preceding night, fired up, and a clank, as a small deck crane jolted into life. Huck had disappeared below through a bulkhead door, gesturing for Denzel to follow him.

Denzel nodded and joined him in a foul-smelling corridor, where the stench of stagnant water and rotting seaweed filled the cavities in his head.

"Okay, time to tell me what the hell's going on?"

"Here's the deal. We've got a friend of ours arriving with a truck in ..." he glanced at his watch "... fifteen minutes. We need to raise the hatch covers to give us access to the hold. There's a hydraulic power unit, controlled from a box somewhere. Billy'll find it. The hatch covers move on rollers along a track and tip onto a stowage rack. We've greased 'em an all, but it's still gonna make a noise. Can't be helped.

"Okay, the truck's bringing us three crates up from the Freeport, each one's about eight or nine metres long. We'll get them off the wagon using its tail lift, then use this deck crane to stow 'em in the hold. That's tonight's work done." Denzel was curious.

"What's in the crates and whose ship is this?"

Huck said over his shoulder: "You'll soon find out what's in the crates. And the ship? *The Jewel of the Islands* is the latest, and probably the cheapest ever, addition to the United States Navy. I mean, not that any registration records'll show that. The only things that work on this tub are the hydraulics on the hatches, that deck crane and those items we've fixed. The rest's junk. Even the john's busted. Come with me."

By the light of their pen torches, Huck and Denzel cautiously worked their way down steep companionways towards the hold area, stepping over piles of rubbish and abandoned clothing. The ship had a heavy, pungent, musky stench.

"Phew, that's a strong smell of rat piss," Huck observed.

Denzel gagged.

Eventually, they found the heavy bulkhead door that led into the hold. Billy had located the power supply and opened the covers that had folded noisily into one another and stacked themselves neatly upright, at the stern end of the hold. When they opened the door, such light as there was over the harbour turned the open space into a grey box. Above them, isolated stars shone in the black night sky. In one corner of the hold was a pile of brand-new work tools and collapsible workbenches.

"I hear you're into motor bikes?" Huck said to Denzel.

"Well, I used to be, until I nearly killed myself on the Coast Road a few years ago. Now, I've got myself a car."

"Okay, but you're handy with a tool kit?"

"Yeah, I'd say so."

"Good. We've got some work coming our way over the next week or so – it'd be good to have extra hands."

They heard the clanking of the deck crane as it started to move above them. Billy's head appeared, looking down into the hold.

"Okay down there? The truck's here. Five minutes and the first load'll be on its way."

Two hours later, the ship was sealed up, with some serious but discreetly placed locks securing the hatches and doorways. Some small CCTV cameras, connected to motion detectors, covered the corridors and the deck hatches, and were linked to Huck's phone. Satisfied the load was safely in the hold and as secure as it could be, they climbed back into the van and returned to the apartment.

CHAPTER 43
NATASHA BONNICI
OFFICE OF THE PRIME MINISTER, VALLETTA, MALTA

Two weeks after the dinner with Fedorov, Natasha was walking up the steps into Castille, brandishing a new security pass, giving her entry to the prime minister's official office. She was led to the cabinet room, where the Emergency Management Committee was holding its first meeting. She walked into the room and plonked her soft calfskin folder onto the table between Colonel Fedorov and Prime Minister Refalo. The prime minister's face was a picture. Nobody had told him his former boss from MalTech would be joining them.

She smiled at him and said: "Be a darling, Edward – shove up and fetch a lady a chair, would you?"

He had little option but to comply. As he rose to bring a chair from lower down the table, she pushed his further away, positioning herself directly to Fedorov's right hand, effectively demoting Refalo.

Fedorov looked on, mildly entertained. Admiral Berezovsky hauled himself out of his chair and extended a beefy paw. Natasha held it for a second, bowing her head slightly. Ambassador Buzilov stood erect and bowed from the waist, before offering her his hand. Natasha turned to Fedorov and observed, "I know George, of course. He and I are old and trusted friends, aren't we, George?" she added pointedly. "As for Ms Baldacchino, we haven't met, but I'm sure we will become close colleagues."

Fedorov explained, with a touch of sarcasm in his voice, "Police Commissioner Mallia sends his apologies; he has a painful and persistent stomach bug. Such a recurring ailment must be most distressing. I'll send him a note saying how much we miss his contribution and wishing him a speedy recovery."

The committee dragged on late into the afternoon. They discussed the attack on the mast and George's report on the tunnels. He wanted to demonstrate he had acted decisively, so had rounded up six junior police officers he knew were involved in a cigarette-smuggling ring and were also known for their idleness and general dishonesty.

He proudly told the committee: "*Mela*, we broke up this highly organised and dangerous ring of activists, hiding in plain sight, within police ranks. All have been taken to Camp Azure where they'll be questioned. I feel sure they know more than they were letting on. I've got an instinct for these things." The ambassador grinned, showing prominent incisors.

"An instinct? How interesting. Do you have everything you need for enhanced interrogation?" George was confused.

"Enhanced interrogation, George. You understand me? It is the only way to loosen tongues."

"Absolutely, Ambassador, we will ask them the sternest questions."

Fedorov said: "Grigori, I'll have a chat with George. There's a chap on the *Putin* who has experience of this sort of thing. Used to be a dentist. Doesn't need much equipment but gets excellent results."

George still did not understand.

"I don't think we need worry about that – no one's complained of toothache."

The Russians laughed. The admiral slapped his slab of a hand down on the table.

"Hah, toothache ... that's a good one, George. I like you!"

As the meeting ended, Natasha walked out with him and they stood on the steps of Castille, watching the crowd in the square looking up at them. George could not truthfully say he was pleased to see Natasha Bonnici again. Instead, he said hesitantly: "I was surprised to see you walk in. I mean, especially after the last time I saw you. What's your interest in all this?"

She looked older than he remembered her, more lines around her eyes, which seemed to have sunk into her head. She was thinner, her plain black trouser suit having been altered to fit her new body shape.

"I was invited, George, and my interest is that these people have waltzed in and taken over our island. I find it all a little strange, don't you?"

"Well, frankly, yes, although you've got to be careful what you say these days."

"What? Or you'll arrest me, now you're in charge of Home Security?" She looked George up and down. He had put on a little weight, but then again, he had never been trim. His hair was thinner, and she always imagined him to be taller than he was. She had known George for many years, but still could not say she had the measure of him. It was easy to dismiss him as a fool but, sometimes, he had the ability to pull off the biggest surprises.

"You're going to have to be careful, George. You're playing with fire, getting involved with those three. They're bad boys and, if they think you're messing them around ... well, I dread to think what they might do."

"*Mela*, I'm not. Messing them around, I mean."

"Don't con a conner, George. That bullshit about pulling in six bad apples and calling them *activists*? If I can tell it's rubbish, I'm sure they can too."

George looked sheepish.

"I didn't ask for this job. I don't even want to be here. I don't even know how it all happened. First Gerald died, then the Commissioner himself resigned and *he's* now being held aboard one of their ships. Then Mallia steps up ... well, enough said. So that left me!"

"Poor George. All that worry and responsibility and I bet you haven't even asked for a pay rise?"

He thought for a moment. It had never occurred to him.

"A pay rise?"

"Don't go repeating my own words back to me, it really gets on my nerves."

George's expression changed. as he addressed a serious subject.

"Anyway, the last time we met ..."

"Yes, at the Sliema Tower? I was injured. That madwoman with Savi assaulted me, stabbing me with knitting needles, and you didn't offer to help. I haven't forgotten. I needed police assistance and medical treatment, and you just left me."

"Police assistance?"

"George, you're repeating my words at me, again!"

"Sorry. But you made threats to kill and unlawfully discharged a gun in a public place. You resisted arrest, then ran off! I didn't *leave you*."

"What're you talking about: *unlawfully discharged a gun in a public place*? There's no such offence. Maybe there should be, but I've never heard of it. I certainly was unlawfully in *possession* of a gun, and I *did* make threats to kill Savi Azzopardi. In fact, I deeply regret that I didn't, but so what? What're you going to do about it? Tell my new friend, the colonel, you've arrested me? Or just send me to Camp Azure? It must be getting a bit full by now. My point is, we need to be friends here, George. It's us against them, that's how I see it."

He was not at all sure that was how he saw it.

CHAPTER 44
NATASHA BONNICI
CAFÉ CENTRAL, VIENNA, AUSTRIA

Natasha decided there was no time to waste, so she told Marco she was in the mood to spread her wings a little and take a weekend break to Bad Gastein in the Austrian Alps. There were thermal baths, and she said she might have a trip up into the high mountains, if the weather allowed. Marco suggested she take Asano with her, but the look on her face made him laugh out loud.

"Well, maybe not! I just thought …"

"Yes, you just thought you'd send your snitch along … no! If you must know, I've booked the Miramonte. It's got thermal baths and treatment rooms, so I'll probably end up relaxing in the spa."

Marco was pleased to see that Natasha was confident enough to make the trip and raised his hands in surrender.

"Well, you are supposed to be taking it easy. You are still not one hundred percent better, you know."

"So you keep telling me. I feel fine and I'm getting seriously bored."

That weekend, she made sure she left her boarding pass for a Salzburg flight in plain view, together with some Googled printouts of the Miramonte Hotel. Then she boarded a plane for Vienna.

Four hours after leaving Castello Bonnici, Natasha was inside the Palais Florentine, a Renaissance-style mansion that once housed the National Bank of Austria and the Stock Exchange but was now more famous for the stylish coffee house on its ground floor. It was here she had arranged to meet Leopold Kruder, leader of the so-called Hussars. She was becoming angry. He was fifteen minutes late and the small cup of perfectly made coffee she had ordered was sitting on the marble tabletop empty, except for the layer of rich dark foam that clung to the shining white porcelain cup with its rim of twenty-four-carat gold.

She sat sideways on to the entrance, so she could keep the door in her peripheral vision, and finally saw him enter. He was tall, lean and particularly good looking. He wore a navy blue suit, which he buttoned as he entered the café. He had the sort of easy confidence that stopped just short of swagger and stemmed from generations of wealth and entitlement. His thick, wavy, light brown hair was fashionably long and parted to one side, to flop over his brow. He saw Natasha immediately and presented himself at the table, with a supercilious smile and a curt bow.

"Miss Bonnici, my apologies. I see you have already had coffee. Can I get you another?"

He unbuttoned his jacket and sat facing her, hands clasped on the table. There was no chitchat. She smiled at the boy's self-assurance. How dare he keep her waiting, then swan in as if he owned the place?

"No more coffee, thank you, Leo. A sparkling water will be fine."

He casually looked around the café.

"You know, Trotsky and Freud probably sat where you are sitting now. Idiots, of course, both of them!"

"Well, if they did, I hope it wasn't at the same time." He

smiled at her little joke, but there was no humour in his expression.

"You probably don't know, but we own this place."

"Really? Who's we?"

"The Family. So that certainly includes me, but maybe *not* you these days? It is tied up in a portfolio of property assets somewhere."

Natasha drew breath sharply and stayed silent. She was taking a strong dislike to this precocious boy.

"You know my father hates you with every fibre of his being? Not only does he accuse you of the murder of his best friend, Wolfram Schober, but also that of Phillipp Von Wernberger, when you blew up the Croce Bianca. Another good friend of his." Leopold paused, sitting back and crossing his long legs, adjusting the crease in his trousers. Looking at her down his nose, he added: "I only went to the club once; it was the most important day of my life. And you destroyed it."

"I'm not here to argue about the past, Leo. Although, yes, I was involved in the deaths of the Wise Men, just look at the wealth I managed to generate, once I shook the Family out of its casual, sleepy, conservative mindset! You should thank me. Then, your father and his lily-livered friends got scared and threw it all away. That was *your* future they destroyed – not mine. And, for the record, I had no involvement in the destruction of the Croce Bianca. Frankly, I don't care whether you believe me or not – it's just a fact."

Leo Kruder shifted in his chair. She knew she had touched a nerve and continued her pitch.

"So, I'm interested in the Hussars. From what I hear, we have common ground. We believe the money in the Family should work harder. We don't want to see our best years wasted, sniffing round antique shops, hoping to build a legacy of gloomy paintings and Chinese pots. I think you recognise the limitations of the Family's 'old guard' and their inability to thrive in the modern world. You're like me – you think they're spineless, talentless, lazy and, more to the point, frightened. Frightened of change. Frightened of risk. They've retreated. Left the battlefield. They sit on their padded arses, doing nothing, weeping and wailing about the loss of the Croce Bianca, when they should be out there building a new one."

He looked at her down his long straight nose, a half-smile on his face.

"You are quite right, of course. Everything you say is perfectly correct. It is just a question of whether we would choose to bring you along with us for the ride. The one good thing the Family has achieved in the last few years is to distance itself from you. Your reputation is toxic. Any association with you would devalue everything we stand for. Why on earth would we have anything to do with you? We have significant support: friends, mentors, leaders – not within the Family, but on the outside – who see what we want to achieve. People who share our values and who we can work with, but who would not put a bullet in us, if they did not get their own way. You are a rare creature, Ms Bonnici – a known murderess, who is allowed to walk the streets. If you have come here looking for some form of alliance, you can forget it. I would rather do a deal with the devil."

Natasha smiled and shook her head.

"Oh, dear, Leo. So much to learn." She paused and thought for a minute while he looked around the café, clearly not interested in continuing the conversation. "Well then, you've been very clear, and I can see we're not going to be friends. I misjudged you. I thought you might be smarter than your father. But you're not. I've wasted my time. Farewell, Leo. You can buy the drinks, given you own the place. I'm sure you'll get a discount." She stood and slung her bag over her shoulder. She was about to leave, when she turned back to face him.

With a smile, she said: "By the way, if you go to the Café Opera, there's a tall waiter with blond hair, who usually does the pre-performance shift. He's about your age. I thought you might like to know, your father's fucking him – has been for years. I'd lock your bedroom door if I were you. That's unless you and Daddy are already at it! *Ciao!*"

She walked from the café into the old town and found her way to the Gothic masterpiece that was Saint Stephen's Cathedral. Gradually, her shock and anger at the encounter subsided. Never before had she been spoken to like that. Naturally, the foolish boy did not realise it, but he had just made an enemy for the remainder of his much-shortened life. Taking a deep breath, she stood and looked up at the roof of the cathedral. That was what she had come to see.

The roof of Saint Stephen's was ornately patterned and covered by thousands of glazed tiles. She walked around to find the south side of the building, where the tiles formed a colourful mosaic of a double-headed eagle, symbol of the empire ruled from Vienna by the Habsburg dynasty. These were her ancestors; in their time, the princes and dukes of the Habsburgs had been at the heart of the Family. It was their stupidity in backing Emperor Franz Joseph in the First World War, with massive loans for his war chest, which had nearly ruined them.

Natasha never considered herself a sentimentalist, but she felt a sense of pride in the knowledge that she had led the Family, an organisation that had its origins represented by the crest on the roof of one of the most iconic buildings in the world. It steeled her resolve that nobody, let alone a fatuous youth like Leo Kruder, would ever take that away from her.

Putting thoughts of revenge out of her mind, at least for the time being, she turned her back on the building and started to walk back to where her driver was waiting. She wondered who these friends, mentors and leaders that Kruder had referred to were. Her next step would be to try and find them.

CHAPTER 45
COMMISSIONER FOR HOME SECURITY GEORGE ZAMMIT

ZAMMIT FAMILY HOME, BIRKIRKARA, MALTA

GEORGE ARRIVED HOME EXHAUSTED, stressed and hungry. He parked the car in the basement garage and made his way up the concrete ramp to his front door. Usually, when he opened it in the evenings, he played a game with himself, called Guess What's for Dinner. He would stand in the small entrance hall, inhale deeply, and try to think what might be cooking in the kitchen. Fridays, it was usually an enormous pan of spaghetti, served with meatballs in tomato sauce, which Marianna crafted from the contents of spicy Maltese sausages. When they had been on more friendly terms with the Mifsuds, George could guarantee at least one night in seven he would be greeted to the rich aromas of frying rib eye steaks, which his wife would serve with piles of mushrooms in a garlic and cream sauce.

Given the time of year, he wondered if it might be lampuki pie. The cheap, oily fish usually made an appearance in Maltese waters at the end of the summer. Marianna would add the fillets to a mix of tomatoes, vegetables, olives and herbs from her own pots, before covering the dish with a layer of pastry. But tonight, he smelled nothing. He sniffed, in several short bursts, and could only identify the disappointing aroma of lemon furniture polish. However, he did hear the mumbling of low voices coming from the kitchen.

He walked down the corridor and entered the room to be greeted by a strange sight – Marianna holding the rotund shape that was Josette Mifsud, who was sobbing on her shoulder. Gina sat red eyed in the rocking chair, with Baby Joseph on her knee, munching his way through a packet of digestive biscuits. Giorgio was leaning against a kitchen unit, arms folded, glowering at the floor. He said nothing to George when he entered.

He stood there, expectantly. Nobody spoke. "*Mela*, what's going on here?" It was Gina who cracked first.

"How could you, Dad? Locking up Joe, Baby Joseph's grandpa, who's been nothing but kind to us. You were always happy to take all his meat."

George guessed Inspector Chelotti had got the list and must have acted promptly. He felt a sinking in his stomach.

"Girl, you're talking in riddles. Will someone please tell me what's happened!"

Marianna stood back and freed herself from Josette, who regarded George with her weepy face, clouded with the deep suspicion of someone who had been doused with iced water, on the last occasion they had met.

Marianna said, very matter-of-factly: "Karl Chelotti and two officers came to the Mifsuds' house and have taken Joe to Camp Azure."

George feigned surprise.

"Why?"

Giorgio stood erect, no longer able to contain himself.

"You know why! Don't act stupid with us. You're harbouring one of the Resistance. That's why! And Dad knew. You got him locked up, so he couldn't tell anyone."

A guilty look spread over George's face. He could never hide his guilt; he was just surprised that Giorgio had got to the gist of things so quickly. George had always thought the lad was a bit dim.

"A terrorist? What, here in this house? Go have a look, Giorgio. Be my guest, see what you can find."

Then he saw Marianna look pointedly at the tearful Gina.

"George, you be quiet. Giorgio, can you tell me how this ... misunderstanding's come about?"

Giorgio glanced sideways at Gina and slumped back against the units, silent.

Marianna fixed her eyes on their daughter. "Gina? Can you help me understand all this?" She snivelled and started crying again.

Marianna had had enough. She raised her voice.

"Stop it, this minute, girl. Tell me what's happened. This is serious!"

Baby Joseph looked from one adult to another, then at the biscuits.

Gina started to speak.

"We were talking about the Russians and Joe said the Resistance were all idiots who would get themselves killed. I said he was the idiot, not the Resistance. Then he asked me what I knew about the Resistance, and I said they were very brave ... and it slipped out."

"What did?"

"That Den was in the Resistance. Joe asked how that could be 'cos he was in Libya. I said, 'That's what you think.' I was angry he'd called our Den an idiot.

"So then he said, like, 'Ha! So, he's here then?' And I said he was and doing all that brave stuff." Gina looked at George. "Afterwards, I spoke to you about it, Dad, and you said you'd take care of it."

All eyes were fixed on George. He looked around him, his face colouring with shame. He had put Joe Mifsud's name on the detention list for personal reasons and now he had been found out. Marianna said, in menacing tones:

"George, you didn't, did you?"

He sighed deeply and said: "Josette, come and sit down." Josette Mifsud sat down gingerly next to her nemesis.

"How close is Joe to the Russians? I know it's good business to sell meat to them, but he doesn't really support them, does he?"

"No, he hates them. He only joined that local liaison group to get in deeper with them, try to get the orders that Oliver Calleja's shop gets. You know, that fancy shop in Balzan?"

To give him time to think, George went to the sink and got himself a glass of water. Josette watched him anxiously and moved her chair back slightly. Then he asked, "*Mela*, would he give our Den up to the Russians?"

"No! He loves Denzel like a son. I mean, he always had his suspicions that Denzel might be involved with the ... you know, those people. But Joe wouldn't say anything to the authorities. Never. When the mast got blown up, he was laughing for all he was worth, wasn't he, Giorgio?"

He glared at George and said: "We've got to get Dad out of there. He's not a well man. He's on tablets, you know, for his waters."

Gina looked up hopefully, her puffy face pleading with her father. There was a sudden movement from by the sink, as Marianna sprang forward and walked right up to her husband.

"George Zammit, you're a commissioner in the *Pulizija*, in charge of Home Insurance or something. Now, you've got to put this right. You've wronged a member of our family who needs your help. Because Joe Mifsud's part of our family. So, you look Josette in the eye, and you tell her that, first thing tomorrow, you'll go to Gozo and get that man out of that wretched camp.

"And Josette, Giorgio? You swear to me now, on everything that's holy, you'll never breathe a word about our Den to anybody. And, when George brings Joe home, you make sure he knows that's what families do. They trust each other and help each other. Is everybody clear?"

There was a moment's silence, as emotions calmed. Then Giorgio came across and shook George's hand and kissed Marianna. Josette warily approached George, who still had the glass of water in his hand, and they kissed briefly on each cheek.

Marianna said: "Right, that's that. Now, I've got to get George's dinner ready, not that he deserves any, so off you all go. And Gina, Baby Joseph looks hungry ... perhaps get him a small snack?"

CHAPTER 46
SERGEANT DENZEL ZAMMIT
JEWEL OF THE ISLANDS, GRAND HARBOUR, MALTA

DENZEL and the others had been working in the hold of the *Jewel of the Islands*, off and on, for nearly a week. They staggered the time they spent there, so as not to create a regular pattern that might attract attention. They had asked Silvia to do drive bys of the ship during the day and at night, to have some sort of counter-surveillance operation but, as far as anyone could tell, nobody was showing any interest in the vessel.

Within the hold, something interesting was taking place. The team had unpacked three top-of-the-range SeeDoo jet skis and were busy assembling a large kit of extras. The boxes had contained pre-formed matt black, aluminium sections that were glued into place with construction adhesive to form a skirt around each jet ski, extending the nose cones. When the work was finished, they looked like long missiles.

The jet skis were powered by standard jet ski petrol engines that drove a water jet to provide the propulsion. Each had a series of complicated electrical additions, including a satellite transceiver aerial and an infra-red camera mounted at about a metre above sea level. There were no seats for passengers and no steering column. Denzel recognised immediately what the vessels were, and gasped. "My God, they're drones!" Billy smiled.

"Yep, USVs. Unmanned Surface Vehicles. Aren't they beauties? They're the same as the ones Uncle Sam gave to the Ukrainians to sink the Russki flagship, the *Moskva*."

"What're we going to do with them?"

"We don't have orders yet, we just gotta build them. But I could make a fairly good guess! You seen the size of the fuel tank?"

Denzel had not noticed.

"It holds about five litres. Usually, these things can hold two hundred litres of fuel, which would give a twelve-hour sailing range, at forty kilometres per hour, on open sea. So, these here bad boys are going nowhere near the open sea." Denzel immediately saw the target.

"*Peter the Great*! The battlecruiser. We're going to hit the battlecruiser."

Billy raised his eyebrows and said: "Maybe. My guess is we reduce the size and weight of the fuel to leave more room and weight capacity for the explosives. A bigger bang! In the nice, smooth water of the Grand Harbour, these things'll easily hit eighty kilometres an hour. Once they're on their way, there ain't nobody stopping them."

Denzel went and took a fresh look at one of the sleek, stealthy cigar-shaped pods. He ran his hands down its perfect lines. On its nose were two shiny plates.

"What're these?"

"Those there are a pair of impact detonators. You've got two 'cos you don't want a wave, or boat wash, accidentally triggering one of them.

Denzel was captivated.

"These USVs ... can they sink a battlecruiser?"

"I guess. Battleships have pretty thick armoured sides and the warhead detonates on the surface, outside the hull, so most of the blast heads away from the point of impact. Now, if the

USVs were armed with a missile, they'd detonate inside the vessel and there'd be a whole lot more damage. But I reckon we'll punch a big old hole in the side, on the waterline. And remember, that was enough for the Ukrainians to sink the *Moskva*, with one USV – and we've got three of the mothers!"

Denzel was excited.

"I can't wait. Who's going to control them?"

"I dunno that, either. They're radio-controlled, so they need line-of-sight signals, but that could be from a plane or a static point. If they wanted to, they could put a datalink up to a satellite and someone in Signorella could operate them through the camera. My guess is, given how little time these babies will be in the water, we'll get the job."

Denzel was like a schoolboy, fizzing with nervous energy.

"When will this ..."

"Den, enough, you've asked way too many questions already. We haven't even got the explosives yet. We're going to need at least half a tonne."

Two nights after the completion of the build, Billy, Huck and Denzel were once again onboard, waiting for Silvia to turn up with the explosives. She had flown to Catania two days earlier and taken delivery of a modified Toyota Land Cruiser. A team of mechanics at Signorella had stiffened the suspension, fixed removable panels in the wheel arches, installed false footwells, a fake spare tyre, a new internal roof space and a false floor in the boot. All these cavities were filled with aluminium tubes of TNT and RDX explosives.

Silvia had then calmly driven the Land Cruiser to Pozzallo, where she had boarded the *St Jean de la Valette* catamaran and sailed to Malta. The Russian soldiers on the dock there were more interested in the contents of her handbag and wheelie bag than what might lie within the structure of the vehicle.

That evening, exactly at the appointed hour, the Toyota Land Cruiser drove slowly down the rubbish-strewn road, alongside the derelict power station, and stopped. It flashed its lights three times and waited for twenty seconds, before flashing its lights again and moving. As the Land Cruiser crept forward, Billy kept one assault rifle trained on the vehicle, while Huck swept his across the nearby buildings.

Once the vehicle had pulled alongside the gangway, Huck said: "Den, tell her to take a walk to the top of the road with the walkie talkie. She's gotta stay out of sight. We're going to unload the SUV. Billy, you go and drop us a cargo net and open up the hatches. We're going to have to work quickly and in the dark. We can't take any chances."

The next hour was spent unloading over half a tonne of explosives in aluminium tubes.

Billy had taken the job of packing the explosives into each USV and connecting the detonators. With that done, the drones were good to go. Except nobody knew exactly when that might be.

CHAPTER 47
COMMISSIONER FOR HOME SECURITY GEORGE ZAMMIT
CAMP AZURE, GOZO, MALTA

MALTA WAS a tiny island of 300 square kilometres, while Gozo was smaller still at 70 square kilometres. Karl Chelotti had collected George in the black BMW that used to be Gerald Camilleri's car. As George approached, his friend lowered the window and said with a smile: "George Zammit, don't you dare sit in the back! I'm not here as your bloody chauffeur!"

Chelotti drove the car carefully onto one of the battered old car ferries that criss-crossed the Gozo Channel, making the twenty-minute trip to Malta's sleepy sister island in the north. As they leaned against the rail, watching the pleasure boats crowd into the Blue Lagoon on the tiny, ruined island of Comino, George recounted the conversations at home the previous night and how they now had to get Joe Mifsud out of Camp Azure. Chelotti whistled through his teeth.

"Well, that could be tricky. It's easy to put someone inside, but getting them out ..."

George then played his trump card.

"Well, actually, as I'm now the Commissioner for Home Security, Camp Azure falls within my responsibilities. I rang them this morning. They're expecting us. At first, I thought of saying we were taking Mifsud back to Malta for enhanced interrogation."

"What's that?"

"I don't know. Apparently, it involves a dentist. Then, I thought it might get complicated. If someone found a transfer order mentioning 'enhanced interrogation' and acted on it … well, I can't imagine Joe being very pleased about that! So, I think we'll just say we – or rather you – arrested the wrong man. Makes you look bad, but it's simpler." Chelotti was thoughtful.

"So, you're a full commissioner now, eh? I can't believe it. Why am I still only an inspector?"

"Well, yeah, but only for so long as the Russians are here." Chelotti looked at him and sighed.

"That could be some time."

When they reached the town of San Lawrenz, George told Chelotti to stop the car, and he got into the back seat.

"Sorry, Karl but, if I'm going to pull rank, I've got to at least look the part."

The entrance to the camp was at the top of the road that wound down the steep limestone hillside to a rocky platform at the base of the imposing promontory. The area still had a collection of small cottages, car parking, a chapel, bars and other facilities from its days as a tourist attraction. With the sea to one side and surrounded by steep limestone cliffs and hillsides, it now made a perfect setting for a low-security prison camp.

They were met at the gate by Captain Louis Scicluna of the Correctional Services Agency, who had been seconded into Home Security to establish and run Camp Azure. George noticed the motto of the Agency painted onto a wooden board, by the rolls of barbed wire. *Suavis Ex Aspero*, meaning Firm but Gentle, which was nothing like what went on in the main Corradino Correctional Facility on the mainland.

They descended the road into the camp itself. The inmates

were housed in the odd collection of tents and buildings that had been requisitioned from the café owners and holiday makers, while rows of new block housing were being constructed on what used to be the old car park.

Given the chaos within the camp, the arrival of George and Chelotti went largely unnoticed, but George spotted several high-ranking politicians, including Michael Cini, formerly the Minister for Home Affairs, recently removed from the Russian frigate, some members of the judiciary and about a hundred or so other middle-aged and elderly men. The detainees were allowed to wear their own clothes, and many sat around in small groups, resting against the walls of the buildings, sheltering from the heat of the early-morning sun.

George asked Captain Scicluna where the women were being held and he replied that there were not many, but they were being detained in a ward of the old psychiatric hospital at Mount Carmel, on the mainland. He walked over to where Cini was standing, talking to another man who turned out to be the deputy principal of the University of Malta. He had made his views on the Russians' presence rather too freely known. George introduced himself to Cini, but the captain was on to him in a flash.

"No speaking to the prisoners, sir. It's forbidden."

"I beg your pardon, czaptain! Don't you dare get above yourself. I'm the Commissioner for Home Security. I'll speak with whoever I wish. Now, make yourself useful and go and find me Joseph Mifsud. He arrived yesterday. I'm afraid the local police brought you the wrong man. My Inspector has papers for his release into my custody."

Chelotti grimaced at the phrase 'my inspector'.

George turned his attention to Michael Cini.

"Well, well, George Zammit, here doing the Russians' bidding. I never thought I'd see that day. I always felt you and Camilleri just about kept on the right side of things."

"I'm sorry to see you here, sir. Is there anything I can do, within reason, to make things more bearable?"

"Within reason? Interesting qualification. But yes. Visits and telephone connections, so we can keep in touch with our families. That'd be a start – if that's *within reason*. Establishing a tribunal to hear what charges, if any, are being brought against us, if that's *within reason*! At the moment, we're being held without any information as to cause whatsoever."

George looked him in the eye and said quietly: "Some of us are doing our best, sir. Don't give up hope. I'll look into visits and telephones."

As he turned to leave the bemused former minister, he heard the raised voice of Joe Mifsud coming towards him.

"It's you! Come to gloat, have you? You bastard! I know what you've done and don't think I'm not going to tell …" George advanced on him hurriedly.

"Shut up, Joe! I've come to get you out, you fool! So be quiet or I'll change my mind and lock you in one of those caves."

Joe looked around him.

"Which caves?"

"*Mela*, do you want to find out?"

There were no caves, of course. George had simply said the first thing that had come into his head, but it seemed to have quietened the butcher. They got into the car and headed back to the ferry terminal. Once on board, Joe Mifsud said he was going to the cafeteria for *pastizzi*, as he was starving. Normally, George would have followed anyone who suggested going for *pastizzi*, but he needed to speak to Karl Chelotti.

"Karl, did you see the people in there? Ministers, priests, judges, lawyers, teachers and professors – they've locked up anybody with half a brain."

"Then why aren't you in there?"

"Ha, ha. Don't joke, I'm serious. We've got to do something

... more than we're already doing. There's nobody of any stature left to run the country."

Karl Chelotti looked at him.

"Careful, George, or you'll find yourself in there with them. But I agree, it's a mess."

"A mess? That's what you call it? It's more than that – it's a tragedy. Thank God some of us are not going to stand idly by and watch it happen."

CHAPTER 48
THE RESISTANCE

JEWEL OF THE ISLANDS, GRAND HARBOUR, MALTA

As it turned out, instructions came the next day to launch the attack the following morning, at dawn. In the early hours, Denzel, Billy and Silvia went to the *Jewel of the Islands* to lower the USVs into the water. Huck had received instructions and set up the command equipment inside them, then taken the van to a seldom-used spot of rough ground above the grain silos to the south of the harbour. He had placed some stolen barriers across the bottom of the road, on the off chance anyone should choose to drive down it. From there, he had a perfect view of the *Jewel of the Islands*, across a kilometre-long stretch of water, lined up with Pinto Wharf, where the *Peter the Great* was moored.

One by one, Silvia fitted the webbing straps to the USVs, and Billy worked the deck crane to lift them out of the ship's hold and lower them into the inky blue-black waters of the Grand Harbour. Denzel was in a small kayak, which Huck had dropped off, manoeuvring around the USVs to release the straps and attach a double-braid nylon rope to the prow of each one. Then, he silently towed each vessel a few metres to a quiet disused dock, where they were secured and hidden beneath two large canvas deck covers, awaiting the arrival of first light. Huck had set up a camera to record the attack for the attention of the world's media.

The early morning sun was just creeping over the hill behind them as they locked up the *Jewel of the Islands* and gathered their things. Huck had set incendiary explosives all over the ship, timed to detonate eight hours' later. This would alert the Russians to the origins of the attack but would also erase all physical evidence of their presence. Silvia and Billy drove the Land Cruiser to Senglea, one of the Three Cities, opposite the *Peter the Great*. In thirty minutes, they would take a seat at a waterfront café for a coffee and wait for the fun to begin.

Denzel sat in his kayak, gradually getting colder and colder and increasingly nervous. He rocked his body back and forth to try and create some warmth and begged the hands of his watch to move more quickly. When his walkie talkie finally crackled into life, he was shaking so much – whether through cold or nerves, he could not tell – he could hardly loosen the knots on the ropes that held the USVs in place.

Once the tarps were dumped and the USVs floated freely at the entrance to the dock, Denzel gave Billy the signal they were good to go. Almost immediately, the engines fired, gently putt-putting their way out of the dock, small squirts of water jetting from their cooling systems. Immediately, the lead USV nosed ahead and started to make its way into the open water of the Grand Harbour. The other two fell in behind it, in an arrowhead formation. The harbour was quiet at that time of the morning and there was no other traffic on the water. In a matter of seconds, the three drones roared into life and picked up speed, flying in a straight line across the still waters of the harbour. Denzel traced their wakes and, as agreed, began his journey by kayak to Senglea, to meet up with Silvia and Billy.

He paddled slowly, unable to take his eyes off what was unfolding in front of him. The *Peter the Great* sat, massive and imposing, its four twin-gun turrets idle and slightly dipped. There was a thin black ribbon of exhaust rising vertically into the morning sky. Its crew of 750 would be having breakfast or finishing watch, getting ready to start another day. There was no sign that anyone on the battlecruiser had seen the three USVs bank heavily and alter their course, in preparation for hammering into their midships at over 80 kilometres an hour.

There was no time for an alarm or defensive fire. Denzel stopped paddling, transfixed by the spectacle of the three huge explosions that seemed to throw half the water in the Grand Harbour up into the air, bursting the ship from its moorings. The blasts smashed it against the wharf, leaving it to sink back into the vacuum created by the explosions, breaking its spine. It was then tossed upwards by the resurgent waters and left rocking, a huge, jagged tear along its waterline.

The force of the blast and the shearing of the metal dissipated, and, for a time, calm of a sort was restored. The only sound was a bell, somewhere deep inside the ship and the wash of displaced water. Denzel paddled more quickly, remembering to pull on the balaclava he had in the pouch of his life vest. Huck went to remove the *Road Closed* signs and drove back into town. In the café, Silvia and Billy stood with a crowd, gathered to check out the cause of the explosion.

"Well, that sure was one helluva bang! That mother's going to the bottom," he told her.

There was a murmur among the crowd, as they realised that the mighty ship was starting to list to port. Then a solitary cheer, then another, and another. Silvia took her seat and ordered a coffee, watching the scene across the harbour develop. Billy stood at the waterfront, transfixed. Aboard the *Peter the Great*, the crew could now be seen on deck, scurrying around, undertaking their damage-control duties. There was a fire somewhere below deck. Thick black smoke started billowing out of the open wound on the side of the ship.

Silvia had worried about the risk of radiation contamination from the nuclear reactor that was part of its power plant. Huck had assured her the US Navy engineers who had planned the strike were confident that the reactor containment arrangements would survive the blasts and remain tight enough to minimise any risk of leakage. The reactor would have to be removed and dumped later, in deep water, as part of the salvage operation.

Along the dock, the first emergency vehicles started to arrive, blue lights flashing and sirens wailing. Silvia made an effort to keep an even, unexcited expression on her face. She need not have bothered, given that all around joyous and excitable crowds were celebrating the strike. She could hear car horns blaring in celebration, across the south of the Grand Harbour, where the spectators were the first to realise what had happened. Initially, only one or two horns sang, in discordant harmony. Then, gradually, others joined in, and, within minutes, it seemed every car in the Three Cities had joined the cacophony. People had come running from all over to see the slain beast slowly sinking into the waters by Pinto Wharf.

It took several hours for the ship to finally settle on the floor of the Grand Harbour. The water had risen over the level of the deck and up to the lower reaches of its superstructure. When the water had surged through the largest section of the gaping wound along its side, it had extinguished the fires that must have been raging below deck. There had been a mighty hiss, and a cloud of steam had tumbled out of the jagged slash, which obscured the scene from view for several minutes. The crew abandoned ship.

Denzel had watched as much of the action as he dared, and had then completed his trip to Senglea, where he had hauled the kayak up the slipway and stashed it in amongst the racks of canoes, kayaks and paddle boards belonging to the Senglea yacht club. He ditched his life jacket and pulled on a jacket he had taken from the store beneath the kayak's hatch. He walked along to the café and joined the others standing near the water's edge. They could not resist exchanging a collective smile.

CHAPTER 49
NATASHA BONNICI
OFFICE OF THE PRIME MINISTER, VALLETTA, MALTA

COLONEL FEDOROV WAVED the letter from the EU Commission in the air and laughed.

"Have you read it! They're so spineless!" He read the last paragraph out loud.

"'... and refer the matter to the European Parliament for Members to consider what aid and assistance they must provide.'"

"What do you think that means? A few more lacklustre sanctions?"

A loud bang echoed across the square outside Castille, causing the tourists to flinch. The Maltese just ignored the deep resonant booms of the fireworks that villagers used, at all hours of the day, to frighten off the evil spirits that might disturb their religious festivals.

Admiral Berezovsky ducked and looked towards the window.

Fedorov laughed.

"You're not on the bridge now, Aleksandr – relax, it's a firework!"

The admiral scowled, embarrassed by his show of weakness.

"Easy for you to say from behind your big desk, Igor. But

listen. We can't just mock and dismiss this letter, Igor. The EU are telling us they're asking their members to consider how they can act against us. They believe a fellow member is under attack. You and Christa Baldacchino need to get together and make a point-by-point response. Answer those accusations. Is that the correct approach, Edward? Kick the can down the road?"

Natasha sat next to Fedorov, as before.

"May I suggest we appeal against the conclusion? There must be a mechanism. We can say Ray Farrugia was a criminal who fled to Brussels to escape scrutiny of his corrupt actions. To start with, we can argue he had no authority to represent the Maltese government. I'm sure the president and the prime minister," here Natasha glanced at Refalo, who squirmed in his seat, halfway down the table, "would both say there's been no armed aggression on Maltese territory and the Russian forces are here at the invitation of the government, in a capacity that does not violate any constitutional provision. Or some such form of words. They could send a further document saying they're making all statements of their own free will and not acting under coercion – couldn't you, Edward?"

Refalo cringed, his body folding in on itself. Natasha looked at Fedorov and shrugged.

"Just a suggestion."

Admiral Berezovsky grunted.

"Why don't you draft it then? That sounds fine to me. Grigori?"

The ambassador agreed.

"I could not have put it better myself."

Suddenly, the doors burst open, and a naval rating came rushing in, bending down to whisper into the admiral's ear. His usually florid face turned white, and his lips started to quiver.

"How did this happen?" Then he screamed at the rating: "Go! Get out!"

Admiral Berezovsky grasped the edge of the table, to try and maintain his grip on reality.

Fedorov calmly said: "Well, Aleksandr, are you going to tell us, or should we wait to read it in the *Moscow Times*?"

"There's been an attack on the *Pyotr Velikiy*. She's holed below the waterline. Listing to port."

Fedorov shuffled his papers, sitting in silence for a moment, and then fixed the admiral with a cold stare.

"I suggest we adjourn. Aleksandr, I want an initial report on the damage, within the hour, and an explanation of how this was allowed to happen. I suggest you go to the quayside and bring yourself up to speed. Meanwhile, have someone pack your belongings. You know Moscow will require a full explanation of this, in person."

Colonel Fedorov looked at George, who was studying his shoes, as the consequences of the attack started to become apparent.

"Commissioner Zammit, go to the Grand Harbour immediately. I want a full cordon around that ship as soon as possible. No photographs, no film crews, no drones – nothing. This is a matter of national security, and we can't be humiliated in the world's press. Do you understand?"

George hesitated, then said: "Can I just say, this isn't Maltese national security, is it? Shouldn't your navy be getting on to this?"

Natasha felt Fedorov's temper rising. She laid a hand on his wrist for just a second, then rose from the table and walked down to where George was sitting.

She turned to face Fedorov.

"Commissioner Zammit and I will get on to this immediately. I think you've got enough to do, Colonel. We'll leave you to it."

She led George out of the room. As soon as the door closed behind them, she shook his arm hard.

"For God's sake, George, that man could've shot you where

you were sitting. Didn't you see his face? This is the ultimate humiliation for them. Their careers are going to be tarnished forever, so they're definitely in the mood to lash out. Come on, let's get out of here and get a coffee."

"A coffee? I thought the ship was sinking and we had a job to do?"

"Of course, but we want to make sure there's plenty of footage in the can before we shoo them away, don't we? Whose side are you on? Oh, this is hilarious! Who did it, do you think?"

George made the mistake of swallowing and hastily looking away, a sudden reflex movement that Natasha was on to in a shot. She grabbed hold of him again, grasping both his shoulders and pushing her face close into his.

"My God! You know, George ... you know exactly who did it! You bad man!" She shook her head in disbelief. "Well, well. George Zammit, you never cease to surprise me. Now's maybe not the time, but soon you're going to tell me everything; I mean, absolutely everything, or I'll find time for a chat with my new best friend, Colonel Fedorov. And, after that, he'll probably pull your fingernails out – before he shoots you." George felt hot and cold, at the same time.

They made the short walk from the Auberge de Castille to the Upper Barrakka lift that dropped them immediately opposite Pinto Wharf. There, the pair of them listened to the creaks and groans of the battleship's demise, as it split and buckled under the weight of the water it had shipped. The crew had thrown as many lines as they could from ship to shore and the winches screamed, as they tried to pull the twenty-five-thousand-tonne vessel closer to the huge cast iron bollards embedded in the wharf. Eventually, two tugs appeared and nosed against the off side of the ship, their powerful engines labouring to budge her the few metres to the dockside. It did not work – the battlecruiser was firmly grounded, only three metres away from the wharf and still listing heavily to port.

The crew rigged precarious ladders and gangways between the ship and the dockside, so those not involved in damage control could scramble ashore. Soon, it became evident that there were many casualties on board. The paramedics from Mater Dei arrived with their large green shoulder bags and clambered across the ladders to lend what assistance they could. Later, the wounded and the body bags would be placed on stretchers and mobile cranes would swing them ashore in cargo cages.

Pinto Wharf was sixty metres below the Upper Barrakka Gardens that sat atop Valletta's enormous bastions. The gardens gave the best views over the Grand Harbour, looking towards the Three Cities. Hundreds of tourists made their way to the St Peter's and Paul's Bastions where, on the lower tier of the gardens, the Saluting Battery fired a cannon every day at noon. George raised his head to see several hundred faces looking down at him. Natasha followed his gaze and realised what he was seeing.

A major road ran around the peninsula of Valletta, only separated from Pinto Wharf by cast iron railings. To George's dismay, he realised there were hundreds of faces pressed up against these. Traffic on the road was gridlocked, as drivers abandoned their vehicles and flocked to the railings to witness the remarkable scene taking place before their eyes.

Whereas the harbour had been quiet when the stealthy USVs had skimmed their way towards the doomed ship, now the waters were alive with traffic. Dozens of inquisitive small boats and yachts sailed close to the *Peter the Great*, getting in the way of the two tugs frantically churning the water, as they tried in vain to save the ship.

To his horror, George saw the early morning tourist boats, which did the harbour cruises, taking their hundreds of passengers to within metres of the stricken vessel, excited commentaries in a variety of languages adding to the cacophony of sirens, voices, blaring car horns and George's own groans.

Worst still, every person, be it up in Upper Barrakka Gardens, looking in through the railings from the roadside or gawking from the pleasure boats, had one hand held aloft, holding a small glinting square: filming, posting, streaming and snapping the very scene George had been ordered to keep secret. A helicopter from one of the news channels buzzed overhead while several small drones whizzed above, diving in and out of the airspace around the *Peter the Great*.

Natasha said to George: "Well, what was it the colonel said? *We don't want to be humiliated in the world's press.* I'm not sure what you can do about that now. But it's interesting, isn't it? I think this car horn protest could become a *thing*."

All around, the horns blared incessantly. George could not have foreseen it, but Natasha was right: the loud, medium pitched blare of car horns was to become the soundtrack of the popular protest against the Russian occupation that erupted on that day. The Maltese loved their car horns, with football victories, election successes, graduation parades and weddings all being celebrated by cavalcades of cars, trumpeting their way through the island's streets. It was a safe way to protest, given that the volume and density of traffic on the island made it impossible to identify which cars were sounding their horns at any one time. Over the coming weeks, the island resounded to the cacophony of protest, almost twenty-four hours a day, to such an extent that the moment became spoken of as the beginning of the Car Horn Revolution.

Karl Chelotti arrived on the scene and turned to George, a half-smile on his face.

"Any orders, sir? I take it you're in charge."

George scratched his head and puffed out his cheeks.

"*Mela*, I've no idea where to start."

Natasha nodded at Chelotti and told George: "Well, I think I've seen enough. I'll leave you gentlemen to get on with things. I'm sure you'll have everything under control in no time, George, I haven't forgotten what happened earlier. I'm going to ring you later – you've been a naughty boy! *Ciao!*"

Karl watched her, as she walked back across the wharf, swinging her hips as she went.

"Who's the hottie, George? Ooooh, have you been a naughty boy?" He fluttered his eyelashes and laughed.

"She's no hottie, Karl. That's Natasha Bonnici. I'll tell her you're a fan, shall I? I can ask her if she'd go with you to the Bocci Club for a can of Cisk. Maybe you can treat her to *pastizzi* afterwards."

"Shit, is that her?" He took another quick glance over his shoulder. "Better not, eh? Don't want to end up dead in a ditch."

George slid his thumbs behind his belt and looked around. "What the hell are we going to do about this lot?"

CHAPTER 50
GRECA ROSSI
HOTEL FOUR SEASONS BELLA, VISTA, TAORIMINA, SICILY, ITALY

When Greca wanted to relax and get away from the dirty business of being a *capobanda*, she would go to Taormina, an upmarket Sicilian tourist town, north of brooding Mount Etna. There, she pretended to be a film star: throwing her money around, dressing outrageously, behaving as if she did not have a care in the world. Not for her the sandy beach looking out on the rocky mound known as Isola Bella, nor the bustle of the upmarket boutiques and cafés of the Corso Umberto. Greca liked the hotels. Not the chic boutique ones, with handsome young men in polo shirts and freshly pressed chinos, but the huge grand establishments that hung to the cliffside, where snooty reception staff flicked their fingers to summon bellboys, and middle-aged waiters, in white jackets and bow ties, delivered ice-cold prosecco and coolly palmed her fifty-euro tips.

It was late in the season, but the last of the summer sun still bounced off the Ionian Sea and lit up the elegant resort. Greca had emerged an hour before lunchtime, wrapped in a floor length black cheesecloth kaftan worn with oversized sunglasses and designer heels. Her long black corkscrew curls had been gathered up on top of her head and secured by a long silk scarf. Under her arm, she carried a small pile of glossy magazines. The pool boys shed their studied insouciance and rushed to assist her, organising her lounger and positioning the umbrella exactly where she wanted it. Several blue twenty-euro notes changed hands. An ice bucket appeared, and a bottle of prosecco was opened, as she settled herself with her phone to read her horoscope.

Thirty minutes later, a languid youth appeared, dressed in Chipkos flipflops and matching Versace shorts and shirt, printed with a funky floral design. He was thin and pale and even his sunglasses could not hide the wasted look on his long face. Greca watched him slowly move along the poolside and lowered her glasses to flash her cat's eyes at him.

"Why, my love, you look positively destroyed."

"I feel as though I have not slept a wink. I am exhausted!" She laughed.

"I know. Fun, wasn't it?"

Leo Kruder flopped onto a sun bed and closed his eyes. He waved away the attentions of the pool boys and groaned. Greca examined him. He was not her type at all: a skinny, anaemic Austrian, with lily-white skin and the sex drive of an eighty-year-old. She thought wistfully of Ituah, whom Natasha had killed simply because he had wanted a bit of fun. There was a man! But never mind, business was business, and Leo was business. She taunted him.

"You take a nap before we have lunch and some wine. Afterwards, we can go back upstairs for a siesta and maybe your strength will have returned by then?"

He took her hand and kissed it. "Greca, please, not again. Can we just rest for a little bit longer?"

"Hmmm. I was led to believe you young things thought about nothing else. Here I am, all revved up, and you're letting me down. You'll be wanting to talk about tomatoes next."

"Well, that is what we said we would do."

"There's nothing to talk about, it's all done. The purchases are going through and, within the month, we – or rather, you –

will own nearly all the tomato processing plants in Italy – fifteen percent of world production! Aren't I clever?"

"And we will owe you, and the banks, a fortune! There are so many zeroes involved, I can't even find the words to express them."

"True. But won't your daddies be surprised at what their little boys have pulled off?"

"Yes, it will show them what is possible with a little effort." He laughed and gestured to a pool boy. "A glass for the prosecco and a *lit* cigarette."

"I love the way you don't even say *please*."

"I tip, don't I? You need not say any more."

She took her sunglasses off and turned on her side to face him.

"Did you meet Natasha in Vienna?"

He stayed very still; not a muscle moved in his face. "How on earth did you know about that?" She ignored him.

"What did she want?"

"The same as you. To use the Hussars to get back into the Family."

"And?"

"I told her to rot in hell."

"Oh, she'd like that. How did she react?"

"She said some nasty things about Father."

"You mean about him screwing that boy in Café Opera?" He glared at her.

"Don't look at me all offended. Everybody knows about that!"

The pool boy arrived, and Leo took a long draw on the cigarette, blowing two perfect smoke rings that floated up into the azure sky. Greca unbuttoned his shirt and ran a hand over his concave, hairless chest.

"Did you sleep with her?"

"What ... Natasha? No! We met for coffee! And I got the

distinct impression she did not like me. Is that all you think about, who is fucking who?"

"I like to know these things; I've got a strong libido. Let's talk about tomatoes, I can feel a need coming on. It'll take my mind off it."

"Not yet! Please, let's have lunch first."

"So, tomatoes. Have you thought about how you're going to meet the loan repayments?"

"Won't the operating profits be sufficient?"

"Well, yes, for the banks, but not to repay me. The total debt's enormous."

"I thought ... well, I didn't think you were going to want repaying immediately. That *is* what you said. We talked about a debt holiday – for a while – a year or so. So that is what I told the banks."

"I said I'd *consider* a brief payment holiday. And I *have* considered it, and I'm not sure it's such a good idea."

"What? You can't just change your mind, like that! It ruins everything."

Greca smiled at him and said nothing.

Leo was leaning on one elbow looking at her. He did not like her. What had started as a laugh, had turned into something else. He felt used.

"What can we do? What do you suggest?"

"I can reschedule the repayments but, to do that, I'll want something in return." Leo sat up.

"Oh, no! They will never agree to let you in. You know that. So you are wasting your ..."

"It's up to you to persuade them then, my love. Otherwise, I'll be the one who'll own all the tomato processing plants in Italy and the banks will chew your little balls off, while Daddy – well, he'll probably make you work for a living. Now, drink your prosecco, then we can get some lunch. The sooner we eat, the sooner we can ..."

CHAPTER 51
MARCO BONNICI
THE ROSENGARTEN, BERN, SWITZERLAND

Marco was due to meet Mary-Ann Baker in the Rose Garden, high above the Old Town in Bern. There was nothing accidental about the choice of venue, as Marco was a student of botany, biology, ecological environmentalism, indeed everything touching and concerning the natural world.

On his Serbian estate, he had created an alpine garden of some renown, with undulating walks through meadows and forests. For those strong enough to climb to the craggy summit of the hillside, at just the right time in late spring, a further magnificent display of alpine flora and fauna awaited, carefully composed amongst an outcrop of glacial erratics.

Marco had arrived early, to wander around the gardens and enjoy the hundreds of varieties of roses, irises and rhododendrons. He made a mental note to return to the park in the spring when the cherry trees – which were spectacular enough with their orange, copper and deep-red autumn foliage – would be resplendent with billowy pink and white blossom.

To his surprise, he recognised Mary-Ann Baker, sitting by the waterlily pond in contemplative mood. She had a tendency to hunch her shoulders and that day, despite the stiff back of the wooden bench, she sagged forward, with her long straight hair hanging loose and covering the sides of her face. She seemed to be looking out over the jumble of buildings comprising the Old Town, but he could see her thoughts were miles away.

"A penny for them."

She spun around and brushed her hair behind her ears. Marco was well acquainted with Mike Lloyd, formerly Mary-Ann's boss, but was only just getting to know his replacement. He had contacted her and offered his help, once he had become acquainted with Fedorov, on a hunch that the Americans would be interested in knowing what the head of the Russian military in Malta had to say after two bottles of red wine. He had not been wrong.

He now told Mary-Ann exactly what Fedorov had told him about the Russian's long-term ambitions for the island. She pulled a face when she heard about the African Gateway concept and the prospect of Malta becoming a new Dubai or Singapore in the Mediterranean.

"I don't get how the Russians are going to create an ultimate free-market country when they've taken theirs down the road to serfdom. But it's interesting to hear that's what they're saying."

Marco explained how the Russians had more or less taken complete control of what was previously a free, democratic country.

"They have suspended the constitution, forced the president to declare a state of emergency, prevented the House from meeting to vote it down, detained all those who have the ability to mount any meaningful protest – without trial or any judicial recourse ... and apparently the EU Commission has written to the other EU members, saying it is up to each country to do something about it!

"Meanwhile, we have several thousand mercenaries turning the tourist districts into no-go areas, half the Russian fleet in the Grand Harbour and the other half protecting a sanction-busting, oil trading free for all on Hurds Bank. They are walking all over us.

"The UN cannot do a thing, given Russia has a power of veto on the Security Council, and the proposed General Assembly resolution, telling the Russians to get out, was rejected, as there had been no request by Malta even for it to be proposed. Nobody is doing anything, and the Russians are getting themselves more and more ensconced."

Mary-Ann Baker sighed. Marco sat back on the bench and raised his eyes to the heavens.

"Okay, you feel better for blowing off some steam?" Marco said nothing. "Good. First, we've been busy behind the scenes. As we sit here, contemplating this pleasant view of the Aare Valley, in Malta, I can guarantee you, there'll soon be chaos. Check your phone when we're finished here. I'm saying no more, but we've rocked the boat a little bit. You'll feel better for it, I'm sure."

"Second, y'all chose not to join NATO. You decided you'd be neutral and non-aligned so, when the bully boys come down the pike, it's a bit rich of you to come running to us. Remember what your man said to Zelensky, the Ukrainian leader, when he begged your government for help? Your PM stood there, watched by the international press and, with a straight face, whined, 'We can't, we're neutral, our constitution won't allow it.' He publicly washed his hands of any show of sympathy or support. So, what d'you want us to do – go to war with Russia to save your sorry, corrupt mess of a country?

"Third, if you wanna do something useful, ask this Colonel Fedorov what he *really* wants. He doesn't want a naval port. Well, he won't this time tomorrow. His Singapore-in-the-Med is a pipe dream, and he knows it. The Russians couldn't stand by and let it do its own thing. Nobody would believe that ... everybody understands they're a bunch of thieving pirates." She snorted. "They could never create a Shenzhen freeport like the Chinese, because they couldn't keep their grubby hands off the money.

"But you're right about one thing. Once the big boys start playing, the EU and UN are a waste of time. They'll send the Brits or some other third world troops to minor flash points but, when stuff gets heavy, well … it's us, the Russians and the Chinese who've gotta sort it out. You know, in 2021, we spent 742 billion US dollars on defence? That's billions, not millions. What did you spend?" She shook her head. "No wonder you came to us."

She sighed and Marco was struck by how tired she seemed. She looked at him for a moment, weighing him up, then said: "If things've gone the way I expect them to have, go meet your guy, Fedorov. He'll be rattled. If you wanna help, stick yourself in the middle of this. Find out what it's gonna take to make him go home. He'll know your credentials, he's not stupid. Just tell him straight. But watch your back – the Russians have a real mean streak. We want this to be done quietly. We don't want anyone knowing we're in dialogue with these people. That's why you're useful. Back channels and all that.

"Thanks for bringing me here though – it's a nice spot. I'll have to come back in better days." She cast a wistful glance around the park and down at the Old Town with its jumble of grey-green sandstone streets. "Sometimes, I wonder if there'll ever be any."

That evening, Marco took Laura out to dinner. They planned to spend the rest of the weekend at her family's weekend chalet, high in the Bernese Oberland. Marco was in an optimistic mood.

"I want you to do me a favour."

"Hmm. Interesting. You know I will, if I can. What is on your mind."

"Can you find me a flat in town?"

She had the ability to arch her eyebrows when she wanted to question something. It made Marco smile, and he carried on: "Somewhere discreet, modern, nicely furnished and secure. I would like to see more of you, and I could do with a base here in Bern. I am going to tidy things up in Malta – I have been asked to do some work over the next few weeks, nothing too arduous, and I can make sure Natasha has settled properly. Then, I plan to split my time between here and Ticino, if that suits you? The manager of the Family Office is confident I can get Swiss resident status. We can have a proper relationship, like two grownups. I can meet your friends, take part in your life. None of this creeping around. What do you think?"

Laura grabbed his hand across the white linen tablecloth and said softly: "You know what I think." She took a sip of wine. "I still worry about Natasha, though. What will she think? How will she react?"

"Natasha has other things to think about just now. She has agreed to go back to work." Laura pulled back.

"Oh, Marco, no! It is far too soon. Any sustained stress could bring on a relapse, and you know she never addressed the root causes of what happened to her. I am not happy about that – I am really not."

"We cannot pussy foot around, worrying about Natasha. I wasn't going to tell her about us but, when she hears I am moving to Bern, she will put two and two together. It will be fine." He raised his glass. "I promise." Laura pursed her lips. "I hope so."

CHAPTER 52
PETER CALLEJA
GROUND-FLOOR APARTMENT, SIĠĠIEWI, MALTA

PETER CALLEJA WAS the motor mechanic who had the ground-floor flat in the block where Denzel and the others were staying. He had been outside, at the back of the apartments, winding back the mileage on an old Toyota, when the old guy from the floor above shouted down to him to get inside and turn on his TV.

For news and current affairs, Peter only watched ONE TV, the Labour Party's own TV station. He turned it on and sat stunned, watching the scenes from the Grand Harbour. He could not believe what he was seeing, and the thought crossed his mind that it might be a film, with a scene shot in Valletta. He rang a friend he knew who lived in the Three Cities. He could hardly hear the guy speak for the background noise. The car horns nearly drowned out all the conversation, but the gist was plain. The scenes he was seeing on the TV were in real time.

He grabbed an espresso and settled down to watch the drama unfold, all thoughts of the Toyota forgotten. He was listening to a live interview by some policeman or other, who was something in Home Security.

"… what people need to do is go home and let the emergency services get on with their job. There's nothing to see here."

He heard the interviewer laugh on the other side of the camera. The police guy looked uncomfortable.

"Commissioner, you say *'There's nothing to see here'*, but take a look behind you! Someone has just sunk the pride of the Russian Navy in the Grand Harbour, in broad daylight! It's incredible, isn't it?"

George stumbled on his words.

"I can't hear you too well, the cars ... well, er, it's not something you see every day ..."

"Do you have any intelligence on who might've done this? It takes a lot of planning to mount such an attack."

"Well, not really, but you know, we're not living in normal times. I've been told it could be some people from the camps in the south. You know... migrants."

"You don't really believe this attack could be done by anyone without access to sophisticated military equipment and support? Reports say the ship was attacked by three drone ships. Can you comment?"

"ISIS build bombs."

"So you think it was Islamic State? Have they claimed responsibility?"

"No, not yet. But maybe they will. Then we'll know for sure."

"So, you have no idea who did this, you're just going to wait for someone to claim it?"

"No! Enquiries will begin shortly, but ... anyway, the important thing is, everybody has to leave and stop turning this into a public spectacle."

"I think it's a little late for that, don't you? George Zammit, Commissioner for Home Security, thank you."

The camera panned away from George's unhappy face, across the stricken vessel, the fleet of emergency vehicles with their winking blue lights, the crowds clamouring at the gates to the music of a thousand horns, and the rescue teams carrying the dead and injured down improvised gangways. It was, indeed, a public spectacle.

Peter Calleja sat back. There was something niggling him. He had seen that man before and it was nothing to do with policing. He got up and walked around the flat, pausing to look out of the front window. Then it came to him. That man was the one who was bringing supplies to the three guys in the upstairs apartment. He had told Peter some rubbish about how they were Serbian gangsters. Well, he had heard them talking in the stairwell, and there was no way they were Serbians. In fact, he was fairly sure some of them sounded like Americans.

That evening, Peter Calleja called in to the offices of Herman Bros. Construction, where Herman Bartolo was the owner and managing director. He was also the local liaison officer for the town of Siġġiewi and a source of much information to the Russians, most of it concerning rumours of misdeeds by other building contractors.

Herman had an enormous office with a huge photograph of his face, set in acetate, embedded in the marble floor. He leaned well back in his expensive high-backed, swivel chair, behind his two-metre cherry red desk, while Peter told his story, which made Herman Bartolo extremely uncomfortable. It was one thing to pass on information about two Americans behaving suspiciously, but it was another to accuse the Commissioner of Home Security, no less, of being involved. That could cause all sorts of trouble.

He thanked Peter for his trouble and promised to find out if there was a reward for such valuable information. He decided that he needed a second opinion on what to do with something as potentially important as that, so he decided to call a fellow liaison officer whom he had met a few times at training events and who seemed to know what was what.

Joe Mifsud was only a butcher, but Herman thought he talked a lot of common sense and seemed to have an inside track with the Russians. The next day, he rang Joe, who was in his shop. Joe said he was busy serving customers but promised to find a minute and ring back from the privacy of his car. Herman was also rattled when he saw what had happened in the Grand Harbour. The thought crossed his mind that, if the Russians were ever to leave Malta and he lost his special status, who knew what might happen to him then? He recalled pictures he had seen of what the French Resistance did to collaborators after the end of the Second World War and could not shake off the image of Mussolini, swinging upside down from an iron girder, after being shot by Italian partisans. Maybe Joe could reassure him that he was worrying unnecessarily …

Joe eventually rang him back and sounded a little cagey, but Herman pressed on with his story. When he came to the part about how his *source* had recognised the Commissioner for Home Security as the man who was delivering food parcels to the gang of *terrorists*, which was what they had now become in Herman's mind, Joe became quite agitated.

"Well, that's all well and good for your man to insinuate, Herman, but you … you're a respected member of the community. Your word counts for something, so you've got to be one hundred percent sure before you start casting aspersions on senior police figures. My God! Can you imagine what'd happen if you were wrong? It could be the end of you! A word from this commissioner fella and you'd be blackballed from all government contracts. Then, where would your business be?"

"Well, this source was pretty sure it was him."

"Pretty sure? *Pretty sure*? Is that good enough for you to be staking your reputation, your future, on what this *source* says? No, no, Herman, you need more information. Why don't you ask this … source, to take some photographs of these men, and particularly this senior policeman? Then you can be quite sure before you act. That's the answer."

Herman saw the sense of this and was pleased he had made

the smart move of ringing Joe Mifsud. He asked his final question.

"Do you think the Russians will ever leave Malta?"

"Of course not. The weather's fantastic, they've got the beaches to themselves, and everybody loves them like brothers."

Herman could not be sure whether Joe was being serious.

Having been detained and taken to Camp Azure, Joe had realised that the whole Russian thing had gone way too far. He had heard about the camp on Gozo, but never realised the implications of it. People he admired, names from the newspapers, important people, priests, all manner of decent individuals, had been taken, just like him, and left in that limbo. If it could happen to him, it could happen to anybody. Also, the car horns worried him. He was unsure what sort of future they presaged.

He made his way back into the shop and immediately sent Giorgio to find Gina and have her run home and tell Marianna he needed to speak to George urgently. *Most* urgently.

CHAPTER 53
COMMISSIONER FOR HOME SECURITY GEORGE ZAMMIT

PINTO WHARF, VALLETTA, MALTA

GEORGE HAD SPENT a difficult few hours on the quayside, doing what little he could to control the circus that had developed around the southern bastions of Valletta. He had closed the road that ran parallel to the wharf, causing traffic jams throughout the city, and ordered the closure of Upper Barrakka Gardens and other parts of the walls that afforded a viewpoint of the stricken battleship. The Grand Harbour itself had been closed to all recreational traffic, including the fleet of pleasure boats and the harbour cruises. He had been forced to field a call from the millionaire owner of the largest boat trip company, arguing his human rights had been infringed, as he could not earn a living. George responded that, if he wanted to see what an infringement of human rights really looked like, he could arrange a one-way lift to Camp Azure.

As the day wore on, he noticed the nature of the activity around the harbour had changed. Ratings were being ferried out to the frigates and minesweepers. A blue smog from ships' exhausts started to develop, as engines were fired up. The bunkering vessels that fuelled the larger ships out on Hurds Bank began to make trips back and forth and the tugs returned, towing lines of huge fenders, covered in lorry tyres, that prevented ships scraping against one another, as they rafted up on the shallows. George realised the fleet was on the move.

He phoned Natasha who could neither confirm nor deny what he had asked, simply saying: "I don't know if they're leaving, George, I really don't. But I'd like to hear what you know about the attack?" George squirmed.

"Well, my investigations ..."

"I don't give a damn about your investigations – tell me what you *know*!"

"I can't hear you too well, Natasha ... the car horns... We'll have to speak later ..."

"George, don't you dare hang..."

George could not see it, but the battlecruiser, the *Admiral of the Fleet, Putin*, had already left Hurds Bank, together with half its regular battlegroup, on course for their port in Tartus, Syria, such was the panic caused by the attack in the Grand Harbour. George had been correct. While the emergency services and the crew of the *Peter the Great* battled to contain the situation aboard the battlecruiser, Moscow had ordered the admiral to withdraw all vessels out of range of any further drone attacks and remove the carrier group from Hurds Bank. It had been decided that their naval assets were sitting ducks, if a hostile population, armed with such sophisticated weaponry, surrounded them.

George clenched his fists and stamped his foot in glee.

"Yesssss!" he hissed.

Throughout the day, his mobile rang incessantly. If it was not some rude junior officer attached to Colonel Fedorov, demanding hourly updates, it was a staffer from the prime minister's office, insisting on knowing whether the 'terrorists' had been apprehended yet, or even Commissioner Mallia, who raised himself from his supposed sick bed to ask what the hell was going on and could George do something about those incessant car horns, which were disturbing his rest? It seemed all media requests were also being directed to him. So far, he had spoken to Reuters, the *New York Times*, *Der Spiegel* and a nice British lady, from *Cosmopolitan*.

Amongst it all, he noticed several missed calls from Marianna and, later, from Joe Mifsud. He was just about to call home when he received yet another call from Fedorov, who brusquely informed him a derelict wreck of a ship had just burst into flames at the Southwest Extension and demanded to know what the situation was. George had a line of sight down the Grand Harbour and noticed the plume of oily black smoke that rose vertically into the evening sky from the bottom end.

George forgot all other matters, domestic or otherwise, and set off to the Southwest Extension. His thinking was, he might at least get some peace and quiet from the car horns perpetually ringing in his ears. They were stopping him from being able to think and made conversation within thirty metres of a main road nearly impossible.

The interior of a breaker named *Jewel of the Islands* was burning fiercely and tugs were busy placing a boom around the perimeter of the ship to contain any fuel spillage. George looked at the trajectory from the burning ship to the prostrate *Peter the Great*. Instantly, he knew this was the origin of the attack and quiet satisfaction flowed through him. He could see the fire burning away any inconvenient forensic evidence before his very eyes.

He phoned Fedorov and told him what he had found. The colonel slammed down the phone; his day was going from bad to worse. George sat on a nearby wall, to take the weight off his feet, and looked through the many missed calls on his phone. Now he had a minute to himself, he rang home, feeling quite relaxed. Marianna answered within five seconds, her voice high with anger and excitement.

"Where've you been? Joe Mifsud's been round … you and Den are wanted terrorists!"

"We're what?" His heart skipped a beat.

"You heard, terrorists! There's some man who reported you being at the apartment in Siġġiewi."

"*Mela*! What's that idiot Joe Mifsud done now?"

"Don't have a go at Joe. He's the one who's saved your bacon. Anyway, get Den and come home. We need to be together. Joe's here. He'll explain."

"Is it safe to go to the apartment?"

"I don't know, but you need to get our Den."

George rang Denzel, who was watching events unfold on television in the apartment. He felt his phone vibrate and saw who the call was from. He put a finger in his ear to help block out the sounds of the car horns and answered.

"There's trouble," his father said tersely. "We need to meet back home. Tell the guys you've been spotted. Leave the Americans to bail out of there. They'll have an extraction plan of some sort. Come to the house and we'll take it from there."

"How long've we got?"

"I don't know any more than I've told you, but my guess is, not long. Where're you anyway?"

"I'm at the apartment."

"I'm just leaving the Southeast Extension. Stay put, watch for me outside. Give me fifteen minutes."

"What're you doing at the Southeast Extension?"

"*Mela*! A ship was set alight, I think it was linked …" Suddenly George realised exactly who was responsible for the sinking of the *Peter the Great*. "You know perfectly well, don't you? *Madonna mia*! I'm on my way."

With that, he cut the call and ran towards his car.

George was right. Billy and Huck did have an extraction plan.

After his call, all it took was a nod from Billy and they both immediately gathered their laptops and hard drives, packed a rucksack each and disappeared out into the evening gloom. The container in the quarry was already rigged with packs of explosives, so all they needed to do was connect the detonators to a two hundred-metre fuse line, and a battery-operated switch would do the rest.

On their way out, the Americans saw Calleja lying low, trying to stay out of sight in the Toyota he had been working on. When he saw them, he ducked down into the footwell. Huck and Billy spotted the movement, looked at each other and nodded. Billy sighed.

"The guy's an idiot."

"He's worse – he's a douche. A talkative douche."

Billy walked over to the car and tapped on the window. On the passenger seat, he spotted an old SLR camera, lying out of its case, with the cap off. Peter lowered the window and Billy stuck his head in and pointed to the camera. Calleja cowered even further down into the footwell.

"You've been a bad boy, dude," Billy said, then promptly stepped back.

Peter Calleja was about to remonstrate, plead, beg, anything to be able to make his escape, but Huck appeared at the other side of the car and opened the passenger door. In one fluid movement, a gun fitted with a suppressor appeared in his hand and he shot Peter Calleja in the head.

Huck surveyed the damage and said:

"Sorry man, but you can't go around saying Uncle Sam's been here."

Billy took the camera and rang Denzel, telling him the death of Calleja would be enough to convince the Russians that George had been helping the resistance – but better that, than having the shmuck give details and descriptions. He suggested that they all lie low, and he would work something out to get them off the island as quickly as he could. Billy said they had to leave to go and blow the container and 'juice the mechanic'. Huck turned the key in the Toyota and the ignition fired.

He called to Billy: "Hey, he must have fixed it! Get in the back, we'll take him in this. Front seat's a bit of a mess."

An hour later, a crowd had gathered in the garage under George's apartment. Upstairs, the house was locked and in darkness, giving the impression to any unwanted visitors that it was empty. As well as the entire Zammit household, there was Giorgio, Joe Mifsud and Josette, who took a position where she could keep an eye on the hosepipe that hung on the opposite wall, dripping threateningly.

George held up his hand and asked for quiet.

"Listen, we've got to think clearly. Joe, who knows about what Calleja suspected?"

Joe Mifsud stroked his chin.

"I'm not sure, but I think only Herman Bartolo, the Siġġiewi liaison officer. That's how I found out. I told him to keep it to himself and get some photos to buy some time, give me a chance to speak to you."

George looked at Joe and nodded in appreciation.

"Where's Herman now?"

"At home, waiting for me to call him and for Calleja to get him the pictures. Word'll soon get round that the mechanic's been shot. That sort of thing doesn't happen every day in Siġġiewi."

George said: "Right. First of all, I'm going to ring Karl Chelotti and get him to arrest Herman Bartolo and take him to Corradino. He'll put him in isolation, in Block C. That'll soften him up a bit!"

"Can you do that? He's a liaison officer," Joe Mifsud said.

George smiled.

"Exactly! One who has systematically abused his position by making false reports about business competitors, to advance his own interests. I'll have Chelotti tell him he could be shot under the Emergency Powers Act. Then, after a day or so, I'll arrange for you to visit him in Corradino and suggest you can get him out, *if* he can put certain things out of his mind. Can you do that?"

Joe Mifsud laughed.

"George, you're a hard man. Never had you down as being so devious. But, yes, I can have a word with him. I'm sure he'll see reason." Joe furrowed his brow. "You could have him shot, you say? Really?"

"Emergency Powers, Joe. I'm the Commissioner for Home Security, I can do just about anything. Crazy, isn't it?"

Josette piped up: "Then why don't you arrest those Russians sitting in Castille? They're the ones creating the emergency!"

George paused and concentrated on the oil stains on the concrete floor, before he looked up at her.

"You know, whenever there's a tricky question, I always think: what would my old boss, Gerald Camilleri, have done? I think he'd have thought about the two thousand Russian mercenaries on our streets, the size of the Black Sea Fleet sitting a few kilometres off our shore and decided to wait a little, before doing anything like that. But, when I think we can get away with it, I'll be straight there."

Marianna could not restrain herself.

"George, don't you go getting any ideas. I'm not having you doing your hero thing again. You'll get yourself killed! You do nothing without asking me first, and that goes for you, too, Den. You're in enough trouble as it is. And don't go listening to your father. What a mess we're all in! You've got responsibilities here. Baby Joseph needs his uncle and, God help him, poor thing, even his *nannu*."

The baby squirmed on Gina's lap, as he tried to grab more of the loaf that she was holding. George shook his head and turned to his son.

"Den, we'll wait and see what the Americans can arrange but, in the meantime, I'll see if we can get you back to Libya or somewhere, as a back-up plan. For now, you'll have to go back to Karl's uncle's house for a couple of days. Straightaway. Obviously, the apartment's compromised and you can't stay here. But otherwise, no one knows you're back in Malta." He looked pointedly around the assembled group. "Except for us, that is."

There was a moment when everybody looked at each other, then their gazes collectively settled on Gina.

"Why's everybody looking at me?"

It was Marianna who changed the subject.

"Ignore them, my love. What I want to know is, Liberia! Why always Liberia? Why can't he stay here?"

Joe Mifsud muttered to Josette: "What's Liberia got to do with anything?"

Josette shook her head. Denzel erupted.

"You don't mean Liberia, Ma! But I'll go wherever I have to, even Liberia, because if somebody wants to find me, the first place they'll come looking is here!"

George looked around the group, satisfied with his evening's work.

"*Mela*, that's all sorted out nicely then. Everybody knows what they're doing. Let's go upstairs and turn the lights on. We've bought some time. What's for dinner? I'm starving."

CHAPTER 54
MARCO BONNICI
CASTELLO BONNICI, IL-WARDIJA, MALTA

Asano was serving his take on classic French cuisine to Colonel Fedorov, Marco and Natasha. They had already enjoyed foie gras with slender fingers of toasted focaccia, young leeks smoked with juniper wood, and a crushed truffle condiment. He was now presenting, with the usual expressions of faux humility, his wagyu beef cooked over an arang-wood fire, with salsify, yuzu bark, sea gel, and a seaweed samphire pesto.

Natasha looked at her father, who seemed to be enjoying observing the irritation the Japanese housekeeper always caused her. Marco smiled slyly at her and started enthusiastically praising Asano, who said nothing but, like a cat, reverberated with a deep-seated inner purr of satisfaction. He had the cheek to make eye contact with Natasha, for a fraction of a second, just long enough for her to know he had registered her annoyance – and was enjoying it, too.

Fedorov was in a foul mood. He had greedily scoffed a bottle of expensive Meursault, helping himself to refills without offering to top up anyone else's glass. On seeing the empty bottle, the colonel had demanded that Asano bring another. The houseman glanced towards Marco, who discreetly nodded his assent.

Marco could guess the reason for the Russian's poor manners and bad temper.

"Colonel, you do not seem to be your usual self this evening. I assume, with the episode in the Grand Harbour and the population suddenly springing to life, it must have been quite a week for you?"

"My apologies, Marco. I shouldn't have come this evening. I've a lot on my mind. I make for a poor guest."

"Unburden yourself. You are amongst friends here."

Fedorov scrutinised the pair with his steely blue eyes. Marco relaxed back in his chair, his hands clasped in front of him, while Natasha easily held his gaze.

"It's curious, isn't it? *Friends*, you say. Interesting. Why would you be friends with me?" Marco smiled.

"Because, Igor, I would not want you as an enemy. Also, this island has been heading down the wrong track for many years and I am interested to see where you want to take it. But mainly because I am a commercial man and, in time, there may be opportunities that present themselves, where having a friend on the inside can do no harm." He paused for a second, then raised his glass and finished with: "And, of course, because I always enjoy intelligent company."

Fedorov twisted his mouth in a sour attempt at a smile.

"Well, I don't mean to be an ill-mannered guest but, given the fiasco with the *Peter the Great*, I'm not sure how much longer I'll be here, so don't invest too much time in cultivating my acquaintance. Admiral Berezovsky and the ship's captain have already presented themselves at the Admiralty Building in St Petersburg and, according to my sources, have yet to emerge."

He raised his eyebrows and sighed.

Natasha pushed her food around, then put down her knife and fork. Asano, who had been hovering in the background, glided forward to take her plate, thinking she had finished eating.

"So sorry, food not to your taste? I bring something else?"

Natasha's patience snapped.

"Oh, get lost, Asano. We're talking. When we want you, I'll shout, loudly. Now just go!"

Asano hurriedly backed away and, with a small bow, left the room.

Fedorov spluttered into his napkin, then barked a laugh.

"Good for you, Natasha. He's got a way of getting right under your skin, hasn't he?"

Natasha shook her head and said: "There're times I could cheerfully throttle him. It's like having a ghost in the house. I find myself constantly looking over my shoulder to see where he's lurking."

Fedorov laughed even louder.

In Asano's absence, Marco sensed the mood around the table change and felt confident enough to bring the conversation back to the point of the evening.

"Listen, Igor, I need to talk to you. Cards on the table." He pulled his chair forward and cradled his glass in both hands. "No one here is a fool and I assume you know as much about us as we know about you – you said as much the last time you dined here. We know about your political connections and your rise through the KGB and FSB. Top of your year in the Academy of Foreign Intelligence, youngest-ranking colonel in the FSB, one of the Kremlin's *silovik*, 'the men of force'. We also know you do not come here just to drink our wine and enjoy our company. Information, they say, always passes two ways."

The colonel's face gave nothing away. Marco continued speaking.

"I have been approached by people who are interested in knowing what it is you really want to achieve here. Believe me, I was surprised to hear from them. I am not usually the sort of person they do business with, but we live in extraordinary times, do we not?" He paused for a second. Natasha was aware of a clock ticking loudly in the hall. After a second or two of silence, while the men watched each other for a reaction that did not come, Marco pressed on.

"To be blunt, they ask what exactly you want. If they know that, maybe they can help you and we can resolve this … mess. Because, frankly, that is what it is. If you do not agree with me, I can open the windows and I guess we will hear the car horns blowing, even from up here."

Natasha held her breath, as the colonel's smile vanished, and his ice-blue eyes glinted behind narrowing eyelids.

After a few seconds, he said: "You want to open a backchannel? Well, well, Marco, I obviously underestimated the extent of your connections. I don't dismiss the approach, as yes, *frankly*, it's all become a bit of a mess. First, I need to know who *they* are? There can't be a backchannel, if we don't know who we're speaking to."

"If I say they are not Europeans, does that help?"

"Please, I'm not playing twenty questions with you, Marco. Is this an approach from the Americans?"

There was a silence, while Marco considered what he could and could not say. He nodded in the affirmative, then said: "It comes from the top. I would not get involved, if I thought it was a time-wasting exercise. Believe me, I appreciate the dangers inherent in meddling in your affairs."

Fedorov relaxed slightly. As the conversation developed, Natasha thought he looked slightly less likely to pull a gun and shoot the two of them.

"I can only speak for myself, but I need something to take back home – otherwise this episode will be seen as a stain on my record. Things aren't going well, as you can see. Or rather, as you can hear." He smiled self-deprecatingly. "So, you know what we want … what we've always wanted. Access to the Mediterranean, to be able to seek influence in North Africa, supply our forces in the Middle East. Keeping access through the Bosphorus and the Dardanelles has been the primary strategic goal throughout the three hundred and fifty years of the existence of the Russian Navy."

Marco knew that the next problem for Russia's sea borne forces was the imminent completion of the Kanal Istanbul, the new thirty-kilometre, modern waterway that would run parallel to the Bosphorus. It was believed that, once the new canal opened, the Turks would stop dredging and maintaining the Bosphorus Straits, which in time, would become unnavigable to heavy shipping. The few rights of access the Russians had would not apply to the new Kanal and Russian overtures about establishing access for their warships through it had been strongly rebuffed by Ankara.

It was this situation that had prompted the plan to build a strategic base and resupply facility in Malta. It would service the combined Black Sea and Mediterranean Fleets and strengthen their regional influence along the north coast of Africa and the Middle East.

Natasha asked Fedorov: "Why do you think it is that Turkey won't give you terms to use the new Kanal?"

"The Ottomans and the Russian Empire have been at war, off and on, since the time of Peter the Great. Even before that. There's a historical prejudice against us. Muslims and Christians are never destined to be friends – so many killings and massacres, there's no trust. The Turks are the gate keepers. They'll never surrender their stranglehold on us. It's their way."

"But, if a third party could intervene on your behalf …?"

Fedorov's eyes turned towards Natasha. Marco knew what she was thinking.

"You've got such connections?"

"Actually … yes. Although I haven't used them for some time. But I think we could do enough to bring the three interested parties into a room together. The Turks, the Americans and yourselves. You've made your point, even if you've had setbacks. The Americans, NATO and the EU have all sat up and paid attention. This is no longer a local southern Mediterranean matter. You've shocked the West, and they'll push or bribe the Turks into giving you a deal on the Kanal. I'm almost certain of it."

Fedorov snorted.

"Hummph. Well, if you're serious, then open these discussions and see if it's a possibility! If you can succeed where others have failed, of course I'm interested."

Natasha left the room to instruct Asano to bring them champagne and vodka.

CHAPTER 55
COMMISSIONER FOR HOME SECURITY GEORGE ZAMMIT

ZAMMIT FAMILY HOME, BIRKIRKARA, MALTA

IT WAS a quiet Sunday afternoon and George was sitting in the family dining room of his apartment. He did not have a study as such, there was no need. Paperwork was not something that came easily to him. The dining room was the family's 'best' room and Marianna kept the plastic covers on the upholstered chairs and plastic runners on top of the tiles, to stop them getting scratched. The dining table was covered with an old sheet, and slatted wooden shutters kept out the worst of the cruel summer sun that had the strength to fade uncovered fabric.

In an impulsive moment, Gina had thought it a good idea to aid Baby Joseph's development by getting him some zebra finches. As she and the baby spent more time in her mother's kitchen than they did in their own home, she decided it was best to keep them there. She claimed the tweeting and sociability of the birds would create a fun and relaxing environment that would be good for her son. The two birds sat happily in a cage in the kitchen, kicking their seed onto the floor and shedding their feathers, which gently floated around in the currents of warm air in the busy kitchen. Their cheeping was drowned out by the constant conversation between Gina and Marianna, and the noise of the television, so all was well, initially.

Unfortunately, Gina had once made the mistake of letting them out of their cage. She insisted they needed exercise, so the door was opened, and the birds fluttered around, chirping excitedly. Much to Marianna's horror, they started depositing their droppings across her kitchen table and work surfaces, which provoked shrieks of outrage. One perched on top of a gilt-framed wall mirror and immediately started pecking off flakes of golden paint, which drifted glittering to the floor.

A chase ensued, with Marianna flapping a tea towel at the terrified songbirds, who fled from cupboard top to light fitting, to the mirror and back again, to escape the brutal assault. Baby Joseph, disturbed by the chaos around him, began to howl. Then Gina, who saw it was all her fault, also started to cry. George had been summoned home to deal with what he was told was a "family matter of the gravest importance". After banishing the semi-hysterical women and the chocolate-covered child from the kitchen, he had coaxed the quivering finches onto his hand with bits of bread and some soothing clucking noises.

From then on, the songbirds enjoyed a sun-filled, happy life in the dining room, unmolested by the Zammit family, with the exception of George, who would sometimes secure the doors and windows, open the cage and take a nap in the single armchair while the birds sat on his head, contentedly chattering to each other.

That particular Sunday was different. The finches were happily bathing in the shallow dish of water he had laid out for them, but his focus was on the box of documents he had received some weeks earlier from Michael Agius, Gerald Camilleri's notary. George and Marco Bonnici had been appointed co-executors of the estate, but George, for one, remained in complete ignorance of what that entailed. Both the lawyer and Marco had been messaging him, saying they all needed to meet to discuss the matter, but with the situation on the island, he had not, as yet, had a chance to arrange it. He always found it difficult to be enthusiastic about administrative tasks such as this but, conscious that it was a last request of Gerald's, had that day felt obliged at least to open the box of papers.

The first document in the list was the will itself. George scanned it, confused by the convoluted legal language, the strange words and the enormous paragraphs of unpunctuated text. From what he could gather, there was money and a house for Carmella, and what was left went to Silvia. There was a list of investments, bank accounts and gifts to various charities including, appropriately, the Hospital of St Anthony of Padua, which was where Gerald had spent his last days.

However, what caught George's eye was a gift to Camilleri's godson, Joseph George Zammit, of 34 Oleander Street, Birkirkara, of 50,000 euros. For a moment, George thought Joseph George Zammit was a lucky man and wondered if he might be a distant relative. Then, he realised what this meant. It was a gift to Baby Joseph! Camilleri had given George's grandson 50,000 euros! His sudden movement, thrusting back his chair and jumping to his feet, disturbed the finches who flapped across the room to huddle together on top of the dresser.

He was about to rush into the kitchen and share his news with Marianna, Gina and Giorgio, who were watching a banal game show on the television, when something stopped him. He had to be sure. He needed it confirmed by Michael Agius and Marco Bonnici. They were serious people, who understood this sort of thing. For a start, was there sufficient money? It was one thing to promise a bequest once dead, but was the money there to give? George did not know. And were there conditions attached? Who could spend it and on what? Did Baby Joseph need to reach twenty-one, or some other particular age? Did he need to marry first? All these were possibilities. George needed answers, before he could tell the family. It also crossed his mind that Marianna and Gina might well just think the money was theirs to spend on the baby's behalf. He could already hear Marianna telling him: *Baby Joseph wouldn't mind. It's only a few thousand, isn't it, Gina?*

Then, there would be the Mifsuds to manage. Josette Mifsud certainly had some fancy ideas, definitely above what might be expected of a butcher's wife. And George knew, from experience, she could be as unreasonable as his own wife. They would feel entitled to have as much say as the Zammits in what happened with the money. Giorgio was not the sharpest knife in the block but, after all, he was the child's father. No. George needed to speak to the lawyer and Marco first.

It took him a little time to compose himself, but eventually he managed to put the thought of the money to one side and continued rooting through the box. A lot of the papers seemed to be of little interest. Files of tax returns, documents relating to various properties, records of dividend payments from investments. But at the bottom, marked *Private and for addressee's eyes only*, was a large buff envelope, sealed with parcel tape and addressed to George.

He weighed it in his hand. There was something heavy inside the envelope. For some reason, he sniffed at it, trying to guess its contents. Then, taking a knife from the best set of cutlery in the dresser drawer, he sliced into the tape. The first document he extracted was a letter.

Dear George,

As you are reading this, it means that my days are now over, and you and Marco Bonnici are burdened with the task of winding up my affairs. For that, I am sorry.

First, I thank you for your years of loyal service. I have enjoyed the times we worked together, especially the last few. It has been a privilege to know you.

Secondly, there is a grave responsibility that I have to pass on and I can think of no better person to carry this out than yourself. As you know, I have always tried to moderate the excesses of those in power, to ensure stable and responsible government. Malta is not unique in having a political class that seems to think achieving high office means unlimited personal access to the public purse. But, I am sorry to say, that this island seems afflicted with an elite class that needs constant supervision.

It has been necessary, on occasion, for me to remind certain of our political masters of the wider responsibilities of their office and, to do that, I collected information that I could use, when necessary, to persuade them to do the right thing.

This information might be in the form of recorded telephone conversations, intercepted mail, bank records, email threads – all of which I obtained illegally, but only ever used when necessary for the public good.

I was often asked why I never sought promotion within the force or high office myself. The reason was that I felt I could best serve the country by operating in my own way, as a check on the misuse of power.

However, I was not as clever as I thought and a year ago, to my horror, my office was broken into and the locked cabinet where I kept my private files was forced. The files themselves were not touched, only a collection of hard drives was taken, which I kept as a backup to the paper files. These drives contained copies of the material I had on: Edward Refalo, our prime minister; Raymond Farrugia, his chief of staff; Michael Cini, our minister for home affairs, national security and law enforcement; and Alfred Fiteni, the leader of the opposition.

I did not raise the alarm at the time, as I did not wish to disclose the nature of what had been taken. I thought I would watch the behaviour of the men concerned and try to detect any changes that might suggest the information was being used against them. This would then enable me to see who might be benefiting from such actions and I would have my culprit.

Now, in the later stages of my illness, it has become apparent to me that Refalo, Farrugia and Cini are all, to some degree, complicit in allowing the Russians to infiltrate our institutions. I have neither the strength nor, at the time I write this letter, the proof, to take the matter further, so this is the burden I pass on to you, George. Look at what has occurred since the date of this letter. Is there more evidence that Refalo, Farrugia or Cini are acting as facilitators for the Russians?

If so, read the material in the files in this box – hard copies of the digital files that were stolen from my office. If things have reverted to how they were before the arrival of the Russians, or if you do not have the appetite for the task, please, as one last service to me, destroy these papers. It is dangerous for you to have them in your possession.

I would suggest, if you feel the need to take action, you consult Marco Bonnici (I have always found him a good and reliable person, despite his other activities). There is a person who can evidence the authenticity of the documents. I still hesitate to name that person, as to do so would put them in peril and, unlike you, they might not prove to be such a resilient survivor! So, I must trust your deductive powers to identify the person concerned.

Once you have done this, you can choose to approach either a responsible person in the EU or in the United States security services, as these are the only two bodies who will be able to bring enough pressure to bear on the Russians. It is likely the drives in my office were stolen, or acquired, by agents of the Russian Federation and used to coerce the most senior officers in our government into allowing them access to our country. Subsequently, they were forced to collude in subverting our constitution. I wish you luck!

You will see that I have left a legacy to my godson, Joseph. I have never been blessed with children and it gives me pleasure to provide the young lad with the start in life that I never had. In the detailed provisions of my will, I have appointed you as a trustee of the legacy and I am confident you will make sure the money is spent wisely until he achieves the age of twenty-one, when what is left is his absolutely.

Yours in friendship,

Gerald Camilleri

Tears welled up in George's eyes. Gerald had spoken to him from beyond the grave. He could hear his friend's voice echo through his head as he read his words. There was no doubt things in Malta had become much worse since Gerald's death and George had often wondered why Refalo had allowed himself to be manipulated by the Russians. It now seemed obvious that he had been blackmailed.

It was not only a question of the disclosure of what might be in Gerald's files; speaking out had other risks. Ray Farrugia, of course, had been murdered on the streets of Brussels, when about to address the European Commission, and Michael Cini had languished in a cabin aboard a Russian warship and then been incarcerated in Camp Azure.

George decided to speak with Marco Bonnici and seek his counsel. He would not look at the files until he had done that. He knew that, once he looked, he would be burdened with that knowledge, whatever happened. He wondered how Gerald had managed to keep sane over the years, knowing so much, and yet saying so little. George slipped the envelope with the files into an old brown leather briefcase and pushed it under the dresser.

He then wondered how Gerald managed to get access to such inflammatory material. He was a senior policeman, that was true, but there were still limitations to what routinely passed over his desk – George knew that from his own experience. The only way Gerald could have got access to such sensitive material was by working with a government official. That must be the person he had referred to in his letter. George wondered who it might be?

One of the blue and red songbirds flew from the top of the dresser and settled on the table in front of him, cocking its head to one side. It looked at him through its black beady eyes, coyly turning its head one way then the other. It chirped and warbled for a bit, and, then, George would swear the damn' bird laughed at him.

CHAPTER 56
COLONEL FEDOROV
OFFICE OF THE PRIME MINISTER, VALLETTA, MALTA

DENZEL NEVER DID MAKE it to Libya, or even Liberia. Such was the outcry following the sinking of the *Peter the Great*, it proved almost impossible to leave the island. Every marina was crowded with volunteers and all recreational sailing was prohibited for a period of twenty-one days. Fedorov was determined to find the cell responsible for the attack on the battlecruiser and, against the constant drone of the motor horns of Malta's more than four hundred thousand vehicles, had decided to wage war on the civilian population.

He had found the spot above the grain silos in the Grand Harbour from where Huck had controlled the attack. By using the exact time of the impact, Fedorov managed to get the cyber warfare teams in the Army's Main Intelligence Directorate, back in Moscow, to locate the text message Huck had sent to Denzel, waiting in his kayak. There were very few messages sent in that area during the ten minutes either side of the first USV hit on the *Peter the Great*. The text read: *Let the babies fly.*

It stood out, not just because of what the message said, but because it was not sent in response to any earlier message and there was no response received from the recipient. The text stood alone. Crucially, the time it was sent was less than two minutes before the first strike. From there, it was straightforward to identify the phone numbers of the sender and recipient and track the source of both burner phones to the small shop in Sliema where Denzel had purchased them.

The owner of the shop, who employed no other staff, remembered the sale very clearly. A tall, good looking, thirty-year-old Maltese man, with short black hair, had bought his entire stock of twelve prepaid phones, paying in cash, something that had never happened before. He also remembered the man did not need a bag for the phones, as he dropped them into a yellow and red Birkirkara Football Club sports bag.

Fedorov then had his own men comb all CCTV footage in the area, including passing buses, trying to find the man who had purchased the phones. He was finally spotted, in images time-stamped ten minutes after the till-roll recorded the purchase, carrying the distinctive sports bag. He was walking along the promenade in Sliema, heading towards the car park opposite the ferry terminal. Unfortunately, the only images available were all rear view. It proved impossible to get a clear picture of his face.

George's team had been reviewing all the images from CCTV cameras around the Grand Harbour. It proved to be a massive and fruitless task, apart from one file, from a camera on Coal Wharf, which showed a solo kayaker making his way from the Southeast Extension, towards Senglea. A young female police officer kept excitedly stressing how the kayaker seemed to be waiting and that his gaze followed the line of the USVs, as they headed towards the battlecruiser. After the explosion, she noted, almost as an afterthought, the man felt in his pocket and donned a full-face balaclava.

Chelotti tried to ignore her and, when she persisted, scoffed: "Well, if you were on the water and saw three unmanned jet skis flying around, in formation, I bet you would take a second look."

The young constable was not convinced and continued to peer at the screen.

"I knew he reminded me of someone. It's funny, but doesn't he look a bit like Sergeant Zammit? You know, Denzel Zammit? Is he still on the run?"

Chelotti casually strolled over to the screen, a cup of coffee in his hand. He examined the image.

"Don't be ridiculous. I know young Zammit, and it looks nothing like him. How long have you been on duty? You're seeing things. Go on, take a break. I'll take over for a while."

The constable left in a huff, to go to the canteen, while Chelotti took her seat. He considered deleting the file but decided against it. It could only lead to more trouble. He had to warn George. That was the best thing he could do. He cursed Denzel's stupidity.

Right at that moment, Fedorov stormed into Police HQ, making straight for George's office, where he found him enjoying his second breakfast of two ricotta and pea *pastizzi*. The Russian slapped a file onto the table in front of George, who hurriedly brushed the crumbs off the front of his shirt.

"There, take a look. That's what I've been doing. How about you?"

George blanched, as he read the report confirming the discovery of the man who had purchased the burner phones. He looked at the photos captured from the CCTV and felt his heart leap in his chest. The red and yellow sports bag was at that very moment lying in one corner of their kitchen in Birkirkara, containing Denzel's washing from the apartment.

"Er ... *mela*, very impressive. I suppose we concentrate our search on looking for a tall Maltese man?"

"No, you fool!" shouted Fedorov. "We get a photofit picture from the shopkeeper, who appears to have half a brain, and we organise a door-to-door search in Birkirkara, wherever that is, and stop everybody who's carrying a red and yellow sports bag! I want it done immediately! Put a cordon around this

Birkirkara place, search every house with a thirty-year-old male in residence, and compare all of them to the photofit and the images grabbed from the CCTV. Ask if anyone in the house owns one of these red and yellow sports bags! We're going to get this character."

As he spun on his heel to leave, he shouted: "I sometimes wonder what you do all day!"

With that, he stormed out, leaving George red-faced with embarrassment, still chewing the remnants of the pastry. Chelotti entered immediately afterwards to tell him Denzel had been spotted, kayaking of all things, across the Grand Harbour, at the very time of the attack.

"How stupid can you get?" the inspector hissed. "He knew there must be CCTV all over the place. Listen, I can't delete the file, it's too obvious, but you'd better do something – and quickly."

George shook his head in disbelief, then thanked Karl Chelotti and immediately rushed to Chelotti's uncle's house to bundle Denzel into the back of his marked police car and drive, with the blue light turning, to St Paul's, where his brother Albert kept his fishing boat.

The boat was out of the water, perched on high blocks, in the back of an old scrapyard. Wrecked cars and commercial vehicles sat quietly crumbling, while the salty wind stripped their paint and turned steel into flaking red iron oxide. The nasty looking dog that was supposed to guard the place lay in the sun, a length of chain attached to its collar, idly flicking its tail in welcome. His brother could not afford the fancy boat-yards and marina facilities.

Denzel clambered up into the cabin and tried to make himself comfortable. George told him to be quiet and keep inside. He then set off to find Albert and explain what was happening, before working out their next move.

The Car Horn Revolution had been reported globally and every radio, TV and video report in Malta featured the backing track of thousands of car horns. Reports of Malta's resistance to the German and Italian Second World War bombing campaign was cited as evidence of the doughty Maltese resilience.

The sinking of the *Peter the Great* was big news around the globe and reported with glee in the Western media, which themed it as a David and Goliath story. Despite Fedorov's injunction, images of the stricken warship, lying on its side in the Grand Harbour, had become a symbol of the failure of Russian power and were seen by an audience of countless millions.

Whatever the Russians had thought they might achieve in Malta seemed to be slipping through their fingers, like so much dry sand from Golden Bay beach. Criticism of them from countries on all continents was now unanimous and unrelenting. NATO had assembled a formidable naval fleet, at Souda Bay in Crete, that planned to position itself off Hurds Bank, in close proximity to what was left of the Russian battlegroup.

The NATO and American bases at Ramstein, Germany, and Signorella in Sicily, were alive with the sound of racing engines, rushing aircrews and multiple take offs and landings, as jets from across Europe gathered in a formidable show of air power. The *Admiral of the Fleet, Putin* had fled Malta, following the attack on the *Peter the Great* but, in its haste to escape, had suffered a mechanical failure in its propulsion system and was in the process of being towed to the Russian naval base at Tartus, Syria. It was shadowed by several US destroyers that constantly buzzed the labouring Russian convoy, offering assistance on a twice-daily basis, to further humiliate the Russian officers.

Ambassador Grigori Buzilov had been temporarily recalled to Moscow and, on his return, had a tense meeting with Colonel Fedorov, in the Russian Command's restored eighteenth century town house, Casa Gwardamanġa – the villa, just outside Valletta, which was beloved by the late Queen Elizabeth II and her husband Prince Philip. It had been their home during the early years of their marriage, when the prince was an officer in the Royal Navy stationed in Malta. As soon as Igor Fedorov had heard about the villa's history, he had gleefully requisitioned it as living quarters for himself and his aides.

Ambassador Buzilov was lounging in a soft leather armchair, one arm draped over its side. Colonel Fedorov was pacing the room, the steel tips on his heels clattering against the mosaic flooring. The ambassador told Fedorov that Moscow was alarmed by the way the project had backfired and, after the embarrassment of the 'special military operation' in Ukraine, deeply concerned about further damage to the country's already rock-bottom reputation, thanks to evidence of yet more shortcomings in its armed forces. He smiled at Fedorov and said he had a feeling they were looking for scapegoats.

Fedorov decided there was no one else he could trust, so related the conversation with the Bonnicis to him.

The ambassador listened and smiled.

"The famous 'off-ramp'! A possible way out, negotiated by the Americans and the EU? I cannot see what will be in it for us, but there is nothing to be lost from seeing what comes back from them. Press on, Igor, but keep me informed. You will need my help to deliver on this one. Moscow will not want to be forced into a climbdown, but I fear they may have little choice."

Fedorov was left to gaze out of the window, deep in thought. His musings were interrupted by an aide lightly knocking on the door. A young officer entered and stood stiffly in the doorway. Fedorov glared at him from his position by the window.

"Well? You've interrupted me. It must be urgent, so out with it. What do you want?"

"We had a call from a constable in Commissioner Zammit's Home Security Command. A young officer, Rita Bonello. She's certain she's identified one of the attackers, but her superior, Inspector Chelotti, disagrees. Anyway, she's gone over his head and brought it directly to us. We've sent a car to fetch her."

Fedorov looked interested.

"A breakthrough, perhaps?

The messenger shuffled his feet nervously.

"We hope so. The inspector doesn't think it's Denzel Zammit and is furious the constable's making such a fuss. But he did say, he'd forgotten his spectacles this morning and ..."

Fedorov froze, not believing what he was hearing.

"Denzel Zammit? What're you saying, man? The man spotted in the canoe is *the* Denzel Zammit?" For a moment, Fedorov was speechless.

The messenger cringed and said:

"That's what she's saying and the time stamp, is, well it's ... it's the exact time the ... the battleship was hit."

"*Da ty chto*! You're kidding me! Zammit?" Fedorov was furious. "Well, don't just stand there, get out and find him! And, where's his father, the commissioner, I want him here, now!" he screamed.

The messenger stuttered: "Er ... of course, we've looked for the commissioner, sir, but he's disappeared... he took a car and ... well, he's gone."

Fedorov slammed his hand against the desk.

"How big is this island? Thirty kilometres by fifteen. It's tiny! Find the car, find them! I want every man we've got out there looking. No one is to stop until they're found!"

CHAPTER 57
MARCO BONNICI
CASTELLO BONNICI, IL-WARDIJA, MALTA

Marco and Natasha were sitting at the breakfast table. Marco had a copy of the *Malta Telegraph* in front of him, while Natasha was looking at her phone. She had found herself reverting to her old habit of browsing the online versions of the *Financial Times* and *New York Times* each morning. The atmosphere was relaxed when Marco folded his newspaper and asked if they could chat.

Natasha laughed and said of course they could, but five minutes later, all laughter had faded from the room and the atmosphere had become ominous. Marco had eventually got round to telling her about his plans to take a flat in Bern and his deepening friendship with Laura.

At first, she listened carefully and nodded along, to indicate that she was following what he was saying. Gradually, as she started to put the full picture together, her demeanour changed. She wanted to be reasonable, to take account of her father's position, but the old feelings started to reassert themselves. What began as an uncomfortable sensation in her gut, grew into an irresistible pulse, beating in her temples. She felt all reason abandon her, leaving only the need to hurt and wound, to make her father feel what she felt.

"It always happens like that, doesn't it? Just as I'm starting to feel better and happier, you kick me in the guts. Again! You just toss me to one side, like you did before. You never intended to stay here – you can't wait to leave and be with her. I get it. You were just hanging around until you got up the nerve to tell me about it."

"Natasha, that is not it at all …"

"Oh, but it is. And that duplicitous bitch wearing a white coat, too! To think that I trusted her … So, tell me, were you two at it while I was lying in hospital and she was raking around in my mind, asking me the most personal questions? Were you?"

"It was not like that, Natasha …"

"Oh, I bet it wasn't! Did the two of you meet up afterwards for a good laugh at what the madwoman was saying? And you paid her many thousands for shabby psychotherapy and second-rate accommodation … just a proxy payment so you could screw her! She's a whore! You disgust me!"

"Natasha, stop, enough! Laura acted in a totally professional way – you have to believe that. And she cares about what happens to you."

"Oh, she cares about me, does she? That's a lie. She doesn't give a damn! All she's after is you and your filthy money. Does she know about that? I bet she does …"

"You are so wrong. She sees you only as a patient, someone who needs help. She does care what happens to you, and so do I. We want to try to be a family for you."

"A family?" Natasha screamed. "What a joke!"

"Look, you are a grown woman, and you are a hundred times better than you were before – you have even returned to work. I now lead a different life, remember? A life I chose for myself to preserve my own sanity, after what happened in Milan. Remember that? But here I am, nevertheless, supporting you. A word of gratitude would not go amiss."

"Gratitude? When you're screwing my psychiatrist, or

whatever she is. You think *I* should show gratitude? Who's the crazy one here? I knew what was going on, but I didn't think anything would come of it. I didn't think you'd leave me for her! I still can't believe it."

The tears rolled down Natasha's face and her fists bunched at her sides.

"Just go, Dad, leave me alone. I don't want you to hang around if you'd rather be somewhere else. It's always me who's left alone."

At that moment, Asano appeared between them, carrying a tray containing a small, blue-patterned teapot with a bamboo handle and two drinking bowls. He hesitated, but eventually moved closer and placed the tray on the breakfast table.

"So sorry to interrupt, but I bring yuzu tea. Is good to reduce stress and to balance mind, body and spirit. And please forgive intrusion. Also, Signor Bonnici, Commissioner Zammit and Sergeant Zammit wait in library. They have no appointment but say they need to speak urgently. Please forgive, if I make mistake."

He bowed and backed out of the room.

Natasha's tear-stained face was averted. She stared out into the early autumn sunshine.

"Off you go, Dad. See what they want." She took a napkin from the breakfast tray and dabbed her eyes. "They wouldn't be here unless there was trouble." Marco took a deep breath.

"Yes, I suspect you are right. But one last thing you should know – Laura is coming to Malta the day after tomorrow. Her sole purpose is to talk to you. She wants to assure herself that this can all work out."

"Well, Dad, tell her from me – it can't and it won't!"

Asano was hovering a few paces back from the table, hands clasping the opposite wrist.

"Shall I pour tea?"

Natasha told him: "Asano, just fuck off, will you!"

George knew from Denzel that Marco was hiding Huck and Billy. They had fled the apartment in Siġġiewi and hidden out in a hot and uncomfortable disused outbuilding, concealed on the agricultural terracing that was part of the *castello*'s estate. The provision of this safe house had been agreed between Marco and Mary-Ann Baker, as emergency fallback accommodation, in the event the Siġġiewi apartment became compromised. Baker told the men she was reluctant to take them off the island just yet, as she sensed they were now in the endgame, and she would rather have them in play.

He also knew from his conversations with Natasha that she and her father were sympathetic to the resistance cause so, in the absence of any other alternative, he had made immediately for the *castello*, to ask Marco for help in hiding Denzel and himself. Marco had sighed and asked Asano to conceal George's car in the garages, covering it with tarpaulin.

"You know, I cannot become the first port of call for everyone who is fleeing from the Russians, or I will end up in Camp Azure myself."

George wrung his hands, "*Mela*, I know, Marco, but we've nowhere else to go right now. And we need to contact Huck and Billy and see if they can help us, or at least get Denzel off the island. Denzel said that you …"

"I will stop you there. Huck and Billy are one hundred metres down the hill, in an old barn, so your luck is in. You had better tell me what has been going on and I will speak to my American contact and see if they can arrange something for you and Denzel. I will make a call but can give no guarantees. You understand?"

Denzel said: "Of course we do. We're very grateful." Marco smiled.

"Well, when the history of this episode comes to be written, just make sure they give me a mention.

"In the meantime, Asano will show you to the west wing, where there are a few spare rooms. Some friends of Natasha stayed there a while back and made a bit of a mess, so forgive the smell of bleach. It lingers. Best keep your head down and avoid my daughter. She is not in the best of moods. In fact, George, you and Denzel could do me a favour.

"Tomorrow, a special of friend of mine is arriving. Natasha has rather taken against her. Could you keep an eye on my daughter, please, just in case ... well, you know how she can be."

George knew exactly how she could be.

That evening, Natasha took dinner in her room. George, Denzel and Marco ate in the back kitchen, while Huck and Billy lay around in their stone hut, down on the terraces, eating noodles brought to them by Asano. George was explaining about the contents of the box he had received from Gerald Camilleri.

"... so, you see, Marco, it was all there! Copies of the bank statements, transcripts, emails, documents ... all together. Gerald had constructed a complete chain of evidence – everything you'd need to *prove* Refalo, Farrugia, God rest his soul, and Cini were corrupt and being blackmailed by the Russians! He even had a file on Alfred Fiteni, the opposition leader."

"I know who Fiteni is, George. But where is this box now?"

George looked sheepish and took a deep breath.

"I'm afraid it's in my dining room."

"And we can assume your apartment is being watched?"

"Well, yes, of course. That's what I would do in their position."

Marco realised getting hold of the documents could well prove difficult.

Asano had presented them with a strange-tasting spicy soup, with what George thought of as overcooked pasta in it, oddly sweet pork and undercooked vegetables. Denzel saw the confused expression on his father's face and asked: "Are you enjoying the ramen, Dad?"

George waited till Asano had melted away before he replied: "*Mela*, it's a little odd, but maybe the main course will be more to my taste. No offence, Marco."

"None taken, George, but I am sorry to say that *was* the main course. We had the sushi as a starter, if you recall."

"Oh! Yes, that cold fish and rice thing. Do they actually eat that in Japan?"

Marco smiled at Denzel.

"George, they eat sushi all over the world. Listen, I can see you are not a fan of Japanese food. Shall I ask Asano to rustle up a cheese board for you?"

George smiled, happy at the prospect of proper food.

"Yes, please, that would be good. Er … this Asano, he seems to be listening to our conversations. I know we're in his kitchen and it can't be helped, but all the same … do you trust him, Marco?"

"Don't worry about Asano, he is completely reliable. I am more concerned about how we retrieve the papers from your apartment."

There were a few moments of silence. Then, George said: "You know, one way we could get those papers is to find someone who could slip past the watchers unnoticed and smuggle the papers back to us. I might know exactly the man for the job."

At that moment, George's mobile vibrated. He removed it from his pocket and glanced at the caller ID. It was Marianna. There were over a dozen messages asking him to ring HQ, Mallia, Fedorov, Marianna and Gina – all of which he had ignored. He stood and said to Marco:

"Excuse me. My wife's probably wondering where I am. I'd better tell her."

Marco raised an eyebrow.

"No, I don't mean tell her ... just let her know we're safe!".

George walked to the hall and accepted the call.

"Don't say anything. Den and I are alright. We're safe. We can't talk – they can trace calls. You've seen it done on TV ..."

"I'm not bothered about TV, you can't just run off like that, without a word ... I've been worried sick ... and we've had the Russians round. That 'Federcoff' man. I know he's a Russian, but he was ever so nice to Gina and me. Polite, and handsome too ... lovely eyes. You know, the uniform really suited ..."

"Marianna, enough! I'll get messages to you, but this phone isn't safe. Please, just be patient."

"Well, it's alright for you to say that, but anyway, they had a nice man with them who fixed the phone. Said it needed something doing to it ... it didn't take him two minutes ... I didn't even know there was a problem ..."

"My love, I'm going. Don't worry, we're both fine." George hastily cut the call and returned to the kitchen.

Marco asked: "Everything ...?"

"Yes, yes. Bit tricky, but all okay. Sort of." Marco took a deep breath.

"So, you were telling us how we could get the papers out of your house, without attracting attention? How would that work?"

"*Mela*, I think I could persuade Father Peter to go to our friend's second-floor apartment on the opposite side of the block. We could get Joe Mifsud to deliver a message to Marianna about the plan. She could put the papers into a bag and take the bag into the courtyard, where the priest would lower a string from our friend's apartment window. He could then pull the bag up two floors and transfer the papers into his own bag. Then, he'd bring them to a nearby meeting place and pass them to Asano. Easy peasy!"

Denzel blew out his cheeks on hearing the plan. "Well, what can possibly go wrong with that!" As it turned out, quite a lot.

CHAPTER 58
THE ZAMMITS
ZAMMIT FAMILY HOME, BIRKIRKARA, MALTA

FOR MANY YEARS, a considerable amount of ill will had existed between Marianna and another neighbour of theirs, Karmenu Cardona, who lived in the apartment on the first floor, beneath that of the Zammits' friend. Karmenu was a dirty, bad tempered old widower, whose apartment was opposite the Zammits' kitchen window. If he raised himself over his sink unit, he could just about peer down into Marianna's kitchen. He rarely bothered putting on a shirt and, all summer, could be seen in a yellowing string vest, which failed to cover his coating of straggly, grey body hair, some baggy stained flannel trousers and open sandals that revealed his thick, clawlike toenails.

Marianna had long suspected him of being a Peeping Tom and had repeatedly warned Gina not to run around the kitchen, searching for clean laundry, in her underwear. One day, Marianna was sure she had seen his face pressed to his window, staring into their kitchen, and had rounded on the malevolent old man in the local grocer's, calling him a 'disgrace and a pervert'. Then, to the delight of the other shoppers, he had retaliated with a barrage of foul-mouthed obscenities, calling Marianna an evil bitch and a small-minded, malicious gossip, who should wash her mouth out and seek Confession, if she could find a priest who could bear to listen to her.

Karmenu Cardona happened to be at his sink the evening the plan to collect the bag was put into action. The first thing he noticed was a length of blue twine dangle past him as it descended into the rear courtyard, to which only the Zammits had access. He had long found their exclusive use of the courtyard a source of deep annoyance. Over the years, he had watched George snooze away the weekend afternoons out there or spend evenings drinking beer with his son, and seen the voluptuous Gina grow into a fine figure of a woman.

Always a curious – some would say nosy – man, Karmenu hoisted himself up onto the draining board and looked out to see Marianna tying a red-and-yellow Birkirkara F.C. sports bag onto the end of the twine. She had felt the bag was the strongest option for the weighty pile of papers they needed to move, so had emptied out Denzel's laundry and plonked the documents inside it. Karmenu pulled back from the window and, a moment later, the bag floated upwards past his kitchen, secured to the string. He had immediately gone to the front door and looked up the staircase to the landing where, shortly afterwards, the door of the upstairs apartment opened and Father Peter, from the Parochial Church of the Assumption, appeared, carrying the bag.

Father Peter hurried past, muttering: "Good evening, Karmenu."

He immediately knew something was wrong, as Father Peter had a reputation for engaging all his parishioners, and anyone else who might listen to him, in long and tedious discourse.

Karmenu called down the stairs after him: "Father, have you got a minute? What's the big secret? What're you hiding in that bag?"

The guilty look on the priest's face told Karmenu he was onto something. As usual, the old man was dressed in a yellowing vest and greasy slacks, his wispy white hair uncombed and his sagging chops covered in four-or-five-days' growth of white stubble.

"Father, why're you running away? What've you got to hide?"

Karmenu started to descend the steps methodically and shuffled after the priest. Eventually, Father Peter scurried around the front of the apartment block and moved quickly past the two soldiers, sitting in an Armed Forces of Malta jeep, who were watching the Zammits' front door, in case George or Denzel decided to return. They were amused to see the old man tottering after the priest, heckling him as he moved off down the road.

"Come on, Father, what's in the bag? Come back! Priests shouldn't have secrets. What's that cow, Marianna Zammit, given you, eh?"

The soldiers' ears pricked up. They looked at each other, then at the priest, as he crossed the road ahead of them.

The first soldier got out of the jeep and called after Karmenu.

"Hey, old guy! What's going on?"

Karmenu loved an audience, and he was out of breath from chasing the priest, so was happy to stop.

"The priest's hiding something in that bag, something he shouldn't have, I know it. They hauled it out of the Zammits' courtyard – you know, the policeman – and up two floors. And you know the trouble that Denzel Zammit's in – they say he's resistance, they do. I mean, I don't like you lot, nothing but trouble since you arrived, but the Zammits ... getting far too up themselves!"

The second soldier was looking down the road at the departing priest, who had broken into a jog to hasten his escape. Suddenly, he grabbed his colleague's arm.

"Look! The priest's got a red-and-yellow bag, see?" He pointed towards it, the priest having made the basic error of failing to empty the contents of the sports bag into one of his own. He was, by now, at the end of the street. "Remember those CCTV pictures?" The soldiers exchanged a glance. The penny dropped. "He's got Zammit's bag! Let's go!"

The pair of them sprinted after the priest, who had rounded a corner up ahead of them. As they ran around it, they saw Father Peter hand the sports bag to a slightly built, far eastern-looking man, dressed in black clothing. The man ushered the priest to the passenger seat of a white Range Rover and shut the door. He turned to watch the two soldiers approach. They did not break stride, nor did they unholster their side arms, but ran right up to him.

Taekwondo is perhaps the most lethal of the martial arts. It focuses on the practitioner's striking ability, with elegant and quick footwork. Exponents use their feet to gain an advantage over opponents and the force of their strikes can render an adversary unconscious. Asano used a *Dollyeo Chagi*, or roundhouse kick, to flatten the first oncoming soldier. Then a lightning fast *Mureup Chigi* or knee strike, straight into the chest, to halt the second. As they lay prostrate on the ground, with two quick and deadly moves, he struck the soldiers on the side of their heads, as hard as he could, with the heel of his foot. He heard bones crack and they lay still. Calmly smoothing his hair back into place, he took a breath and glanced around. It seemed there were no witnesses to the entire incident, save for Karmenu Cardona, who quietly turned away and resolved to mind his own business in future – at least, in so far as the Zammit family were concerned. Asano got into the Range Rover and unhurriedly drove away.

Father Peter directed Asano to a monastery near Rabat, which was part of the Carmelite Order, where the terrified priest said he would seek refuge, claiming ill health, until the Russians had left and it was safe for him to return to his parish. As the priest left the car, he turned to Asano and made the sign of the cross, saying: "May the Lord forgive you your sins."

Asano smiled. He needed neither forgiveness, nor the blessing of a priest. He then drove back to the *castello*, where George, Denzel and Marco were waiting.

As Asano handed Marco the red and yellow sports bag, Marco asked him: "Any problems?"

"No problems. But best to keep Range Rover in garage for little time. Sorry to cause inconvenience."

CHAPTER 59
NATASHA BONNICI
CASTELLO BONNICI, IL-WARDIJA, MALTA

Laura Weber had arrived at the *castello* late in the evening. Anticipating the event, Natasha had withdrawn to her room earlier than usual. She had lain awake, waiting for the Mercedes to arrive, listening out for the sound of the metal gates swinging open and the car rolling to a halt under the imposing stone portico. She pulled the bedclothes over her head, as she heard the sound of car doors opening and closing. There were muffled voices, as the car was unloaded and then she heard the creak of the large-leafed, solid wood entrance door swing open on its huge hinges.

All was quiet then for at least an hour, until there was a low murmuring and suppressed laughter, while her father led Laura past Natasha's bedroom door, on their way to his rooms on the east side of the house. She squeezed her eyes shut to fight the tears and her fists gripped the bedsheets until her knuckles were white. Finally, she succumbed, burying her head in her pillow, and started to sob.

It was even harder to bear than she had imagined it would be. She tried her breathing exercises. In – one, two, three, four; hold – one, two, three, four; out – one, two, three, four; repeat. Again, and again. Eventually, sleep did come, but it was disturbed by dreams of betrayal and banishment, being lost and alone in strange, distant places.

When morning came, Natasha made sure she was down to take her seat at breakfast in good time. It was a Thursday and her day to take classes at the gym in one of the big hotels in St Julian's. She had tied her hair back and wore sporty leggings with a bright red branded sports top, looking the picture of health. Inside, she was exhausted and in turmoil.

To her surprise, Laura walked into the room alone. She was a woman who understood good posture. She had a straight back and a long neck, which made her look taller than she was. Natasha noticed at once that Laura was dressed entirely in white, which had echoes of the surgical gown Natasha was used to seeing her in. Natasha knew the scheming woman would have thought carefully about her wardrobe and immediately took the white cashmere jumper and white flared trousers as an opening gambit in the game that was to come. The costume was there not to complement Laura's ash blonde hair or peaches and cream complexion, but to remind Natasha of their respective roles as doctor and patient and all the imbalance of power that came with that.

Laura forced a smile and went straight to Natasha, to kiss her gently on both cheeks.

"Natasha, lovely to see you again. And thank you for welcoming me to your home. It is even more beautiful than I was led to believe."

Natasha fixed her gaze on Laura's pale blue eyes.

"It's only a building – it's the people who make it a home."

"Quite so. I wanted a chat before Marco came down. Just you and me."

"Do normal confidentiality rules apply? I mean, apart from the fact I tell you everything and you then immediately share it with my father? Also, if this is a professional chat, who's paying, me or Dad?" Laura sighed.

"Please, Natasha. I understand this is a tricky situation and

I am sorry if you are upset by it. I can understand your confusion. But, despite our age, Marco and I have fallen in love." She shrugged and shook her head. "I know it sounds strange, but it is true. There was nothing we could do about it. I wish the circumstances were different, but they are what they are. I was hoping you might find it in you to be happy for us."

Natasha scoffed: "Spare me the schmaltz! You're not fifteen. Listen, if you two are going to be together, carrying on like a pair of schoolchildren, there's nothing I can do about it – but I don't have to like it and I don't have to like you. The best thing you can do, if you want to make me happy, is for both of you to disappear back to Bern and let me get on with my life here."

"Maybe you are right, Natasha. I just wanted to see you, face to face, and offer to do anything that might bring us a little closer together – mainly for your father's sake. He worries about you."

"Worries about me? I don't think so. Anyway, I've decided I don't care what you and he get up to. It's your business. Just don't involve me or pretend that I'm part of your new happy family. Do you have children?"

"No, I am afraid not."

"That's a mercy. Anyway, don't think you can adopt me to fill that particular hole. Get a cat!"

With that, Natasha threw her napkin down onto the table, pushed back her chair and left, barging into George in the doorway, as she did so. He was helping Asano and bringing a flask of coffee through to the breakfast terrace. George and Denzel ate in the kitchen, where there was a servants' staircase up to the rooms in the west wing. George was happy with the arrangement, as he did not want to impose on the family, and it also allowed him to keep a wide berth from Natasha. It was also a convenient exit, up to their rooms, in case of unexpected visitors.

Natasha snapped at him.

"And you – I don't get what you're doing here! Don't you

have family of your own somewhere? When my father leaves, you and those goons in the barn can all sling your hook and find somewhere else. I don't see why I should risk my neck for you lot."

George was speechless, and stood holding the silver coffee pot, his mouth gaping.

Natasha stormed off up to her bedroom to brood. As she ran up the stairs, she found herself standing on the half-landing, between the twin white marble flights of stairs leading up from it. It was the very spot where her mother had died.

Natasha knew she was responsible, that she had pushed Sophia but, after so many years trying to remember the details, with only imagination filling the gaps, fact and fiction had become blurred and she could not, in truth, recall exactly what had happened. All she knew was that her innocence had been lost that day and Marco's heart had been broken. Recently, Laura had picked and worried over that episode, trying to elicit some memory, some emotion attached to the events. But Natasha was too wary to be drawn into giving any details.

She looked up the nearest flight of stairs. The door to her bedroom was a few metres away from the top. It would only take three strides from there to reach the first step. When she had spent nights in the *castello* by herself, she had armed herself with a wooden axe handle. The weight of it balanced beautifully in her hand and she was sure that, should any interloper happen to come up those stairs, a blow from her cudgel would be more than enough to crack a human skull. The thought of it in readiness under her bed had provided comfort when the wind blew and whistled down the dark stone corridors of the drafty old building, and the midnight creaks and groans of the timbers sounded like an army of approaching demons.

She stood very still for some seconds, then quickly turned back and went down the stairs to the entrance hall. She opened the door onto the front drive. There was a flower bed by the gate, which contained a huge bougainvillaea and a mature japonica tree. Natasha clumped about in the bed, picking up as much mud and dirt on her trainers as possible. She then slipped them off and ran back inside to the foot of the stairs. Carefully putting the shoes back on, she deliberately left a trail of dirt all the way up the stairs. Satisfied with her work, she then slipped off her shoes, and went back down the staircase, in bare feet, and into the kitchen, where Asano was loading a dishwasher.

"I'm sorry, Asano, but I've trailed mud all the way up the stairs. You couldn't run a mop over them, could you?"

Asano said nothing, but bowed slightly and nodded his assent. Natasha smiled sweetly.

There was nothing more slippery than wet marble.

She sat behind her bedroom door on a stool that was usually kept at her dressing table. The old wooden door was ajar and, like most of the original fixtures in the *castello*, was a poor fit, so there was a gap between the hinged side of it and the architrave. This narrow aspect afforded her a view of the hall below, so she could see someone approach the stairs and ascend to the first landing. The staircase then split to the left and right. A gallery ran around three sides of the main entrance hall. The left-hand flight of stairs served the side closest to the west wing, while the right served the main bedrooms on the east side, including Natasha's and Marco's rooms.

Natasha's dirty footprints had marked the right-hand branch of the staircase. She sat, watching and waiting. It only took a minute before Asano appeared with a galvanised janitor's bucket and a classic wooden-handled mop. He had slipped off his straw soled sandals and set to work, bare foot. Natasha leaned the axe handle against the wall, within easy reach. Asano was thorough in his work, slopping copious amounts of water on every step. Natasha smiled.

When he had finished, he disappeared, only to return

seconds later with a bundle of cloths and a large blue roll of commercial kitchen paper. He used the first of the cloths to soak up the film of water from each of the steps. Then, he tore off lengths of kitchen roll and meticulously dried every square centimetre of every step, pushing the crumpled balls of damp paper into a black bin bag. Taking the softest of the cloths, he slowly polished each step till it shone. Natasha chewed the inside of her cheek. That man – she hated him!

Asano examined his work, gathered together his cleaning equipment and made to leave. Suddenly, he stopped and turned to look up the staircase, directly towards Natasha's door. He was like an animal in the bush, unexpectedly alert to a danger as yet unseen. His black irises, unblinking, seemed to see or sense her, through the wood of the door she sat behind. She did not move or breathe. Slowly, he turned away and made his way back towards the kitchens.

Natasha remained perfectly still, watching through the crack between the door and frame. Her stomach churned and lurched, her breathing quickened. She could not believe what she was about to do. A feeling of nausea rose in her throat. She dismissed it as excitement and took a firm grip of the axe handle. She waited, playing the game of predator and prey.

CHAPTER 60
COMMISSIONER FOR HOME SECURITY GEORGE ZAMMIT

CASTELLO BONNICI, IL-WARDIJA, MALTA

MARCO JOINED LAURA AT BREAKFAST. He saw immediately that her facial muscles were taut and she was looking pained. "So, how did it go? Was she at least polite?" Laura pushed out her bottom lip.

"I am sad, Marco. I had hoped for more." She took his cup and poured the rich, dark coffee she knew he liked. For a moment, the roast and smoky aromas filled the space between them. "I think maybe you are right. There is too much there to unpack and a lack of trust at a basic level. She feels misunderstood and I am certain I am now part of the problem, not the solution. Until Natasha wants to resolve her issues and will commit to the process of therapy, there is nothing I can do for her." Laura paused in her diagnosis. "How is the coffee?"

"It is good." Marco knew there was more to come. So, he sat back and waited, letting Laura work things through in her own mind. She poured herself a coffee.

"Was I vain or naïve, thinking I could help? I was certainly wrong. And now, loving you, how on earth could I hope to do any good, when Natasha's negative feelings towards you are transferred onto me?

"I have never given up on a patient before, but I have to

accept, Natasha has given up on me – if she was ever committed in the first place."

Laura smiled and Marco reached across the table, taking her hand.

"I am glad you tried. If you had not, you would always have wondered what might have been possible. I think it is best you return to Bern. There is nothing to be served by staying here. I have to spend some time working this morning, then I will show you Valletta. There are some good boutique hotels. I suggest we stay in the city tonight, until your flight. I will get Asano to make a reservation. I know we will be more relaxed there and can have dinner overlooking the Grand Harbour. It is an absolutely wonderful view." Laura smiled.

"You understand me so well. You go and do what you have to do. I am going to have a walk around the estate; then I will pack."

Marco checked his watch and went to meet George and Denzel in the *castello*'s library. That room was Marco's favourite. The tall stacks of ancient leather-bound tomes had been cured by generations of tobacco smoke and stoked wood fires. The heavy dark mahogany furniture and brass fittings created an almost ecclesiastical atmosphere. George had been in the room several times before and had been intimidated by the aura of scholastic devotion and learning that had been absent from his own mediocre performance at Saint Aloysius College.

Marco had spent the early part of the previous evening, before leaving to collect Laura from the airport, examining the documents that George had received from Gerald Camilleri. On one level, he was horrified to find what Refalo and Farrugia had been up to, but on another, their subsequent actions now all made perfect sense. They had put themselves in thrall to the Russians. It was apparent to Marco that the misdeeds of the prime minister and his chief of staff had pointed the Russian cyber agencies in the direction of any additional hard evidence they needed for their blackmail dossiers.

The criminal enterprises that Refalo and Farrugia had undertaken for their own financial gain were reprehensible enough, but the way they had used their office to advance Russian interests, whether through the disclosure of NATO naval exercises, of which the Maltese government became aware, or the exercise of Malta's vote in the European Council, to frustrate the imposition of restrictive measures or sanctions, was most certainly a breach of the Americans' widely drawn Espionage Act and a host of European and Maltese laws.

On reading the papers, it had become apparent to Marco that Camilleri must have had an inside source, someone who had sat in cabinet and who was somehow privy to Refalo's misdeeds. Marco, George and Denzel had been in the library since early that morning, glued to the paperwork. Marco had only stepped out briefly, to catch up with Laura at breakfast. On his return, he found George and Denzel in jubilant mood, their faces flushed with excitement.

"We think we know who Camilleri's mole was, or rather is," said George.

He ushered Marco into his seat and Denzel pulled up a number of documents and pointed to the initials ER/RAF/MRC/CB/LtC.D. Denzel gave the background.

"These are the minutes of a meeting, marked 'Top Secret', in Castille, to discuss the refuelling of NATO vessels on Hurds Bank, during the Operation Windstorm exercise – back end of last year. Refalo agreed to support over twenty NATO vessels that would muster, refuel and restock on Hurds Bank, as part of an exercise to retake Tripoli in Libya. You remember, there was talk that it was at risk of being overrun by Russian volunteers and Benghazi government rebels?"

"So what?" said Marco.

"*Mela*," explained George, "you remember the whole thing was a disaster, because the Russians had two submarines waiting on Hurds Bank, the day before the first NATO ship turned up? The Russians surprised them – it was a real embarrassment for NATO. Somehow the Russians knew what was going on."

"Ha," said Marco, "and now we know *how* they knew."

Denzel was getting excited.

"Yeah, but look at the names on this circulation list. We know Edward Refalo is 'ER'; Ray Farrugia, 'RAF'; 'MRC' is Michael Cini; Lieutenant Colonel Debono, the head of Armed Forces Malta, Maritime Squadron, was also there. And finally, 'CB'."

Marco raised his arms. "Well, who is that?" George looked triumphant.

"'CB' is the State Advocate, Christa Baldacchino, who must've been acting for Camilleri. Gerald always held her in high regard. I had no idea what she was doing cosying up to Fedorov so blatantly during meetings – now I can guess! If you look at the minutes that are on that drive, Christa Baldacchino was at every meeting. She fed all this stuff to Gerald – nobody else would. Remember, she was a law officer and worked with him as a public prosecutor in the Attorney General's office, before her promotion. Not only that, she was appointed on Gerald's recommendation. It has to be her! She was collecting evidence!

"The last time I saw Gerald," George continued slowly, "just before he died, he said something cryptic to me that I didn't understand. He said he feared it'd come to this and that I should speak to those he trusted. He assured me there were people who could help and in his letter to me, with the box of personal papers, he said I should use my detective skills to find out who it might be. I thought he was rambling, given his illness, but he wasn't! Now, it's all become clear."

Marco looked at Denzel and George, who seemed pleased with themselves. He was still confused.

"Well, I see all that, but is it enough? And what do we do with it?"

Denzel said: "Nobody else in that room would've given Gerald a copy of those minutes. It's the same story for all the documents in the file. Christa's the common link. That, with all the financial stuff, is proof that our government's executive was blackmailed into allowing a takeover by the Russians, who sacked off our constitution and claimed Malta as their own. Gerald Camilleri knew exactly what was happening, but he was a dying man. So, it falls to you, and Dad – sorry, the commissioner. As I said to Dad, sorry, I mean … well, that's why Gerald left you the papers. He trusts you to do – something! But I don't know what. Tell the Americans?" Marco looked at them.

"And tell them what? We must get this Christa Baldacchino to confirm she was the source. Otherwise, we have nothing. Yes?"

George nodded.

"I know how to find her. I'll see if I can get her on board."

"I hope you're right, Dad, otherwise you'll be going back to Camp Azure, but not as commissioner," Denzel said.

George swallowed.

"Madonna mia!"

CHAPTER 61
MARCO BONNICI
CASTELLO BONNICI, IL-WARDIJA, MALTA

MARCO MADE his way down the terraced fields of vines to the hut where Billy and Huck were still whiling away their time. Further down the hill, he could see Laura wandering through the terraced vineyard, filled with the local variety of Gellewza grapes. They exchanged a wave. The Americans were lying on the roof, their shirts off, enjoying the morning sunshine and discussing the merits of pizza. They had spent the last two days arguing about the best way to prepare Southern Fried Chicken. It was a serious discussion, and the men had gone deep into it late into the preceding night.

This morning's pizza debate had only just got going when Marco approached. Huck was considering the drawbacks of using Monterey Jack instead of Mozzarella.

"Problem, as I see it, is it's an American cheese so, to start, it's not pizza authentic. Not *I-talian*. Know what I'm saying? Okay, it's got high fat, so a good melter, but I'm seeing Mexican food here, not *I-talian*."

Billy's ears pricked up.

"Shush! Someone's coming."

They heard somebody sliding down the path towards them.

In one smooth movement, Huck rolled over, took his pistol out of its holster and trained it on Marco's head.

"Shit, Marco, don't creep up on us that like that. I could've blown your brains out!"

"Good morning to you, too. I need to speak to Washington. Can I use the satellite phone?"

"Use the phone? Whaddya you think this is, a booth? And it's four in the morning in DC."

"Well, I have to wake somebody up and make a secure call. Can you bring it up to the *castello*? We need George in on this."

They all gathered in the library, while Marco made the call. Huck and Billy poked about the shelves, casually flicking through three-hundred-year-old books, as if they were shopping for paperbacks, while Denzel perched on the antique Tuscan desk, swinging his legs. George and Marco huddled around the phone.

Marco did wake Mary-Ann Baker, who was a famously deep sleeper. He explained who was on the call. She told him to hold on, as she went to the bathroom for a pee and to splash cold water on her face. Marco told her what had been found amongst Camilleri's papers.

"It is firm evidence that the Maltese prime minister and key members of the cabinet are being blackmailed and acting under coercion. That is how the Russians effected control over the legal and constitutional processes of the island."

"Okay, okay, I get it, I get it. Wow, it's a lot to take in at four a.m., but the first thing is – we need this lawyer lady on board. She needs to present this evidence to us. Then we can work out how to play this farce. Are our special forces guys still with you?"

There was a shout from across the room.

"Sure are!"

"Listen guys, we need an exfiltration plan for you, Denzel and the lawyer lady. Get me some ideas, by the end of the day.

I assume this lawyer can be trusted?"

George admitted: "Well, there's a reasonable chance …"

"What! You're ringing me before the cock crows and the main act isn't even on board? You've got some work to do, Marco." Mary-Ann sighed wearily.

"Listen, I'll give those who need to know a heads up, but you'd better confirm we've gotta game here or we could waste a lot of valuable time. Time, I don't have."

She added wistfully, or sleepily, Marco could not tell which: "You know, in the US, a conviction of espionage carries the death penalty? That man, your PM, screwed us around and made fools of us in front of the Russians. That's bad news in my book. Maybe, if you get the chance, make sure your Refalo guy knows we'll push for it, if he doesn't change sides – fast."

The call ended and Huck and Billy went back down to resume their sunbathing and make plans, while George and Denzel went to sit out on the terrace to consider how to approach Christa Baldacchino. Marco remained in the library, wondering if he had made the right decision to bring in Mary-Ann Baker, when Asano suddenly appeared beside him.

"So sorry to interrupt, but Miss Natasha made me clean stairs. I make sure I dry them well, but I wonder why she would make dirt and tell me clean stairs. Then, sir, I see she is hiding behind door in bedroom. She is waiting for someone to walk upstairs. So sorry to disturb, but something is not right, and I am afraid. I hope I wrong, so sorry."

Marco looked at Asano and tried to make sense of what the man had said to him. He felt something terrible was about to happen, but he did not know what. Then, it started to fall into place. The blood drained from his face and his breathing became fast and irregular.

"Where is Dr Weber, Asano?"

"She is not in house, sir. I think she is in gardens."

Asano made a little bow.

Marco ran out onto the terrace, followed by the houseman,

hoping to catch a glimpse of Laura, down amongst the terraces. There was no sign of her. George and Denzel looked on wondering what was happening.

"Quickly, follow me!" Marco and Asano ran up to the house and in through the kitchens. There was no sign of Laura downstairs in the house. Marco turned into the servants' staircase that led up to the east wing.

"I'll take care of Natasha. You go to the back gardens and stop Laura going up those stairs."

Marco was breathing heavily, but forced himself on, two steps at a time. He turned into the corridor on the first floor that led onto the gallery and jogged along it. He rounded the corner and leaned against the wall, his eyes swimming from the effort of the run. He felt sick.

He slowly approached Natasha's door, which stood ajar. Between the door and the architrave was a gap of a centimetre or so. Through this narrow crack, he saw a flash of red move, only a metre away, on the other side of the door.

He called softly: "Natasha?"

She pulled the door back and stood facing him, the axe handle swinging loosely at her side. He looked at her, realising, possibly for the first time, that she was nearly as tall as he was and, as she stood there coolly appraising him, there was nothing frail about her. She exuded a sense of latent menace. Her expression was detached. Suddenly, Marco felt scared. He had no idea what was happening.

He looked at the axe handle and said, more forcefully: "Natasha!" hoping to shock her out of the strange mood that seemed to possess her. "What is going on?"

She said calmly, in a voice that seemed to come from somewhere deep within her, "I'm waiting for Laura. She can't win, you know. I won't allow it. She can never win."

"Natasha, stop it, whatever this is. You are scaring me. Give me that ... thing."

Marco made to grab the axe handle. He held it horizontally,

across his chest, in both hands. Both of Natasha's also grasped the stave. He started to pull it towards him. Natasha's expression did not change, but she held on tight, while her father tried to tug it out of her hands.

Suddenly, Natasha exploded out of the room towards him in an incredible burst of speed and momentum. Marco still had tight hold of the wooden stave. Natasha loosened her grip on the handle and, using her forward impetus, put both hands on his chest and pushed him away, with all her might. He staggered backwards across the gallery, flipping slowly over the low marble balustrade. His torso went first, arms outstretched, windmilling to try and get a grip on something, his feet seemingly stuck to the floor of the gallery. The leverage of his falling body slowly lifted his legs into the air, and he fell, horribly, onto the marble floor below.

There was a distinct crack as he landed and a deep groan, as the air was forced out of his lungs. His broken body lay perfectly still, arms outstretched and both legs bent. The stave clattered to the floor beside him, striking melodious notes that echoed around the cavernous hall. The fall broke Marco's back and the force of the impact fractured his skull, killing him instantly. Natasha would always remember his expression, as he toppled over, staring into her face with a look of horror on his own.

She went slowly down the stairs to retrieve the stave. She took one of Marco's feet and pulled her father's body across the smooth marble floor, towards the bottom of the central staircase, to make it look as if that was where he had fallen. Positioning his limbs in the same way as she had found them, she took the axe handle and went back upstairs to replace it under her bed. Then, she sat on the top step and looked down at her father's body.

There was a satisfying neatness to the fact that he had died on the stairs, as had her mother, Marco's beloved Sophia. She was his first and, until Laura Weber came along, his only love. Natasha thought he would have appreciated that things ended that way. She studied him for a moment, without any emotion. He looked comfortable, almost as though he were asleep. It looked a bit *too* comfortable, so she was about to go and rearrange him again when she realised there was still work to be done.

With a sigh and a small shake of the head, she started screaming, calling for Laura and Asano. She went out of the front door and shouted repeatedly. George and Denzel came rushing in from the terrace. George felt his knees go weak when he saw Marco sprawled at the bottom of the white marble stairs. Denzel quickly hurried to check the body for signs of life. He looked back towards his father and shook his head. George wondered where Natasha was. Then, he heard her, outside in the gardens, calling for help.

At that moment, Asano entered with Laura, coming from the kitchens. She gasped and her hand went to her mouth. She ran to the body, kneeling beside Marco, realising the worst had happened. She cradled his damaged head and softly kissed it, muttering to herself in German. Still keeping tight hold of Marco and sobbing gently, she started looking around for someone to explain what had happened.

Natasha burst in through the front door, tears streaming down her cheeks. There was an expression of the most profound grief on her face; she wailed like a woman possessed. She went straight across the hall to where Asano stood and slapped him as hard as she could, with an open hand. He was rocked back on his heels but made no move to defend himself.

"You killed him, you fool," she screamed. "He slipped on the stairs. You didn't dry them, did you? Now he's dead! This is all your doing!"

She started wailing again and launched herself at the housekeeper, beating him with her fists. He moved his arms to protect his head, but otherwise let her take out her grief on him. Denzel was the first to restrain her, and he and George took her to the library, where she curled up in an armchair, tucking her feet beneath her.

Conscious of the fact he and Denzel were wanted men, George phoned Inspector Karl Chelotti and asked him to come, by himself, to the *castello*. He took a white-faced Asano and a tearful Laura into the kitchen, while Denzel sat with Natasha in the library. Denzel spotted a red tasselled damask throw that was covering one of the library sofas and went back into the hall to drape it respectfully over Marco's body.

George told Asano to make tea, while he listened carefully to Laura's account of the morning. The more he heard, the less comfortable he became but, considering the circumstances, he knew he could not push an investigation into Marco's death, not with the house full of fugitives from the police and the Russians.

Chelotti arrived and made a cursory inspection of the body. He pronounced Marco to be dead and read the statements that George had taken, signing his own name at the bottom. He moved on to speak privately to Laura Weber and Asano, to confirm their accounts. When he was certain he understood the facts, he and George took a walk in the gardens.

"Well, George, this is all a bit of a mess. There's something not right here, I can feel it. Before we get into it, they've got CCTV on Denzel in a canoe, in the Grand Harbour. Fedorov's like a man possessed. The heat is on, for both of you." George shook his head.

"That's all we need! So, that's it – we're wanted men now – definitely?"

"Definitely! I only just escaped with my head on my shoulders. I tried to distract that stupid Rita Bonelli, but she went over my head, direct to Russian liaison. Imagine how that went down with Fedorov!"

George sighed.

"We need to get this wrapped up, but I'm not sure how. What can we do? We've got to get Dr Weber out of here. Maybe the housekeeper'll stay, but I'll make sure he doesn't start causing trouble. And Natasha Bonnici ... well, I've no idea what to do with her. Never have done."

CHAPTER 62
COMMISSIONER FOR HOME SECURITY GEORGE ZAMMIT

CASTELLO BONNICI, IL-WARDIJA, MALTA

GEORGE WAS IN A DILEMMA. He was in the middle of a family drama – a serious family drama, probably involving murder – yet all around him the country was in turmoil, and he had found a key he could use to free it from its troubles. He knew he had to act but was not quite sure what to do first.

Best to deal with Laura Weber immediately, he decided. She was the one most likely to make life difficult and put himself, Denzel and the two Americans in danger. She had gone to her room and locked the door. Nobody had seen her since the shocking discovery of Marco's body. George had no idea how much she knew about Marco and his involvement in the resistance, or indeed the Family. He decided he would play it straight with her.

George knocked on what had been Marco's bedroom door and asked Laura to come downstairs for a chat. She agreed: "As long as that psychotic, murdering woman remains in her room, and you do not leave me unattended." George was relieved when she appeared in the library with her case packed and her coat on. She was ready to leave. They had just sat down when Asano ghosted in, as if nothing had happened, with two tall glasses containing light brown liquid. He bowed and said:

"I offer a ginseng, schisandra and botanical infusion, to balance mood and body, counter stress and exhaustion. It is good for time like this."

He bowed and backed out of the room. Laura took a glass and drank deeply. George sniffed at his, screwed up his face and pushed it to one side, wondering how people could drink such stuff.

"I see you've packed, Dr Weber. Does that mean you're going home?"

"Yes, that was our plan – to leave today – only we did not do it soon enough." She caught her breath on a slight sob. "We gave her time to get to us."

A shiver ran down George's back.

"*Mela*! You mean, you think Natasha Bonnici played some part in Marco's death?"

"I do not think so. *I know so*. But, of course, I cannot prove it. You know she is a killer, don't you? She has done it before, several times, and got away with it. Now she can add patricide to her list. She is terrifying. I was her psychiatrist, you know."

The doctor's face was without colour and her pale blue eyes were bloodshot from crying.

"Oh! No, I didn't know. So, you know Miss Bonnici well?"

"Only too well, which is why I ask you to drive me into Valletta tonight – now, in fact. I will take a plane back to Switzerland tomorrow. I get the sense there will be few formalities requiring me to stay and I shall not be returning for any funeral. I will mourn Marco in my own way. I understand what is happening in this house, with your son and yourself, and I wish you luck. My presence here will only confuse things and put me at risk by association. I must leave, and frankly, will be happy never to set foot on this accursed island again."

George could only mutter: "I understand. I'm sorry."

He asked Chelotti to take Laura to Valletta and post a uniformed officer within the small boutique hotel, where a room had been booked for her by Asano. He stood at the door and watched Karl's car leave the *castello*. The large iron gates at the end of the drive clanged shut, shuddering slightly on their hinges. It occurred to George that they were as effective at keeping insiders in the *castello* as they were at keeping intruders out.

Next, George asked Asano to join him in the library, when he was ready. George was browsing the bookshelves, wondering why anyone needed so many books, when he realised Asano had somehow entered the room and was perched, his back perfectly straight, on the first two inches of a leather armchair, his hands clasped on his knees.

George smiled and took the seat opposite. Asano had no expression whatsoever on his face. His large black eyes were fixed on George.

"A terrible day, Asano. I'm sorry, I know you liked Mr Bonnici."

"He was good master; I was happy to serve." George nodded.

"You said you made Mr Bonnici coffee at breakfast, then later he sent you to find Dr Weber in the gardens. Why did he send you and not go himself?"

"Yes, I explain. After breakfast, Miss Natasha ask me to clean marble steps, after she make mess there. I did, but I think she is ... unwell, so I found Mr Marco. He tell me to find Dr Weber, tell her to keep away. Mr Marco went to see Miss Natasha."

"You said to my colleague that Mr Bonnici could have slipped on the wet steps?"

"Yes, is possible. I try to make dry, but ..." He cast his eyes down. "So sorry. So sorry."

"Have you spoken to Miss Natasha?"

"No."

"What's your plan, Asano, now that Mr Bonnici's dead? Will you stay?"

"A house needs housekeeper. I am housekeeper. If Miss Natasha wishes it, I will stay. If not, I go. She will decide."

"You said you thought Miss Natasha was unwell and you were so concerned you went to get Mr Bonnici?"

"Yes."

"What was the matter with her?"

"She lose colour and her pupils very big, like in shock. You know, her mind has not been good, so I look for these things. I make tea and traditional treatments, for mood, to help. But she was watching me clean stairs, from behind door, and looking at me through crack. Very strange." George thought about this.

"Yes, most strange indeed, but nothing concrete to indicate she had anything to do with Mr Bonnici's fall?" Asano was silent.

George could think of nothing further to ask the little man, so he thanked him and watched him silently leave the room.

George was starting to feel that things might just work out. He only had Natasha to speak to now. The other two people in this weird household had been strangely accommodating. Natasha had been wandering around the gardens, while he spoke to the others. Despite the warmth of the afternoon, she had draped a blanket around her shoulders and, when she sat down, pulled it over her head, like a shawl.

This was how George found her, sitting on the back terrace, watching the sun disappear behind the ridge to the west.

He took a chair across the table from her and the pair of them sat in silence for a while. Eventually, he said: "I'd like to make a suggestion as to how we should manage this situation."

"Situation?"

"Yes, your father's death." He paused. "It was a terrible accident. Slipping like that on those wet stairs. Asano is distraught."

He swallowed, feeling wretched at the thought he could be helping this woman get away with the most terrible of crimes. But his and Denzel's safety required it.

"Yes, terrible, isn't it? Distraught, is he? I should fire him at once. How's Dr Weber? How does she feel about it?"

"I don't know. She's left. Gone back to Switzerland. She asked me to tell you not to contact her again." Natasha nodded slightly.

"Hmmph. I won't then."

"My colleague, Inspector Chelotti, has arranged for a funeral director to collect your father, unless of course you have your own people?"

Billy and Huck had moved the body into the garage, where it lay on an old door, covered by the red damask throw.

"As the death was an accident and not the result of natural causes, there'll have to be a postmortem and a magistrate will have to review the report. But, in light of the statements Inspector Chelotti's gathered, I don't envisage any difficulties."

Still Natasha said nothing. George asked: "Do you blame Asano?"

"Blame? I don't know. He can't have dried the steps properly."

George was curious.

"He seems very loyal to the family. He says he saw nothing to indicate any other person had anything to do with your father's fall and assumes Marco slipped on the wet stairs. He said the last he saw of you, you were in your room and looked unwell."

There was a pause. Natasha thought of the moment her eyes had met those of the housekeeper, through the crack in the door. The man had superpowers. He could walk through walls, see inside minds. She would not be surprised if he could levitate. She wondered why he was making this so easy for her. It was as if he had another agenda.

"Yes, I watched him clean and dry the staircase, but he

must have missed a step. I was upset. I'd had an argument with Laura, so I went to my room for some privacy, then into the gardens to clear my head. That was when I came back in and found Dad."

"An argument?"

"She was my doctor, and I didn't agree with her screwing my father."

"Ah, I see. I can understand that."

George weighed his next words carefully.

"So, everybody concerned seems to agree on the unfortunate circumstances that led to your father's death. It appears there's no suggestion of foul play. If you're content, I can ask Inspector Chelotti to get on with the formalities?"

"Foul play?" She barked a laugh. "I've been the victim of that all my life."

Natasha pulled the shawl over her head and slumped back into her seat, refusing to say another word or even acknowledge George's presence.

Once the house was quiet and everybody had retired for the night, Asano left the kitchen and went into his *kamidana*, locked the door and sat cross legged on the mat. He took out his phone and rang the number.

"Asano, do you know what bloody time it is?"

"So sorry to disturb, but there is terrible and important news. Mr Marco is dead."

There was silence on the line.

"Dead ... how?" the familiar voice asked finally. "He die in fall down stairs ..."

"Oh my God, just like his wife? Was Natasha nearby? Was it her?"

"I did not see it happen but am certain it was. I see her wait for him, in her room, with wooden stick in hands. Her eyes were dead woman's eyes. Killer's eyes. I think she wait for Dr Laura Weber, Mr Marco's new companion, but he came first ..."

"New companion?"

"Yes, the doctor for Miss Natasha. They share a room, Mr Marco and Dr Weber."

"Right. And Natasha didn't like that!"

"No, she had much bad feeling for Dr Weber."

"I bet she did. And the police?"

"The policeman Zammit is staying in house. He make problem go away. Miss Natasha say I not dry stairs properly and Mr Marco slip on wet marble. This is official story."

"Is it true?"

"It is true I clean stairs, but I clean and dry every step carefully. I am very good houseman."

"Are you sure?"

"Yes, because I think how strange Miss Natasha make stairs dirty and wet when everything dry outside. We all say to policeman stairs were wet and Mr Marco fell. I apologise to Miss Natasha, policeman, everybody, very sorry for mistake. But there was no mistake by me. They say it best not to invite trouble into house.

"I know what I see. Miss Natasha in her room, with long wooden sword, like *bokken*, then it was falling, and I hear sound of wood on stone, bouncing like taiko ... drum. When I go and see, Mr Marco is lying in hall, dead. There is no *bokken*. It is back in Miss Natasha's room. This is how I know, but I do not tell policeman this."

"She was hiding in her room, waiting for this woman or Marco to come close?"

"Yes. I not sure who is the one she wait for, Marco or the lady."

"Asano, you did the right thing. Poor Marco, what the hell's going on? He was a decent man. That murdering bitch – she killed her own father. Incredible! God forgive her. Where's Natasha now?"

"She is in her room. Upset, I think."

"Hmmm. Thanks, Asano. Wow, what a thing! Ring me again tomorrow. I need time to think – there're too many loose ends."

Greca plumped up her cushions and raised herself in her bed. She took a tube from her bedside cabinet and gently rubbed some more serum around her eyes. Her beautician had told her that, at her age, she had to take steps to avoid the onset of wrinkles, although she wondered if using a tube a day might be too much.

With Marco dead, she pondered whether her chances of taking her father's place in the Family had improved or not. Who would be his likely successor? Would he – it had to be a 'he', there were no women on the Committee – be more, or less amenable towards her? They were not able to agree on who should lead them last time, which was why they begged Marco to return, so why should it be any different this time?

The one mistake she had made was in bragging to Natasha that she had destroyed the Croce Bianca. If that got back to them, any hope of ever joining the Family would be finished. She had been drunk when she had blurted that out, but it was no excuse. She did not believe for a moment that Natasha had forgotten her confession. She just had to push on with her plan and see how the cards fell.

With a sigh, Greca replaced her eye mask and turned off the light.

CHAPTER 63
COMMISSIONER FOR HOME SECURITY GEORGE ZAMMIT
OFFICE OF THE PRIME MINISTER, VALLETTA, MALTA

THE OFFICE of the State Advocate was in a narrow street, off some steep steps that led into the heart of old Valletta. Traditional, multi-coloured Maltese balconies projected out above street level, with narrow doorways and carved frontages completing the classic Valletta look. There was even a vintage bright red British pillar box outside the office, an echo of the city's colonial past.

George knew he was taking a big chance going into an area where there were numerous government offices. He was still a wanted man. Valletta was a small capital city, and everyone tended to know everybody else. He took the liberty of going into Marco's dressing room and rummaging around in his wardrobes. There, he found a long steel blue Burberry raincoat, a paisley silk cravat and a rather dashing Fedora. A pair of gold-rimmed Gucci sunglasses added to the detail of the character he was trying to build. In a moment of inspiration, he grabbed an ebony walking stick from the back of a cupboard and resolved to alter his gait, to complete the image of a sophisticated artist or film producer.

He walked downstairs, tapping the cane on the marble stairs as he did so. In the entrance hall, he ran into the housekeeper who was carrying a vase filled with freshly cut flowers. Asano looked straight through him, his only comment being "Good morning, Mr George", as he passed by. George was mildly disappointed that his disguise had been ineffective.

Asano caught his hesitation and said: "May I be of help?"

"Er ... yes, I need to borrow a car. Please."

Half an hour later, George was standing on Mikiel Anton Vassalli Street, outside the office of the State Attorney, leaning nonchalantly against the bright red pillar box. It was not long before he saw Christa Baldacchino tottering across the ancient and treacherous stone paving slabs, in a pair of black high-heeled shoes. Her whole style was smart business, featuring a black pencil skirt, cropped black jacket and plain white high-buttoned blouse. Her shiny jet-black hair was, as always, pulled back into a ponytail that bobbed up and down as she walked. It was an austere look. In meetings, she would wear owlish, black-framed spectacles, which magnified her large chestnut brown eyes. Maybe it was from youthful insecurity, but she worked hard at presenting the image of a mature professional.

As she approached, George waved his cane to get her attention. She looked at him askance, hesitating for a fraction of a second to check what her brain was telling her. Then, she glanced around.

"George, what on earth ..."

"It's good, isn't it? Did it have you fooled?"

"No, not for a minute! You look ridiculous ... that coat's down to your ankles! It's obviously you."

"Oh! You're the second person who's seen right through me. Pity. Look, can we talk?"

She glanced around again, to see if anyone had noticed her in the company of this oddly dressed individual.

"You walk on. I'll follow. If I'm seen with you ... looking like that, it'll only raise questions – or downright laughter!"

At the end of the street, up a steep hill, was Hastings

Gardens – a small public space on top of Saint John's and Saint Michael's Bastions, to the west side of the City Gate. The garden offered panoramic views of Floriana, Sliema and Manoel Island, and hosted a rumbustious annual wine festival. The pair of them took seats there. George felt silly, so took off the sunglasses and the Fedora.

"*Mela*! You know I'm now the sole executor of Gerald Camilleri's estate?"

"I'd heard that Marco Bonnici was a co-executor ..."

"I'm afraid he died yesterday ... a terrible accident."

"Really? How awful! I'm so sorry."

"Of course, thank you. But that leaves me with a dilemma." He glanced around him, checking nobody was within earshot. "Gerald left me a file of papers – confidential papers. I'm wondering what to do with them. You see, for them to be of any real value, I need someone who can attest to the provenance of those papers. Evidentially, that is."

"And you want my legal advice?"

"No, I want to know if you gave Gerald those papers. Because me and the late Marco Bonnici both thought that you did."

He watched her face keenly. She took a quick breath and stared out over the bastions, across the waters of Marsamxett Harbour.

"How do you know it was me?" George smiled.

"Because I'm a detective and I work things out."

"George, Gerald Camilleri was a detective. Did he tell you about me? You notice, I'm not denying it."

George was hurt to be discounted by her in such a way, but she had at least admitted to her involvement. It was a remarkable display of candour, given what an objectionable front she had previously put on, toadying up to Fedorov and the rest.

"If you gave Gerald those papers, it must've been for a reason. You've got to be prepared to help us get rid of these people."

"Careful, George, you're presuming a lot here. *If* I was involved in getting those papers to Gerald, what more would you want from me?"

"I'd ask you to come with me to Brussels, to meet the Americans and the EU, tell them what really happened, what a criminal Refalo is. That he and the others were being blackmailed, coerced, put under duress, whatever, and prove that there's no *legal* basis for the Russians being here. And you can explain how the president was also put under pressure to undermine the country's constitutional safeguards. It's country capture, Christa. And there're only a handful of us who can do anything about it."

"Oh, you're not asking much then, are you? You remember what happened to the last person who fled the country to tell all to the EU authorities?"

She looked away and shook her head. A second or two later, she turned back to face him.

"And how do we even get out of the country?"

"There are two CIA men with me, right now, who're planning just that."

"How convenient! And, if we leave, how and when do I get back in? How do I pick up my normal life? See my family, my fiancé? What happens to them? Don't think for a minute I haven't contemplated it, because I have. I'm just not sure I'm brave enough to do it. And I bet, if Ray Farrugia could have his time again, he'd think twice about playing the hero. Have you thought about that?" George had.

"The difference is, Christa, nobody's aware that you know anything. Gerald was very careful about that. With Ray it was totally different. He walked onto the plane of the president of the EU Commission."

Christa stood up and smoothed her skirt. She walked over to the parapet of the bastion and gazed out over the island. George followed her, his cane tapping on the paving slabs.

"I knew this time would come," she said, "but I thought it

would be Gerald asking. After he died, I didn't know what to do."

"You would've trusted him more?"

"He was a very smart man, George, and did more good than anyone'll ever know. But I suppose I also trust you," she laughed. "After all, you're a master of disguise, so why wouldn't I? I'm not promising anything. It depends on what I think of your plan to get us out. When you know what it is, contact me again. But be quick, my nerves won't hold out forever."

George smiled.

"By the way, I think it's you who's the mistress of disguise. You had me fooled all along. You really got up my nose!"

CHAPTER 64
NATASHA BONNICI
CASTELLO BONNICI, IL-WARDIJA, MALTA

NATASHA WOKE up the morning following Marco's death, feeling much better. She had begun the process of blocking out the patricide. This disassociation had happened in the past, particularly following the death of her former live-in boyfriend, Nick Walker. She had had real feelings for Nick, who had betrayed her for some little floozy. They had both been killed on her instructions. As soon as the deed was done, she had felt liberated. It was the strangest experience, but definitely worth the trouble – and the money!

In Bern, Laura had listened at length to Natasha speaking about her involvement in a succession of murders. Laura had asked why she felt compelled to undertake them and how she had felt afterwards. Natasha did not deny the murders took place or that she might have been responsible for them but had said she could not recall any details. There were gaps in her memory and a sense that events were somehow unreal or dream-like – she was disassociated from her participation in them. Almost blackouts, Natasha had called them. As an explanation, it seemed far too convenient to be true.

Natasha felt uncomfortable with her father's killing and repelled by the thought of the act itself. She could still see the look of horror on his face, as he tumbled backwards over the balustrade. But, at that moment, she had felt she had no other choice but to break the alliance Marco and Laura had formed against her. She could not let her father reject her again – she refused to be cast aside in favour of that manipulative, sanctimonious bitch. There was too much pain, she was not ready for it – she would never be ready for it. They had wanted to steal away to Bern and leave her behind.

The truth was, she had not cared which of them died; either would have suited her purpose. But, in a twisted way, it was more satisfying that it was her father who had crashed down onto the hard marble floor. It meant that *she* was not getting her prize. *She* would have to bear the pain of loss. It was almost worth it for that alone. *She* would feel the guilt for his death, because *she* had put herself between Natasha and her father.

As the day wore on, she relaxed more. George had sorted out the legal position, so she did not have to worry about that. It would be some time before the funeral, so there would be plenty of opportunity for her to find a suitable dress. In fact, her time was her own.

George had been out. She had been at the library window and seen him arrive back, wearing the most peculiar costume. She had put her hand to her mouth and giggled. She had no idea what he was up to, but felt better for seeing him dressed up like a Hollywood rake.

She decided she needed a word with Asano, to make sure the housekeeper was still on her side. She found him outside, squatting on his haunches, tending the herb garden. He jumped to his feet as she approached.

"Asano, I know you were always very loyal to my father. He appreciated that. Now he's gone, can you be as loyal to me? I'll need a housekeeper, and I take it you're available?"

It took him a little while to gather himself. He looked her straight in the eye, unblinking.

"I was happy to serve Mr Marco and he would not want to

see you have inconvenience. So, I stay as long as needed, until you have new person. Then I go. I think you can find better housekeeper than me."

He bowed. Natasha nodded. It was all for the best. She would be glad to see the back of him.

"Good. Then, for the time being, I want things to continue just as before. But can you always carry a bunch of keys, please? I like to know where you are. Attach them to a belt. The sound of them is comforting. Your predecessor carried keys that jangled against her hip. I quite liked the sound. Also, please book me a ticket to Istanbul, for the day after tomorrow. One way. I'll take a suite at the Çırağan Palace Kempinski for two nights. I have some business there."

He said calmly: "I can book ticket, but I cannot wear bell. That is for animals, not housekeepers, and I fear it is not best idea. So sorry."

"Oh! You refuse, do you?"

Asano looked her straight in the face, without any trace of fear or deference.

"Yes, I refuse. I apologise, I mean no insult to you. I try to keep house peaceful and calm, so no bells or ringing keys. It is best."

Natasha chewed her lower lip. The annoying little elf insisted on maintaining his ability to float around the *castello* without being heard. For the first time, she wondered why. She recalled her father saying Katia had appointed him before she had left. It seemed strange she would find time to recruit a replacement in the middle of packing up her things and creeping out of the *castello*, after suffering one shock too many. Natasha would have thought it was the last thing on her mind. The recollection of what had happened between her and Greca's lover, prompted her to ring the only relative she was on speaking terms with, to tell her of Marco's death – her cousin, Greca.

Greca had been wondering if Natasha would call her. They

had not spoken to each other in person since they had stood together on the doorstep of Greca's farm in Sicily, when Natasha had asked her to kill Hakan Toprak's family: an exercise that had gone horribly wrong.

In her heart, Greca still could not forgive Natasha for the death of Ituah. She believed, unlikely as it seemed, he had been her one chance of finding love. His death at Natasha's hand, over what was, after all, a *misunderstanding*, still rankled. In addition, she realised that she and Natasha were in competition with each other to take the top position within the Family. Greca would never give up her claim to her father's share of the Family's wealth, and Natasha would never stop scheming, until she had fought her way back onto the committee and avenged herself on those who had cast her out from their protection, at the very time she needed it most.

That was why Greca had planted Asano in Castello Bonnici. At the time, Marco had gone to Serbia, Natasha had run away from the Italian anti-Mafia police, and Katia, the housekeeper, had conveniently deserted her post. There was no one to stop Greca taking control from behind the scenes.

She had discovered Asano a year before those fateful events, looking after an elderly, but wealthy, farmer in Pachino, tomato country, in the southeast of Sicily. The farmer had made the mistake of setting up in competition to Greca's organisation, supplying migrant labour around the Province of Syracusa. Her fearsome Aye Axemen had paid a visit to the stubborn old man and things had got out of hand. The farmer was no more and Asano, whose mixed martial arts defence of his master had impressed the Axemen, had, with some difficulty, been subdued and bound.

Rather than being killed out of hand, as might have been expected, he had been delivered to Greca, as a curiosity piece, and held in chains to await his fate. She immediately saw the value of the man and, being without a master and in an unhappy situation, he had agreed to serve as her houseman.

Greca thought having a butler was highly amusing, until she realised she had no idea how she had ever coped without him. She grew to trust Asano and, over their year together, he had, as was his way, become devoted to her. She was loath to part with his services, but ensured he was in position at the *castello* in time to greet Marco on his return. She knew things would start to get interesting when the Bonnicis were back in residence, and it would be in her own best interests to have eyes and ears within those thick limestone walls.

So, that afternoon, Greca was not taken totally unawares when a servant handed her the mobile and told her it was her cousin on the line.

"Natasha? You're the only cousin I have who knows this number. I would say, nice to hear from you, but given how things are ... tell me, how are you? Back from Switzerland was the last I heard."

"I'm fine, thanks. But, Greca, I'm afraid I've got some bad news. Marco's dead."

The announcement was met by silence. Eventually, she heard Greca sniff and sigh, before she replied in a softer voice.

"I'm sorry to hear that, Natasha. I know you two had your differences, but he is ... was ... your father. What happened?"

Natasha told her the bare details and Greca listened, holding the phone against her shoulder, while she lit a cigarette.

"It only happened yesterday? Christ! Well, I'm shocked. You must be all over the place. I'm so sorry. How're you, really?"

"I'm feeling better. Much better. The clinic was horrible. But now ... now, yeah, things're okay."

Greca could not believe what she was hearing. It was as though they were having a casual chat about Natasha's health, when Greca already knew from Asano that this woman had just murdered her father. What was terrifying was that her tone did not sound fake. Natasha was being completely herself.

"Well, that's great. I'm glad you're getting back to your old self."

The thought crossed Greca's mind that she might be on medication. But she instantly dismissed it. This was Natasha, through and through.

"Yeah, that's what it's starting to feel like. I know it's too soon to be sure how I am, but, yeah, I'm on the mend. I'm just tidying up some *loose ends*, you know, and then I really think I can go back to work and be normal again. So, you'll come over for the funeral, yes? I need some family here. We'll look great together in black – it suits you so well!" Natasha laughed.

Greca was thinking hard. *Loose ends*? What was going through her cousin's mind? Had she gone completely crazy?

"What about the therapy, Natasha? That can go on forever."

"Oh, I'm done with all that. But the funeral … You'll come, won't you? It'll be fun to spend some time together. You can stay on for a bit."

"Yeah, of course I'll come." *Fun*? she thought. *Loose ends*?

There was something definitely off with Natasha, that much was obvious. Greca might go to the funeral, out of respect for Marco, but she would take her plane from Coniso and be back home by nightfall, taking some muscle along with her, for protection.

Greca was about to ring off after a few platitudes, but then had second thoughts. She was not just going to let Natasha get away with it. This was how she could be brought down. How she could be isolated from the Family for good. She took a deep breath and, before she knew it, the words were tumbling out.

"I'm sorry, Natasha, but I know you killed him, so you can drop the pretence. I know he didn't fall down the stairs, slipping on a puddle of water. You killed your own father! A decent man, who did what he could for you. I don't know what crazy fit of jealousy brought it on, but I think you're still a seriously sick person."

There was pause on the line.

"I didn't... Greca ... how can you say such a thing?"

"I can say it, because I know the truth. I lost my own father, and I still think about him every day. You? You just killed yours and it doesn't seem to mean a thing to you. You're ... I can't bring myself to say the words!" She had done it now, there was no turning back. Greca took a drag on her cigarette and continued. "I don't know whether you hit him with that wooden stick or what, but you ran down, didn't you? Picked it up and hid it back in your room. That's the proof. One minute you were holding it, the next it was lying with Marco, who was dead at the foot of the stairs, and then, suddenly, it was back in your room. How did that happen, Natasha?"

"You can't say things like that ... you've no idea ..."

"You've really screwed it up, now, haven't you? In your twisted mind, it was all about you. Revenge or something, I'll never understand. Did you ever stop and consider – you've just killed another Wise Man, another head of the Family. What're they going to think now, Natasha? And you really thought you'd find a way back in, meeting up with poor Leopold Kruder? What a disappointment for you. And your convenient Russian convict can hardly confess to this one, can he? He's locked up in a Siberian gulag somewhere. What an alibi! You're vicious, that's for sure, but I never had you down as stupid!"

"Where's all this coming from?" Suddenly, Natasha got it. There was a spy in the camp, and it could only be one person. In a flash, it all made sense. "Okay, Greca, it's good to know that's what you think. But, you're wrong and, if I hear any of this crazy rubbish is getting out, I promise you – all the Axemen in Nigeria won't protect you from me. On second thoughts, it's better for you that you don't come to the funeral."

"Natasha, it's *you* who doesn't get it. Of course I'm going to tell the Family. It'll slam the door in your face, once and for all, and open it for me! And then, guess who'll be sitting at the top of that table?"

As soon as she ended the call, Greca did something she had never done before. She rang Asano's phone. It was answered almost immediately.

"Get out of there, now! Natasha's coming for you!"

CHAPTER 65
NATASHA BONNICI
GÜLHANE PARK, ISTANBUL,
TURKEY

BY THE TIME Natasha had made it to the pantry, Asano had gone. In just seconds, he had scooped his most precious items from the *kamidana*, slipped out of the back door with a small rucksack, and started to freewheel down the hill on an old black bike, to a lockup garage in Burmarrad, where he kept a small car. There, he changed out of his bleached cotton traditional clothing and into a pair of worn denims, a creased Hard Rock Café T-shirt, and a battered *I Love Malta* baseball cap. His plan was to find a workers' hostel and lay low for a day or so, and then see what Greca wanted him to do.

Natasha cursed Asano and threw what few possessions of his she could find around the pantry. She took a bottle of wine and went and sat on the rear terrace. It was warm, with an autumnal sun bouncing off the flagstones. She needed to think.

Despite everything, the trip to Istanbul was something that she knew she had to take, otherwise her whole plan for the future would fall to pieces. The conversation with Greca and Asano's treachery had rocked her badly, but she was sure that, once the Family discovered who had really destroyed their precious palazzo, the old men would close ranks against Greca. After all, she was Sergio's daughter – a rough, uncultured and uneducated Sicilian. She was a *cafona* – a boorish peasant! In reality, Greca had no hard evidence of what had happened on the staircase at Castello Bonnici. It was all Asano's interpretation of events and that was unlikely to stand up in a court of law. As the hours passed, her confidence started to return, and she managed to put the annoying conversation out of her mind to concentrate on what needed to be done in Istanbul.

She also thought that it would be a good time to leave the *castello*. The second difficult conversation she had had that day was a call to Fedorov, telling him of Marco's death. The colonel's suspicious mind went into overdrive, and it was all she could do to convince him that the death was a simple, yet tragic, accident and had been thoroughly investigated by the local *Pulizija*. She stressed there was no need for him to despatch a full forensic team and asked to be excused for a period – a week or so – as she needed some time to herself, but also wanted to follow up on some business in Istanbul that might be of benefit to both of them. Reluctantly, he had agreed, though she could tell he was far from convinced that he had been told the full story. Fortunately, he had his hands more than full, coping with the blowback from Moscow about the disastrous Russian showing on Malta and did not make any enquiries about who had handled the official report of Marco's death. So, in a lighter mood, she set off for Istanbul.

Natasha liked the place; it was her type of city: cosmopolitan, rich, wonderfully dynamic, receptive to the best in culture and art from Europe and Asia. After a few hours soaking up the atmosphere, she found herself relaxing, despite the tricky nature of her visit.

She had arranged to meet Istanbul's master manipulator and dealer, Hakan Toprak at Gülhane Park, a popular place in the centre of the Old City, formerly part of the Topkapi Palace gardens. Hakan and she had been lovers for several years and, for a time, had believed they held the riches of the world in their hands. Together, they had been the driving force behind the Family's rise to new mercantile prominence, until press investigations and the forces of the law had closed in around them and Hakan had cut her loose to face the coming storm alone.

The duplicitous Hawk had then cleverly stripped the Family of many of the valuable assets that he and Natasha had assembled. She had felt abandoned, cheated and rejected; an emotional cocktail that had driven her to despair. His actions had been a major factor in her breakdown. In revenge, she had ordered an attempt by Greca's Axemen to kill Hakan's wife and children, as they ate ice-cream in an Istanbul park, but it had failed and there had been no further contact between Hakan and her, since that day.

Natasha saw him ahead of her, sitting alone on a bench, admiring the view, while he ate an ice-cream cornet. Natasha looked around. It was unthinkable that Hakan would have come without backup.

She spotted the man and woman, sitting twenty metres away, rocking an old-fashioned, sprung pram with metre-high wheels. Another man, apparently reading a newspaper, stood beside some railings, at a short distance from Hakan. The couple were not looking into the pram and the man's eyes were not on the paper. There would be others in position around the park, but Natasha intended no mischief. Hakan saw her approaching and dropped the cone into a bin at the side of him, using a tissue to dab his moustache. He stood to greet her. They did not kiss or shake hands.

"You've aged, Hakan, and put on weight. I'm disappointed."

"And you are as beautiful as ever. A little thinner, yet looking more youthful with the new hairstyle. I could fall in love with you all over again."

There was no twinkle in his eye and no smile on his face.

He sighed.

"But ... you tried to kill my family. Butcher them in a public park. I am afraid that was a step too far." He shrugged. "Maybe we had the best of each other. Let us at least be happy about that."

Natasha countered: "And the worst."

"Hmm. I do not disagree. So, what can I do for you?"

"Shall we walk?"

Hakan glanced quickly at the couple with the pram. Natasha smiled.

"It's okay, we'll walk slowly so they can follow. Tell them to leave the pram, there's probably nothing in it."

Hakan held out his arm and she linked it. Immediately, she felt the warmth of his body next to hers and relaxed, as the familiar feel and smell of his presence reassured her. Her head involuntarily rested on his shoulder, when they took their first few steps forward. She took a breath and announced the terrible accident at the *castello*. He drew her closer, the first person to offer real comfort for her loss. The physical contact was what she had needed; just to feel another human beside her.

They walked slowly for twenty minutes or so. He talked to her about grief, the process of healing and coming to terms with loss. In her hatred of him after he betrayed her, she had forgotten how wise and sensitive he could be. He recalled his memories of Marco: showing Hakan around the garden of cacti and succulents at the *castello*; hearing him talk of the development of the Maltese language and other backwaters of learning, which seemed to fascinate him, rendering him oblivious to the bored expressions of his audience. They laughed together. For a moment, she became tearful, accepting Hakan's sympathy, even forgetting whose hand it was that was responsible for her father's fatal fall.

Finally, she pulled away from him, shaking herself free of the confusing emotions that filled her.

"Thanks for that – it was worth the trip. There aren't many

people who understand me like you do. But I'm here to talk business. Serious business."

Hakan buried his hands in his jacket pockets and nodded, urging her to proceed.

She explained the situation in Malta and the stranglehold that the Russians had on the country. She had no idea of the manipulations of Christa Baldacchino, as George and Marco had only agreed that plan of action immediately before Marco's death and George had not revealed to Natasha the existence of Camilleri's files. Similarly, she had not informed him of the reason for her visit to Istanbul, believing the fewer people who knew of her plan, the better.

What she was sounding out was an audacious political move that she thought gave the Russians, and all the other interested parties, what they wanted – to be able to resolve the crisis the Maltese gambit had caused them.

"What I suggest is simple. Why don't you give the Russians the same rights of passage through the new Kanal Istanbul as they've got down the Bosphorus? When it comes to it, that's what they really want. Freedom to use their Black Sea naval bases. In truth, the occupation of Malta's not going well for them, and, my guess is, they'd happily leave, if a respectable compromise was achievable. And the Maltese would be overjoyed to see them go."

Hakan just laughed.

"Come on, Natasha, you disappoint me! We have had every Russian politician, general and oligarch you can name arrive in Ankara, asking the very same thing, since the Kanal Istanbul was first proposed. We took American money to build it, you remember, fifteen billion initially, rising to nearly twenty. I said to the CIA that they were pushing us into a war with Russia, if we were to block the Bosphorus and deny them access to the Kanal. My exact words. And here we are."

"Well, times have changed, Hakan. I think there's something you want badly enough to grant a concession over the

Kanal to the Russians, something that the Americans will accept, given the alternative seems to be a Russian base in the middle of the Mediterranean."

He shrugged his shoulders.

"I am interested to hear your thoughts. Go on."

"Membership of the European Union – a fast track of your application. Your economy is a mess, so changing to the euro will be a challenge, but Greece managed it. You're already NATO members, so that's a plus. Your geopolitical credentials are impeccable, as long as you stop facilitating the Afghanistan heroin trade. Also, you'll have to start behaving better towards your political opponents and realise dissent's a fact of life. And stop being so damn' nasty to the Kurds! If you push on with Kurdish independence, the PKK should be less of a problem. Turkey could be the first Muslim country to join the EU. This could be the biggest moment since Atatürk founded the republic.

"And what're you giving up, really? What's the actual price – nothing, except avoiding further conflict with Russia. Aren't you two sick of fighting each other yet?" He looked closely at her.

"And you can deliver this?"

"I don't know. But it makes sense to me, and, at the moment, I know the Russians'll take anything they can to get out with their heads held high. The Americans don't want the Russians in the Mediterranean and the Maltese situation's making a mockery of the EU. This solution suits everybody. If you're interested, I can take it to Brussels and the Americans, see if it flies."

It did not surprise Hakan that Natasha had such connections. She had once been one of the most prominent entrepreneurs in Europe, wining and dining heads of state, top bureaucrats and leaders of industry. He wondered why it had all gone so wrong for her. Then, he smiled to himself; *he* was probably the reason. In his heart of hearts, he realised he had all but destroyed this formidable woman. What a waste. Hakan took a deep breath and forced himself to consider the proposal impartially.

"I think I can raise this with the right people, but there are no guarantees. Many a good idea has floundered on the rocks of politics. And, make no mistake, there are a lot of politics at stake here. But I will try." He paused for a moment, looking at her, admiring her dark, smoky eyes and cappuccino complexion. He knew her intimately and felt a longing to hold her again. He could have kissed her, there and then, but he held back. "I suppose this means we are likely to meet to discuss my progress? I will look forward to it."

The look exchanged between them lasted longer than it should have. Before he turned to go, he took her cool, smooth hands and gently kissed her on the cheek. She felt the soft bristle of his moustache linger for a moment, and her heart missed a beat. She had often thought of killing Hakan, he deserved no less for what he had done to her but, at that moment, she was glad she had held back. It was true, though, that he was one of her *loose ends*. Maybe his time would come – later.

CHAPTER 66
COMMISSIONER FOR HOME SECURITY GEORGE ZAMMIT

HASTINGS GARDENS, VALLETTA, MALTA

FOLLOWING MARCO'S DEATH, it became a priority to get Christa Baldacchino and the men off the island. The east side of Malta was the developed, commercial side of the island. From Marsacala in the south, through to St Paul's in the north, almost every accessible strip of seafront boasted hotels, restaurants, shops, or mid- and high-rise apartment blocks. The west of the island was more agricultural and rural, but the land was higher, and cliffs made access to the shoreline more difficult.

There were only four sandy beaches in the less populated north-west area, nestling in quiet coves. Each of them was guarded by Russian soldiers. Huck and Billy had conferred with George and Denzel, and they had all agreed that their best chance of getting off the island was to scramble to a headland between Gnejna beach and Għajn Tuffieħa bay, where there was a disused concrete jetty that had formerly served a small fishing community. All that was left of the fishing village these days was a few tumble-down buildings and a treacherous footpath across some unstable clay cliffs.

There, they could meet a high-powered US Navy RHIB that would speedily take them back to a Zumwalt-class destroyer, sent from Souda Bay naval base, in Crete. It would wait just outside Maltese territorial waters. The oddly shaped 'stealth' destroyer, whose sides sloped inward above the waterline, was designed so its radar cross section made it look more like a local fishing boat and was fifty times harder to spot than a conventional destroyer. Should any Russian vessel try to interfere, they would realise the US destroyer was also a formidable fighting ship.

The destroyer would make short work of the journey to Catania, from where Christa Baldacchino and the team would travel to Signorella, to be debriefed by Mary-Ann Baker. That was the plan George outlined to Christa on the second occasion that they met in Hastings Gardens.

She sighed deeply and looked him in the eye.

"George, this better work, otherwise we're all in big trouble."

"Christa, look around you. We're in big trouble now, anyway."

"Okay, I'm in. For better or worse."

George's words were prophetic as, that night, he had to tell Marianna that he and Denzel were leaving the island. They met in the Gardens of Serenity, a strangely beautiful construction of elaborate buildings, shaded walkways, lily ponds and dramatic stone features – a gift from the People's Republic of China to the people of Malta.

The plantings of magnolia, bamboo, olives and azaleas were chosen for form, balance and texture, rather than showy blooms or bright colours. The location of the garden, adjacent to a busy dual carriageway, near the airport, seemed at odds with its stated purpose, but usually ensured it was empty.

Maybe it was the atmosphere of the gardens, but Marianna was calm and understanding. It was just the two of them and they sat on a bench, under the glazed, tubular-tiled roof of a walkway, watching the jets of water oxygenate the ornamental pond.

"Come back soon, George, and bring our Den with you. I can't stand this for much longer. My nerves are playing up."

"I will. With any luck, this trip'll sort everything out."

"We must be in a spot, if there's only you left to save us." George looked at her. She was staring out over the pond.

"Thanks for the vote of confidence."

"So, when'll you be back?"

"When the Americans or the EU or somebody forces the Russians to go home. They know that Den and I've been working against them, and that, in their eyes, he's a …"

"Don't say *murderer*. My son's not one of those! So, it could be a week or two?"

"Hmmm. Or even a bit longer."

Marianna looked downcast. He thought she looked close to tears. Sometimes she would roar like a lioness, terrifying everybody around her. Now, she looked small and defenceless. His heart went out to her.

"I'm sure you'll do your best, George. You always do. You're a good man, but I do worry when you're away. And I worry twice as much when Den's with you."

It was a declaration of sorts, and he left it hanging in the air. Marianna was staring out over the lily pond. After making the most of their special moment together, he said: "So, what're you thinking about?"

She did not turn her head, just frowned, as she concentrated on getting her thoughts together. Insects danced on the surface of the pond and the bamboo shoots rustled in the breeze that crept in through the ornamental arches of the walkways.

"I was thinking … maybe we should have a change from Nerja this year? They say Alicante is nice. What do you think? Will you be back in time?"

CHAPTER 67
NATASHA BONNICI
SIGNORELLA US AIR FORCE BASE, SICILY, ITALY

NATASHA SAT across the white utilitarian table from Mary-Ann Baker. The blinds hanging from the conference room's glass partition walls were drawn. Mary-Ann had flown overnight from Washington and was still dressed in her crumpled black trouser suit. She had bags under her eyes.

"I was surprised to hear from you, Miss Bonnici. I didn't think you and I would ever end up on the same side. I was sorry to hear about your father – I liked him. I hope you've got some of his sense of decency."

"Well, you'll no doubt form your own judgement on that."

"No doubt."

"I've met with Hakan Toprak and spoken to him several times. There's a faction in Ankara that can never forgive Russia for its nineteenth-century crimes against the Ottomans but, in the main, he thinks there's sufficient support to deliver an extension to Montreux, allowing Russian warships down the new Kanal on the same terms as the Bosphorus now, in exchange for Turkey's fast track EU membership. And, by fast track, they *mean* fast track: no conditional terms, such as pulling the economy around, a Kurdish state, human rights inspections, all that procrastinating nonsense. They say they're committed to it and will agree to get on with it all, but no backstop deadlines."

"Yeah, something like that was expected. If they can do it in five years, the EU will live with that. That's fast track when you're talking about this stuff – the Turks know that. The EU still has their talking to do but, after we picked Noémie Minaud up off the floor, she said she thought there was a real chance she could pull it off. So, there's going to be a dead period now, while the big boys and girls sort all the shit out.

You spoke to your Russian friends yet?"

"No, but if you think now's the time?"

"Yeah, we think so. We've looked at some papers we obtained through a third party. They show that the Russians had your PM and two of his ministers by the short and curlies. Blackmailed them to subvert the proper functions of the Maltese Republic. So, yeah, tell them the game's up. Everything they've done since they arrived has been illegal and to no effect. It's been nothing more than a blackmail scam. They're gonna end up in the Hague, if they don't play ball.

"Get it done. Tell the Russians to go home and they'll get their treaty. You gonna hang around the base meantime or you got somewhere to be? We'll need you to bring the Russians on board and one or two more calls with Toprak, then it becomes proper channels, we thank you for your service, and no more back door stuff."

Natasha told Mary-Ann she was going to Catania where there were hotels with five-star rooms and decent restaurants. She said she would ring Fedorov from there.

Natasha was not aware that, by this time, there were also five other visitors on the base. George and Christa Baldacchino had presented their files of documents to the US and EU security teams and were cross-examined on their contents and the sources of the information for several hours. Billy and Huck had largely faded out of the picture and were last seen waiting to be shipped back to the US. Denzel swam in the pool, read thrillers from the extensive library and watched endless movies on the base's TV station. He was hoping things would resolve themselves soon, as the boredom was terminal.

Meanwhile, Natasha sat at a quiet table by the edge of the pool in her five-star hotel and rang Fedorov. From his tone, he did not seem particularly pleased to hear from her.

"So, Colonel, I've got good news for you. You remember the conversation you had with my father, about the Kanal Istanbul?"

"Of course."

"Well, the Americans, the EU and, importantly, the Turks are all ready to begin formal discussions."

"Really! So, you took it upon yourself to step into his shoes?"

"He'd already got the ball rolling, I thought it'd be a shame if his death slowed things down."

"You seem to be holding up remarkably well. Are you sure you're strong enough for such work?"

"No doubt, it'll all catch up with me, but you know what I'm like. Pretty resilient."

Fedorov considered her statement. Then he said: "And us, the Russian Federation ... what's required from us?"

"Well, apparently, copies of the dossiers you collected on Refalo, Farrugia and Cini, among others, are in the hands of the Americans. Nothing to do with me, I might add. There's been some talk of the International Criminal Court, but I'm sure you can deal with that in the negotiations. Anyway, they need you to leave Malta, completely, by the end of the month and pay reparations for damage to Manoel Island and the cost of scrapping the *Peter the Great*. But, back home, you'll be a hero. You'll have brought them the treaty extension! Same terms as now."

Federov was puzzled.

"The dossiers, you say? Any idea ..."

"No, none at all, actually. But my guess would be to look at those close to the late Assistant Commissioner Camilleri."

"It can't be your father as, unfortunately, he's no longer with us ... so who? Not the policeman – Zammit? Surely not? The man's an idiot!"

"I don't think we'll ever find out."

"So, tell me, why've you done this? What's in it for you? I don't understand. You were looking at relaunching yourself, at home and in Milan; receiving an indemnity regarding the murders there. So what do you get out of it all?"

"I still want your Siberian murderer to sign his confession. That costs you nothing and I've earned it. But I came to the conclusion it was only a matter of time before you were thrown out of Malta and I didn't want to be left backing the wrong side when the music stopped. I like you, Igor, you're an attractive man. In other times, who knows ... but you've got your treaty. Retire gracefully, swallow some pride."

"That doesn't come easily to a Russian."

"I wouldn't imagine it would!

"So, Natasha, I think this is farewell. Others will now take over. Expect their call and be straight with them. Unfortunately, not everybody in my country's as reasonable as I am."

In Malta things started to move quickly.

Noémie Minaud had contacted President Mizzi, who eventually agreed to come out of his shell and convene the House of Representatives to vote to remove the corrupt prime minister, pending elections. Within days of the colonel's conversation with Natasha, he and Ambassador Buzilov left Villa Gwardamanġa, on instructions from Moscow, rapidly followed by the remaining Russian forces and the volunteers.

Refalo used what time he had left to approach the UAE about moving some money – a lot of money – and acquiring rights of residence. He then left the island, travelling first-class on an Emirates flight to Dubai, courtesy of the government's travel budget. Malta and the United Arab Emirates have no extradition treaty.

CHAPTER 68
COMMISSIONER FOR HOME SECURITY GEORGE ZAMMIT

POLICE HQ, FLORIANA, MALTA

GEORGE AND DENZEL returned to Malta on the same day that Refalo left for Dubai, walking off the Sicily catamaran late in the evening, to be met by the entire Zammit and Mifsud families, holding *Welcome Home* balloons. Also on the quayside were Karl Chelotti and Commissioner Carmel Mallia, whose stomach ailment suddenly seemed to have disappeared. The commissioner thought he had better say a few words, but the noisy Zammit and Mifsud families ignored him, so he stopped talking and faded into the background.

Within an hour, the crowd were crushed around Marianna's kitchen table, feasting on the finest cuts from the Mifsuds' cold store. There were piles of cans of Cisk and bottles of sparking rosé. Josette made sure the jug of water was always within her reach and that she was in sole charge of refilling glasses.

The men toasted the return of law and order, free elections, the end of corruption in all its forms, for now, and good riddance to the Russians. George toasted Denzel, who toasted Democratica, who were in turn applauded by Marianna, who asked where they would all be without the Catholic Church. There were some confused looks, but nobody spoiled the good mood, and the party continued into the early hours.

As the days passed and the old institutions cranked back into life, the details of how Refalo, Farrugia and Cini were manipulated and blackmailed by the Russians into giving up the Maltese state became known. The backlash against both political parties was severe, and a new centre-left party was formed, fielding candidates of good standing on a far-reaching anti-corruption ticket, breaking the hegemony of the two-party system that had dominated the political landscape since the founding of the republic in 1974.

Natasha Bonnici had stepped forward and, because of her extensive business knowledge, her lack of any association with either of the two political parties and the good name of the illustrious Bonnicis, was appointed co-leader, alongside a primary schoolteacher from the small southern town of Żurrieq.

By the time of the election, George and Karl Chelotti were actively investigating thirty of the seventy-nine members of the House of Representatives and their trusted advisers, who were facing prosecution for various offences of graft and corruption, ranging from bribery, extortion, fraud, theft and nepotism to subordinating the public interest to their own private aims. This related both to acts carried out before the arrival of the Russians and those occurring during the occupation.

George had summoned Natasha to Central Police Headquarters, to meet with him and the commissioner. The top man sat wringing his hands together and perspiring, while George addressed her.

"Thanks for coming in to meet us." He gestured around the sparsely furnished corner room, with the long rosewood conference table. "This used to be Gerald's office." He pointed out of the window that faced out over Marsamxett Harbour. "He would stand there and look at that view, working out how to approach all the problems people dumped onto his desk." Mallia shifted uncomfortably in his seat.

Natasha smiled at George, putting her Hermès Birkin

handbag on the table and taking a seat, after brushing off some pastry crumbs.

"It's the first time I've been inside this building. Gerald was always courteous enough to come and see me. What do you want, George? Have I suddenly become a problem that's been *dumped* on your desk?" He swallowed.

"It's very simple. We want you to stand down from becoming involved in the new Social Democratic Party. We've decided you're not a fit and proper person and, in due course, we'll pass on our assessment to whoever's governing the party – unless you choose to stand down first." Natasha laughed.

"Are you telling me what I can and can't do?"

"*Mela* ... yes. That's what policemen are for."

"George! What do you think you're doing?"

"Something that should have been done a long time ago, Natasha. The old days've gone. Gerald's way of doing things has gone. The Russians brought out the worst and the best in the Maltese and now we've had a clean out, we can start again and not make the same mistakes."

"Well, George, maybe *you* should stand for election! But you know me? You know I won't be told what to do by anyone." There was menace in her voice. "I like you, but I won't stand by and let you steamroller me."

"I don't want to run you over, I want you to avoid being run over ... by stepping to one side, as it were. Run your businesses or do something else – you can't go into politics. Not after what we've just been through. So, that's all I've got to say. Please think about it and do as we ask." He glanced at Mallia, who nodded his head.

Natasha took her bag, put her sunglasses on and paused, glancing around the room before she departed.

"So, this was Gerald's office, was it? Miserable little place, isn't it? I can't imagine what yours must've been like, George. You're making a big mistake."

The door closed behind her and George and Mallia looked

at each other. The commissioner's bulbous, slightly bloodshot eyes were mournful.

"Well, you've done it now! What do you think she'll do?"

"Probably order a hit on us."

Mallia gasped. "You really think so?"

George responded with a withering look.

As the months slid by, the island cleaned itself up, both literally and metaphorically, and the tourists started to return. The occasional Russian tanker could still be seen lurking off Hurds Bank, but changes to the Maltese constitution had now allowed a small NATO naval force to take over the facilities at Manoel Island and more effectively police illegal maritime activities. It had been agreed, by the required two-thirds majority of the House of Representatives, that the principle of neutrality and non-alignment had run its course, and it was time for Malta to become fully European and join the alliance. An application by the Republic to join NATO was duly sent to its headquarters in Brussels.

The Maltese Armed Forces Maritime Squadron had been gifted a dozen aging American corvettes, to patrol Malta's significantly reduced maritime search and rescue area, and a new, more benign regime by the EU for the management of migrants arriving from North Africa had been put in place.

As memories of Camp Azure and the Russian occupation faded, there were those who said that Malta, post-occupation, was an infinitely better place than it had been before. It had taken the arrival of the Russians to reveal the depth of the previous corruption and the extent to which it had undermined the country.

To the surprise of many, Natasha Bonnici withdrew from being a candidate of the new Social Democratic Party, citing a wish to resume her business career and an inability to do that and simultaneously serve in the House of Representatives. She sent George a bottle of Maltese wine, together with a note reading: *Thanks for the advice. Don't think I've forgotten.*

He opened the wine the following Sunday and, after only a moment's hesitation, poured himself and Denzel a large glass each, to accompany a bowl of rabbit pasta, studded with green peas.

CHAPTER 69
GRECA ROSSI

ROSSI'S VINYEARD, NOTO, SICILY, ITALY

Greca was having lunch with Bernd Kruder on the loggia outside her farmhouse. He had insisted on the meeting which, in truth, she had been expecting. Temperatures had dropped, so outdoor dining had become comfortable. On the estate, the migrant pickers were busy dropping this year's crop of Fragolino grapes into their baskets. The sun had developed the sugars and Greca was expecting a fine vintage.

She did not eat with the same enthusiasm as the skinny, pale Austrian sitting opposite her, who had emptied his plate at least twice.

"Excellent *porchetta*, Greca. I thought we Austrians were the experts in pork cuisine, but we could learn a thing or two from your kitchen."

She dabbed her mouth gently, so as not to smudge the cherry red lipstick she had applied earlier.

"Yes, it was a cute little piglet. It was running around out here for the last week, just to finish it off, eating everything. Then, one of the boys shot it. Not how we used to slaughter pigs when I was a girl. Anyway, figs, Bernd. Let's try some fresh figs, – fat and juicy. They're from my orchard." She lazily gestured over her shoulder, calling for the man who served in the house.

"Asano! Coffee, please, and figs for Herr Kruder."

"Already waiting on side table, Miss Greca. I come now. So sorry for delay."

Greca turned and smiled at him indulgently. He was an excellent houseman, very loyal, with many skills. "Thank you, Asano."

Bernd shifted in his chair.

"To business?"

"Of course. I didn't think you'd come all this way just to enjoy my *porchetta*."

"Greca, these loans – the boys had no idea what they were signing up for. They had no authority to do what they did. They thought they were being clever and duped our bankers by padding the business plan. The rest of the Family are furious with their behaviour and have no intention of supporting them. It is all most unfortunate. Surely something can be done?"

Greca took a fig from the plate and lustily bit into it. She dabbed the juices from her chin with a napkin.

"*Unfortunate*? Not really. It'll allow me to foreclose and become the owner of almost all the tomato processing plants in Italy. That's a big deal. My associates and I are perfectly happy with the way things've turned out. In fact, that's what we expected to happen."

"Your associates?"

"Yes, you didn't think I could raise all that money myself, did you? I called in a few favours from some *very* cash rich people I know in Naples, Palermo and Calabria. They all saw the upside to the deal, and they went crazy when I told them it was the tomato business – but they can be *very firm* when it comes to borrowers sticking to their obligations. Anyway, they were happy to lend to the brave Hussars, knowing exactly who their daddies were! Those *boys* aren't children, just arrogant and stupid young men who deserve to learn an extremely expensive lesson. You should thank me!"

She smiled at him, green almond-shaped eyes flashing like gemstones.

"Look, Greca, I will put my cards on the table. Now that Marco is gone, I could well become the next chair of the Family and this ... well, it is an embarrassment. And some do say that you led them on ... well, Leo that is ... and you definitely took advantage. Leo is, shall we say, impressionable?"

"*Impressionable*? Personally, I found him pompous, entitled, self-opinionated and unwilling to listen to good advice. He must've got that from somewhere, no? And while we're speaking of advice, I'll give you some. Natasha Bonnici's coming for you. She's back, she's mean and she's looking for revenge. She was the one who killed Marco. She topped her own father – that's how crazy she is! Another Wise Man to add to her tally. She's dangerous. As if you didn't know." Bernd froze, his napkin midway to his mouth.

"You are kidding me? I had not heard that. I am shocked. Poor Marco! It is unbelievable – his own daughter!" Kruder sighed. "Mind you, she also ruined the relationship I have with my son. Said things to him she had no right to say. Now the damn' boy has disappeared. Stomped off in a huff. We have not seen him for several weeks. His mother is worried sick. Probably in Antibes, he likes the South of France at this time of year."

Greca snorted.

"No, Bernd, *you* ruined your relationship with him when you started screwing boys his age."

"I ... how dare you?"

"Give it a rest. It's old news. Anyway, trust me, Natasha threw Marco over the balustrade in the *castello*. Simple as that. Asano was there. He used to be Marco's butler, didn't you?"

Asano turned away from the side table, where he was preparing the coffee. He nodded. Bernd Kruder looked the inscrutable butler up and down. A dozen questions flitted through his mind. Asano bowed his head, ever so slightly.

"I had privilege to serve Mr Marco, but his death was ... very bad and I could not serve Miss Natasha after that."

He gracefully brought over the small coffee cups from the side table, arranged on a silver tray, and placed it in front of them, together with a closed silver cloche.

Greca laughed.

"Hear that, Bernd? *Very bad*! I suggest the Family might need some enhanced security. Say, two hundred Aye Axemen, loyal and willing to do whatever it takes. They'll wipe the floor with any other organised crime group, even take out Natasha Bonnici for you, if that's what you want. The world would be a better place for it.

"Marco's gone, you're free to redefine yourselves. No more lurking in the shadows, collecting boring old paintings and scribblings, like frightened little boys. You could have a controlling stake in all of my tomato processing plants, plus a business that controls all the migrant labour in Sicily and southern Italy." She studied Bernd Kruder's sour expression. "That'd give you effective control over the price of tomatoes in the biggest market in Europe – it's worth billions. It'll put the Family back on the map and restore the Hussars' tarnished reputations, so their daddies can be proud of them again. I can arrange all that, at a price. Let's say, you pay me my dowry. Let me in. I want my seat at the table. I know how to behave, Bernd. I really do – I'm a lady now!"

"Well, Greca ... it is not as easy as that."

Meanwhile, Asano had finished depositing plates and glasses on the kitchen worktop. He walked out into the large rear courtyard and through a locked door leading to the cellars beneath an old barn. Originally, they were cool rooms, used for the maturation of wine, but recently they had been boarded with hygienic white panels and used for an entirely different purpose.

Strapped to an old dentist's chair with wide cable ties was Leo Kruder. His mouth was stuffed with tightly rolled cloth and grey gaffer tape was wound across it and around the back of his head, which had slumped to his chest. His left hand was dripping blood from a soaking bandage, where Asano had, with surgical precision, removed his little finger, just below the joint of the proximal phalanx. The idea was not to inflict unnecessary pain, so Asano had injected him with a local anaesthetic of lidocaine. Nevertheless, Leo had still found the sound and sensation of crunching bone upsetting and was in shock.

Asano felt the vibration of the pager on his hip. He had been summoned.

Once he was back at the table, Greca lifted the silver domed lid and Bernd saw the finger, lying on a bed of chopped lettuce. Greca had not been expecting the garnish and had to snort back a laugh at the bizarre sight. She would have to have a word with Asano – jokes like that caught her unawares and that was not good!

Greca kept her tongue in one side of her mouth, to control her laughter. Bernd Kruder's eyes bulged and his mouth fell open.

"Asano, I think Herr Kruder wants to know what this is?" She glared at the houseman and pointed to the finger.

Asano pulled an expression meant to convey confusion. He said, as if speaking to a five-year-old: "So sorry to confuse, but is Herr Leopold's pinky finger."

Greca covered her face with the linen napkin and started rocking with silent laughter.

"His *pinky* ... oh, Bernd, I don't mean to laugh, but you've got to see the funny side." Asano looked at her.

"Sorry to do something wrong? I have cut off wrong finger? I can cut another?" he added helpfully.

"NO!" cried Bernd. "Where is he, I want to see my son!"

Greca stopped laughing and any humour or trace of compassion left her face.

"Bernd, I'm keeping him here and I'm going to cut something off him every three days, until you sell my very generous deal to your pals in the Family. I also want some figures about how much my father's share is worth, in today's money.

"If my guys even get a sniff of strangers in the area, police or private military, whatever, they'll kill them. Then, tell your gang of sad old men, my Axemen will come for them, their children, wives, mothers, and cut them all into pieces, too. Believe me, I'll do it. Then, I'll just walk in and take what's left. It's game on, Bernd – and I bet I know who'll win." She paused to let the threat sink in. White faced, he stared at her in disbelief. Greca continued speaking, in a lighter, more jovial tone.

"Just sign me up! It can all be avoided and then ... won't we have some fun together? Now, come with me."

She held out her hand, so Bernd could help her from the chair. Like the gentleman he was, he instinctively obliged.

"We can both go and see Leo and explain to him why he had to lose his *pinky* finger. He's downstairs. And, be warned, he's not very happy."

CHAPTER 70
NATASHA BONNICI
CASTELLO BONNICI, IL-WARDIJA, MALTA

NATASHA WAS DRIVING BACK to the *castello* from an exercise class when, to her surprise, she received a call from Bernd Kruder. The imperious Austrian and she had many reasons not to be civil to one another, so she was intrigued when his caller identification popped up on her screen. She pulled over and parked.

It was only a day or so since Bernd had returned from the nightmarish visit to Greca's farm in Sicily to his Austrian home, nestled in the undulations of an agricultural area, south of Vienna.

He had tearfully promised Greca he would do what he could to restore her to her father's former position within the Family and begged her not to harm Leo any further. He pleaded for time, stressing the difficulty of the task he had been given. Greca had cheerfully said she understood perfectly, pointing out that, as Leo had nine fingers left, that gave Bernd nearly a month to make the arrangements.

Bernd knew that the blackmail would never wash with the committee – the members would never welcome Sergio's unhinged Sicilian daughter into their midst. After a sleepless night spent pacing the corridors of his ancestral home, he gave up. Early the next morning, he rang Natasha.

"Well, well ... Bernd. What a pleasure! How're things between you and your young Hussar? When we met, I found him a surprisingly graceless young man."

Bernd ignored the taunt and carried on.

"It is time we talked, Natasha. I need some assistance from a woman with your particular skills. I am in serious trouble, but I think we can help each other."

Natasha smiled to herself. She had no idea what was happening to him but was certain this conversation was going to be fun. She started by injecting as much fake concern as possible into her response.

"Oh, no! How terrible, what sort of trouble? And what can I do to help?"

"Okay, Natasha, there is no need to humiliate me. If you help me resolve my troubles, in a satisfactory manner, your reward would be my sponsoring your return to the Family. It is not a guarantee but, now your Italian legal troubles seem to have been cleared up, I might be able to do something. I am more than likely to become chair of the committee, following Marco's unfortunate ... accident. I am sorry for your loss, by the way. But, without me, you have no hope of *ever* making a return. So, listen – here is your incentive – it is either you back in the Family or your cousin Greca."

Natasha's mood changed in an instant.

"What're you talking about? How on earth would Greca find her way into the Family?"

"She has my son, plus a lot of tomatoes."

Natasha shook her head in frustration.

"Let's, for the sake of advancing this conversation, try a different question. What do I need to do for you to choose me?"

"Simple. Kill her and bring my son back to me. She is holding him hostage on her farm in Sicily."

"Poor Leo! I hope she's being kind to him."

"No! She is not, far from it! The other thing you should know is that she is going around telling people you were responsible for Marco's death. You defenestrated him or something. I should have thought you would want to put a stop to that."

Natasha drew breath sharply.

"Yes, I do." It made her blood run cold to hear her father's death described so callously. The scene on the landing flashed through her mind, as well as the image of his face, as he fell backwards over the balustrade. An accident, that's all it was.

"It has to be done within days. She is slowly dismembering my son."

There were choking sobs from him. Natasha sighed.

"For Christ's sake, Bernd. I know Greca – she won't hurt him unnecessarily. Pull yourself together."

"I cannot! Her Japanese butler has already cut a finger off and they are due to do something else the day after tomorrow! You have to …"

"Listen to me. There's no way I can charge into that farmhouse and pull Leo out. I wouldn't get through the gate. You've got to tell Greca to bring him to Switzerland, or wherever you hang out these days. Tell her she needs to talk to the committee about … what is it?... *tomatoes*, or whatever you've got going on, and discuss her joining terms.

"She'll come with bodyguards, but that's okay. There's far more chance to do something away from her home territory. If she won't bring Leo, get Bohdan to organise some mercenaries. Tell him there're still some Russians hanging around Malta looking for work. Have them raid the farmhouse, while she's away. They'd better know what they're doing, though. They'll be up against the Axemen, who'll happily cut them to pieces. It'll be a firefight, but everyone'll think it's just some Sicilian gang thing.

"As for our Ms Rossi, leave her to me."

Natasha thought about her conversation with Bernd. It was odd. If he wanted to dispose of Greca and get Leo back, he had many other options. Why ask for her input? Also, even if she could put a plan together and it all worked out, would the wider Family agree to her return? She knew Bernd did not have as much influence as he thought. Also, if Greca was spreading the word that Natasha was responsible for Marco's death, then the Family would be even less likely to take her back.

The thought did occur to her that he was setting her up, in some way. What he was promising was undeliverable. She realised there was something wrong with the whole idea, but the fact that Greca was making a further concerted pitch at membership herself, kidnapping Leo and instigating the *tomato* thing – whatever that was – unsettled Natasha.

She took coffee on the terrace and thought through the best course of action. Without further hesitation, she decided there was only one thing to do. She rang the same number that the police had rung from the superheated station in Greece, back in the early springtime. As before, it rang and rang.

Eventually, a voice with an East Asian accent answered.

"Hello, how may I be of service?"

"It's me, Asano. You've found a new hole to squat in, I hear. Be a good little toad and take this phone to Greca, please. Hop to it!"

There was a pause. Natasha listened to Asano's footsteps pattering through the house in Sicily. A hand covered the mouthpiece and there was some mumbled speech. Then, a husky female voice spoke to her.

"Hello, my darling cousin. It's just as well I keep this phone charged up. What can I do for you? How're you holding up?"

"I am fine, thanks, but listen – I think we're being played. A rather desperate and unsubtle Bernd Kruder has just rung and offered me untold riches for the return of his son – oh, and your head."

There was deep throaty laughter and the flare of a light being applied to a cigarette.

"What a slimeball. I hope you didn't agree?"

"You'll get a call shortly, inviting you to go to Ticino. That's where I'm supposed to … do something."

"Exciting! How do I meet my end? I'd love to know."

"Listen, I'm being serious. We can carry on like this, at each other's throats, or we can work together. I'm sorry about Ituah, but I'd do the same again tomorrow, if I had to. You know that. But I also know we both want to get into the Family and take what's due to us. So why don't we work together, rather than fighting each other? I don't want to fight you."

Greca exhaled cigarette smoke.

"Well, we've tried that once. How did Greece work out for you?"

"This is different. We've got a second chance. Listen, the Family're a bunch of deadbeats. You and I couldn't bear to sit at the same table as them. I don't even know why we're both so obsessed with them. I've been thinking, there's another way we could build ourselves a base and take them on. You've got your business and the Axe guys …"

"And the tomatoes!" Greca injected.

"Yes, of course, those damn' tomatoes, how could I forget! Why's everybody going on about tomatoes? You'll have to explain about that sometime, but I know exactly how we can set ourselves up to beat the Family at their own game."

"Are you being serious, or will I need to keep three of my boys behind me at all times?"

"We should be allies, Greca. We were good friends once, until that awful Ituah business spoiled everything. We're better together than apart. Think about it. What's going on with Leo, by the way?"

"Oh, he's fine. He and I're having breakfast together. He's just gone for more coffee."

"Breakfast? It's nearly two o'clock!"

"Well, we had a late night."

"Greca – you're kidding me! You aren't …?"

"Well, he's no Ituah, but I'm teaching him."

"So you're not chopping him up?"

"No, relax. I took a finger, or rather Asano did, to scare Bernd. But Leo and I have had a long chat and got past that. It's all good!"

"Oh my God! You're awful!"

"I know!"

They giggled together like schoolgirls.

CHAPTER 71
COMMISSIONER FOR HOME SECURITY GEORGE ZAMMIT

ZAMMIT FAMILY HOME, BIRKIRKARA, MALTA

Baby Joseph was growing into a rumbustious toddler. He had graduated from grabbing and pulling over furniture, to thundering around the apartment, colliding with walls and doors and terrifying the finches. The family doctor had been alarmed by the child's weight and had recommended a strict diet. Gina had been mortified, saying that she thought it was positive that he was such a good eater. The doctor had not been impressed and, from then on, Gina spent hours peeling fruit and hiding biscuits. The child's pasta portion was carefully measured at forty grammes per meal and the rest of the plate filled with green vegetables. George looked on suspiciously, as the doctor had suggested that this new regime might benefit a few other members of the family.

Gina had proudly announced that she and Giorgio were expecting again, and Baby Joseph was going to have a brother. George hastily persuaded her it was time to start living full time in their own apartment, round the corner from George and Marianna's. He said that, with his new responsibilities, he needed more thinking time and opportunities to work at home – something he had never done and would never do, but Gina tearfully agreed it was time for them to be independent.

"You're only going round the corner, not to Australia!" Denzel told her.

"Oh, but Baby Joseph's so upset. This is his home."

George slipped the child a segment of apple that he immediately threw on the floor in disgust.

"*Mela*, it's time for him to get used to his new one. See you all tomorrow."

Denzel shut the door behind them and threw himself against it, arms outstretched, legs apart, as if to barricade it against their return. He and George started laughing and found they could not stop. Marianna folded her arms across her bosom.

"Den, don't be horrible about your sister!"

Then she grinned at the two men, as they rocked with laughter.

"Listen," she called out, "do you hear that?"

"What?" said Denzel.

"That – the sound of silence!"

All three of them started laughing again.

"Anyway," Marianna said to her son, "I'm glad to see you smiling again. You've had a face like a wet feast day recently."

"I'm just a bit bored, that's all, since the excitement ended."

"Well, I've got something to liven you up. I was talking to your Auntie Gracie, and she's got a nice Italian girl, helping her out, and I said you might …"

"Ma, don't meddle, or I'll move out, too. Then where would you be, eh? With only Dad for company."

"Ooooh! You shouldn't be so horrible to your poor mother!"

George went to the fridge and pulled out two cans of Cisk. He threw one to Denzel, pointing to the wicker seats in the back yard.

"C'mon, let's celebrate the arrival of peace and quiet."

They took their respective chairs and sipped cold beer. George was in reflective mood.

"You realise that, with Karl's promotion to superintendent, there's an inspector's post vacant within Organised and Financial Crime? You should go for it."

"I'm too young. I've only been a sergeant for a couple of years. People'll say it's a stitch up. Like Karl's promotion. And that's the very thing we're trying to stop, isn't it? Blatant favouritism!"

"Well, there're always exceptions. People might see your promotion as acknowledgement of what you did with the Resistance. Why don't you let me test the waters?"

"No, Dad, I don't think so. Anyway, I've been meaning to talk to you about something. I think the time's come for me to spread my wings a bit. After what I saw in Syria and this episode, I'd like to get some more experience abroad. Say within OLAF, Interpol, or a field job in one of the Brussels based agencies. I need something different. Malta's a small place; I'd like to try somewhere new."

"Well, well!" George clasped his hands behind his head and pondered how he would feel if Denzel were to leave. His son was probably his best friend. To see him go abroad would be … well, awful.

"Your mum won't like that. I'll have a think. It's a good time to be asking for favours, after what you've been through. Leave it with me."

"And what about you? What's it like being the big cheese?"

"*Mela*, Mallia's suddenly recovered, but he doesn't bother me. One of Gerald's files concerned certain matters that … well, I can't say, but he knows I know, which puts me in a very satisfactory position." He smiled knowingly at Denzel.

"Also, Karl Chelotti's a very able superintendent – and happy with his promotion. He loves paperwork, strategy papers, going to meetings and so on, so that suits me. And you wouldn't believe it but, since the elections and the focus on corruption, everybody's really behaving themselves. It's incredible! People actually phone me to ask if it's okay to do things.

"Also, I was thinking about Gina and this new baby. When it comes, your mother'll be full on helping again. So, I thought we'd go on a little holiday together, before it arrives – just the two of us, your mum and me. There's this cruise, around the Canaries and Casablanca. We've never been anywhere like that – what do you think?"

"Mum, in Casablanca?"

George rubbed his chin, deep in thought.

"Well, yes – but we don't *have* to get off the boat there. Then, I thought, if we're going to do something different, there's another idea I've got. I'd like to know what you think about it …"

CHAPTER 72
NATASHA BONNICI
PIERRE LOTI HILL PARK, ISTANBUL, TURKEY

IT WAS A SUNDAY MORNING, just into the New Year, and Hakan and his wife, Elif, were walking with the twins in Gülhane Park, the same place Hakan had met Natasha several months earlier. Emir and Erin were nearly three now and full of energy. It was a bright winter morning with a low cruel sun. Elif sported sunglasses and a full-length sable coat. The boys did not feel the cold, as they jostled each other at the little stall that sold *halka tatlisi*, the Turkish version of sweet, syrupy *churros*. Elif pulled the deep-fried dough hoops into little pieces and blew on them, before popping them in her sons' mouths. Hakan grabbed a piece.

"Stop it, Hakan, you have to start watching what you eat. You're putting on weight."

He thought about the last person who had said that to him. Contrary to what he had hoped, he had not seen Natasha again. The negotiations with the EU were conducted by bloodless, grey-suited bureaucrats and the discussions with the Russians in the company of loud, argumentative, chain-smoking military officers. On balance, he preferred the Russians. At least he knew where he stood with them.

The whole project had been seen as a remarkable success

and his star had risen even higher than before. He had money, position, reputation and his family, yet he remained restless. For Hakan, it was always about the journey, never the arrival. There was nothing he could not fix, no problem that could not be resolved, except for the feeling of a life left incomplete. He wondered if it was Natasha that he missed; his one failure. He had been clumsy there, he had panicked, had cheated and disrespected her – yet he had also become fabulously rich. His boys and their families would never, ever need to worry about money.

Yet, it cut both ways. Natasha could be impossible and, when her temper spilled over, beyond reason. He had left her for his own sanity and to protect his wife and the boys. He knew Natasha could do them harm; that had been proven when the Aye Axemen attacked Elif and her parents, while they sat in a café, the boys with them in their pushchair. Hakan had only just saved them in time. He shuddered at the memory.

Emir had made a run for the play park, while Erin stayed close to his mother. Hakan smiled. Two boys, so similar, yet so different. Emir, bold, reckless even, and Erin, quiet, sensitive, never far from his mother's side. Elif hurried along, pulling Erin behind her, to try and catch the other toddler, before he threw himself into something perilous.

Hakan felt his phone vibrate. He studied the strange text message from an unknown number: *It had to end like this one day, Hakan. Such a shame.*

For a moment he was confused. He read it three times and then glanced around him. Suddenly, he understood. The large old-fashioned pram stood unattended, fifty metres behind him. The female agent, a member of MIT, sat unnaturally still on the bench, not moving, arms hanging limply at her sides. Of the male agents, there was no sign.

Elif was placing Emir into a small swing, Erin at her side. There were two or three couples in the play park, parents with children. He turned round again, his heart beating rapidly. He saw what he feared and was momentarily confused. Waving at him, a big smile on her face, was Natasha Bonnici. She wore a long camel teddy bear coat, open so he could see she was unarmed, no weapons holstered at her hip. Her leather trousers were skin-tight and her black, fitted rollneck sweater allowed for no concealment. Hakan felt the rapid thumping of his heart and glanced around, looking for accomplices.

"Hakan!"

He heard her call from ten metres away. He turned to check the play park, then realised his mistake. By the time he faced her again, she had walked right up to him and drawn a suppressed pistol from her sleeve, holding it in her right hand. He opened his mouth to speak but, before he could utter a word, she shot him clean between the eyes. His last image was of Natasha's broad smile, her sparkling eyes and the curl of her short brown hair. She did not break stride, as she walked straight past the body of her former lover, looking into the play park where a tall slim woman in a black fur coat was pushing a child back and forth in a small boxy swing, while another stood by, patiently waiting his turn.

Poor Elif.

A car was waiting at the gate to whisk Natasha back to the airport, where she took a small private jet out of the country. There were no CCTV cameras and no witnesses. The driver smelled the acrid gunshot residue when she climbed into the back of the car but dismissed it as a waft of diesel fumes from a passing truck.

It was all as simple as that. Once Natasha was seated in the cabin for the flight back to Malta, the steward brought her a gin and tonic and she opened a magazine.

She breathed a sigh of relief, of freedom. That had been long overdue. She had tried not to do it, she really had. But therapy just made her ill, unhappy. It did not work for her. No, she refused to feel guilty about her actions. She felt much, much better – freer, happier, ready to pick her life up again.

Once Hakan's body had been placed in the family tomb at the Karacaahmet Cemetery, Elif, her lawyers and brothers had sat down to work through the complicated legal maze that was his estate. There were groups of companies, some trading, some not. There were holding companies, investment companies and trusts in a dozen different jurisdictions. There was cash, but some was needed for creditors, some for tax, some for future liquidity.

Elif was assured that, under the terms of the will, she owned it all, somehow and in some way, but the lawyers and accountants said it would take time, a lot of time, to unravel the ball of string Hakan had wound together. In fact, many of the complications flowed from the assets, companies and trust structures that he had secretly acquired from the Family, for a song, when a process of disinvestment had been agreed with the Anti-Mafia Direzione Nazionale, so as to avoid prosecution.

It came as a relief to all concerned when a Swiss private bank approached Elif and her advisers with a cash offer for all the assets that Hakan had bought from the Family, at the exact same price, plus a ten percent uplift. Within a month, the money had been paid and all documentation was completed. Elif settled down again with her family and advisers to decide what to do with the hundreds of millions they had just been paid, while in Castello Bonnici, Asano was opening a bottle of Fragolino wine.

Greca and Natasha clinked glasses, and he backed away, bowing slightly as he went.

"So, cousin, we're now the owners of one of the largest portfolios of oil and gas assets in Europe."

"Yep," said Greca, "and, don't forget, also the largest tomato processing business!"

"You'll have to tell me about that sometime. Speaking of squishy red things, where's Leo? I haven't seen him around much."

Greca frowned and shook her head.

"Oh, he finished his apprenticeship and I sent him home." Natasha laughed.

"So, is he a Greca-trained master of the bedroom now?"

Her cousin fluttered her eyelashes, green eyes glinting wickedly.

They both raised their glasses and laughed. Then, Greca became more thoughtful.

"Actually, no, I'm afraid not. No happy endings there. He made progress, but... maybe it's just Austrians ... there was just no passion! And, believe it or not, he has a thing about his missing finger. Insisted on wearing that wretched black glove. I told him not to – it's a real turn off, having that cold, clammy leather all over you. But he wouldn't listen. He got quite upset at times. It spoiled the mood, you know?"

Natasha bit her bottom lip and put her hand to her mouth.

"Greca! You're such a bad woman. I'm shocked, but I'm not really sorry – I didn't like Leo much. Long streak of misery. Anyway, would now be a good time to tell me about the tomatoes?"

"That can wait. We've made a very good start, so congratulations to us, but I'd rather talk about how we're going to screw the last cent out of that bunch of inbreds in Switzerland."

Natasha settled herself into a leather armchair and soaked up the atmosphere of the library, with its rich aroma of leather, tobacco and woodsmoke. Greca edged forward in the matching fireside chair.

Natasha looked at her. Greca looked at Natasha. Behind the smiles and laughter, there was mutual wariness.

Natasha wondered what the future might hold for them. How long would it be before this woman let her down, betrayed her, cast her aside, just like all the rest – she was capable of it, Natasha knew that. It was only a question of when. Then what?

Greca held the gaze of the woman opposite; the woman who had killed her own father and her former lovers, even Ituah who was Greca's, not to mention a string of business rivals. Greca easily maintained her smile and tried to put those thoughts to one side, but she saw Natasha's face tense and darken, just for a fraction of a second, as doubts flashed through her mind. Then, just as quickly, they were both all smiles again.

"Okay, Greca, I do have some thoughts," Natasha said. "But first ... Asano," she called out, "please fetch another bottle of Fragolino!"

She whispered to Greca, "I can't believe you brought him with you. It's like having a ghost in the house!"

Greca shrugged. Moments later, Asano silently appeared at the occasional table beside Natasha and started to open the bottle.

"So, Asano, how does it feel to be back at the *castello*? Is Greca treating you well?"

His eyes flickered towards Greca, who was looking relaxed and smiled back at him.

"Very pleased to be of service to Miss Greca. Hope wine is correct temperature – if not, so sorry."

Natasha looked at Greca and pulled a face.

Holstered in a leather strap on Asano's upper left arm, he felt his *kanabō* press against his taut bicep. When Greca had instructed him to accompany her to the *castello*, he had decided to arm himself with the short, iron-tipped cosh. He had learned that in proximity to Miss Natasha, you could never be too careful.

EPILOGUE

GEORGE HAD REALISED he could not persuade Marianna to make the trip to Libya using reason or by pleading so, after consulting with Denzel, he had resorted to trickery and subterfuge.

"You know, Abduallah made Den and me promise we'd go to Libya this year – for a holiday?"

His wife was at the sink, doing some hand washing, and immediately sensed trouble.

"I didn't know that. But you're not going, are you? Why would you? Not with Gina being pregnant and everything."

"Well, it's a bit tricky. He wants us to go for three weeks. He says not a day less will do. I mean, he and Rania helped hide Den when we really needed it. I feel I can't say no. Den feels the same. He wants to say thank you properly. Take some presents and stuff. I mean, you're invited too, of course."

"What! To Liberia? No, no, no! I'd rather stay here."

"*Mela*, you'll have Gina, I suppose. I mean, she won't go, given that she's pregnant."

"What! You'd go without me? Just leave me behind?"

"I feel … we feel, that's Den and me … that we have to." George gritted his teeth. "Also, it means this year's holiday allowance is all used up. I'm sorry about that. You know how much I enjoy going to Spain, but..."

As George had expected, this had not gone down well. The two men had to endure a period of sulking and bad temper unlike any they had experienced before. Of course, they could do nothing right, and every conversation came back to their selfishness in giving up the family holiday to Spain, just so they could get rid of Marianna and Gina and go to Liberia to be with that terrible man. Finally, after several days, Denzel told his father he could not stand the atmosphere in the house anymore and urged George to move on to the next part of the plan.

Over dinner that evening, when cutlery was clattered around the table and bread and salami was served, as Marianna was 'too busy' to cook anything more substantial, George announced that he had a suggestion to make – a compromise even. Marianna avoided eye contact, but he could tell she was listening intently.

If his wife was prepared to go to Libya for *one* week, he could explain to Abdullah that she could not spend any more time there, as she did not want to be away from Gina for too long, due to her pregnancy. And obviously, he and Den would not want the family to be apart at such a time, so they would all have to return to Malta after seven days – *seven days*, he stressed. This, he proudly exclaimed, as if surprised, left two weeks of holiday allowance for a family trip to Spain!

Marianna knew she had been backed into a corner. She said nothing and bit her bottom lip, but both Denzel and George noted the slight nod of the head, which they took to be her unequivocal consent. It was the best they were going to get! Denzel left the table, a smile on his face, to fetch some take out pizzas, saying: "Thank God that's over!"

The flight between Malta and Tunis had been without incident, but the connection between Tunis and Tripoli was on a local airline, which had led to an unseemly scene at check in, where Marianna voiced her doubts about the airworthiness of foreign aeroplanes and pilot competence.

Eventually, the three of them found themselves in Abdullah's Range Rover, as it pulled off the Coastal Road from Tripoli and sped up a long dirt track towards his isolated and heavily fortified compound, throwing up a shower of stones and dust behind it. Both Denzel and George had previously spent many weeks enjoying Abdullah and Rania's hospitality, so were used to the security arrangements at the compound. To Marianna, the sight of so many armed militia fighters, dogs and razor-wire fences, made her even more fearful than she already was.

Rania was waiting by the door to welcome them with hot towels and cold drinks. Much to Marianna's consternation, Denzel and George immediately changed into the long and loose-fitting cotton *djellaba* robes that had been laid out for them and joined Abdullah on the terrace for more tea and hours of conversation and laughter. For a short while, Marianna sat with them, in her best dress and black patent shoes, clutching her handbag, watching the dogs and the staff's children scamper around the dirt compound. Jamal's return from work added a further male voice to the conversation, which flowed freely.

Rania, sensing her female guest's discomfort, beckoned her into the large modern kitchen. She introduced her sister, Dihya, who had just arrived, together with their elderly mother. The old lady sat quietly at the table, dressed in black clothing and a headscarf, slowly peeling carrots with a paring knife. Rania apologised for asking, but said they were running behind with preparations for dinner and whether Marianna would be insulted if she was asked to lend them a hand.

Delighted to escape from the men, Marianna accepted an apron from Rania, changed into some sandals and set herself to work, sieving tomatoes, crushing garlic, chopping onions and making the tomato sauce that would go with Rania's famous spiced lamb and rice dish. Almost immediately, she relaxed, chatting away, as she went through the familiar motions of preparing food, explaining the difficulties of Gina's pregnancy, the outrageous price of lamb in Malta, the shortcomings of Maltese men – and George, in particular.

The sisters were highly entertained by their guest, prompting her with questions about her life in Malta, her neighbours, the wider family, their apartment, and what Abdullah had got up to during his prolonged stay there when he had fled the hostilities in Libya. Even the old woman chuckled to herself, as she continued to peel carrots, while Marianna became ever more expansive and less discreet in her responses. Soon, the kitchen was rocking to shrieks of laughter, sufficient for Abdullah to make a rare appearance and ask them for some consideration – the men were having a serious conversation! Much to Marianna's delight, Rania and Dihya pelted him with vegetables.

After another half hour, as Dihya filled in their guest with a rundown of the Belkacem family and their Berber heritage, Marianna noticed that the old lady had at least three kilos of peeled carrots in a bucket by her feet. She nodded at Rania, suggesting that might be sufficient.

Her hostess shook her head and whispered: "Let her carry on. She likes peeling carrots, that's all she does. It keeps her happy. We have to buy a sack a week. We feed most of them to the horses!"

As the sun set, a long table was laid on the terrace and large trays of spiced roasted vegetables and fried fish were served. The undoubted highlight, which was presented with much ceremony and applause, was the fragrant slow-cooked lamb and rice platter, with Marianna's velvety smooth tomato sauce. Abdullah was overly effusive in his praise for it, telling Rania she had been embarrassed by this guest who had only just arrived and put her kitchen to shame! Rania wagged a warning finger at him, while Marianna blushed, unable to conceal her pleasure at the flattery.

Tired from an evening of talking and eating, the family and their guests retired. As George and Marianna lay in the enormous bed, under the glossy weave of the Egyptian cotton sheets, watching the fan cast its patterns over the ceiling, he asked her how she was enjoying the stay.

"It's not as bad as I'd imagined, and I like Rania and her sister. But that Abdullah … he's still a terrible man. Did you notice, he ate with his fingers?"

"That's what they all do, they use bread instead. You got a fork, so that's alright."

After a pause she added, sleepily: "Hmmm. Saves on washing up, I suppose. We're still going to Spain though, aren't we?"

"*Mela*, of course, love. Anywhere you like."

"That's good."

AUTHOR'S NOTE

EU sanctions are voted on by the European Council and require Members' unanimity. Malta has never exercised its right of veto. At the time of writing, Germany has proposed a gradual transition to majority voting in common foreign policy and other areas, such as tax policy. Malta, as the smallest country in the EU has objected and stands by the veto system.

The war in Ukraine has brought the 1936 Treaty of Montreux into focus. The Kanal Istanbul has long been the subject of discussion, but there are no plans to begin construction. In the current situation, the Turkish government finds itself in a difficult position, as both Ukraine and Russia are important partners in critical energy and military trade agreements. Its control over these key straits is testing its balancing act.

Similarly, Turkey's decade long drive to join the European bloc is at a standstill, amidst concerns over democratic governance and human rights.

ABOUT THE AUTHOR

AJ Aberford is a former corporate lawyer and retired business entrepreneur who moved to Malta several years ago, although he still keeps a house in Yorkshire. He is enthralled by the culture and history of the island that acts as a bridge between Europe and North Africa. Its position at the sharp end of the migrant crisis and the rapid growth of its tourist and commercial sectors provide a rich backdrop to the Inspector George Zammit series.

AJ Aberford is married and has two grown-up sons, as well as grandchildren. He is a keen cook, an adventurous traveller and enjoys cycling, as well as daily swims in the Mediterranean Sea.

To keep up to date on AJ Aberford's fiction writing, please subscribe to his website: **www.ajaberford.com**.

Reviews help authors more than you might think. If you enjoyed *The Car Horn Revolution* or any of the previous books in the series, please consider leaving a review on Amazon and/or Goodreads.

You can connect with AJ Aberford and find out more about any of George's future adventures by following him on social media. Better still, consider subscribing to his mailing list.

When you join the mailing list you will get a link to download a novella, *Meeting in Milan*, a prequel to the Inspector George Zammit series.

X: @AJAberford
Facebook: AJ Aberford
Instagram: @ajaberford
TikTok: ajaberford109
Threads: ajaberford

ACKNOWLEDGMENTS

The Car Horn Revolution is the sixth book in the Inspector George Zammit crime series and what started as a Covid lockdown hobby, has now become a way of life. The same tight team have helped to bring each of the books to fruition, and I am grateful to each and every one of them.

My editor, Lynn Curtis, patiently studies the plot of each book, checking the structural and thematic content, before moving on to work the prose into something more readable. I have learned so much from her frank and honest critiques.

My wife, Janet, brings her forensic proofreading skills to bear on the later drafts, reading each book many times over. She also acts as a publicist and marketeer, tirelessly reminding the world that a humble Maltese detective has exciting stories to tell. It has become a joint venture – which means we have something else to argue about around the dinner table!

I thank Adrian and Rebecca, of Hobeck Books, who took a chance on publishing the first Inspector George Zammit book and have enthusiastically supported the rest of the series. I respect their honesty and integrity in educating me about the business of publishing and selling books. It is not easy. Catch up with them on their weekly podcast: The Hobcast Book Show.

Another pleasant surprise has been the level of support and friendship offered by fellow authors, particularly those from the Hobeck stable, and the book blogging community. Writing is a solitary endeavour, so all support is doubly appreciated. Also, a shout-out to Josh Collins, who has designed the covers of the last two books in the series – we loved them!

Finally, a word to all the friends I have made in Malta, due to the books being widely distributed in the Agenda chain of bookshops. We have lived in Malta for ten years, but it was with trepidation that, as an outsider, I dared to write about this proud island community. I thank all those Maltese readers who have made themselves known to me, saying how the books capture the spirit and character of this remarkable island. Particular thanks go to Peter Portelli, Rita Camilleri, Marisa Farrugia and Mike Mercieca who kindly read an early draft of this book and provided invaluable feedback and encouragement.

For a definitive view of political corruption on the Maltese Islands, I would recommend the excellent and highly readable book written by Carlo Bonini, Manuel Delia and John Sweeney, *Murder on The Malta Express: Who killed Daphne Caruana Galizia?* Truth is, indeed, sometimes stranger than fiction.

For now, we will let the Zammit family rest and recover from their latest adventure. Is this the last we will hear from them? I don't know, but in any event, I wish them well.

AJ ABERFORD

THE GEORGE ZAMMIT CRIME SERIES

Meeting in Milan (short story prequel)

Bodies in the Water
Bullets in the Sand
Hawk at the Crossroads
Fire in the Mountain
The Last Bird of Paradise
The Car Horn Revolution

MEETING IN MILAN

Short-story prequel available for free: www.ajaberford.com.

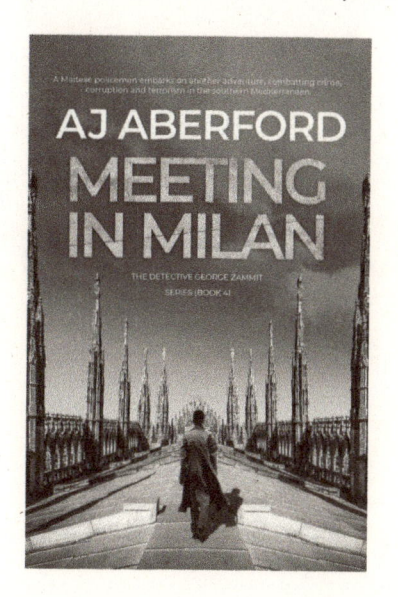

What is a family?

Two very different cousins, one from Malta and one from Sicily, are brought together to embark on their university studies in Bologna.

While spending time with their uncle and dying aunt in Milan, they learn some truths about themselves and realise that family is not what it seems.

In the space of a few short weeks, they have a decision to make. It is a choice that could change their lives forever and, once made, there will be no going back …